DARK SCRIPTURES

Deo de Wit

Dedication

To my Family

"All wickedness is but little to the wickedness of a woman: let the portion of a sinner fall upon her." Ecclesiasticus 25:19 King James Version (1611)

All biblical verses within Dark Scriptures are from the Douay Rheims Bible 1610

1

Innocence Lost

23 May 1670

The walls of St Raphael, cannon-scarred by centuries of repelled invaders, rose from a thick mist blanketing la Loire. The first yawning rays of a spring sun pierced a red sky, casting long shadows of three men who were standing on the bank, peering down into the fog.

"A body! Floating. Down there," pointed an agitated, weathered white beard holding a fishing pole; his breeches wet to the waist. "If you walk down this path, you will see him; just beyond the lilies."

Commandant Bertrand Duval, his suspicions heightened, scrutinised the elder and surveyed the surroundings. "A boy you say?"

"Yes, about eleven or twelve." The white beard stepped back from the bank. "I must be gone; my wife will question why I have lingered so long. You should have no trouble finding the poor wretch."

Duval's questioning brown eyes, hooded by bushy black brows, locked the fisherman. "You appear to be in some haste. And not one fish for your morning endeavours?"

The white beard surrendered the stare to his feet. "Yes, that is correct. When I saw the boy, I stopped my fishing and waded in for a closer look. I swear, Commandant, I have not touched any of the evidence."

Duval rubbed his clean-shaven chin, contemplating his suspect. "You may go. I am aware of your place of residence if I have a need to speak with you again. And do not forget to tell the boatman to come this way."

The white beard nodded and without another word or backward glance strode off towards the city gate.

"Thomas, we should proceed immediately to inspect this corpse."

Lieutenant Thomas Beaufort, a rotund, bald man, led the way down into a shadowy, damp haze where only the murmur of a myriad of unseen creatures and the occasional squawk of a river frog defending his territory broke the stillness. Blurred contours initially slowed progress through a tangle of drooping, faintly mint scented willow leaves, which brushed their faces and hands. The path, however, was well trodden, and they soon felt the squelch of river mud beneath their leather boots. They stopped at a line of lilies and peered into the mist.

"There it is, sir," Thomas pointed. The mist had lifted just above the water's surface and a partially submerged object floated, motionless, just beyond the lilies. A few dark shadows scurried over the shape.

"Yes. Yes. We must go immediately to inspect this corpse."

"But Commandant, should we not await the boatman? We are ill prepared for wading in this river." Thomas with eyes wide, spread out his arms displaying the pristine grey uniform of St Raphael's constabulary; la Maréchausée.

"If we delay any longer, those river rats will soon devour all the evidence," Duval replied over his shoulder as he strode towards the river's edge; a coarse, rumpled jacket hanging loosely on his tall, lean frame. Without hesitating, he plunged into the icy shallows, disturbing the floating duckweed and releasing its pungent perfume.

The muddy river soon covered their boots, and a few steps further, the cold seeped through their stockings and breeches. The pack of squeaking vermin abandoned their meal when the ripples of the gendarmerie lapped against the cadaver. Waist deep and shivering, a rotting egg smell assailed them as they reached the bloated, naked body of a young boy. His head was submerged.

Duval's experience triggered an explanation. "See how it floats, Thomas? A dead body first sinks, but as it decomposes, gases are released and fill the tissues, causing the body to rise. Considering the reasonable condition, I would venture that this unfortunate lad died about three days ago. Come, let us pull him up on the bank."

They floated the body between them till the mud compelled them to carry him. The blond-haired boy was light and easily carried up the track and out of a dispersing mist. Laying him carefully on the bank, they turned their heads to one side and pulled out their handkerchiefs as the smell of putrefaction intensified. His glazed eyes bulged from their sockets and a large, bruised wound covered most of the left side of his face. Morsels of the lips and nostrils had been taken by the rats.

Duval confidently pointed to the child's shoulders. "Thomas, these bruises on either side are of interest. These will be the hand marks of the assassin as he forced the boy down under the water. The shape of the bruise suggests the thumbs were to the rear. This would imply he stood behind his victim when he pushed him under."

Duval put the handkerchief back in his pocket, held the boy's nose and chin and prised open the mouth. "These dark red dots across his gums are the result of internal bleeding as he died. And those loose teeth on the left side of his mouth are likely the result of a blunt instrument or fist that caused the wound on his cheek. If the blow was struck by the assailant as he stood behind, it may indicate he is left-handed."

"Yes Commandant, an horrendous death of an innocent, committed by some degenerate fiend. It is unlikely we will ever find the murderer."

"You are probably correct, Thomas, just another of our many unsolved river deaths." Duval studied the ashen mask and brought his face so close that his bristly moustache almost touched the boy's chin. "Well, well, well, what do we have here?" Duval drew a white cloth from his jacket pocket and, with his other hand, pulled at something between the boy's left incisor and canine. He laid a strand of hair on the white cloth. He examined the mouth again and pulled another hair from between the left canine and premolar. The sun had risen enough to warm their wet backs and start drying the two short strands of hair. "It would appear that this boy put up a good fight. Putting this all together, I would wager that there is a scoundrel somewhere in St Raphael with an incriminating bite wound on his left wrist." Duval looked again at the two pieces of dry hair and his muscles tensed. "Thomas, I believe we are looking for a fiend with red hair."

"The evidence would certainly imply that, Commandant."

"Let us turn him over."

They easily rolled the waif onto his stomach. A glaring patchwork of blue-black bruises spread across the top of the thighs and both buttocks. Duval's eyes widened, and the bitter tang of disgust filled his mouth. He pushed one outspread hand through his thick, black mop of hair as he considered the abused child. "Mon Dieu Thomas! We now seek a monster. A deranged, red-headed monster."

2

The Kings Messenger

23 May 1670

Bishop Victor Bernard's chubby face and bald head sat perched directly atop a black, ankle length cassock. A gold crucifix swung from a thick chain against his chest as he shuffled sideways, studying the wall-to-ceiling bookshelves.

A tall, trim, red-jacketed soldier with a loping stride considered the bishop as he approached. "Good morning, My Lord, I hope you have found something of interest while waiting. I am Colonel Valentin Montpellier."

Bishop Bernard turned and nodded to the colonel. "You certainly have a wide selection of books and manuscripts. I was not aware that soldiers were such avid scholars. But it is pleasing to see that the men of our la Maréchausée are so well informed."

"Our King expects a well-rounded soldier. Our work is sometimes brutal and perilous, but there are times when it requires thoughtful and careful planning."

"You wished to see me?"

"Yes. I will not waste anymore of your most valuable time. I have recently been despatched to St Raphael on the instruction of King Louis himself. The King requires absolute commitment and duty from his soldiers. For this reason, the leaders of la Maréchausée, in cities such as St Raphael, are entrusted with direct access to our King. I had private counsel with His Majesty before my departure from Paris."

"You move in very illustrious circles. But I fail to see how this involves me."

"Our King is deeply concerned about the recent rise of devilish activity in la Loire valley, particularly around St Raphael. I have been personally selected to wipe it out."

"Again, Colonel, I fail to see how this concerns me."

"You are the clerical trial judge. The King requires convictions."

"I judge each and every case on its merits. I believe in fairness and the pursuit of truth."

"And so you should. We certainly do not want any innocents going to the fire. But the King has suggested that if he finds pleasure in your fairness, he may then look upon you favourably."

Bishop Bernard's eyes widened below raised brows. "Was he more specific?"

"He only said, in passing, that a new Archbishop of Paris is soon to be selected. As you are no doubt aware, the current one is of older age."

Bishop Bernard tilted his head and pulled his mouth. "It is clear that you and our King are well acquainted. Yet you appear so young. Are you from a noble house?"

"To the contrary Bishop. I was born in the worst slums of Paris. The military was my escape and my path to a life where I did not have to beg for every scrap. The King has entrusted me to this mission and I have no intention of failing."

"I can see that our King has selected a very determined soldier for this task. And yes, I do agree with you and our King concerning the current surge of apostasy in and around St Raphael."

Montpellier smiled and stroked his goatee as he fixed the bishop. "Can I suggest that you and I have regular weekly meetings to consider the situation and assess new suspects? I am confident that we will make an excellent team."

"As a servant of both God and King, I will certainly offer my services. These women are the gate of the devil, and this heresy is a plague on our land, and an insult to our God."

At that moment, a grey-jacketed soldier entered the library with two glasses of sherry on a silver tray. Montpellier handed one to the bishop and took the other and raised it. "To a successful association. Perhaps you would like to take a seat and discuss this in some more detail?"

An hour later, their discussions complete, Montpellier watched the bishop depart. This alliance would ensure his success in St Raphael and the chance of further promotion. He still had one more task to complete and proceeded through the warren of corridors and down two flights of stairs to the ground floor. He knocked at a door bearing a sign: Commandant Bertrand Duval.

"Come in, it's open." Duval sat at a desk, head down, buried in a clutter of papers.

"Good morning, Commandant Duval."

Duval lifted his head, recognised the uniform, and stood. "Good morning! You must be Colonel Montpellier. I had heard you had arrived. This is a surprise. How can I be of service this morning?"

Montpellier's eyes darted around the small, stuffy room noting along one wall, a bench, stacked with four neat piles of paper, standing next to a glass-fronted cupboard filled with books. A window behind the desk looked out onto a small parade ground. The opposite wall was bare except for two portraits next to the desk. "We have not had the opportunity to talk since my arrival. As you are my second in command, I thought we should speak frankly."

Duval took his seat, pointing to a chair on the opposite side of the table. "Yes, certainly. Please take a seat."

"But first; I have heard that you come from a very illustrious military background. Your father, I believe, was involved throughout the Franco-Spanish war from 1638 to 1659. As a result of his valour, he was appointed colonel here in St Raphael and served till 1664 before retiring.

He would have been only forty-five at the time and it seems strange that he retired so early."

"Yes, his time here was cut short. He had suffered considerable injuries during the war with Spain, which made him old well before his time. He was given an army pension and moved to Tours to be with some of his war comrades. Unfortunately, one month ago he suffered a sudden apoplexy and now lays in an unarousable, unconscious state. This was my father." Duval pointed to the portrait of a highly decorated, red jacketed soldier.

Montpellier scrutinized the painting. "Yes, that is most unfortunate news for one of St Raphael's greatest war heroes."

"Yes, it is sad and unfortunately his wife; my mother passed while he was away fighting for France. This was my mother." Duval pointed to the portrait of a dark-haired, sombre woman dressed in black.

"Well, Commandant, that is indeed a tragic family history, but I must now speak about the current leadership of la Maréchausée. I am aware that you have worked in St Raphael most of your life and slowly worked your way up through the ranks. I have heard that after the previous colonel retired, you had aspirations for this position."

"Yes, there is some truth in that, but I certainly hold no animosity towards you. I can assure you of my trustworthy allegiance"

"That is good. Well, now that we understand each other, I felt it best that we define our roles. I have been sent by King Louis to quell the witchcraft in St Raphael. This will be a merciless task and my methods may at times appear brutal. However, I must make it clear that I will not tolerate any interference about the methods I use or dissent from subordinates. Those suspects that I capture and bring for interrogation in the Tower cannot be questioned by anyone other than myself unless you first seek my permission. Is this clear?"

"Absolutely Colonel."

"This process will undoubtedly consume most of my time and therefore you should deal with all other forms of crime in St Raphael. If you have any concerns, please do not hesitate to come and see me."

Duval sat upright in his chair and only a slight twitch of his moustache betrayed something of the thoughts within. "This arrangement suits me perfectly Colonel, as I have absolutely no belief in witchcraft. It was my father who provided me with wise counsel on this matter."

The colonel's face reddened, and eyes bored into Duval. "I feel certain that once you have heard the confessions and the diabolical practices of these servants of Satan, your beliefs will change." Montpellier stood; Duval followed and straightened; half a head taller. They shook hands, and Colonel Montpellier turned and left the room.

3

A Night Call

25 May 1670

The midnight tolling of the distant St Raphael cathedral confirmed Jules was overdue and heightened his anxiety. He dismounted and handed his frothing, sweat-drenched mare to the Laughing Waters stable boy. Without hesitating, he plunged into the crush spilling out of the front door. The alehouse was filled with pipe smoke, laughter and the clamour of intoxicated men, each rising louder to be heard. Barmaids squeezed amongst the patrons and a few harlots plied their trade on expectant laps. His face flushed, riding scarf askew and youthful innocence scarred, Jules escaped from the rank of sweat and approached the bar. "Would you be the publican, Sir?" he asked a jovial, large, bearded man pouring a mug of ale.

His joviality changed to a half smile with raised eyebrows as he looked down at Jules. "What is a young fresh-faced lad doing out at this hour? Is your mother aware of your roaming?"

"Please sir, Monsieur Duplessis is in very poor health and I have been instructed to find Dr Pierre Laurent. I have visited his house in St Raphael and other places he frequents but cannot find him. I believe he may be here."

The publican's eyes widened. "Is his presence essential? Our young doctor has just paid for a young lady with whom he wishes to spend the night." He raised his eyes and thumb towards the ceiling. Jules confirmed the urgency with a nod. "Well, he went upstairs about ten minutes ago. If you are brave enough, he is in the first room on the left. I must warn you though, he can be in a filthy mood once he has had a few."

"Thank you, sir. For the health of my master and to avoid the wrath of his wife, I will have to take that risk." The young horseman turned, jostled through more revellers and mounted the stairs two at a time. He knocked hard three times and pressed his ear against the door.

"Who in God's name is that at this hour? Fuck off, I'm busy."

With his face turned to the door Jules shouted against the din from below. "Doctor Laurent, Monsieur Duplessis is very ill and desperately requires your assistance, even at this late hour."

From behind the door Jules heard irritated mumbling and the shuffling of bedsheets. The door jerked open and Pierre Laurent stood bleary-eyed, brown hair ruffled, reeking of alcohol and his manhood beginning to sag. "How can I visit a patient in this state, at this godforsaken hour and with her ripe, ready and paid for?" His arm stretched back across the room to a young bare-breasted maid, sitting in bed, smiling back at Jules.

Jules forced his eyes back to Pierre as his face reddened. "Sir please, I can see that this is a most inconvenient time. My master shits and vomits constantly. He is confused and my lady believes it may be his diabetes."

"His diabetes! He always has a few turns with his diabetes, but always gets better. Now go! Let me enjoy the few pleasures that I have." He threw the door to close and Jules winced as he stopped it with his foot.

"The madame said that if you did not come, she would have to inform your father."

"My goddamn father! How does she know? That will not work, you little shit," and he pushed the door again. Jules again put his boot in the way and with nervous determination fixed the blazing green eyes that burnt into him. Pierre's well-trimmed moustache began twitching, his set mouth slackened, his shoulders drooped in resignation and his member reduced to total disinterest. "I regret the day I chose this profession. All right, all right. Just allow me ten minutes."

"Thank you, sir. I will wait outside. By the way, my name is Jules." He offered his hand, but Pierre grunted and turned inside. Jules pushed back through the clamour and, once outside, sucked hard to feel the pine-scented night air cleanse his lungs. He crossed to the stable and, with the assistance of the stable hand, expeditiously prepared a horse and carriage.

As Jules pulled the reins in outside the tavern door, Pierre appeared from the smoke; barefoot, shirt unbuttoned and partially tucked into his breeches. In one hand he carried a pair of leather boots and in the other a tankard of ale.

"Alright, let us get on with this absurdity." Jules watched as Pierre stumbled headlong into the carriage, spilling his beer across the floor. "Dam, what a pity. Some say that the last sip is the best." He clambered to his feet and when he fell across the carriage seat, Jules flicked the reins from the driver's bench.

"You said your name was Jules?" You have the face of a child; shouldn't you be home in bed asleep?"

"Yes, Jules is correct. I may look young, but I happen to be fifteen." He pushed the horse into a canter.

"Well Jules, you may call me Pierre. It would interest me to know how Madame Duplessis has knowledge of my father. That bastard resides in Paris and still watches and meddles with my life. He drove my mother to so such madness that she killed herself. At least, that is what the magistrate said."

"I have heard he is a very wealthy businessman?"

"Businessman! That is a joke. He is a scoundrel and as slippery as a snake."

Jules smiled to himself and couldn't resist one last gibe. "Madame says that he sends you money to keep you in the manner to which you are accustomed?"

"Merde! How does she know that? Is nothing private anymore?" Pierre sighed and put his head down on the seat. Jules watched him slip into a coma and snapped the reins across the mare's rump, urging her into a gallop. With nostrils flaring and mane flying, they charged past open fields and through the blackness of a forest. Pierre bounced and slid on the carriage seat as it jolted and twisted along the country road. Jules finally pulled the horse in outside the front of a large country house.

"Wake up Doctor, we have arrived." Jules gently shook him by the shoulder, and through an inebriated haze, Pierre squinted at his surroundings.

"Well, it is about time we got here. And not a very comfortable journey, Jules."

"Yes, sir, let me help you out of the carriage."

"I can do it myself, young man," and he pushed Jules' hands away. Staggering to his feet, he missed the step, fell headlong out of the carriage and sprawled out on the driveway. Pierre groaned once and then passed out.

As Jules rushed to assist, Madame Duplessis appeared from the front door. "Don't worry Jules, I will deal with this inebriate. Go to the stable and change the horse. You will most likely have to take him home once he has completed his duties here."

***

After some minutes Pierre stirred and peered through slit eyes to discover the feet of two stout legs inserted into slippers. His gaze moved upwards to a large bust and the chubby face of an unsmiling Madame Duplessis.

"It is high time you arrived, Doctor. Judging from your appearance and condition, I must assume that Jules found you in an alehouse somewhere. Wait till I inform your father how you spend your leisure time. Come on, get up and follow me. Quick, quick, he may be dead already."

Pierre followed obediently, barefoot across the stone driveway, up the steps and through the open front door. He stumbled up the broad staircase, resolutely following the ample posterior. A thick, pungent stench floated out of an open bedroom door and smothered them as they reached the landing. The alcohol and added fetor turned Pierre's stomach. The bile rose in his throat and an uncontrollable projectile of vomit poured onto the landing. He pulled a handkerchief from his waistcoat pocket, attempted to wipe his mouth but only managed to spread the spew over his moustache and long sideburns.

"Oh my God, young man. You can suffer for your overindulgence tomorrow. But now you have a patient to see." She grabbed Pierre by the arm and dragged him into the room. "Now get to work!"

On the floor in the middle of the room, Pierre contemplated a naked, obese man, fitting and salivating from the corner of his mouth. He staggered towards him and knelt by his side, feeling for a pulse, listening to the chest, all the while mumbling and shaking his head. Pale gums showed small haemorrhages and the whites of his eyes had a yellowish tinge. Both ankles were swollen and discoloured. Pierre gingerly stood up and surveyed the room. The bed was soaked with urine and faeces. Across the floor a trail of vomit and excrement led to a large, high-backed mahogany chair with armrests and a hole in the seat. He was drawn back towards the bed. On a bedside table stood an open, seven compartment pill box and a small, brown, glass stoppered bottle. "When did all this start?"

"Hugo was well when I brought up his meal at about six this evening. We no longer sleep together, so I am uncertain when it started. I heard a noise at about eleven and came to have a look and found him on the floor. I helped him up, took him to the privy, and waited. It was like water and the noise and stench were sickening. He was sweating and complained of terrible stomach pains and vomited. I managed to get him back to bed and then ran downstairs and arranged for Jules to find you. When I returned, he was on the floor again, having a fit. I felt helpless. There was nothing I could do."

Pierre shook his head again. "Madame Duplessis, it pains me to say this, but your husband is terribly ill. He appears to be bleeding internally, there is fluid on his lungs, his heart is failing and perhaps his diabetes is out of control. I fear he is about to die. There is nothing I can do to change that."

Madame Duplessis placed both hands over her open mouth but could not contain the high-pitched, hysterical scream that filled the room. Pierre wrapped his arms around her trembling shoulders as she sobbed into her open palms, watching her prostrate husband. Monsieur Duplessis' breathing became shallower, his fitting ceased and then, one last cough, followed by the gasp of his final struggling breath.

Pierre held her. Neither spoke for the next few minutes, and he guided her from the room onto the landing. "I am truly sorry, Madame. He was a good man and I am certain he will find peace with his maker."

"But why? He was so well just this afternoon."

"I am uncertain of the cause of death, Madame, but I will call in at Commandant Duval on my way home and ask him to come by first thing in the morning. Do not touch or clean anything. Just walk out and close the door behind you."

"Commandant Duval of la Maréchausée! Why?"

"I cannot say too much, but his sudden deterioration, the pillbox and the small bottle makes poisoning a possibility, and that makes everyone a suspect."

"Poisoning? Suspects? Surely not? That is ridiculous!"

"I am sorry Madame Duplessis, but close the door and do not go back in. Go to bed. I will ask Jules to take me home."

Pierre held the banister, and one tentative step at a time, negotiated the stairs. He found Jules standing at the front door, holding his boots. "You may need these, sir. Do you wish to return to your lady at the tavern?"

Pierre took his boots and climbed into the waiting carriage. "No, thank you Jules. I am in dire need of sleep, but first we must make a stop at the house of Commandant Duval."

4

The Sabbat

25 May 1670

Mara lay awake, restless. A foreboding had settled on her, squeezing her heart and chest. Painful muscles in her neck, tightness across her forehead and a queasiness in her stomach prohibited sleep. She waited. A full moon entered through an open window, creating ghostly, serpentine shadows in the cracks of the bare stone walls. She stared blankly, through wide, azure eyes, at gnarled, timeworn beams and musty thatch. She listened. The dread that consumed her made the usual hum of the surrounding forest seem louder. Even the occasional, delicate ooohu of the eagle owl seemed sharper and persistent. Her mother's warnings reverberated through her thoughts. *Never, never wander beyond our front gate in the darkness. La Maréchausée and their informants are everywhere amongst us. We have even seen them in St Joan. They will seize you and torture you in the Tower for even a suggestion of suspicious behaviour.*

Mara forced Maman's caution from her conscious and focussed on a competing peril. She had paid little attention to Celeste's incessant chattering over the past months. But this afternoon, Celeste, with Francine and Isabella in tow, had rushed past her on the last day of school, whispering. *Do not forget! Tomorrow at dawn. I need you there.* Then they were gone.

Recollection of Celeste's previous babbling came in fragments.

My initiation ceremony will be on the first full moon. It would help me greatly if you could be there, she had pleaded.

What ceremony?

You know, the last six months of my training? For admission to our society? You take no notice of anything I say. You are my dearest friend;

closer than both Francine and Isabella. But you are always so busy with the things you find in the forest and with the strange plants you grow in your garden.

The blackbird's fluted first song pierced the murmur of the forest. *At last!* Mara silently lifted the cover. She removed a faded red dress hanging over a chair and pulled it over already stockinged legs. The rough oak floorboards creaked as she moved her feet while tucking in a white shift. She froze, waited, listened, moved a few paces to the left and pulled on a white, collarless blouse over which she tied a bodice, cross laced at the front. From her dress pocket, she removed a pre-written note and placed it on the bed. Creeping towards the door, she stopped, turned, and from the chest beside her bed grasped a belt with a large hunting knife. With trembling hands, she strapped it around her waist. As expected, the door squeaked when it opened. She waited, rigid, and then continued down the hallway. Mother's door was open, and Mara cautiously avoided the creaky floorboard outside her room. *Please do not be angry with me, Maman. I hope you can understand.*

Grandmère's snoring poured out of the next room as Mara hurried past on her way to the kitchen. She pulled on the soft leather boots she had left there the night before, opened the kitchen door and stepped out into the moonlit courtyard just as the robin and wren joined the blackbird. Across the yard, she was relieved to see that Simon's window above the stable was not yet flickering with candlelight.

The crisp air and the subtle, aromatic smell of lavender and angelica drifting across from the kitchen garden settled the tight knot in her stomach. She strode up the garden path, tentatively opened the gate, turned, and stared at the painted sign as she closed it. *Maison Diana.* Hesitating, she placed her hand back on the gate to return. Suspended, her entire young life tumbled past confused, uncertain eyes as she forcefully disengaged her hand and mind. She stepped out into the road as the pygmy owl's high-pitched, clipped song drifted down from a huge pine to join the chorus. Mara avoided the moonlit dirt road with its deep cart ruts and moved quietly and swiftly on the grass in the shadows.

It must be a full moon, Celeste had said. *If not full, the ceremony will not be recognised and all my training will be wasted.*

Running, she soon reached la Loire and le Pont St Joan. She crouched; hands pressed against the cold stone side walls of the uncovered bridge. Moving slowly forwards she attempted to prevent her blond head from bobbing above the parapet. A pine scented mist, draping the river as it flowed quietly through the lilies near the shore, provided Mara with some calm. But on reaching the middle, the deafening water charging through the gothic arches completely drowned out the growing choir but could not still her pounding heart.

On the opposite bank, Mara reached the crossroads and the hamlet of St Joan. The fork to the right led to the city of St Raphael, with the Laughing Waters Tavern standing hushed between the road and the river. Mara took the left fork where the village school, Celeste's home, and a few other scattered dwellings stood dark and silent in the moonlight.

Suddenly, a creak of a door and a slight movement at the school-house. An icy chill slid down her spine as a silhouette emerged from the shadow. Mara flung herself down the bank, tumbling and sliding until she felt the wet of the river seep through her bodice and blouse. Jumping up, she stumbled blindly through the murkiness and then cautiously climbed back up the bank. She lay flat in the long grass and scanned St Joan. The schoolhouse was silent, but a shape in a long coat stood on the bank squinting down into the fog. A musket at the ready was held in both hands. She stifled a scream, and the breath caught in her throat as it turned and moved towards her. Instinct overcame fear and, with a trembling hand, she removed the knife from her belt. After a few paces, the menace stopped, peered into la Loire, shook its head, and turned back towards the hamlet.

Mara waited till the threat was back in the shadow of the school-house. In front of her, the exposed road swung away from the river and up a long hill. She chose instead to follow the cover of the river and its forest and then climbed out, ducked under a wooden fence, and entered an open, ploughed field. The farmland provided little cover, and she moved quickly between isolated trees towards a dense forest at the top of the rise, leaving the river and the escalating orchestra behind her.

What will happen at this ceremony?

There will be much eating and dancing, and at the end our commander will take me.

Take you! What does that mean?

You know, she had said, with a smirk and sideways glance.

But you are only 16!

It has been part of my training, particularly the mental part. Maman says the first time is the most beautiful moment in a maiden's life.

Maybe if you love the boy.

Do not worry, the night before, Maman and the rest of the women will prepare my body with special oils, and just before the ceremony, Maman will put in a small poultice of herbs and fragrant oils that will make it easier.

A new choir was already in full song as Mara reached the hilltop woodland surrounded by an impenetrable bramble bush. Entry points had been cut at intervals, but a robed guard stood at each. Celeste's instructions came back. *The main entries will be guarded by men who will sound the alarm and probably cut your throat if you try to enter. You should use the small, secret tunnel we made.*

Mara parted a small stand of purple foxglove that disguised the entry and crawled cautiously through as thorns scratched her skin, ripped her clothes and caught her hair. Breathing heavily, she emerged on a mat of leaves under a canopy of oaks and pines through which only a scattering of moonlight could enter. Mara knew this forest. She had explored and hunted here since childhood. The chorus above drowned any sound made by her soft leather shoes. At intervals, she stopped and listened. Then she heard it. Music and laughter. Distant at first, but growing louder with every step. And then, a dim light through the undergrowth to which she was drawn. When every word could be clearly heard, she climbed a large oak and crawled out on one of its higher branches.

Smoke, music, singing and a babble of voices rose through the branches, competing with the aviary. She inched forward, away from the safety of the trunk towards an opening in the foliage. The branch narrowed and began to sway. Mara paused, held tight, her pulse racing. With a trembling free hand, she pushed a thatch of leaves to one side. The glade below formed an almost perfect circle within the blackness of the forest. Five long tables laden with food, fruit, and flagons stood evenly spaced around the periphery. To one side, a bass drum pounded out a relentless beat, accompanied by a vibrant violin, a rich flute, and a deep brass horn.

An assemblage of about thirty white-robed figures gathered in groups, drinking and talking excitedly above the clamour. Others sang and danced to the rhythm of the ensemble, while a few lone souls shuffled haphazardly amongst the crowd, chanting to the heavens.

Two tables, just out of view, aroused her curiosity and forced her to stretch further forward. The branch again creaked and swayed. Heart racing, she gripped tighter and waited till her hideaway stabilised. Spread across the tables, Mara recognised the lobed leaves and funnelled cream flowers of the henbane scattered amongst the tortured roots and blue, bell-shaped flowers of the mandrake. Both plants soaked in two large vats from which the drinking flagons were being continually refilled.

Smoke from a central fire rose into a transforming sky; blackness giving way to a red hue from a yet unseen sun. Just south of the fire and almost directly below Mara, a gleaming sword lay on a bed of straw and blankets atop a raised platform. Celeste and her mother, Bella, were nowhere to be seen, but her grandmother sat chatting with a small group, sipping from a pewter cup.

A loud, protracted drone of the horn brought the hubbub to a sudden halt. The forest choir ignored the command as the male birds continued to advertise their fitness and territory. A tall, silver-haired woman draped in a red robe entered the circle and raised both arms.

"Welcome, my dearest brothers and sisters. Thank you all for your gracious presence on this most sacred occasion. As the high priestess of our society, it is time to cast the circle and begin the initiation of our newest convert, the virgin Celeste Lemaire. She has completed six months of intense training and passed all our most arduous tests. She is ready to join us."

The drum beat four times, followed by the horn commanding the assembly of white robes to rise as one. They moved from their tables, formed a circle, and joined hands.

"This circle we cast will contain the energy required and create a sacred space that will provide mystical, emotional and physical protection for our Celeste."

The high priestess moved to the altar, clutched the sword, and held it high above her head in both hands. She strode past the fire to the northernmost point of the circle where she was handed a glowing green candle which she placed on the ground.

"I welcome you, spirits of the Earth from the North. I ask you to provide your power and protection and bring your gifts of patience, discipline, endurance and prosperity so that Celeste can complete her journey."

To the slow beat of the drum and a low drone of the horn, the high priestess brought the point of the sword down to the ground. She drew the circle in a clockwise direction inside the silent, standing participants. On reaching the eastern point of the circle, the music stopped, and she placed a yellow candle on the ground.

"I welcome you, spirits of the East and Air. Please bring your gifts of wisdom, creativity, intellect and inspiration to guide Celeste tonight and in all her future practising."

To a delicate flute and austere violin, the sword drew the circle and stopped at the southernmost point, directly beneath Mara. The high priestess was given a blue candle which she placed on the ground.

"I welcome you, spirits of Fire from the South. I ask that you bring your gifts of passion, strength, energy and determination to guide Celeste tonight and for the rest of her life."

She continued to draw the sword along the ground to the accompaniment of the whole but subdued ensemble. At the westernmost point, she stopped and placed a red candle on the ground.

"I welcome you Spirits of Water from the West. I ask you to bring your gifts of emotion, pleasure, empathy and fertility to give Celeste understanding and many like-minded descendants."

The ensemble struck a loud, joyous beat as the sword completed the circle back to the northern starting point.

"The circle is now cast. I call again on the spirits of the North, East, South and West and welcome you to the centre of this circle."

With the music building, the high priestess moved to the centre and raised the sword up to a rose-coloured sky. Conjointly, the participants jumped into the circle singing, chanting, and holding their hands upwards towards the sword.

"Centre spirits, I ask that you bring down your cone of protection on these most sacred proceedings. I now call upon the virgin Celeste and I call upon the Horned God to complete and ratify this life-changing occasion."

The eastern point of the circle parted, and Bella walked barefoot into the ring. A wreath of flowers held down black, grey streaked hair, which fell over an orange patterned dress. Mara held her breath, this beautiful free spirit, now hardly recognisable from the poor wretch, whose daily existence Mara knew to be a bitter struggle. Within her ringed fingers, she carried a single red rose. Her feet, colourfully painted and her favourite horned ring, as always, on the right second toe.

Celeste entered wearing nothing but a crown of white flowers and a gilded, golden snake encircling both forearms. Long, black ringlets, outlining high cheekbones, fell across slender shoulders and over full breasts. Her pale skin and oil impregnated black thicket glistened in the firelight. Trembling lips and an occasional shiver belied her purposeful steps as wide, brown eyes fixed on the altar ahead. She stopped when she reached her mother, received the red rose in her right hand, and continued forward. In front of the altar steps, she turned to face directly south, raised her eyes, searched the trees and smiled. The trembling settled as she found the holdfast in Mara's eyes.

The chanting of the convocation grew louder, the dancing more erratic. The dawn chorus, however, grew quieter as the light unveiled the glade. Then four beats of the drum directed them to shed their robes, exposing their nakedness to the dawn chill. Another horn blast and the ring parted at the western point and a naked male, his head adorned by two long antlers, strode across the circle and halted in front of Celeste. The music and assembly fell silent.

"I am the servant of Satan. It is my power that will change your maidenhood, Celeste. I am the dark hunter and this morning you are my prize. Are you ready? Are you willing to undertake this ceremony which will fix you on a path from which you can never return?"

Celeste, in a loud and determined voice that belied her pallid face and trembling chin; "I am ready, my Lord and Master."

"Let it be known to all those assembled that Celeste is a willing participant." The beast stretched out his hand and laid his open palm on her crown of flowers. "Do you, Celeste, vow that every part of your body and soul that lies beneath this hand shall forever belong to Satan, and I, his servant?"

"Yes, my Lord and Master."

"You may now recount your vows."

"I, Celeste, forsake the one they call Creator. I renounce his temples and all their holy ceremonies. I also forswear my mother, my father, my family, and my ancestors. In their place, I swear total and unwavering loyalty to you, my Master and to Satan." Celeste turned and took two steps onto the altar and lay down on the bed of straw with her toes pointing south. She smiled directly into Mara's wide, tear-filled eyes.

The ensemble fell silent. The morning chorus was mute, except for the high-pitched trilling of the blue tit and whistle of the finch.

"Northern spirits of the earth give me, The Prince of Darkness, the power, the virility and the wisdom to complete this initiation of this our new servant of Satan."

He climbed the steps and stood on the altar with his arms stretched out. The convocation erupted, cheering and urging him on. The Horned God knelt between Celeste's parted thighs and pushed his instrument into her. Celeste's mouth opened and eyes widened at the pain of the intrusion, but unwaveringly held Mara's gaze.

The drum thundered again, and violin, flute and horn joined in an exuberant chorus. The climax of the morning had arrived, and the unrestrained assembly responded. They burst into spontaneous singing, dancing, kissing and coupling, in twos and in groups. The movements of the Horned God and his servants became faster, frenetic and in tune with the rhythmic pulse of the instruments.

Tears streaked down Mara's cheeks as Celeste's agony and torment looked back at her. She wished with everything that the beast would finish, and Celeste's ordeal would be over. But then, the initial pain in Celeste's contorted face faded and with every movement was replaced with a smile and then, pleasure. Her hips moved in unison with the monster, faster, eager, till finally she screamed her first fulfilment.

Mara's disbelief lasted a second. The snort of a horse. An escape of birds from the trees. The glint of steel on the forest floor. Swords. Pikes. A bustle of hats. A white stallion carrying a red-jacketed soldier brandishing a sword above his head bolted from the woodland.

"No-one must escape. We want them alive. Use your weapons wisely."

Behind the rider, twenty grey-jacketed soldiers of la Maréchausée emerged in a line. With black tricornes low over foreheads and muskets and swords primed, they charged into the clearing.

Copulating bodies disengaged, music and dancing ceased abruptly, and the convocation retreated as fast as possible to the assumed safety of the forest. The beast withdrew, unfinished, leapt off the altar and scurried northwards, but was mercilessly brought down by a club to the back of the head. Most of the coven failed to reach the edge of the glade. A few quicker, less intoxicated members reached the forest, pursued by the foot soldiers. Their flight ended with the sound of musket fire. Mara, fearing detection, retreated slightly along the branch. Celeste lay unperturbed on her bed of straw, paralysed with pain and contentment.

The red-jacketed leader drew his horse up beside the altar, rubbing a goatee and stroking a meticulously trimmed moustache as he considered the prostrate Celeste with open amusement. A lewd smile revealed perfect white teeth and a small gold filling in the left incisor gleamed in the early sunlight. "Well, well, what have we here? It appears to be a pretty young witch who has just had her first fuck. Would you like to tell Colonel Montpellier what it was like?"

Celeste, wide eyed and silent, fixed his gaze.

Montpellier's smile transformed to a snarl as a rumble surged upwards from deep within his chest and escaped as a bark as sharp as the blade he waved above his head. "So, that devil fucked the tongue out of you, did he? What is your name, you loathsome, Satan's whore?"

Stirred by his anger, Celeste rose, flaunting her full nakedness. She smiled and looked down at him. "Celeste, Sir."

Temporarily disarmed, the leader slowly lowered his sword. "Celeste? Not very celestial behaviour here this morning, was it? Go and stand in the front of all the other witches!"

A horseman pulled up beside the colonel. "Sir, we have rounded up twenty and five are dead. All men, sir, who wished to put up a fight. There are still some concealed in the forest. A few men will remain to scour these woods for the rest of the day. I can assure you, Colonel, we will extract every last one."

"Good Sergeant, we will march them through this wood and take them to the river as planned. Bring all the bodies to the river when you have finished your work. And put the little slut into one cart on her own. I wish to keep a close eye on her."

Mara remained silently anchored to her branch. *Did the oak's foliage provide enough cover?* When all was quiet, inch by inch, she began to move. Then a single musket shot, followed by a human cry, broke the stillness and instantly stopped her progress. She waited again. Then another shot and another shriek. *Would it be safer to leave?* First, a few tentative inches backwards and then, as the swaying stabilized, quicker and more purposeful movements. On the lowest branch, she hesitated, listening and scanning the foliage for the searching guards. Satisfied, she jumped into the mattress of decaying leaves on the forest floor. Then another musket shot, close, to her left. A sudden dread triggered Mara to move; running as fast as possible through the dense scrub. The concealed tunnel was easily found, and she emerged amongst the foxglove, bathing in the morning sunlight. To her left a blood soaked, robed sentry lay motionless at the forest entrance.

The column had reached the road and was advancing towards the river. Montpellier, resplendent in his red coat, white breeches and knee length leather boots, rode upright at the head of the train. Celeste followed, unbound and holding the sides of the bouncing cart. Grandmère led the procession, followed by Bella and the devil. Guards flanked the assembly, swords in scabbards and pikes upright, shouting abuse at any captive that stumbled or complained. The commotion attracted curious peasants from roadside shelters and farmers abandoned their early labour in the fields to climb the fences and line the road.

Mara chose an alternate route, running from tree to tree diagonally across the field. She soon reached the safety of the thick riverside undergrowth and waited. By the time the procession reached her, it had grown to a boisterous horde of about fifty. Enveloping the procession, the crowd had supplemented their obscenities with projectiles of vegetables and rotten fruit. The clamour provided Mara with sufficient security to emerge and mingle.

The fog had lifted by the time the parade reached le Pont St Joan and the churning waters of la Loire. Montpellier raised his hand, bringing the procession to a halt. The crowd fell silent as the colonel turned his horse and stopped at the middle of the troupe, facing the bedraggled captives. "I observed all your heinous acts of devilry this morning, so there is no doubt that you are servants of Satan. Therefore, you should all be burned at the stake this very afternoon." He paused as he scanned the procession with burrowing dark brown eyes. "But, by the grace of our good King Louis, our laws state you should all be allowed a fair trial to convince us you do not hold such satanic beliefs. So, raise your hands if you are a witch."

Silence. Not a single member of the of the congregation or the surrounding mob uttered a sound or moved a muscle.

"As you now deny your witchcraft, I have the authority to invoke the ancient trial by swimming. This will give you one last chance to save yourselves. You will each be bound and thrown into la Loire." He paused, smiled and scanned the procession again. "As we should all know, witches have denounced all the holy rituals of the church, including baptism. Therefore, if you are a witch, the water of la Loire will reject your body and prevent you from drowning and you will simply float on the surface. You may then be entitled to repent your ways and receive a fair trial before the bishop and magistrate. Unfortunately, if you drown, you are not a witch. Now this hardly seems fair, does it?" Montpellier paused in the ensuing silence, then laughed, flashing his full toothed grin. He turned and signalled to the sergeant. "We have wasted enough time with these harlots. Let us swim these witches. Start from the front. That old woman. She is of no use to anyone."

Celeste stood tall, outwardly calm but wide, horror-filled eyes, could not hide the inner turmoil that tore at her very soul as two guards grabbed Grandmère by each arm. Long silver hair fell down her aging nakedness as they guided her to the centre of the bridge. There was no struggle. She seemed at peace, almost ethereal as they laid her on the ground, bound her hands to her feet and fastened a rope around her waist. She was lifted onto the bridge parapet and, without a moment's hesitation, pushed over the edge. Tumbling, turning, hair flying, and finally an anguished primal cry escaped before being swallowed by the turbulence. Disappearing momentarily, she popped up like a cork, rotating in the water, alternately exposing buttocks and head to the crowd who stared from the shore in disbelief. After a few long minutes, the partially submerged lifeless body drifted into a quiet section of the river. Both guards returned to the river bank still holding the rope and dragged the lifeless matriarch onto the bank. Mara stood paralysed, open-mouthed, her face pinched by the fear and panic that consumed her.

The swimming continued and as the news of the heinous acts in the Glen permeated the crowd, initial disbelief mutated to retribution. The cheering grew louder with a united chorus as each accused plunged to their death. Montpellier, astride his horse in the middle of the road, watched, expressionless and silent.

With the sun now well above the horizon, the rattling of the approaching first carriage of the morning halted proceedings. The driver, his face shadowed by a broad-brimmed hat, pulled up the open carriage and surveyed the small collection of bodies. Foam and vomit dribbled from their mouths and terror still filled the eyes that stared back at him. "Good morning, Colonel Montpellier. This is indeed an extraordinary practice. What have these poor souls done to warrant such barbaric punishment?"

Montpellier, ensuring that his authority was clear and unquestioned, scowled as he looked down from his mount. "Commandant Duval, as your commanding officer, I will not legitimise your impudence with a reply. As I explained to you, not two days ago, and now to all those gathered here, I am under the direct instruction of King Louis to rid all witchcraft from this region. I suggest you move along to whatever trivial business you are engaged with."

Duval again scrutinised the mound of bodies, the naked, waiting participants, the onlookers and the troupe of armed soldiers. His eyes, as expressionless as a gravestone, fixed on Montpellier as a mix of dark thoughts moved across his face. "Yes, I can see that the death of the local landowner, Monsieur Hugo Duplessis, which I on my way to investigate, pales by comparison with the crimes these felons have committed." He flicked the reins and rattled past and up the hill.

Montpellier nodded to his henchmen to continue. One after the other, men, women and young girls were launched off the parapet into the rushing waters of la Loire. It ejected no one. Numerous travellers passed on their way to St. Raphael; their steps quickened and eyes downcast for fear of association. The raucous crowd slowly lost interest as the morning passed into afternoon and gradually drifted away. As the mob thinned, Mara felt increasingly exposed, but was too afraid to move away should she be noticed and questioned. Then, as if some silent prayer had been answered, her anxiety evaporated as she felt the closeness of a man who smelled of horses and a newly ploughed field. She looked up and a corner lift smile brought deep dimples to her olive cheeks. Simon stood tall, bearded, with long, blond hair, greying slightly at the temples and braided back in a tail. His sun darkened skin contrasted with a white linen shirt over which he wore a sleeveless waistcoat. Mara shuffled close till her forearm touched his farm roughened hand. Her dress moulded his black breeches and her leather boots stood next to his. *Why had he taken so long to get here?*

The sun was touching the horizon when the colonel called a halt to proceedings. Through a twisted smile of malice, he examined the disorderly pile of staring corpses that lay beside the river. "Make a huge pyre and see if the real Satan comes out to seek revenge."

The devil, Celeste, the high priestess, and three other women, including Bella, were the only remaining members of the original assembly.

"We will keep these heretics. They could be valuable. After some time in the torture chamber, I feel certain we will extract further information about the whereabouts of more of their kind. Throw them all in the cart with the devil's bitch."

Mara, anchored to Simon's side, watched the cart disappear as a nauseating, putrid smell of burning flesh reached her. A plume of smoke rose into a red sky and then settled as a dark shadow over an angry river that had judged every soul innocent.

5

A Suspicious Death

25 May 1670

Bertrand Duval's thick eyebrow ledges lowered and joined as he squinted into the harsh morning sunlight, up a long driveway towards the distant Duplessis mansion. He had already removed his neck scarf and jacket and gained some respite from a broad-brimmed hat. Seven large doors spread across the front of the ground floor, and above, seven draped windows looked out across the gardens. On the third floor seven dormer windows punctuated the slate tiled roofline.

The events at the river had choked his thoughts, and he could not drive that darkness away. Breathing deeply, he forcibly focused on the events described by Pierre. With a flick of the reins the carriage moved under a cool canopy of grey stemmed elms beneath which stretched a dense growth of blue petalled, yellow throated irises. Their powdery scent, though subtle, was enough to momentarily replace the events at the river with the awakened memory of a failed amour. The hurt was quickly shut out as Duval's attention was drawn to a movement in the middle room of the second floor. *Mmm? The master's bedroom. Laurent said he had instructed no-one to enter?*

The driveway swung away to the left and around a symmetrical hedge-lined garden. In the centre gushed a tall fountain from the middle of a group of granite soldiers on horseback. Sweeping, perfectly manicured lawns ran away from the driveway towards a distant, dark pine forest. Emerging from the woodland, a man, musket over his shoulder, walked with a pack of four hunting dogs. Duval stopped the carriage at the front of the manor and pulled his pocket watch from his waist coat. He had not yet opened it when Madame Duplessis burst out of the door, wiping a handkerchief to both eyes.

"Commandant! Commandant, my poor Hugo lies dead upstairs. What will become of me now?"

"Madame Duplessis, I am truly sorry for your most unexpected loss."

"Thank you, Commandant. I am so pleased you have finally arrived. I could not be certain that the young doctor would convey the message to you. You know, Commandant, he was in a most muddled condition when he arrived. Over indulgence, I am certain."

"Well, you need not have worried. Jules dropped him off early this morning. When I left, he was snoring peacefully in the spare room of my house. Now, let us proceed. Show me to Monsieur Duplessis' bedroom."

"Yes, yes, Commandant, but I have some most important information. Before that drunken doctor left in the carriage last night, he told me that 'everyone is a suspect.' This comment occupied my thoughts throughout the night. Then, this morning, I recollected a visit we had from Madame Macon."

"Madame Macon?"

"Yes, you know. The witch who lives in the shanty on the edge of the river. You know, in the poor quarter."

Duval sighed. "Well, what of it?"

"One week ago, to this very day, she came a knocking at our kitchen door and my poor husband answered. She begged for some food, 'a few scraps' I heard her say. My husband is…., was, a busy man and does not have time for these trivial nuisances. He said to her; I heard it clearly. 'Be off with you, vermin of our land, and do not dare to knock on this door ever again!' And slammed the door shut. I watched through the window. And then, when she reached the garden gate, she turned and cast a most wicked spell."

Duval nodded, but his attention was drawn again to the man with the hunting dogs at the edge of the woodland. "How so was it wicked?"

"She stretched out her arms, wide from her side, like this. Then brought them up in the air above her head, then down across her face, slowly, slowly. When they reached her belt, she suddenly thrust them forward and pointed directly at the kitchen door and shouted, 'With all the power invested in me, may you vomit and shit until you are purged of all your injustice and hatred and all life has been drained from you.'"

"That is all?"

"Yes, it must be her. It is exactly the way it happened. His life just drained from his body. Can you not see that?"

Duval looked back at her with emotionless brown eyes and a fixed mouth; only the bristling of his moustache revealing something of the reasoning within. "Madame Duplessis, I have no interest in witches' curses and will not take it into consideration. Now, could you please take me up to your husband's bedchamber?"

Clearly piqued, that such a valuable observation was cast aside, she sighed, turned and grumbled softly as she led him inside across the entrance hall and towards the stairs. Duval, relieved to be out of the heat, removed his hat and obediently followed. Crossing the tiled floor, an open door to his right distracted him. Madame Duplessis continued to puff up the stairs as Duval turned and entered a musty oak panelled room with floor to ceiling shelves filled with books. Against the window, looking out across the garden and fountain stood a solid oak desk inlaid with green leather. In the middle of the desk lay a large leather-bound journal. He reached out to open it when he heard panting and footsteps at the door.

"That is my husband's journal. No-one but he was permitted in this room. He kept a ledger of all our finances in that book. Lately he spent much of his time in here."

Duval ignored the reprimand. "Madame Duplessis, I will take this back with me and return it when I am finished."

"If that is what you wish Commandant, but I am sure you will not find it of much interest. Shall we continue up to his room? I suggest you leave the journal here and collect it; if you still require it, when you leave."

Duval followed her up the carved wooden staircase and onto the landing. She opened the second door on the left and the contained stench and heat poured out and enveloped them. Duval coughed and gagged as he pulled a handkerchief from his breeches pocket and held it to his nose. Entering, he surveyed the obese and bloated body and the excrement laden room. Eyeing the open pillbox, he stepped carefully over faeces and urine towards the bedside table. With one hand holding the makeshift mask he picked up the box and fastened the gold catch. It was elongated, intricately hand painted and made of porcelain. On the lid was an almost exact depiction of the country house. Two large hunting dogs stood in the foreground. Duval read an inscription aloud. "May we both love and live long in our beautiful home."

"Yes, I gave that to him for our twentieth wedding anniversary. That is now some ten years past."

Duval opened the box again and admired the seven separate compartments, each inlaid with mother-of-pearl. Six of the chambers were empty, and the remaining one held two pills. "Did your husband take his pills yesterday?"

"I assume so, Commandant."

"Who fills the pillbox?"

"The apothecary in St Raphael, a Monsieur Baptiste. His delightful daughter, Isabella, usually comes once every week to fill them. In fact, she should be here this morning. As you can see, the pill box is almost empty. But surely, Commandant, you are not suggesting that someone has tampered with Hugo's pills?"

Duval ignored her question and quickly moved on. "And what of this brown bottle?"

"I have not seen it before. I assume he must have acquired it when he was in the city yesterday. Now that I recall, when he arrived home, he did say he was to return to town for further business in the evening. But clearly, he did not."

"Hmmm?" Duval picked up the bottle, removed the glass stopper and looked inside. Then examined the base and noted a plain pontil scar with no identifying blower's mark. "I see that it is empty?"

"As I have said, Commandant, I know nothing of that bottle."

"I assume those garments belong to your husband," nodding towards some rumpled clothes hanging on a teak clothes horse in the corner.

"Yes, that is correct. I would have tidied up, but that indulged young doctor ordered me to close the door and not enter."

Duval, having seen a movement from his carriage, smiled at the deceit and moved across and rummaged through the pockets of the breeches, waistcoat and jacket. "I am surprised that such a busy man carries nothing at all in his pockets, not even a handkerchief."

"He is most meticulous in his habits. Everything is emptied and placed in the appropriate place as soon as he retires to his room."

"I understand that you and your husband sleep in different rooms. Do you know if he was seeing another woman?"

"Commandant! How could you dare suggest such a thing? My husband was a very important and a well-respected member of this district."

"Madame, please just answer the question."

"I trust my husband implicitly and pay no attention to his life outside our home."

Duval waited and wiped the sweat from his brow with his handkerchief. "Madame Duplessis, you should start being very honest with me. I oversee the criminal arm of la Maréchausée. We take a specific interest in controlling prostitution and we have eyes everywhere. We also know of, but turn a blind eye to kept mistresses of the rich and influential."

"All right, all right. I am aware that my husband keeps a mistress at Maison Claire."

"I think you may know more about this mistress?"

She stared wide eyed with mouth open. "You people are despicable, watching every move of every citizen. Is there no privacy anymore?"

Duval fixed her, his face expressionless, waiting.

"Yes, yes. She is known as Madame Bonnie. I followed her some two weeks ago and confronted her."

"And?"

"She shouted at me in the middle of the street so that all would hear. She called me fat and ugly and said it was not surprising that he did not wish to sleep with me. And then she walked off."

"You were no doubt angry with her and your husband?"

"Yes, of course. That story was soon around the entire city."

"Did you want to kill your husband? It would leave you without that embarrassment and a lot of money?"

"Commandant! How dare you, a mere commandant, suggest that a woman of my standing be party to such a vile act. This is ridiculous."

Duval ignored the reprimand and continued. "I have made enquiries and am aware that most of this wealth is from your inheritance, and that he was a man of modest means when you met. Were you not afraid that he would forsake you for this younger woman and leave you with very little?"

"Commandant, I would ask you to please desist from this line of questioning. To suggest such a thing at this current time is to accuse one of witchcraft."

"If you can think of anything further, please let me know. Now, take me down to your kitchen."

A narrow wooden staircase at the rear of the house took them down and opened into a cavernous, rectangular room filled with a pleasant aroma of smoke and recently baked bread. Although the sun streamed through a large high window, Duval was relieved by the coolness. A long stone fireplace occupied one entire wall. In the centre, a large iron pot hung from a chain and hook over an open hearth with a small bed of glowing coals.

On either side of the hearth, long-handled iron forks, spoons, pokers and coal rakes hung from the walls. An outstretched table laden with pots and pans and recently harvested carrots and potatoes stood in the centre of the room. In a far corner, a young woman dressed in a white, starched uniform bent over an iron pot, diligently peeling potatoes. Duval nodded in her direction.

"Charlotte, could you please leave the kitchen? The Commandant and I have business to discuss."

In one corner, a large dresser with open shelves above closed cupboard doors drew Duval's attention. He walked directly across to the containers and took down a cork stoppered, brown glass jar labelled ARSENIC.

"I assume you will tell me you use this for killing vermin."

"Yes, of course. We have a horrid rat problem and can never seem to be rid of them."

"Madame, are there any servants who may hold a grudge or grievance towards your husband?"

"No sir. Absolutely not!"

"Are you certain?"

"Well, my husband believed in strict discipline and keeping the servants in their place. He often reprimanded them and occasionally struck them if they misbehaved or questioned him. I believe they respected him for his rigid authority."

"Who brought up his dinner last night?"

"Charlotte prepared it and I brought it up to him."

Duval scanned the room once more and then turned towards the stairway.

"If that is all, Commandant, I can instruct one of the servants to make you a cup of tea. You have come so early and you must have a thirst."

"No, thank you Madame. I will contact you if I need anything further." He reached the first step, stopped and turned. "I saw a gentleman with some hunting dogs as I drove in."

"Yes, Monsieur Antoine Bassett. He is an old friend and neighbour who sometimes hunts on my estate."

Duval's eyes locked on hers. Her smile did not reach her eyes, and a slight tremble of her lip and a pink flush to her cheeks suggested some duplicity. He turned again, continued up a short stairway which opened back onto the entrance hall. He gathered the journal from the study and left through the front door.

***

The landscape passed by unnoticed as the carriage jarred and jerked along the potholed road. With one hand he held the reins; the other fiddled with the pill-box and small brown bottle in his waistcoat pocket. Approaching the river, he took the bend to the left, pulled his hat low over his forehead and passed the continuing drownings unnoticed. The pile had grown considerably; those near the bottom now showing signs of early bloating. The village school was silent and Celeste's front door hung on its hinges as two unkempt men carried out furniture. Le Pont St Joan did not carry its usual bustle. The Laughing Water's publican, busy cleaning up the debris from the previous evening, gestured to Duval as he rode past.

The carriage climbed a small rise and St Raphael appeared before him. He pulled the horse up in the shade of a large pine tree, still juggling the objects in his pocket. Staring blankly towards the city gate, he was oblivious to the occasional carriage and country folk making their way towards the city. St Raphael, named after the patron saint of travellers, stood on a wide plain leading north to Paris. In the centre of the wall the city gate stood open and a drawbridge crossed a side fork of la Loire. To the left of the gate, marked by a row of willows, was where he had found the young boy two days previously. To the right of the gate, one section of the wall had succumbed to the pounding of cannons and the shanties of the poor quarter spread out through the chasm. The Tower stood tall and ominous, guarding the right-hand corner, and the barracks of the la Maréchausée spread out behind it. A wide, quiet section of la Loire flowed quietly beside St Raphael's right wall as fishermen with makeshift rods waited patiently in small boats.

A large cart of rowdy farm workers rumbled past and snapped Duval from his deliberations. *An abused young boy and now a possible poisoning. Could they somehow be connected?* He straightened, removed his hand from his pocket, flicked the reins with both hands, and the carriage quickly covered the distance to the city gate. Instead of proceeding to his office, he turned left, following the wall and stopped outside a pink three storey building bearing a sign, *Maison Claire*. He sat paralysed, feeling some guilt as memories flooded back. He had visited there some ten years previously; inebriated after the father of a woman he loved, advised him he was not a fitting suitor for his daughter Giselle. As always, he forced the scar from his conscious and climbed out of the carriage.

On entering the cool hallway, an aromatic, exotic scent reached him. Two women with powdered faces, blackened eyes and covered only by flowing, loose-fitting gowns bustled towards him. They adeptly attached themselves to either arm. "Ah Monsieur, what is your pleasure here this morning? It is not yet midday. You must be in urgent need. You can call me Margot, and this is Lisette."

"My ladies, I am Commandant Duval and unfortunately my business here today is not pleasure. But I can see that I will have to return at a more convenient time."

"Oh, Commandant Duval, you must be sure to ask for me," said Margot. "I know exactly what pleases the brave men who maintain law and order in this fine city. But Commandant, if we are not your pleasure, how is it we can be of service?"

"I would very much like to speak with Madame Bonnie."

"Oh Commandant, surely you do not prefer that witch to me!"

"Certainly not Madame Margot. We have business of a different nature."

At that moment, the front door opened, and a grey-haired gentleman in a fine suit entered.

"Ah Monsieur Romero, I thought you had forgotten me. It has been such a long time." Margot quickly wrapped herself around Monsieur Romero and signalled Lisette, who shuffled across the tiles and up the stairs to call Bonnie. Margot followed with Monsieur Romero, leaving Duval alone in the hallway. He was drawn to a row of paintings along one wall. First a study of the canals and bridges of Venice, the next a wide river with fertile banks and towering pyramids in the background. He was engrossed by a painting of an enormous lion's head emerging from tall, yellow grass, when he was interrupted by a soft voice.

"You are probably wondering about these paintings in an establishment with this reputation?"

He turned to the voice. Madame Bonnie, tall, dark and sensuous, glided down the stairway, hand sliding along the wooden banister. Duval studied her without replying until the sweet smell of jasmine reached him.

"Good morning, Madame Bonnie, I am Commandant Duval," and held out his hand.

She ignored his hand and clasped her gown around her neck. "We cater for customers with a more discerning taste. The paintings give them a sense of the exotic. They feel special and as a result, they come back."

"I agree. They are unusual and captivating."

"A visit from la Maréchausée is not a good way to start my day. What am I being accused of?"

"You are accused of nothing Madame. I have just a few questions to ask regarding Monsieur Duplessis."

Beneath the curl of her lashes, slightly widening pupils were the only sign of recognition. "Yes, he is a regular customer here, but I am certain you are already aware of that."

"Yes, Madame, that is true. Unfortunately, I bring some very sad news. Monsieur Duplessis passed away last night."

This time only a slight twitch at the corner of her mouth as she held Duval's gaze. "Yes, is that all?"

"I understand you had an altercation with Madame Duplessis in the street about a week ago. Would you care to comment on that?"

"There is little to say. Madame Duplessis had discovered that her husband visited me regularly. It seems she had this deluded belief that by insulting me, it would somehow stop his visits. I advised her to lose some weight and provided instruction about her manner of dress, if she wished him to return to her bed."

Duval, hand in his jacket pocket, fiddled with the pillbox and small brown bottle. "There is only one other question I have for you Madam." He pulled the bottle out of his pocket. "Do you know anything about this bottle?"

"Most certainly. I gave him a similar bottle."

"For what purpose?"

"Well, you see, he was having a few problems down below. We see that here occasionally. Some men may see it as a failing on my part and move on to one of my colleagues. Soon the rumour spreads and then I am without business. So, we provide our men with this little remedy, which together with some encouragement from me, usually resolves the problem. I provided him with that medicine yesterday and suggested he return in the evening after he had taken the contents."

"And from where do you acquire this medicine?"

"I do not know, because I get my supplies from Madame Katerina, who departed for Paris some two weeks ago. She informed me she received them from a man who experiments with new remedies. A highly intelligent man; way ahead of his time, she said. I believe she called him Charles, but cannot be certain."

"Have you any further supplies?"

"No sir, that was my last bottle."

"As you have said, you have provided these bottles to other troubled clients. I assume none of them have come to any harm?"

"To the contrary Commandant. They appeared much more spirited, and as I have already stated, their little problem resolved."

"Thank you, Madame. Do you mind if I return if I have further questions?"

"Not at all. Good day Commandant." She held her outstretched palm towards the door, the other still clasping her gown to her neck.

6

The Black Death

12-26 May 1670

Charles Labonne hunched forward in his carriage; a hat pulled low over his brow. His bright blue eyes avoided the sunken, dark sockets of the ragged procession of ghosts trudging in the opposite direction. In the distance, the walled city of la Bastille nestled on the plain in the shadow of the towering crags and peaks of the Pyrenees. The city had for centuries repelled countless southern invaders, but the current enemy had proved invincible. His disquiet and guilt dissipated slightly when he turned off the rutted road and away from the column of wretchedness. The carriage came to a halt in a dense clump of trees where he removed his hat, leather boots, and fine suit. Emerging from the thicket with short cropped blond hair and a dirty white shirt which hung loosely over broken brown breeches, he readily blended with the hapless throng. Only a few gaunt faces stared in disbelief as the tall, unblemished man walked in the opposite direction; towards the doomed city. The ache of stones beneath his bare feet provided some atonement for the deed he was about to undertake.

The wailing of mourners and piercing cries of pain from those in their last hours of life poured out of the main gate and momentarily slowed Charles. A horse-drawn wagon rattled past with blackened, putrid bodies piled five deep above the sides. He stopped and watched the cart jar and jolt towards a group of men emptying a stationary cart of its cargo of human flesh into a large pit.

Once inside the city, the smooth cobblestoned avenue allowed Charles to proceed more rapidly with long, easy strides. Most doors bore the cross of the Black Death and large black rats scurried around bodies piled outside residences.

Another cart trundled towards Charles, the driver shouting through cupped hands, "Bring out your dead. Bring out your dead." A few doors opened and emaciated residents carried out dusky bodies and dumped them into the cart before disappearing back inside. Two men walking on either side kicked at the rats and heaved waiting bodies into the wagon.

The ornate three and four-storey buildings of this once wealthy city were bedecked with roses, carnations, and the purple flowers of la Mentha. Charles shook his head at the desperate and deluded belief that these flowers would block out and absorb the pestilent miasmas that brought the plague. The main avenue opened onto a large town square littered with bodies. A queue of robed flagellants paraded around the periphery, chanting and lashing themselves with leather scourges, seeking penance and hoping to placate an angry god.

As he walked across the square, Charles paused briefly at a barely moving body of a young naked boy with large, black suppurating lumps in his groin and axillae, and fingers missing from both hands. The eyes, large and hollow, looked right through him and the memory of his childhood flooded back; but only for a second. He had work to do and continued on towards the towering cathedral which cynically kept watch over the town. The massive front door was ajar and, as expected, the inside was devoid of priests or any other clergy. History had confirmed that their god did not provide them with special protection from this pestilence. They either died or were the first to leave; justifying their exit by claiming they would be most needed when the plague passed. He strode quickly along the flagstones of the nave's central aisle, traversed the crossing and stopped in front of the altar. There, as predicted, he found the usual bags of coin, jewellery, paintings and title deeds to countless properties. Relinquishing all their worldly goods being a final, desperate plea to their Lord for protection from the unyielding contagion. Sadly, these pleas remained unheard, and the church became the prodigious beneficiary of this scourge. Charles emptied a large sack carrying a magnificent framed mural of Jesus instructing Lazarus to rise from the dead. He smiled at the irony and filled the bag with smaller valuable items. From experience, he knew exactly which items would fetch the best price per weight and discerningly filled the sack. Once full, he flung it over his shoulder and returned to the entrance of the church, where he left his stash just inside the door. His work now almost complete, he walked outside and sat on the steps watching the square. No-one paid him any attention; to them he was just another poor soul trapped in this hell, waiting to die.

Remaining till dark was perhaps the most precarious part of his assignment. Not for fear of being discovered, but more the dread of repressed childhood memories surfacing when he watched the curtain descend on a city. It was no different on this occasion. He had grown up in a town like this, the son of a wealthy trader, and lived a comfortable, happy childhood. The plague also arrived in his town and quickly ravaged their blissful life. His father soon developed a headache, quickly followed by his mother and two brothers and then himself. The black blotches soon covered their bodies, the telltale buboes arrived, and they all lay down to die. He flinched at the memory of the excruciating pain as the buboes grew, and then the sudden relief and loss of consciousness as they burst. He awoke to the rumbling of the carts outside and the rancid smell of his family around him. When the door shattered and the body carters entered, they immediately turned and fled at the sight of the ghost of a boy walking towards them. He was one of a few survivors and struggled in the aftermath and through his slow rehabilitation. But two years later, the plague struck again, and he again watched death all around him, but nothing touched him and he remained when everyone left. He was able to enter houses and take anything he needed or wanted. As a result, in the following twenty years, he followed the plague throughout Europe, slowly accumulating vast wealth and property.

The long shadows of the cathedral slowly crept across the square. Charles was preparing his departure from this misery when the town doctor entered at the far corner, followed by another cart. Charles could not conceive that such learned men had the deluded belief that it was their duty to remain through the pestilence. Most of them perished. Charles had seen them countless times before. It was always the same. The doctor moved from body to body, conspicuous in a wide-brimmed hat, ankle length overcoat, gloves and boots. He wore a most distinctive bird-like beak mask with glass rings to see through. At each corpse, he used a long cane to prod or disrobe and examine the prostrate soul. Once satisfied that they were dead, he signalled to a cart assistant who removed the body. The doctor approached a body at the foot of the stairs and a familiar pungent smell reached Charles. He made no attempt to cover his nose. He knew its origin; a vinegar impregnated sponge in the beak to disguise the stench of the decaying corpses.

By the time the doctor and the cart departed the square, dusk had given way to darkness and a morbid stillness engulfed the city. Charles retrieved his sack and with eyes fixed to the ground, weaved through the rats and carcasses along the deserted streets. The city gate was open and once in his carriage, the Pyrenees quickly disappeared behind him.

***

Two weeks later, Charles stepped out of a large blue door onto le Boulevard du Printemps. He sucked in the honey scented air produced by the yellow and white flowers of the lime trees that lined each side of the avenue. It was good to be back in St Raphael. His last trip had been tiring, and he had vowed that it would be his last. It was time to give something back, something that he had been pondering for some time. He had experimented with various medicinal remedies, none with any great success. This time, however, he was certain he had found a miracle cure. He walked briskly and proudly with his cane, wearing a fine jacket covering a matching waistcoat over black breeches tucked into white stockings and leather shoes. Strutting down the avenue, the black curls of his wig bounced on his shoulders when he tapped his hat and nodded to passers bye. A couple, chatting arm in arm, walked towards him, rousing his aloneness. For that moment, he also wished for someone special to talk to, but quickly locked the thought away.

He stopped briefly to watch a group of four children playing blind man's bluff. They were all neighbours, and he knew them well. Maria, the youngest, wore the blindfold and was covered in the lesions of the chicken pox. The other three children, all a few years older, had unblemished skin. He watched for a few minutes, smiled and then continued on his way along le Boulevard.

He breathed deeply as he reached the last steps of the university, entered the open wooden doors, and found his way to the office of Professor Stefan Dubois. The door was open and a grey-haired, full bearded man sat writing at his desk.

Charles removed his hat, adjusted his black curls, and entered. "Good morning, Professor. I am Charles Labonne and am most pleased that you have so kindly agreed to see me. I guarantee my proposal will not disappoint you."

Professor Dubois looked up briefly and signalled for Charles to enter. "I am rather busy this morning, but I understand you want some syphilis pus from this body." He pointed to a table on the far side of the room where a white sheet contoured a body. "This is a very unusual request, so please proceed and try to convince me."

"Well sir, as you know, I trained in medicine at the University in Paris but have never practiced. I see myself more as a researcher. My preference is to apply my mind to complex questions with the hope of ending some of the immense suffering we see in the world today. I maintain an intense interest in the human body and the diseases that affect it. For some time now, I have observed how people respond to certain infections. Some die and some survive. More interesting is that those that survive do not suffer from the illness again." He paused, waiting for a response from the Professor who, head down, merely waved his left hand to continue and persisted with writing. "Only this morning I observed some young children, one with the chicken pox, while three others who had had it previously, were clean."

"The protection from chicken pox is well established. Surely you have more than that to proclaim."

"Yes, Professor, I have much more. But first I must speak personally about my experience with the plague. I contracted this fatal illness as a young boy, as did my mother, father, and two brothers. They all died, but I survived and since then I have entered and lived in many plague-ridden towns and have never shown any signs of the dreaded Black Death."

"Well, it sounds rational that the very few that survive may develop some sort of protection. But I remain uncertain how this has anything to do with my body. This man here who died of syphilis?"

"Thank you for listening. It is clear that the human body retains some sort of memory of a previous infection. And this memory protects us against the same illness again. But what if we can provide a person with this memory either before or during the course of this illness?"

"Yes, that would be a great medical breakthrough. But, again, how can I be of help?"

"Well, I was informed that you had a body here with the syphilis infection, and I am pleased that you have confirmed that information. He probably has those big buboes, clearly indicating a syphilis infection. The pus will contain the syphilis infestation. I have developed a method where I can mix that pus with water, add specific herbs to retain memory and then dilute it to a point where it is not harmful. But miraculously, the fluid will retain the memory of the syphilis infestation. If I give this fluid to a patient with syphilis, it will provide him with the memory and the protection that is required. It will act like a shield and therefore I have called this fluid Memory Shield."

Professor Dubois sat quietly at his desk, now head up and glaring at Charles. The room was hushed with only the muffled sound of chatting students drifting in from a distant corridor. Dubois rose with both hands fixed to his desk; his eyes blazed brown fire. "My dear sir, I have never heard such utter gibberish! How could water with nothing in it provide a cure for syphilis or protection from it? Not to mention that you may pass on the syphilis infestation to some poor soul."

"But sir, if I could just have some of that pus, I will prove that this is not just a deluded theory. You can then share in the fame that we will achieve."

Professor Dubois straightened to his full, imposing height. "Doctor Labonne, I want nothing to do with your ridiculous and dangerous theories. Please leave!"

Charles partially opened his mouth, but instead turned and left the office.

7

Foxglove

27 May 1670

Commandant Duval raised his head when Thomas Beaufort knocked at his office door. "Well, Thomas, what news have you about the drowned boy?"

"Sir, I have looked through our missing person's file and have found eleven missing persons over the last month. The earliest report is 1 May, and the latest was yesterday. Only two fit the description of our eleven-year-old blond boy who appears to have been abused and drowned on about 20 May. One is Andre Bellamy, and the other is Frank Pelletier. In both cases, the mother came in to report the disappearance. I first visited Madame Pelletier, who advised that her son had already returned after visiting his grandmother in the country. She apologised for wasting the time of la Maréchausée. However, the events surrounding Andre Bellamy are of great concern. I visited his house, a shack in the chasm of the wall. The house was locked with no sign of life. A young boy from the house next door, a Jacques Macon, informed me that Andre was a friend from school who he had not seen for about a week. Jacques confirmed Andre was blond and that Andre's mother had looked everywhere for him."

"Well, the description and timing certainly are in keeping with the poor lad we found at the river. Andre Bellamy? You mentioned they were school friends; what school did they attend.?"

"Yes, it is interesting that both Andre and Jacques attend the village school near le Pont St Joan. Not one of the closer Catholic schools in the city"

"Thank you, Thomas. It appears we may now have a name for the unfortunate lad we found in the river. Tomorrow I will pay a visit to this

50

school. Perhaps there is further information that can shed light on this heinous crime."

***

Mara crouched silently, patiently behind a large elderberry bush in the middle of an open meadow. The sweet smell of its cloak of white flowers effectively disguised her human scent. She tried unsuccessfully to smother the recurring dark clouds of Celeste's recent incarceration while she waited. Her eyes danced with relief when on schedule the fox appeared at the forest edge. First, his elongated muzzle and pointed ears peered through a patch of tall grass and surveyed the open pasture. Cautiously, a red coated, thin frame emerged followed by a bushy tail. The young male moved abnormally slowly across the open ground, stopping occasionally to rest. A fat belly almost touched the grass and a sharp, shallow cough punctuated his progress. Passing a stone pen with an open wooden gate, he stopped and looked inside. He turned and sniffed a breeze wafting towards and rustling the leaves of the elderberry. Satisfied, he rested again. Once revived, he continued and eventually reached a hedgerow lined with a row of purple tubular shaped flowers at the opposite edge of the meadow. He sniffed the foxglove and chewed on his selected leaf. Mara captivated, stared with discerning curiosity at the nibbling fox as the morning sun warmed her back through her white collarless blouse. Her quarry, when finished, lay down, resting, but alert, repeatedly testing the breeze and scanning his surroundings. Finally, he rose to his feet, stretched and ran surprisingly quickly, without pause, back across the field to the safety of the forest. Mara smiled as she vacated the disguise of the elderberry and walked to the hedgerow. This was the third day she had watched this fox repeat his routine. *It must be the foxglove!* As on previous occasions, only the blade of one leaf had been eaten. The midrib remained. Mara plucked about twenty leaves, placed them in her satchel, and jumped over the hedgerow. Her faded green dress swayed from side to side as she skipped in soft leather boots along the rutted country road.

"What have you been up to this morning?" asked Simon as Mara opened the gate. "Watching that sick fox again?"

"Yes, and he did exactly the same again. I have picked some more leaves," her pride filled smile and sapphires danced as she lifted the bag. "Where are Maman and Grandmère?"

"While you were busy with your experiments, they packed some belongings and left in the wagon."

Mara's eyes dimmed, and her smile contracted to a frown. "Why? Where to? They didn't say goodbye."

"I am sorry Mara, but your account of Celeste's ceremony and the drownings troubled them deeply. Because of their own herbal practices, they thought it best to disappear for a while until this witch hunt nonsense settles down. They were certain that you would be safe here with me."

"Disappear! When will they return?"

"I do not expect them for some time. They have travelled about four days east, so perhaps next week, maybe even longer."

Her head and shoulders drooped, and the excitement of her discovery faded. She dragged herself to the south side of the house where previously gathered foxglove leaves had been laid out to dry on a large flat stone. Mara scooped them up and spread the morning harvest out in the bright sunshine. She cut the midrib from one dry leaf and then cut the blade into tiny pieces before grinding into a green powder between thumb and forefinger. With some apprehension, she placed a tiny amount in her mouth and swallowed. The remaining leaves were prepared in the same manner and the pieces ground with a mortar and pestle. The fine ground powder Mara emptied into a small earthenware pot, which she placed in a compartment of her belt.

"That did me no harm," she mumbled to herself after about half an hour. She reached back into the pot and took double the amount. After cleaning and sweeping the kitchen and hanging out washing, she still did not feel any effects. She doubled the dose again, but this time after half an hour she felt a slight nausea and developed a headache. "So that must be the noxious dose!" She returned to the prior dose, calculated the fox's weight and made a comparison with her own. "Now let me see how my little friend likes this."

Mara woke early the next morning, singing quietly to herself as she cleaned the cottage. She mixed the powder with a piece of meat left over from the previous night's dinner and rushed out of the kitchen door and raced towards the garden gate.

"Mara, wait! Where would you be off to so early?" shouted Simon from across the yard. "Not the fox again?" And then added, "You have been tardy of late and have many unfinished chores. Miriam will be furious if she finds them unfinished."

"Yes, yes. I know, but if this works, it will be the last time, I promise. I know you only worry about what Maman says because you will be the one in trouble," she laughed. "Did you fix the trap?"

Simon nodded and smiled as he watched Mara open the gate and run up the road.

She arrived earlier than previously and set the piece of meat covered with the powder in the middle of the small stone enclosure and left the gate open. A piece of string twine attached to the bottom of the gate led back and around the gatepost and the rest lay in a coil against the stone wall. Mara unfurled the twine as she walked across the field and took her position and waited behind the elderberry bush. The fox's muzzle appeared through the grass at exactly the same time as previously and ventured, coughing and resting along his track. He stalled and sniffed the air a few times as he passed the enclosure. The smell of the meat was too tempting, and he turned, entered and swallowed the meat in one quick gulp. Mara pulled hard on the string twine and the gate slammed shut behind the startled fox. He moved towards the gate, sniffed, looked up helplessly at the stone walls, and lay down with his head on his paws. Mara waited, unmoved, behind the elderberry. Within thirty minutes, the fox stirred and again paced around the perimeter of his prison, sniffing for an escape route. With failure came agitation and a more frenetic pace around the enclosure. He again scanned the wall, backed up, and with an immense effort, launched himself at the stone parapet. His front paws just failed to reach the top, and he slid back down into his cell. Mara ran across the field, pulled the gate open, and stood behind it. Within an instant, the fox spotted the exit and was soon running free, across the field and into the safety of the forest. Mara smiled, eyes shining, and raised her hand to wave. "Thank you, my little friend. You have been most helpful."

As Mara reached the front gate, the excitement of her discovery dissolved when she saw a tall man in a black jacket climb out of a carriage and talk to Simon. As she approached, she recognised him as the man Colonel Montpellier had addressed, as Commandant Duval, at the drownings.

"Good morning, Mademoiselle, I assume you would be Mara Mandeville"

Mara's eyes widened at his knowledge of her name. "Yes, that is I. If you are here to see my mother and grandmother, they are away. Only I and Simon our farm hand are here."

Simon interrupted, "Mara, Commandant Duval means us no harm, and it appears he is making enquiries about Andre Bellamy who appears to have disappeared."

"That is correct Mademoiselle, I had information that he was missing and heard that he attended the village school. Unfortunately, I found the school closed but asked the Laughing Waters publican if there were any other school children that lived close. He pointed me in your direction."

"Yes, school closed three days ago, but Andre was not at school for the last three days of school. The children often have to help at home, so no one seemed concerned about his absence."

"Is there anything at all that you can tell me about Andre's behaviour over his last days at school?"

"We are a small school with only one classroom, but our lessons are very different. I hardly ever spoke to Andre, but my good friend Francine has a brother Jacques who always talks to him.'

Yes, we have spoken to Jacques, but he could not provide much information. Please, is there anything, anything at all that you found unusual in Andre's behaviour in his last days at school?"

"Me and my three closest friends Celeste, Francine and Isabella were all so excited that our school days were finally over that we paid little attention to the other students."

"Well, if you think of anything, anything at all, please let me know."

"Sorry. Yes. There is one thing that I noticed that was a little strange. On his last two days after school, he went across the road towards the Laughing Waters tavern where he met a man who I am certain passed him a coin. He then climbed into a carriage that travelled toward his home in St Raphael."

"And would you recognise this man again?"

"Most certainly! He was large with a bushy red beard."

8

The Body Snatchers

29 May 1670

A cold front fell on St Raphael and a thick midnight fog cloaked la Loire and a riverside graveyard. William wiped the sweat from his brow with the back of his arm and took a long swig of water from a nearby flagon. Rested, he continued to dig and repeatedly removed shovelfuls of soil from a hole at the head of a grave. Michael and John stood to one side and squinted through the gloom in every direction; vigilant for any unexpected visitors. Silence was essential. The only sound was the hoot of an owl in a towering oak and the dull thud of the stout wooden spade against the damp soil. Every spadeful was placed carefully on a canvas sheet next to the grave, not a trace allowed on the surrounding grass. The clunk of wood on wood signalled that William had reached the head of the coffin. Michael, the largest of the three, changed places with William. Using a fine saw, Michael cut through and removed the end of the coffin, revealing the bald head and shoulders of the recently buried corpse. With ease and experience, he located the armpits and slowly extracted the body from the casket. The moonlighters hoisted the body up, wrapped it in a cloth sheet and carried it to the graveyard wall, where it was hoisted into a waiting wagon. The hole was refilled, and the canvas lifted to drain the remaining soil. Stacked sods of grass were replaced to complete the deception. Michael stood back, examining their handy-work while stroking his full black beard, and smiled. No-one would suspect that a body buried yesterday was no longer resting in peace.

He scanned the darkness one last time and hurried back to the wagon to join his accomplices. "A good night's work thus far. A nice fresh body. Just what Professor Stefan requires for his students to dissect in the morning. He will pay handsomely. And that decayed old hag we picked up from the potter's field will fetch good money for her skeleton. The teeth shall sell quickly on market day, not to mention what the wigmaker will give us for her hair. But the night is yet young. Let us take a ride back inside along the wall. Perchance there has been a murder or an unforeseen accident."

The wagon slowly rolled through the murkiness, passing dimly lit bars, brothels, and squalid wooden houses. William and John walked on either side of the wagon, searching the darkness of the roadside gutters.

"Got one!" mumbled William quietly. "Drunk as a fish. Passed out but still has breath."

Michael jumped off the wagon and in the pool of lantern light lay a dishevelled, stuporous man, content in his liquid abyss. "I know him; drinks and goes with these women every night. Does not work and has a wife and two young children at home. No-one shall miss him and his wife will do a jig when he has gone. Let's do it!"

John pulled a piece of white cloth from his breeches pocket, knelt next to the inebriate, and pushed the cloth into his mouth. The drunk's eyes snapped open. He grabbed at the vise around his neck and kicked his legs furiously. John's powerful arms had little trouble holding him down and within a few minutes, he was quiet.

"Hoist him up and cover him. Now that should please the good professor. We have one more body to collect. A baby. They were expecting a difficult delivery."

The wagon again moved off through the soup and, before long, stopped outside the door of a small wooden dwelling. Michael cupped his hand around his mouth and copied the owl; "hoohoo… hoooooooo." Within a few minutes, a young girl emerged from the door carrying a small bundle in her hands. "What has taken you this long? The child was born an hour ago!"

Michael didn't respond and looked at the bundle. "Is it….?"

"It is not the whole thing, stupid. Just a few parts. Now hurry on, Madame Macon is expecting it." She placed a single livre in Michael's outstretched palm.

Again, the wagon pushed on down the rutted streets and soon came to rest outside another small derelict cottage within the chasm of the city wall. Michael again cupped his hands, "hoohoo…... hoooooooo," and within seconds a bent, bedraggled women clutching a tattered coat emerged.

"Ah, Madam Macon, we feared you may be asleep."

The wretch ignored the comment. "At last, you have arrived. I have so much to do before dawn." She snatched the small bundle from Michael's hands, turned and quickly re-entered the shack.

The wagon turned away from the gloom of the river and the fog thinned and the air cleared as they ascended to a more affluent district. They turned and crept along le Boulevard du Printemps. The avenue was well lit, but the setback mansions remained in the shadows. Michael squinted into the dark to find the correct address. "Ah, here it is, number 28." He pulled the horse to a stop in front of an imposing three-storey building, jumped off, hustled up the steps and knocked on a large blue door. Within minutes, a light appeared inside and Charles Labonne opened the door carrying a lantern.

"Hello Michael, have you finally got something for me?"

"I am not certain, Monsieur Labonne, but this man is a drunk and a regular visitor to all the whores down by the river. So, I believe he fits your description."

"Let me take a look." Charles pushed past Michael and led the way to the wagon. Under the lantern light, he pulled back the sheet and examined first the left and then the right groin of the drunk and smiled. "Yes, yes, this is perfect. Please, bring him inside. It will not take long. I have been preparing for this moment for some time."

Michael stepped into the lamplight and looked directly at Monsieur Labonne's illuminated face. "I have to sell this body, so no cuts or missing bits?"

"I promise, just a small procedure. Bring him in!"

William and John lifted the corpse off the wagon, carried him into a marble floored entrance hall, down a flight of stairs and into a brightly lit basement. They placed him on a long wooden table in the centre of the room. Tall, glass-fronted cupboards filled with an assortment of containers and instruments lined the walls. Monsieur Labonne took a short quill with a sharpened open end and expertly pushed it into the lump in the drunk's left groin. Thin pus drained freely through the quill and into a small porcelain container. "Ah, at last! This is marvellous. Just a bit more." He squeezed the lump and more pus drained into the bowl. "Yes, that is enough." He pulled out the quill and applied pressure with a small piece of white cloth at the puncture site. "Hold that there for about fifteen minutes and you will not see a thing. Even that bigoted professor will not notice." He held the porcelain container and marvelled at the contents. "You lads can take him out now; I have finished with him."

"You forgot one thing, Monsieur Labonne." Michael held out his hand.

"Oh yes, yes. How could I forget? Very happy to pay for this most remarkable gift. You may not realise this, Michael, but this is the beginning of one of the most stunning discoveries ever seen." He placed two livres in William's hand.

The wagon moved off further up the hill towards the dark outline of the hospital and university. "Alright boys, our night is done. Our children shall have food for a week and our wives may surprise us."

***

.

Monsieur Labonne woke early, dressed, and went directly downstairs to his small laboratory. On the long central table, twenty glass containers stood neatly in a row, each one half full with water. To each, he added a sprinkling of salt. He removed the cover of the small porcelain container and trembled as he marvelled at its miraculous contents. After pouring the pus into the first container of water, he added a pinch of dried rosemary leaf powder and then gently swirled the container for a minute. He then poured half of the diluted pus into the second container, added more rosemary powder, and again swirled the container for a minute. The identical process was repeated twenty times. He held the final container up to the light and smiled. He poured a portion of the final dilution into ten small, brown glass bottles and closed them with a glass stopper. To the neck of each bottle, he attached a label with twine. Memory Shield for the Treatment of Syphilis. Prepared by Dr Charles Labonne.

9

Witch's Brew

30 May 1670

A morning sun bathed imposing, stained-glass windows, highlighting the red, blue and yellow mosaics composing Jesus Christ. A white cloaked bishop stood high in the apse, arms outstretched, interrupting the rays of light and casting a long, monstrous shadow over the pulpit, across the north-south crossing and the assembled congregation.

"We live in the most difficult of times and every day our faith is being tested. But if we follow the one, the true path which God has laid out for us, we shall find the salvation we desire."

The cathedral was bursting. The congregation crammed shoulder to shoulder. There was not a spare seat in God's house, except in the middle row on the epistle side of the nave. There Madame Maxine Macon sat alone with two empty spaces on either side. A black, grey-streaked curtain of bedraggled hair hung across her eyes and face while a prominent, battered nose protruded through the mess. Bony hands fidgeted continuously on her lap. Madame Macon's blue, darting eyes were the only sign that she was younger than her outward appearance suggested.

Madame Macon's mouth was set in a grimace as she scanned the large murals along either wall. This was her first visit after a long absence. Every corner, every painting and every sculpture was as she remembered. Moses still occupied a large section of the right-hand wall with his hands stretched out, parting the waters of the Red Sea. Next to him stood Lot, sculptured in a pillar of salt. A smile broke her set mouth as she fixed on The Last Supper and then The Lady at the Well. Circumstances and knowledge had replaced her previous teenage innocence with scepticism and anger. Her thoughts quietly escaped her lips.

"Yes, I now know the truth. Not as pure as this deluded zealot up there thinks you are."

"Shhh," from the men on either side, two spaces away.

Madame Macon smiled at each one in turn, beckoning them to come closer. They quickly shifted their eyes to the front and squeezed as far as possible in the opposite direction. She had grown up in this city. This church had been her foundation, her justification for everything she did. Her parents sent her to the College of Sorbonne in Paris, where she studied theology and history. While away, the Black Death arrived and decimated St Raphael and her whole family. She returned to a life of destitution, bitterness and hatred of her God. In the gutters and seediness of the riverside, she lost her soul and followed another path.

"To finish, I would briefly like to forewarn you about the sin of heresy. Heresy is the denial of Christ or the denial of his commandments and teachings. Over the centuries, we have seen countless heretics who have attempted to defile our God and our Church. We have witnessed the Waldensians who worshipped Satan, and the Cathars who murdered and devoured babies. Even the Knights Templar were involved in satanic worship, blasphemy and homosexuality." He paused as green eyes, deep-set in a round face, searched his flock. "Men who sleep with men are also heretics, as this practice is strictly forbidden by our Lord. I read from Leviticus 20 verse 13. 'If any one lie with a man as with a woman, both have committed an abomination, let them be put to death: their blood be upon them.'"

He raised his bald head, atop a squat neck, from the huge, open tome and scoured the audience. Not a muscle moved or mouth twitched, for fear it signalled a dark secret. His focus came to rest on two greying women sitting shoulder to shoulder two rows in front of Madame Macon. "Les sapphists!" The words spewed from his mouth, instantly uncoupling the two dames. "Yes, we know of the vassals of the ancient poet of Lesbos. Do not think that you can hide your vile acts behind a shroud of unmarried chastity. We will find you!"

No-one turned to look for fear of association. Madame Macon had recognised them as she entered. Madame Augustin and Madame Blanchet lived not far from her.

"Jews," he spat out the name, "are often regarded as the greatest heretics, as they have adulterated the true word. Association with any adulterers of this most cherished book is a sin against God and his church."

"Then there are also those individual heretics who have achieved greatness before being cast aside. Our very own Joan d'Arc did not lead the King's army because she was some great general. No! We now know that she had secured a pact with the devil and was able to conquer her foes with some satanic magic. This heresy justified her death by fire. The hamlet and bridge that bears her name is not far from our walls. This is an insult to our God and this we must rectify." Bishop Bernard paused, searched the audience again, and took a sip from a glass.

"Central to any heresy is always Satan. As you are all well aware, Satan led a failed revolt of dissident angels in heaven and they were all cast out to pursue their malefice on earth. Here, they regularly tempt innocent souls to renounce their allegiance to God. God allows this. It is a test he has set for us. However, at times he is so angered by our weakness that he sends calamity down upon us. The Black Death, which has caused and continues to cause untold suffering, was brought upon this world because of our failure to hold back Satan. This plague sent by our God occurred not once but multiple times over 300 years. It seems we repeatedly fail his tests."

The perspiration appeared as beads on his forehead; the glittering diamond rings flashed in the sunlight as he paused to wipe the sweat away. Madame Macon felt the hatred of his gaze as he momentarily fixed on her. "Now we are witnessing an even greater heresy. The widespread practice of witchcraft and devil worship. We in the Catholic church have made it God's work to eradicate this scourge from the earth. And let me add, here in St Raphael we get little help from those who call themselves reformists.

So, I ask. No, I demand, in God's name, that you join with God's church in our fight to rid this pestilence from our land. Be watchful, trust no-one, not even your closet friends and family. If you have a suspicion, bring it to us immediately." He paused and took another sip.

"Now, as is the custom, this morning we will perform the Blessed Sacrament. Before doing so, I ask each and every one of you whether you are worthy to partake of this ceremony. All the aforesaid heretics and any non-believers cannot therefore take part in this holy communion. If anyone of you knows in your hearts that you have sinned and are not re-pentant, do not come forward when the procession begins. I repeat, do not come forward!"

The assembly remained closemouthed. Not a muscle moved, but a thousand eyes looked from side to side. The bishop stood with both hands on the pulpit and perused the congregation. At one point his head stopped, and for a brief second Madame Macon felt the full threat of his instruction. Those in the seats on either side shuffled nervously, but she looked directly back at him through her disordered veil of hair. No threat from this deluded prophet would distract her from her morn-ing's mission.

"We partake of The Blessed Sacrament as a remembrance of the blood and body of Christ that was shed on the cross and to show us how much he loved us and to remind us of his suffering. It is also a remem-brance of the Last Supper where Jesus promised, that whoever eats his flesh and drinks his blood shall have eternal life and he will raise them up on the last day."

He paused and stood tall in his pulpit. "It is time to bring your gifts forward."

As Bishop Victor Bernard stepped down from the pulpit, a rumbling of whispers swept through the congregation. A few stood and moved to the rear of the church. Here they collected gifts and food, which they car-ried up the nave and placed on a long table at the crossing.

Silence descended again as the bishop broke a round loaf with his hands and placed it on a silver platter. He then poured a flask of the wine into a silver chalice, dipped his fingers in a bowl of water and sprinkled it into the wine. "The mixing of the wine with water symbolises the union of the humanity and divinity of Christ." He raised the platter above his head. "Blessed are you Lord of all creation; through your goodness this is your body." He replaced the platter and lifted the chalice above his head. "Blessed are you Lord of all creation, through your goodness, this is your blood."

"These gifts of bread and this wine have now been transformed into the body and blood of our Lord. At our saviour's command and by the divine teaching, together we dare to say…" The bishop extended his arms and as one the entire congregation roared,

"Our father who art in heaven,

Hallowed be thy name,

Thy Kingdom come….,"

Madame Macon mumbled under her breath in unison with the rest of the assembly. Her mouth moved, but the words she muttered were very different.

With hands extended, the bishop continued. "Deliver us Lord from every evil, graciously grant peace in our day, that by the help of your mercy we may always be free from sin and safe from all distress, as we await the blessed hope and coming of our Saviour Jesus Christ."

The congregation respond as one. "For the Kingdom, the Power and the Glory are yours now and forever more."

Bishop Bernard continued, "Let us now offer each other a sign of peace."

Every member of the congregation turned and embraced, male to male and female to female, and then kissed each other on the mouth. Madame Macon stood alone, ignored by everyone but keeping her eyes firmly fixed on her goal on the Sacrament table.

The bishop took a piece of bread from the platter and placed it in the chalice, "May this mingling of the Body and Blood of our Lord Jesus Christ bring eternal life to those who receive it."

He stretched out his arms. "I welcome you in the name of our Lord Jesus Christ. Please come forward and receive this gift that his sacrifice has given us."

Row by row and one by one, the assembly stood and started singing,

"Lamb of God, you take away our sins,

Slain for us, we will never forget……………"

Madame Macon fell in line as her row emptied into the central aisle. Her muttering continued, masked by the singing assembly. Her eyes darted from side to side as she recognised more of the sculptures and paintings from her past. A large bust of Constantine stood at the entry to the south transept. She smiled, continuing her jabbering. "The man who expunged women's central role from the church. Not surprising he secures a prominent place."

"Together we take this body of his life,

And drink the blood of sacrifice……"

She reached the crossing, and a painting of Jesus travelling with his disciples appeared in the south transept. Among them a number of women, one with long strawberry hair. "Aah! Yes. Joanna. You from a wealthy family. You funded this rabble of holy-men and peasants. How else could they have survived on the road for so many months?"

Madame Macon could now see the bishop and stood shielded behind a tall, broad-shouldered man. A painting of the Tomb of Jesus, against the back wall of the transept, was now visible. The stone rolled away and three women stood with hands over their mouths. "Aah! Of course. Mary, mother of James, Salome, and, of course, leading the group, Mary Magdalene. His favourite. Dark. Standing tall and strong. No wonder Jesus named her Tower. If women were so insignificant, why were they the first to arrive?"

Her turn was approaching. She concentrated as the bishop offered the chalice to a parishioner, now only two in front.

"The blood of Christ."

The parishioner crossed himself. "Amen"

The bishop offered the bread. "The Body of Christ"

The parishioner crossed himself again. "Amen"

The tall man moved forward, exposing Madame Macon. She shut out all her fear and mumbled incoherently as the assembly continued the procession song.

"We know he will come again,"

"And will join him in the heavenly feast."

Bishop Bernard's eyes opened with surprise as Madame Macon stood directly in front of him. Momentarily distracted from his task, he continued and placed the chalice to her lips. "Blood of Christ,"

"Amen," she replied boldly, without hesitation.

"The Body of Christ," and moved his outstretched hand holding the bread towards her extended tongue. Just as he reached her open mouth, Madame Macon moved her tongue up against her palate and the bread was placed on the floor of her mouth where it mixed with the wine. Bishop Bernard, briefly stunned, opened his mouth to call out, but she had moved on and the next parishioner was already in front of him. She did not return to her seat, but scurried to the entrance and left the church. She crossed the square and disappeared up a small alley. In the shadows, she looked from side to side and then spat out the body and remaining blood of Christ into a ragged piece of cloth. Surveying the alley again, she placed the cloth in her pocket and hastened away.

Madame Macon did not walk directly to her dwelling by the river, but turned towards the higher side of town. The streets gradually widened and finally opened onto the expansive, tree-lined Boulevard du Printemps. The midmorning sun had brought many of the local inhabitants out to promenade and display themselves and their finery. Madame Macon, refused to move over as they approached and steadfastly, held her line on the boulevard, causing sneering strollers to veer towards the centre of the road.

Passing a white three-storey house, she slowed, momentarily glancing at the blue door. Then hurried on as the door opened. In a quieter part of the street, she stopped in front of a much larger four storey building with a gold plaque beside the front door bearing the name *Monsieur Claude Villiers*. On either side of a grand green door stood a large earthen pot, each with a sculptured olive tree surrounded by a low covering of purple, sharp smelling lobelia. She hesitated for a moment, but the thoughts swirling through her head justified the proposed task. "Yes, you deranged pig. This will ensure the end of your vile acts." She pulled the piece of cloth from her pocket and carefully broke the wine-soaked Sacrament into two pieces. With the other hand, she lifted a dead frog from the opposite pocket and placed one half of the Sacrament in its mouth. She wrapped the remaining piece of Sacrament back in the cloth and placed it in her pocket. Scanning the street and repeatedly turning her head in all directions, she stepped up to the front door and placed the frog containing the precious Sacrament under the lobelia. "May you burn in the fires of hell, you depraved soul!" She turned to go, but momentarily hesitated as a curtain moved and a face disappeared in the house across the street. She bowed her head and quickened her pace in the direction of the river.

The streets narrowed again, the clothes more faded and ragged. The faces sadder and harrowed. She entered a darkened warren of streets and laneways where the eves almost touched, and the sunlight struggled to penetrate the gloom below. The maelstrom of the thousand poor souls occupying the decaying three and four-storey tenements poured out of broken windows and doors and bounced off the walls in the confined street. From a fourth storey window a woman appeared, glanced down and shouted "heads up" and discharged a bucket of sludge into the open sewer in the street below. A scantily clad woman stood in an open doorway hoping for custom while children played happily with sticks amongst the muck and putrid stench of the roadway. Through an open doorway, Madame Macon nodded to a tailor who was busy fitting a woman with a garment, and smiled as a baker threw out stale bread into a large wooden container outside his shop.

She entered the light at the end of the street; ahead lay the chasm in the city wall and beyond flowed la Loire. On the corner facing the river stood a wide four storey tenement with a pack of twenty young men loitering outside. She nodded, smiled, but moved on quickly. The Temple of Miracles was home to a hundred families living in cramped, squalid, and fetid conditions. The Temple was inhabited by thieves, murderers and released convicts, but it was most widely known for its perverse reputation as a school of crime. Children were taught how to steal purses and jewellery but also how to simulate blindness, gangrene, amputation and other appalling and frightening wounds and illnesses. These afflictions always miraculously disappeared as they walked back through the front doors after a successful day on the streets.

The Temple of Miracles faced an open strip of ground on the other side of which lay a row of dilapidated, wooden shacks interspersed with remnants of the city wall. Just beyond the shacks, a line of debris showed the high-water mark. Madame Macon walked across to the second dwelling and pulled open a makeshift door made from various pieces of driftwood.

"Pardon Madame." Maxine spun around to see a man in a jacket with a mop of black hair emerging from the shack next door. "Sorry to startle you Madame, but I seek Madame Bellamy. I wish to question her about a blond boy of about eleven. He maybe her son Andre, who I hear is missing?"

Madame Macon straightened, brows knitted, and her bottom lip quivered. "And who, pray tell, would you be?"

"Sorry, I am Commandant Duval of la Maréchausée; but not one of the witch hunters. My colleague, Lieutenant Beaufort, was here a few days ago and found the Bellamy house locked. He spoke to a Jacques Macon, who confirmed Andre was missing. I see that Madame Bellamy's door has now been smashed open, and she has yet to return."

Madame Macon shuddered, and her heart quickened at the mention of Jacques. "In these times it is best not to become acquainted with neighbours as even living next door to a witch may see you in the Tower."

"I mean you no harm. Please, my only interest is the boy."

Madame Macon fixed Duval for a few more moments. "The boy vanished some ten days ago and has not been seen since. My son and Andre play together."

"Yes, I have heard he was well liked in this neighbourhood. And what of Madame Bellamy?"

"She was a broken woman after her son disappeared. She searched everywhere. Then two days ago, la Maréchausée arrived here on horseback, broke down her door and took her away. She did not struggle. She was crushed. It was as if she was expecting them."

"La Maréchausée took her away! That is a tragedy. I must explain Madame. I am not involved in any witch hunting practices of la Maréchausée. I have responsibility only for criminal cases."

Madame Macon did not respond as she assessed the Commandant.

"Well, I must be on my way. Thank you, Madame…....?"

"Madame Maxine Macon, Commandant."

Duval raised one bristling eyebrow in recognition. "Madame Macon! So, you would be the mother of Jacques?"

"That is correct, Commandant."

"I would like to question you on another matter. You visited the house of Monsieur Duplessis some weeks ago, and his wife mentioned you placed a curse on him. She believed it resulted in his recent death. I have no belief in such curses and therefore have not questioned you earlier, but would welcome your opinion."

Madame Macon's eyes initially wide with surprise, relaxed with the commandant's comments, and chuckled. "Yes, such a horrid and spiteful man. His wife and St Raphael are better off without him. However, the curse is not the cause of his death. It was placed in anger and did not match his crime of refusal to help the needy. Mismatched curses are never effective. That fiend held so many other dark secrets that are much more likely to have contributed to his death."

Duval's eyes widened. "Would you care to enlighten me of these dark secrets?"

"Just the usual. He is a regular visitor to Maison Clare and has even been seen parading in the city with women of ill repute. The manner in which he treats those in his employ is despicable. I have heard of horrific beatings. His staff seldom last long and he has difficulty recruiting new ones. Unfortunately, those leaving his service receive a demeaning reference and find it difficult to find work and end up destitute, here in the chasm of the wall. Any of those previous employees would hold a grudge and have good cause to see him gone."

"Thank you, Madame. If you think of anything else, please let me know."

She watched Duval walk away and called after him. "Commandant, there is something that I found rather curious."

Duval wheeled around and walked back towards her. "Please Madame Macon, anything may be of help."

"Some two, perhaps three weeks past, I saw a large man standing across the road," she pointed to the Temple of Miracles. "He signalled to Andre, who approached him. They had a brief conversation, and he then pressed something into Andre's hand; I think it was coin but cannot be certain. He then walked away towards the city gate."

"Can you describe this man in more detail?"

"As I have said, he was a huge man, with thick red hair and a very bushy beard. I have not seen him before or since."

Duval's eyes sprung open and nodded. "Thank you, Madame Macon, that description does fit with someone with whom we wish to speak. Please, if you see him again, please come and speak with me immediately." Duval tapped his forefinger to his temple and walked away.

Madame Macon shook her head as Duval departed and pulled open her door. Inside, beams of light shone through the gaps in the wooden walls and roof. The interior was spartan. A straw bed covered with threadbare blankets lay in the corner to the left of the door. In the middle of the room stood a broken wooden table. Against the right-hand wall was a plain dresser with drawers at the bottom and shelves above, filled with an assortment of stoneware bottles. A solitary pewter mug stood out of reach on top of the dresser. The back wall was missing and framed the gently flowing Loire. In the middle of this canvas hung a heavy, cast-iron cauldron over an open fireplace, next to which stood a small wooden stool, a metal pail and a wooden crate.

The door opened behind her and a teenage girl with cropped dark hair and a blond boy of about twelve burst in out of breath.

"What have you two been up to?"

"We were playing in the street, Maman."

"I hope you did not speak to that rabble across the road."

"No Maman. Not them. Definitely not. Is there anything to eat?"

"You two are always hungry. It has only just past noon. Jacques, go down below the Tower and find some fish. The fishermen often throw some away. And you, Francine, get some scraps at the baker in the town. I saw him throw several loaves away as I walked down. I have had a busy day and need to make a cure that I can take to the apothecary in the morning. Now go!"

Jacques moved obediently back to the door, but Francine stood her ground, her bright blue eyes under full eyebrows fixing her mother. "Maman, we always scavenge, borrow, and beg for food. And look at this house. I get teased every day at school about this shack."

"Well, Madame, what do you suggest I do about our situation?'

"Well, you once said my father had some money. Does he know of my existence?"

"That scoundrel turned his back on us when I was pregnant with you, and I have too much pride to go begging to him. Anyway, I have no idea where he is. The last I heard, he was in Venice. And while we are talking about fathers, Jacques's father died in a brawl and any money he had went to his wife. Now go, before I give you both a hiding!"

When the door slammed behind the children, Madame Macon wasted no time and scurried through the open wall to the river bank where she collected pieces of dried driftwood. These she placed underneath the cauldron and, with a flint and some dried reeds, the fire was soon flickering. She returned to the river and filled the pail and tipped a portion into the hot cauldron. She grinned at the satisfying hiss and steam of the cold water on the scalding pot. Soon the muddy water was bubbling, and Maxine took her place on the stool to prepare the recipe of her gypsy ancestors. She pulled the crate closer and began to drop the contents into the broil. First, a dried wing of a bat, the skin of a small snake and two human molars. With a sharp knife, she cut a mandrake root into small pieces and watched them splash into the broth. She unfurled a hessian package and laid it open on the ground. She picked up the tiny heart and afterbirth, which had been soaked in a mixture of spices and cast them whole into the brew. Finally, she withdrew the remaining Sacrament from her pocket, unwrapped it, smiled and dropped it in. The bubbling potion hissed and spat as she stirred with a long wooden spoon. Satisfied, she lay down next to the cauldron and drifted off to sleep.

It was late afternoon when she awoke to the slamming of the front door. Jacques smiled proudly, holding two small fish above his head.

"Look, Maman, can I cook them now?"

"Well done, Jacques. Yes, go ahead, the fire is still alive. Just add some more wood."

Francine, brooding and grumpy, carried a half loaf of bread in one hand and three brioches in the other. The bread clunked on the wooden table as she threw them down. Madame Macon tried unsuccessfully to press her fingers into the loaves. "I can never understand why people throw away such good food. Where did you get those brioches?"

"I passed by Madame Augustin's house and she gave them to me."

"I have warned you about those two. Keep your distance. Those sapphists are constantly watched by la Maréchausée and all those seen in their company will be questioned. Surely you did not enter?"

Francine looked down, fidgeted with her hands, and moved her feet.

"Well! God help you if you went in!"

"No, no mother. But mother, they are always so friendly and welcoming."

"I have warned you. Have nothing to do with them. Now enough, it is time to eat."

The sun was setting behind the hills by the time they sat next to the cauldron. They quietly ate their simple meal as the darkening river flowed peacefully past.

"I think it is time you both went to bed. I must still complete my new cure; so off you go."

After the children had settled into the rudimentary bed, Madame Macon gathered several containers and a funnel from the cupboard. With a metal ladle, she carefully scooped the mixture from the cauldron and poured it into the cloth lined funnel, which drained into a flask shaped stone bottle. Four similar bottles were sequentially filled, and the rest decanted into a larger jug. Madame Macon stacked them on the cupboard shelves and lay down next to her children.

10

The Apothecary

1 June 1670

The bell jingled as Commandant Duval opened the half-glass door and immediately inhaled the sweet smell of lavender and lemon herbs used to disguise the smell of the tallow soap used to keep the apothecary clean. He was surprised to see, standing with his back to the door, a colossal figure adorned with flowing yellow and orange garments. A chestnut head protruded above the costume and brown, dusty feet filled open sandals. Monsieur Raphael Baptiste's bald head and red beard popped out from behind the giant. "Ah! Good morning, Commandant. And to what do I owe the pleasure of the constabulary at such an early hour?" The hulk turned, surveying the Commandant with one eye, the other covered with a patch. A ragged scar, from underneath the patch, cut a groove across his face to the corner of his mouth, creating a bizarre, lopsided distortion as he smiled. "I have neglected my manners. This is Khan Abas Hassan."

"Good morning, Khan Hassan." Duval held out his hand, and the cyclops crushed it with his.

"Good morning, Commandant. I speak not so good the French. Me from Egypt."

"Khan Hassan is a trader of medicines from the East. He provides me with many new and interesting remedies which I use for my clients. Look, he has brought me these castor beans." He opened a small woollen bag on the counter, inserted his hand and drew out a palmful of brown patterned beans. "The contents of these beans can be ground into a paste and used for a variety of skin ailments. They are also excellent purgatives and have been used to cause contractions of the uterus to remove unwanted babies."

While Monsieur Baptiste spoke, the Egyptian packed his displayed wares into a hessian bag, which he threw over his shoulder. "Monsieur Baptiste, Commandant, it is the time. I go now to Marseille. I catch the boat. Goodbye."

"It was good to see you again. When will you return?"

He held up two fingers. "Two months, maybe." He turned, opened the door, strode across the small square outside the apothecary, and disappeared down a side street.

"Well, Commandant, how can I be of service?"

"I will get straight to the purpose of my visit. As you are no doubt aware, Monsieur Duplessis died under unusual circumstances."

Without a flicker, Monsieur Baptiste's green eyes held Duval's. "Yes Commandant, I am aware and was expecting a visit from you in connection with this tragic and unexpected death."

"I must, in my investigations, pursue every possibility to be assured the pill box beside his bed did not carry a poison."

Monsieur Baptiste nodded and rubbed his beard with his left hand; Duval noting the absence of an injury to his left wrist. "I am an open book Commandant and have nothing to hide. Please continue."

"Thank you. Your daughter visited Monsieur Duplessis a week before he died and filled his pill box. Could you briefly explain how Isabella does this?"

"In the case of Monsieur Duplessis, it is very simple. For him, I prepare two packets, each with a different pill and each packet with seven pills. Isabella then places a pill from each packet into each compartment of his pillbox." Monsieur Duplessis hesitated and then turned and called out, "Isabella, could you please come here for a moment?"

A young, red-headed girl in a red dress appeared through a curtain behind the counter." Yes, Papa?"

"Could you please explain to Commandant Duval how you dispensed Monsieur Duplessis pills last week?"

"Certainly. Papa prepares the packets, each with seven pills, and I place one from each packet into each day of his pillbox."

"That sounds straightforward," nodded Duval.

"In Monsieur Duplessis' case, yes, it is simple. But there are patients with more complex requirements. Those I will pack in the pill box myself."

"Papa, I am preparing for rounds. Is that all you require?"

Monsieur Baptiste nodded, and Isabella disappeared behind the curtain.

"And what do Monsieur Duplessis pills contain and why does he require them?"

"These are questions usually only an apothecary or a man of medicine will understand."

Duval shrugged off the slight with a forced smile. "Please humour me Monsieur Baptiste. Make it simple, for a simple man."

Monsieur Baptiste sighed. "Monsieur Duplessis suffered from diabetes. We confirmed this some fifteen years ago because of his symptoms and his sweet tasting urine. His symptoms were mild, and if he had heeded mine and Dr Laurent's advice and desisted from his gluttonous eating and excessive drinking, he may not even have been plagued by it or needed his medication. As his diabetes was mild, we were able to control it with some age-old remedies. I usually make a mixture of fenugreek, wormseed and lupin, from which I make one of his pills. His other pill is crushed poppyseed, which contains small quantities of opium."

"And you prepare all these tablets here?"

"Yes. I have a small laboratory just behind that curtain. I would be more than happy to show you how these pills are made. It is a long and tedious process and now is not a convenient time as the shop is about to open and Isabella needs to do her rounds. I usually make my pills in the afternoon, and would be happy to arrange a time with you."

"You mentioned his diabetes was mild. Does that imply it was not the cause of his sudden death?"

"I discussed this with Dr Laurent and we both agreed that in view of his mild, stable diabetes, the sudden deterioration and death were unlikely because of his diabetes."

Duval raised his eyebrows. "Yes, Dr Laurent informed me of that same theory, which then raises the possibility of other causes."

"Yes, perhaps his death was by poisoning or perhaps a severe gastrointestinal upset. Dr Laurent and I both agree that a gastrointestinal upset is unlikely, as there was no current sign of an outbreak in the St Raphael community."

Duval held Monsieur Baptiste with a questioning stare. "So, you say you are free most afternoons to show the pill making process."

"That is correct. No need for an appointment."

As Duval turned, Dr Laurent entered the apothecary. "Well, Dr Laurent, Monsieur Baptiste and I have just been talking about you."

"Hopefully, you both spoke well of me."

"Have you had any more thoughts on the Duplessis death?"

"As a matter of fact, I have not been able to shake this tragedy from my thoughts. As we have already surmised, it is most likely poisoning. However, I very much doubt it is arsenic. I have never seen or heard of such a sudden death with arsenic. Furthermore, I doubt one could put enough arsenic into one of Baptiste's pills to cause such a violent death. It is conceivable that the small brown bottle could hold more arsenic. What do you think, Monsieur Baptiste?"

"I am shocked, Dr Laurent, that you could even link my pills with this death. But yes, I agree, you would require a significant quantity of arsenic to cause such a death, and this would require a very large pill."

Dr Laurent approached the counter while Duval stood aside and waited. "Monsieur Baptiste, this morning I require more laudanum. A truly magnificent drug that has allowed surgeries I would never have before contemplated."

"Most certainly Dr Laurent. Be careful with it, as you know it is made from the opium and alcohol and is quite addictive. I have had few fellows from the poor side who have come a begging for it."

"Not just the poor, Monsieur Baptiste, of that I can assure you."

Monsieur Baptiste disappeared behind a curtain and returned holding a small bottle containing a reddish-brown liquid. "I will put in the ledger."

"Thank you, Sir. I must hurry back, as I already have a full waiting room. I should really engage someone who can run these errands for me."

Duval held open the door, and they left the apothecary together and walked, conversing, across the square.

***

Some hours later, Baptiste lifted his head from his journal when the bell jingled again and Charles Labonne entered the apothecary. Labonne immediately appeared distracted by a head, without a nose, protruding from a large wooden box, releasing steam through slits between the panels. Another man sat in a chair, bent forward, moaning as he clutched his leg. He was naked except for a small cloth covering his genitals. He was ravaged with multiple ulcers and raised lumps extending from his bald crown to his black toes. Monsieur Labonne stepped closer to inspect the steaming wooden box. At the rear of the box was a small fireplace, above which was placed a simmering pot of viscous fluid. Labonne's head swivelled back towards the counter when Baptiste addressed him. "Good morning, Monsieur Labonne. It has been quite some time since I saw you last. Are you here for some medications or to enlighten me about another of your most recent discoveries?"

Labonne did not respond immediately and continued to study the wooden box. "This is indeed extremely interesting. May I ask of its purpose?"

"This is the latest treatment for the cursed Grand Verole, or as we now say, syphilis. We practitioners call it suffumigation with mercury. It produces excellent results."

"That is interesting. I have heard of the treatment using holy wood ointment. I am certain you know of this herb." Without waiting for a reply, Labonne continued. "You are no doubt aware it is from the Americas; conforming to the theory that the cure is found in the same land where this cursed pox originated. I have not heard of suffumigation."

Monsieur Baptiste had no wish to be drawn into Labonne's ludicrous theory of the origin of syphilis. "Holy wood may work for early cases, but these poor souls have ignored early signs and have come to me late in their illness. Look at those buboes, their distorted faces, and the agonising groans from the pain they feel deep in their bones. They need something stronger, so we use mercury. It is truly a wonderful discovery. Unfortunately, mercury elixirs and ointments have no effect on late disease. However, breathing in the mercury by suffumigation allows the mercury to enter every pore of their body. But the treatment is long, years in fact. As has been said before, 'a night with Venus is a lifetime of mercury.'"

The bell jingled, and another customer walked in and stood at the counter. "Excuse me, Monsieur Labonne, I must attend to this client."

While Baptiste talked with his client, Charles studied the floor to ceiling medicinal storage behind the long counter. Six parallel shelves stretched above six banks of drawers. Each row was filled with an identical jar, pot, or bottle, perfectly spaced along the length of the wall. He stepped closer so that he could read the labels. Shuffling sideways, he studied every herb and medicine. Towards the end of the shelves, he turned and stood staring at a floor to ceiling mural on the side wall. Four horsemen rode side by side in a headlong gallop.

"Do you like it?" asked Baptiste, who had moved silently beside him.

"Oh, yes. Yes! It is truly breathtaking. It has so much energy and colour. What does it mean?"

"I have only recently acquired it. A close friend painted it and is his interpretation of The Four Horsemen in The Apocalypse of Saint John. Look at the first horseman. He carries a drawn bow and arrow, regarded as an emblem for the transmission of disease. The second horseman holds his sword high in the charge, symbolic of war. Note the third horseman's scales: these represent famine. Finally, the fourth horseman, almost skeletal, is Death. He carries a pitchfork and rides an emaciated horse bareback. All four charging into all forms of disaster."

"It is truly fascinating. But such a cruel fate. Such a sad daily reminder of the delicate balance of our lives. What made you chose this?"

"You are very insightful Monsieur Labonne, not many ask this question. It is a daily reminder of the tragedies of my own life. My wife and son went to visit family in Spain and while there, the Black Death swept through that country. They left immediately, but on their journey home it was clear they had contracted the disease, and died before they could reach St Raphael. I have managed to raise my beautiful Isabella on my own."

Labonne laid his hand on Baptiste's shoulder. "I am truly sorry for your loss. I share your grief. My father, mother, brothers all succumbed in the same manner."

Uncomfortable with the hand on his shoulder, Baptiste pulled back slightly. "So, Monsieur Labonne, what did you say your business was here today?"

"Well, sir, I see that you have an interest in this syphilis. It appears that I have fortuitously arrived at exactly the right time."

"How so is that, Monsieur Labonne?"

"Well, I have discovered a unique method of treating diseases. I call it Memory Shield, and this morning I have brought you the Memory Shield to treat syphilis."

"Memory Shield! Never heard of such a method." Baptiste stretched his open palm to the shelves of medicine. "And as you can see, I remain abreast of each and every new discovery."

"Well, let me explain. We know that many infections only occur once in the lifetime of a patient. They do not even get the illness again if they come into contact with someone with an unrelenting, terminal affliction. It is as if the body has a memory of the illness that shields him from a second infection."

Baptiste, irritated, rubbed his hands together as he listened. "Go on, go on. This is not new, and I do not have all day."

"Well, I have been fortunate to obtain some syphilitic pus and have diluted it repeatedly with water. It is no longer infectious, but with my secret method, I have been able to retain the memory of the syphilis in the harmless water. This memory we can give to anyone, either to prevent or to cure an infection."

"So, you think it will work for these poor souls? Even the mercury suffumigation seems to have lost its bite."

"I am absolutely certain it will work. I would like to try it on these two gentlemen. Here is a first bottle for each of these desperate men; absolutely free, of course."

Baptiste rubbed his chin and looked across at his two patients. The nose-less man lifted the lid of the steam box and stepped out of a small door. Small streams of perspiration ran down his chest and abdomen, changing direction each time another pustule was encountered. He walked across to the counter and picked up a small leather object, placed it where his nose had once been, and tied it behind his head with two pieces of twine. He tripped as he moved away from the counter and fell to the floor. Labonne and Baptiste quickly helped him to his feet. At close quarters, they could observe the man's excessive salivation, the loss of most of his teeth, and the ulceration around his lips and in his mouth. The gentleman with black toes took his place in the box and pulled the lid over his head.

"Alright, alright, I will try it. These poor souls have not much hope otherwise. As you have observed, not only has the mercury lost its effectiveness, but I am afraid some of what we are seeing are toxic effects of the mercury."

"Good, you will not regret this." Labonne held up two small, brown bottles, each with an attached tag. "Here, take these two bottles. They should take a small thimble full once every day. I will return in a few weeks to observe the miracle of the Memory Shield." He placed the bottles in Baptiste's open hand, turned, opened the door, and let it jingle behind him.

The apothecary, now empty, Baptiste retired to a seat behind the counter and squeezed copper rimmed spectacles onto the bridge of his nose. He dipped a goose quill with a few terminal barbs into a pot of ink and began writing in two large journals.

After much coughing and spitting, the black toed man raised the lid and stepped out of the steam, breathing and salivating heavily. As he reached for a towel, his body stiffened, a violent spasm consumed him and he fell writhing to the floor. Both Baptiste and the nose-less man paid little attention. Within a few minutes, the spasms eased, and he dragged himself off the floor. Once dried, he pulled on his clothes.

"Monsieur Boucher and Monsieur Durand, you would have observed that man who came here. Well, he says that he has discovered a new miracle cure for this pox that you suffer so cruelly from."

"If such a medicine exists, it would indeed be a miracle. I do not think I could bear another night of this crippling pain in my……. Aaah!" Monsieur Durand gripped his leg as another spasm possessed him.

"Yes, you are both in need of a miracle. This may be the cure you seek. I will give you each a bottle. I want you each to take a thimble full every day and we will reassess in two weeks"

"Thank you. Thank you for all that you have done for us. And particularly for providing us with this glimmer of hope."

Baptiste returned to the back room as the two men finished dressing. He weighed out some ingredients for a batch of tablets but was distracted by the jingle of the door. Peeping through the curtain, his heart sank when he spied his most unwelcome visitor; Madame Maxine Macon. She was bent forward, bedraggled hair falling in her face, and pulling a few ceramic bottles from her pocket. Baptiste elected to ignore her, but when she approached his two pox ridden patients with bottles held in her outstretched hands, he pulled back the curtain.

"So, you two are here again for your regular pox treatment? You men, all the same. You just cannot keep it in your trousers, and then you try all these mad ideas." She pointed, laughing at the steaming box in the corner. "Probably fallen off by now, has it? But do not despair, this could be your lucky day. I have made a brew that is especially for the pox."

"Madame Macon, so nice of you to pay us a visit. But these gentlemen have had their treatment. They are about to go home and are not in need of your brews."

"But Monsieur Baptiste, this time I have added the missing ingredient. A special blessing from our Lord has been included as well as a contribution from a medicine that is pure, innocent and untarnished by the sins of our wicked world." She winked.

"I am sorry, Madame Macon, but these men have no need of your medicine. I have said many times that I have no interest in selling your concoctions in my establishment. It has taken years to build my reputation and I do not wish that to be ruined by the selling of witchcraft, particularly in these troubled times."

"Witchcraft! How dare you! These recipes are as old as the earth itself and have been passed down from generation to generation by the most revered practitioners of our craft."

Baptiste's patience transformed to anger; his mouth drawing into a flat line and his puce face blending with his beard. "Madame Macon, I will not sell your recipes in my shop! That is my final word on the matter!"

Madame Macon's blue blaze fixed him through her veil of hair. "You will regret this day." She turned, and the door jingled and then slammed as she left the shop. After a few paces across the square, Madame Macon turned to face her antagonist, who watched her through the window. She raised her arms high above her head, then slowly brought them down to her side and with a sudden jerk pointed to Baptiste and shouted, "May the curses of a thousand generations of our teachers fall upon you. May you suffer the same disease and agony of those for whom you knowingly fail to provide the true cure. May your darkest secrets be revealed and may your suffering and misery finally be so great that you die by your own hand." Her hands fell to her sides. She turned and walked across the square, holding up a bottle in each hand, towards a group of well-dressed ladies and gentleman. "Come and try this magical remedy for all your pains, coughs, and maladies. Made from a recipe as old as time itself and infused with a little help from our Lord above."

Baptiste watched as her prospective clients held up their hands and walked away. Then, the clatter of hooves on cobblestones; faint at first, but growing louder. Suddenly, four horsemen burst into the square, pulling up almost on top of Madame Macon. The red jacketed leader glared down at the cowering wretch.

"Would you be Madame Maxine Macon? We visited your dwelling in the chasm of the wall and were informed that you were visiting the apothecary."

"Yes, that is I. Who are you and what do you want of me this morning?"

"I am Colonel Montpellier of la Maréchausée. We have evidence that the recent death of Monsieur Duplessis was as a result of a curse that you placed on him on the 18th day of May 1670. You will accompany us to the Tower for questioning."

"This is outrageous and absurd. That curse did not fit the crime of his refusal to give me a crust of bread. It could not possibly have caused his death."

Montpellier's face was fixed, emotionless. "Take her!" he barked.

Three soldiers jumped from their horses and tackled a screaming Madame Macon to the ground. She cried out as her head hit the cobblestones and her bottles of magical cure shattered and the contents splashed across the square. They tied a rag to muffle her screaming mouth and bound both hands together. Montpellier led her from the square with a rope attached to her hands.

11

Maison Diana

4 June 1670

Simon knelt next to the first calf heifer, guiding his hand through the vulva and up the birth canal. "I can feel the nose and mouth but not the feet."

Mara, mouth set, stomach churning, stared through the dim candlelight as she cradled the cow's head in her lap. "Oh no! That is why she is struggling so?"

The cow had shown abdominal contractions for over six hours and the first water bag had already ruptured. She lay in the straw exhausted; both front legs restrained with ropes.

A gush of fluid spilled over Simon's hand. "That's the second water bag. Keep her calm. I must pull the baby out, otherwise this will end badly." Mara's chest tightened and breathing quickened. Simon grunted and stretched as he searched vainly for the legs. He waited, and as the heifer had more contractions, pushed his arm further. "Got one." A gentle pull and he stretched again. "Yes! Got them both." Pulling steadily, slowly, inch by inch, his arm emerged. Mara's frown softened and breathing slowed as one front hoof appeared and then a smile as both feet, together with the nose emerged. Simon now gained a better purchase on the legs and gradually, the entire head and front legs were out. Then quickly, with Simon's guidance, the bundle of fur covered in slime slipped out and lay on the straw. Simon put his ear to the calf's chest, smiled, nodded, and then gently touched an eyeball, eliciting a blink. With some rags, he rubbed the calf vigorously and then pushed a piece of straw up one nostril, inducing a sneeze. A finger in the rectum produced a steady respiration. "We have

a beautiful baby boy, Mara. Keep mum quiet while I undo the bindings"
Mara's tear-filled eyes beamed back, still cradling the new mother's head.

An hour later, they stood together as dawn broke. The new mother, exhausted, watched on as her child heartily drank the colostrum.

***

After a quick breakfast, a grinning Mara joined Simon in the kitchen garden, hoping to catch up on chores.

"About time Mara. She could be home at any time."

"I know, but won't she be happy with the recent addition to our family?"

"Yes, she will, but do not forget you have to do the rounds tomorrow. Miriam would expect you to visit all her customers."

Mara poked her tongue at him. "I know, I know. I will collect everything now."

The garden had been created to the side of the kitchen door and was surrounded by a woven wattle fence. Within the fence lay four rectangular, raised garden beds with perfectly maintained pathways in between. An internal, woven-wattle barrier surrounded one bed. Simon was busy in the pottage garden. Mara watched momentarily, while the gentle giant hummed a tune and his bare hands gently prised the white garlic bulbs from the ground.

Mara slowed as she passed the scented garden. The white starburst flowers of two angelica commanded the centre. Their aromatic, musky smell permeated the entire garden and wafted through the kitchen door into the house. The fragrance blended perfectly with the aniseed of the yellow fennel, the white flowered anise and the calming, purple lavender.

The medicinal garden was where Mara collected ingredients for her round. The angelica was again prominent and when made as a tea was their most effective remedy for gastrointestinal, respiratory, nervous system, fertility, menstrual and menopausal disorders. Mara picked some of the triangular leaves and purple stems of the rhubarb. Their cathartic and laxative properties would resolve the common problem of constipation. The Alexandrian senna, with its feathery leaves and yellow blossoms, was an effective, gentle laxative which she cut for the children. The succulent aloe with tubular, yellow flowers stood in earthenware pots; their skin healing and rejuvenating properties were a favourite for some of the local women whose skin had been punished during the long, bitter cold days in the fields. The sweetly scented, pink flowers of the valerian were specifically for one neighbouring family who, strangely, all suffered from a fitting disorder. Mara also gathered ginger for digestion, thyme as an antiseptic for wounds, catnip for headaches and migraine, St John's wort for depression and peppermint for calming the anxious.

The fourth garden, surrounded by the separate, woven-wattle fence, was entered through a padlocked gate. Mara pulled on a hessian overall and a pair of leather gloves, which lay on a small table. She lifted a large iron key from a hook and entered the enclosure. The flowers of the opium poppy provided a burst of colour in one section of the garden and were interspersed with the fleshy leaves and purple flowers of deadly nightshade. Her customers would use both plants for pain relief, muscle relaxation and for soothing inflammation. The purple helmeted flowers of the monkshood decried the plant's lethal toxicity. But when used in tiny quantities could slow the pulse, settle fever and, when applied as a tincture was effective for rheumatism and aching joints. A well-pruned shrub of angel's trumpet stood in a large earthenware pot and was the centrepiece and Maman's most prized plant. The pendulous leaves and the orange, trumpet-shaped flowers, exuding a seductively sweet scent, had successfully resolved many cases of asthma, fever, pain and inflammation. The yellow oleander with its erect stem, five lobed flowers and long, narrow seed pods was used to treat heart conditions, asthma, epilepsy and venereal disease: there were a few men who Maman had promised to bring this special remedy for their pox. The last plant Mara required was the poison hemlock. A single plant stood about two meters high at the edge of the bed. Any part of the plant, including the purple, spotted stem, the lacey, triangular leaves and the multiple clusters of white flowers could be used successfully on local children for teething, and for adults it could resolve painful joints, cramps, anxiety and mania.

The feel of the moist soil, the fragrances, the softness of the flowers, and the new calf left Mara content and tranquil. Her mother's absence was momentarily removed from her conscious and Celeste's incarceration pushed transiently to the back of her thoughts. With her work complete, she opened the gate, placed the wicker basket brimming with plants on the small table and removed her gloves and overall.

Then, a sudden clatter and voices at the front gate. Mara turned abruptly, her serenity evaporating as Colonel Montpellier and four grey jacketed horsemen entered the yard. Broad-rimmed tricornes shadowed their faces, but the muskets in their hands and the scabbards at their side made their intentions clear. Simon had already left the pottage garden, pitchfork in hand, and strode towards them. Mara hurried to catch up.

"Good morning, Colonel. To what do we owe this pleasure?" Simon smiled, leaning on his pitchfork.

"This visit is not for pleasure. It is for a matter of extreme gravity. We seek the mother and grandmother of this house; Maison Diana."

Simon spoke as Mara opened her mouth. "They have gone to visit family to the North. At least two days travel from here. We expect them back any day. I would be happy to send on a message to not inconvenience you to return. I feel certain la Maréchausée have many more important things to attend to."

Montpellier sneered at Simon. "I hope that is not the acid of sarcasm I detect in your tone? Do not dare treat me as a simpleton! I understand you are only a hired labourer here?" Without waiting for a reply, the colonel turned his glare to Mara. "And this, I believe, is the daughter, Mara?"

Mara baulked. *The executioner at the river, has knowledge of my name?* "Yes? Yes, sir, that is who I am."

"Well, now that we have become acquainted, I will advise you of the purpose of my visit. A reliable source has informed us that your mother and grandmother have been practising witchcraft for many years. Even prior to coming to this district some seventeen years ago. Is this correct?" his eyes still focused on Mara, ignoring Simon.

"I believe you are mistaken, sir. Maman and Grandmère are not witches, but do treat the common folk with herbs that they grow in this garden." Mara's arm outstretched behind her pointed towards the wattle fence.

The colonel looked across at the plants jutting above the woven fence and signalled to one of his soldiers. "Go! Have a look! See what witchery they grow there!"

A short, thin soldier dismounted and walked towards the fence. Mara noted he bore several open sores on his face and on the back of his hands where they protruded from his uniform.

Montpellier scanned the house and the stables and turned to a tall, rotund soldier. "And you have a look through the house and in the barn for anything suspicious."

Colonel Montpellier again fixed on Mara. "I am also aware that you mother bore you out of wedlock?"

Mara's eyes widened. "That is untrue, Colonel. My father died when I was but one-year-old."

Montpellier sniggered. "Well, that is strange. I have been unable to find any marriage certificates involving your mother anywhere in France. As a matter of fact, I could not locate any for your grandmother, either."

Mara stared, open-mouthed, her thoughts scrambling to understand the colonel's words.

"Colonel, Colonel!" All heads turned to see the soldier returning, his face hidden by an assorted bundle of plants clutched against his chest. Mara recognised the monkshood, arum, deadly nightshade and angel's trumpet. "Sir, I recollect these plants are those used in witchcraft ceremonies." He spread the plants on the ground next to the captain's horse, squinted at the sun, and then rubbed his eyes. "I have heard that a mixture of these plants is made into an ointment. They then rub this on and so allows them to fly to gatherings such as the one we witnessed some nights ago!"

"What do you say to that young Mara?"

"Yes, these are highly dangerous plants, but we use them for medicinal purposes." Mara looked away from Colonel Montpellier and eyed the skinny soldier, addressing him directly. "Why did you not use the gown and gloves that were set aside?"

The guard eyed Mara askance and squinted in the midday sun as his pupils dilated. He looked at one of the other guards and asked for water, which he guzzled without taking a breath.

The colonel continued his questioning. "You are aware that if your mother is a witch, that this heresy can be passed through generations. Which means, at the very least, you may be tainted by it."

Mara did not respond, preoccupied by the guard. Simon remained silent as ordered.

The tall guard returned. "Sir, there is nothing untoward in the house or the barn other than a newly born calf."

Montpellier sat bolt upright in his saddled and turned to Simon. "A newborn calf! What has been done with the afterbirth farmhand?"

Simon frowned and shuffled his feet. "The afterbirth? We always throw it on the fire, sir. For fear it may attract foxes and other vermin."

Montpellier's eyes narrowed, holding Simon's hesitancy. "So, you, a mere peasant labourer, expect me, Colonel Montpellier, to believe that it has not already been used in some witch's brew?"

Before Simon could respond, the skinny guard, now disengaged from the questioning, began to mumble and walk around in small circles, staring up into the sky. "There are so many clouds in the sky today, my Colonel!"

"Silence. Did I ask you to speak? And stand at attention!"

"Look Colonel, there is one that looks like a cat, and one like a dog, and God have mercy, another one like some hideous monster!"

"Shut up you idiot, you will spend time in the Tower if you do not hold your tongue."

The guard released a hideous, high-pitched scream and pointed anxiously at a floating cloud. "Oh my! Colonel, look there! There! Can you not see it? A vicious-looking group of witches led by a horned goat coming down on broomsticks. They come directly towards us. See their anger! They come to protect their kin and have their retribution. We must leave Colonel, immediately."

Montpellier and the other guards scoured the sky, and the floating clouds, shaking their heads. Then, another sharp scream and the guard shook violently and fell to the ground, his face contorted and body convulsing. Mara rushed to him, turned him on his side, and held him there as he regurgitated his last meal. She looked back at the colonel. "It is the angel's trumpet. It should pass."

The colonel and the company looked on wide eyed, paralysed by the bizarre proceedings. The fitting ceased after a few minutes and morphed into a restless, twitching stupor and quiet wheezing. Montpellier, initially silenced by the unfolding drama, straightened in his saddle and gathered his authority. "This is no angel's trumpet. I know what you have done. You have placed some of your evil magic on this poor soul and it has brought him to the brink of death. It is only because of his demanding military training that he has been able to stave off certain death."

"No, no, sir. I have seen this before. That is why we lock that gate and put on gloves and gown before handling those plants!"

Montpellier moved his horse closer and bent down towards Mara. "Shut up witch!" Mara felt the sour spittle spray her face. She paled and her lips trembled as the colonel licked his lips at her weakness. "I saw his hallucinations. It is clear to everyone here that witchcraft was involved. Tie her up and attach the rope to my horse. We cannot allow such evil to escape and contaminate good citizens. It is time to go. And you farmhand, stay and watch over this poor soul. When he wakes, give him some food and send him home on his horse. If he is not back by the morrow, we will be back for you."

Paralysed with fear, Mara did not struggle as they tied her hands behind her back. Simon held her eyes, but did not move. She was led out of the gate by Montpellier and the three remaining horsemen, who turned towards la Loire. On reaching le Pont St Joan, Colonel Montpellier called the squad to a halt. "I have given this matter more thought. This little witch has attempted to kill one of the king's men with her sorcery. This is indeed a heinous crime, worthy of an equally gruesome punishment."

The three soldiers looked at each other and nodded enthusiastically, but not a word dared pass their lips.

"Good. So, you agree that punishment is required but cannot venture an appropriate method. Well, look around. We have a bridge, a fast, flowing river and a manifestly guilty witch. Let us swim this little bitch."

The threesome again nodded in agreement.

"Good. Let's get started."

The guards jumped from their mounts and grabbed Mara by the arms. The rough surface of the bridge tore painfully at the skin of her legs and feet as they dragged her towards the middle. With Colonel Montpellier's words ringing in her ears, and the clear intent of the guards, the gravity of her immediate plight was apparent. Sweat trickled down her neck and brow, her breathing became faster and shallow as the centre of the bridge approached, and la Loire thundered beneath her. They forced her to the ground, tied her hands to her feet and another rope around her waist. The guards raised her up and laid her on the parapet. Her wide eyes and dilated pupils desperately scanned the bank and her trembling lips muttered. "Oh Simon, where are you now? You promised me!"

The colonel, still on horseback, approached the executioners. "Very well, men. Now we will see if the water rejects her. If not, and she drowns, then unfortunately we would have drowned an innocent. What a shame that would be."

Mara's teeth drew blood from her lips. The inevitable end of her life brought the bile to her throat and her vomit exploded and poured into la Loire. A gentle push, and Mara was launched off the parapet. She tumbled over and over and then silently plunged into the surging, muddy water. The sudden coldness reclaimed her senses, and she struggled frantically but hopelessly with her bonds. She bobbed to the surface, face up into the sunshine, gasping for breath, but immediately turned, swallowed water and was engulfed again by the raging torrent. Her breath was fading, and she was about to abandon herself to the watery grave when a hand grabbed her wrist and frantically undid her bindings. Through the murkiness, she knew it was Simon, and immediately, all fear and trepidation vanished. Within seconds, the ankle and wrist bindings were gone and the rope around her waist drifted away. As suddenly as he had appeared, Simon let go and vanished into the turbulence. Mara drifted away with the current and her head bobbed up about twenty metres downstream. Exhausted, she swam to the nearest side, clambered up a muddy bank, and sat on a large rock. Head held in both hands, she sucked in deep breaths as she watched the soldiers and their leader on the bridge; initially shouting, pointing and then mounting their horses and riding towards her.

The trio had caught and bound her when the colonel arrived. Mara stood straight, the water dripping from her face and clothes and could not hide the satisfaction that welled up inside. "Wipe that smile off your face, you little witch. You now think you are very clever, but you have just confirmed your own guilt. This water only rejects heretics. You will go on trial in six days and then, almost certainly, it will be the fire for you!" Then to the soldiers. "Throw me that rope. This witch will not be smiling by the time we reach the city gate."

As she was wrenched towards St Raphael, Mara looked across the river and smiled inwardly as she saw Simon's blond head peeking out from behind one of the arches.

12

The Tower

5 June 1670

Unrelenting moans of torment, punctuated by piercing screams of pain, echoed through the stone corridors as a daily reminder of Celeste's future. The wailing had been relentless since her incarceration ten days previously. Nightfall brought some respite, but each morning, the same anguish broke through her sleep and into the nightmare she now found herself. She lay on a bed of straw and inhaled the pungent smell of the excrement in the wooden bucket against the opposite wall. A small opening high in the wall partially illuminated her cramped stone cell while a solid iron door filled almost one side of the dungeon. A hand bearing a metal bowl, filled with her only nourishment, appeared through a hatch at the bottom of the door. She grabbed the rations, placed it to her lips, and drained the slop. Once finished, she removed the remaining gruel with her fingers and sucked them clean.

A key turned in the lock and a dishevelled jailer with a bare stomach protruding through his unbuttoned leather vest entered the cell. He jangled the ring of keys in his hand, sighed and shook his head as he considered the empty bowl in Celeste's hand. "Ah, ma Cherie, it seems I have been a little tardy and have missed our morning entertainment."

Celeste's unblinking brown eyes glared at the sloth through a rat's nest of black hair. She knew well that this lowly oaf could not influence her escape from this hell. She had refused his advances the two previous mornings when he tried to bargain with her food. This morning, his tardiness and the reek of stale alcohol affirmed he had overslept and failed to wake before the kitchen staff.

"So, you think your silence can save you? You are not the clever little witch you think you are. If you leave me nothing to bargain with, I will just have to take what I want." With a wry smile and outstretched hands, he moved towards Celeste, who scrambled backwards into the corner. Breathing heavily, he bent down to grab her wrist when the door opened behind him.

"What is happening here?" a loud, deep voice commanded.

Without turning, the guard took Celeste's wrist and pulled her to her feet. "I was just helping her up, my lord. She complained of some stiffness and possibly requires a little exercise." The brute turned to face the colonel.

"You can go. I will deal with her now."

Colonel Montpellier waited for the oaf to leave and the door to close. "This is not a welcoming visit. I am to take you for your first lesson in interrogation. Can you hear those screams? That will be you. Pleading for mercy, if you do not repent of your witchcraft."

Obediently, Celeste rose and followed the colonel through a maze of dark stone tunnels toward progressively louder screams. She had seen this man's influence. *Was he her only chance? Could he get her out of this nightmare?*

The tunnels finally opened into a large arched cavern in the middle of which lay the High Priestess on a wooden rack. Her arms were bound above her head and her legs tied to a rope, which was coiled around a roller with a handle. A massive man with a bare, sweating torso and a leather hood with cut out eye and mouth holes slowly turned the handle. He hesitated when his colonel entered the room, his blue eyes instantly registering recognition and obedience. Colonel Montpellier signalled for him to stop as he stepped up beside the High Priestess. "Are you willing to repent your sins this morning, or are we going to let this poor innocent experience your torture?"

The High Priestess looked across at Celeste and back to the colonel. "Do your damnedest! I have nothing to say to you or the priest or your fucking God! And if this young debutant is true to her teachings, she will have no trouble watching me being torn apart."

The colonel signalled to the persecutor, who clasped the lever and recommenced rotating the wheel. Her arms and legs tightened as her body stretched. Her eyes squeezed tight and her mouth contorted, attempting to halt the screams of pain building up within.

"This is your future, Celeste. This is what you will have to endure if you do not repent your ways."

Celeste felt faint, but did not respond to the taunt and continued to look defiantly at the strained face and lengthening body. She would not fail her teacher and was determined to summon the inner strength of her previous training.

The colonel raised his hand to stop and again warned the Priestess. "This is your last chance. The next turn of the wheel will tear at least one limb from your body!"

She opened her eyes and, with the only energy left in her tortured body, she sprayed his face with spittle.

Without speaking, Montpellier drew a handkerchief from his pocket and wiped the drool from his cheek. He nodded to the torturer.

The wheel turned, the body stretched, and her face grimaced. Questioning eyes peered from the mask towards his commander. Montpellier nodded, and the wheel continued the suffering. Then, an ear-splitting howl escaped the victim's set mouth as her left arm dislocated from her shoulder. The sudden release of tension caused the rope to slack and the wheel to slip a cog. The colonel raised his hand to stop and walked to her side and whispered. "We will not stop until every limb has been removed."

She could not speak or spit; wild, defiant eyes provided her answer.

The brutality of the rack and the pain of the High Priestess forced Celeste to look away. But the sight of other instruments of torture against the wall did not offer any solace. A large iron chair armed with spikes in the backrest and seat stood at the centre of the wall. A group of skinny rats scurried around a cage on top of a wooden trunk next to the chair. She shivered.

"Well, in that case, I might try something else, which might at the same time convince your student here of the futility of any similar stubbornness." He looked towards the hooded brute. "Let us try the Pear."

The torturer turned to the wooden trunk against the wall and pulled out a metal object, the size and shape of an elongated pear, with an extended ratchet mechanism protruding from one end.

"Madame, this instrument we call the Pear of Anguish. It is inserted into your vagina and slowly opened until it splits you apart."

The High Priestess didn't blink and glared back, but with fading defiance; the torture appearing to have finally fractured her conviction. Celeste, who had maintained some composure, felt the nausea in the pit of her stomach. A shiver permeated her body; her knees buckled, and she fell to the floor.

The colonel let her fall and placed a small wooden stool next to the High Priestess' hips. With hands under each armpit, he dragged Celeste off the stone floor and planted her on the stool. The hooded man handed Montpellier a small jar, which he held under her nose. The smelling salts would never allow a victim to escape a painful death. Celeste would be compelled to watch. Once alert, Celeste looked directly at her mentor's shaved mound. Montpellier signalled the torturer to continue.

Celeste shuddered as the pear was inserted into her teacher's womanhood. Once inside, the protruding ratchet turned, and the leaves opened. Another harrowing scream escaped the High Priestess as the pear expanded and tore at every tissue, muscle, and bone of her core. When the blood drained from her orifice, Celeste collapsed onto the cold stone.

***

Celeste woke some hours later in her cell; the memory of the chamber churning her stomach and chilling her body. Some hours later, she heard the key in the lock and the door open. She was strangely relieved when the colonel entered and not the jailer returning for another attempt.

"I acknowledge the brutality of what you have observed. But I needed to demonstrate what will become of you if you do not repent and comply with everything we ask. You will most certainly suffer worse or the same punishment. Do you understand?"

Celeste's eyes widened, her lips parted slightly, and she nodded. She rolled onto her side and one breast slipped out of her loose hessian rags. "I understand, my Lord, and will do whatever you ask of me. I believe I have made a terrible error of judgement and I will repent." She rose to her knees and moved across to the standing colonel. Placing both her hands on his knees, she looked up at him imploringly with wide, gullible eyes. "Please my Lord, I beg of you. I will do whatever you ask."

Montpellier stalled, unable to turn away as he knew he must. The pleading eyes, the inviting, shameless mouth and the exposed, firm breasts inside the loose-fitting rags held him there. His mouth opened to say no and his hands found her shoulders to rebuff. Instead, Celeste rose slightly and her open mouth met his. Resistance was no longer possible, and Montpellier abandoned himself to the ripeness of the young temptress. Celeste responded entirely, unreservedly, taking him and racing with him in untamed union until his final shuddering gasp. When the colonel lay finished on the demolished straw cot beside her, she smiled: he was hers and she fell into an exhausted and contented sleep.

***

Colonel Montpellier closed the iron door behind him. The turnkey could not hide the smirk as he pulled the key ring from his belt and inserted the key in the lock. "If I hear of this little tale from anybody, I will come looking for you. I will ensure your screams are even louder than those of the High Priestess. And you will suffer the same fate if you lay one finger on her. Now take me to the Devil."

The jailer inserted the key in an identical door further along the corridor. In contrast to Celeste's putrid pit, they entered a large room filled with sunshine from a window overlooking la Loire. The Devil, clean shaven with a mop of black curls, sat at a table, dressed in jacket and breeches, eating from a plate with a fork.

"Ah, good morning, Colonel. I have not had the pleasure of a visit from you since my incarceration." He stood, a head shorter than Montpellier, and held out his hand.

Montpellier ignored the gesture and did not return the pleasantries. "Monsieur August Moreau, I have been instructed to ensure that you remain in good health and to inform you that you will face the magistrate in five days."

"So soon? That is good news."

"And I believe you have something for me?"

"Ah yes. The list." He pointed to a rolled-up parchment tied with a red ribbon at the far end of the table. "I am sure that document will provide a useful list of names."

Montpellier grasped the scroll. "Thank you, Monsieur Moreau. I will pass it onto the magistrate." Without waiting for a response, Montpellier turned and left the room.

***

Colonel Montpellier still had to make one more visit. He proceeded through the warren of corridors and down two flights of stairs to the ground floor. He knocked at Commandant Duval's door.

"Come in, it's open." Duval sat at his desk, head down, studying one of the files stacked on his desk.

"Good morning, Commandant Duval."

Duval recognised the voice, lifted his head, and stood. "Good morning, Colonel Montpellier. This is a surprise. How can I be of service this morning?"

"Since our initial conversation, we have not had an opportunity to talk. We need to speak frankly."

"I agree entirely." Duval held out his hand to a chair on the other side of his desk, and Colonel Montpellier took a seat.

"First, I make no apologies for the orders I gave at the drownings some ten days ago. The tracking and processing of witches remains my sole responsibility. We discussed this previously. I will tolerate no interference in this task. As we arranged, all other crime in the city remains your sole responsibility. Do I make myself clear?"

"Yes Colonel. That seems like a very reasonable arrangement. As a matter of fact, there is one such crime that you may be able to help me with. I am currently investigating the death of a young boy. I believe his name is Andre Bellamy, but am not entirely certain. Some five days ago I received information that a Madame Bellamy was recently taken from her shack in the chasm to the Tower by la Maréchausée. I have up to now not been allowed to see her. Can you shed any light on this?"

"Yes, a most unfortunate event. We were aware that her son had disappeared and heard rumour that he died in a witch's ceremony; the body subsequently found in la Loire by a fisherman and reported by yourself. We extracted a such a confession of Andre's death from her but unfortunately Madame Bellamy died here in the Tower. You need not concern yourself with this matter; as we have just discussed, it clearly falls under my jurisdiction."

Duval's smirk signalled his knowledge of Montpellier's deceit. The colonel shuffled his hands, averted the gaze and stood up. He moved towards the door, hesitated, stopped and turned back. "You wear civilian attire and not the uniform of la Maréchausée. I find that unusual. I have always felt that we gained the respect of the people when in uniform."

Duval ignored the veiled order and again held the colonel. "My experience is vastly different, Colonel. I find that witnesses shirk away from a uniform, whereas by wearing the attire of the common folk allows one to gain their trust."

The colonel stared brown fury back at the commandant. Neither flinched until a cold, sneering smile changed the colonel's face. "I understand you are unmarried and not currently courting. Rumour amongst the troops is that you once wished to marry a young lady but were rejected by her father. I believe her name was Giselle."

Duval's eyes widened, and moustache twitched. "I was not aware that my personal circumstances were the subject of so much speculation."

Montpellier's sneer confidently transformed as he eyed his prey. "Perhaps if you wore the uniform of la Maréchausée, future fathers may find you a more respectable suitor? Good day to you, Commandant."

Duval remained seated as Montpellier left the room; fists clenched on the table and a heavy, aching heart pounding in his ears. The anger he felt for Montpellier could not smother the regret of his lost love.

13

The Malleus Maleficarum

10 June 1670

Ten black robed seminarians stood motionless, waiting. Centuries of protocol prevented them from using the hard wooden benches behind them. All heads faced directly to the front. All eyes deviated to the left and fixed on a single door on the front side of the room.

"What is this all about so early this morning?" Gabriel pondered aloud.

Louis was the youngest of the students and still half asleep. "Probably the same old lecture. You know, masturbation, wet dreams and carnal thoughts."

"Yes, that old priest talks about nothing else," Thomas agreed, and the rest of the group nodded.

Elias, a tall, thin, young man, provided some support for the bishop. "Do not be so hard on him. He has been good to me."

"Yes Elias, we all know why he was good to you. Unfortunately, you are now too old to be his favourite."

The door handle moved. The door opened and ten pairs of eyes snapped back and focused directly on a crucifix on the front wall. "Good morning, Bishop Bernard."

Bishop Bernard, clutching a book under one arm, shuffled across the room in an ankle length cassock covered from shoulder to waist by a black cloak. A young blond boy, in a white cassock, walked close behind, holding a tray with a silver carafe and cup.

"Good morning, my young seminarians. I hope I have not kept you waiting too long?" He didn't wait for a reply and gestured with both hands to sit down as he slumped in one of two chairs at the front table. The altar-boy dutifully removed the cloak from his shoulders and hung it on a hook against the wall. With small, delicate hands, he then poured water from the carafe and placed it in front of the bishop.

"Thank you, Robin." The bishop gestured him to sit in the adjacent chair.

With hands folded on the book, he faced his attentive audience. "You no doubt wonder why I have called you here this morning?" He scanned the room, searching the faces for an answer, but all ten mouths remained shut, with eyes locked firmly on the cross. "Well, today, we are going to witness the trial of four heretics accused of witchcraft. The background and the manner in which this trial will be conducted is essential for your training. You will be tested on every aspect of witchcraft and every detail of these trials." He searched each face again and smiled. He had their attention.

The bishop held the book aloft with one hand. "This is the Malleus Maleficarum. A glorious manual and informative record that will help rid the earth of these pagans. This masterpiece was written by two priests in 1486 and has been the cornerstone for fighting witchcraft since then. It has served as my guide and inspiration in my role as the ecclesiastical magistrate in St Raphael's court room. It is essential that you all know every detail of this book by the end of this semester. Today in court will be a practical introduction. I brought you here this morning so that you could ask questions before the trial begins."

Immediately, Paul, a tall, frail boy with his head completely shaved, stood up. "Father, why is it that God permits such evil as witchcraft? We have been taught that he provides and controls all things. If he cares for us, why would he not keep away all evil?"

"A difficult and thought-provoking question, my dear Paul. Our Almighty God does not wish evil to be done, but allows it because it is necessary for the perfection of the universe. God allows sin in the world, but has provided man with all he requires to fight against it. And those that pass this test will enter the Kingdom of Heaven. To repeat, he permits sin, including witchcraft, for the purpose of perfecting humankind."

A stocky, thickset boy with dark unkempt hair and rumpled robe stood and raised his hand. "You have said that witches are heretics. Why is that?"

"My dear Emile, did I not ask you all to attend the last Eucharist? It would appear that you were not there or fell asleep. I discussed heresy at length. I do not intend to go over it again. For your slothfulness, you will provide me with a five-page dissertation on heresy by this evening. Next question!"

Elias raised his slender frame from the bench. "Father, why is it that there are certain persons who are protected from the power of witches?"

"An excellent question, Elias, but much simpler to answer. In essence, there are three classes of men to whom God has given this unique protection. The first are those who play a part in the administration of justice against witches. This includes the witch hunters, the inquisitors, the judges and court officials and also those that are charged with executing the punishment. The second group are those that make use of certain powers which are embedded in holy customs such as Holy Water, the taking of Consecrated Salt, bearing Blessed Candles on the Day of Purification of our Lady and carrying Palm leaves on Palm Sunday. In the case of Holy Water, it is well established that wherever sprinkled, all defilement is purified, all mischief is repelled and a witch cannot remain there. The ultimate protection from witchcraft is given to those blessed by having a special Angelic guardianship provided by the Powers that move the stars. Other than these three classes of men, non-one is safeguarded from witchcraft."

Dominic, a tall, handsome adolescent with black, curly hair, raised his hand. The bishop gestured for him to speak. "My Lord, why is it that by far the great majority of those that practice malefice are women?"

"That is a very intuitive question Dominic, as I would expect from our top student who has passed all his exams, and I am informed, is due for ordination shortly. You and I probably find it impossible to understand how anyone can be drawn to witchcraft and become a servant of Satan. But then you and I are men. Women are made differently. First, women are more credulous and therefore, Satan targets them. Women are also more impressionable and more susceptible to accept an evil spirit. They are weaker, powerless in mind and body and therefore easily fall into the bewitchment of the devil. This vulnerability, this imperfection, was easily exploited by the Serpent in the Garden. Eve failed that test and committed the first sin that has put humanity on a treacherous path. Women naturally follow their own foolish impulses with no thought of the consequences. They are difficult and most times impossible to discipline. Women also have slippery tongues and cannot smother evil knowledge. This then ensnares friends and acquaintances in their mischief. Above all, however, women are naturally wicked and are accomplished at concealing their wickedness."

Dominic again raised his hand. "My Lord, we are here because of our chosen path and therefore have very little experience with women. Accordingly, we cannot verify these characteristics of women. I accept that what you say is correct, as you are a man of great experience and wisdom. But what does God say on this matter?"

"Dominic, I take no offence and I am pleased that you seek the truth from the highest authority. This sorry portrait of women is well described in The Holy Bible. I will read selected verses from Ecclesiasticus 25.

'17. The sadness of the heart is every plague: and the wickedness of a woman is all evil.

18. A man will choose any plague, but the plague of the heart: And ally (any) wickedness, but the wickedness of a woman.

22. There is no head worse than the head of a serpent:

23. And there is no anger above the anger of a woman. It will be more agreeable to abide with a lion and a dragon than to dwell with a wicked woman.

24. The wickedness of a woman changeth her face: and she darkeneth her countenance as a bear: and sheweth it like sackcloth. In the midst of her neighbours.

26. All malice is shore (sand) to the malice of a woman, let the portion of a sinner fall upon her.

27. As the climbing of a sandy way is to the feet of the aged, so is a wife full of tongue to a quiet man.

28. Look not upon a woman's beauty, and desire not a woman for beauty.

29. A woman's anger, and impudence, and confusion is great.

33. From woman came the beginning of sin, and by her we will die.'"

Beads of perspiration appeared on his brow as his face reddened. Taking a deep breath, he lifted the water glass to his lips. He signalled to Robin, who took out a white cloth and gently wiped his forehead. "Is there another question?"

Silence for a few moments and a small red-haired student raised his hand.

"Yes Randolf? Speak!"

Randolf looked furtively from side to side and then at the bishop. "I have heard that there is much debauchery in their meetings and even copulation with devils. Is this true?"

Bishop Bernard sighed, frowned, and his head drooped. "I had hoped not to expose you to this, but I am afraid the courtroom will not be so guarded. What you ask is true. Carnal acts are at the centre of all witchcraft. The reason for this disgusting behaviour is, however, not surprising. Women are much more carnal than men because they have a natural, insatiable, licentious appetite. For the sake of fulfilling their lusts, they consort even with devils. The devil knows this full well and aspires to wrap them in his allegiance by such delicious pleasures." The bishop's voice rose and his hands balled into fists. "Through this insatiable lust, they become the perfect gateway to wickedness. These servants of Satan repeatedly ensnare men into sin, ruination and away from their beloved church and

God." His voice grew louder, his nostrils flared and his teeth bared. "This factual knowledge of women is not just gossip or rumour, but based on the findings and teachings of many learned men." Bishop Bernard breathed deeply and reached for his glass of water. The perspiration ran down his forehead and the back of his neck, and Robin once more wiped his brow. The students sat rigid, unblinking, daring not to speak. Robin's attentions soothed the bishop and his composure partially returned. "The core of the carnality of women dwells in a devious instrument deep in their abdomen. A woman's womb is unique, not being present in men. This organ, made entirely of nerves and delightful sensitivity, will compel their whole bodies to shudder, urge them to abandon their senses to a verbal and physical frenzy and unleash them to indulge all their passions. We now know that, unlike men, this organ gives women the capacity for multiple orgasms. As a result, they will cravingly and callously exhaust the male to satisfy their own licentious appetites."

The tirade complete, he gasped deeply and his flushed, sweating bald head fell into his arms. Robin jumped to his assistance with his cloth and whispered in his ear. The bishop nodded and rose slowly. "I will see you at the trial in an hour. I need to prepare myself for the faithlessness and treachery that lies ahead."

Robin removed Bishop Bernard's cloak from the hook and led him from the room by his hand.

14

Justice

10 June 1670

Dr Pierre Laurent shuffled along the cobblestones, head down and occasionally side-stepping freshly scattered horse droppings. An unbuttoned waistcoat and rumpled jacket suggested it had been another night of revelry. He rubbed each eye with the pulp of a fingertip and yawned as he reached the square. The twin spires of the cathedral on the east side cast a long shadow, reaching almost to the doors of the courthouse on the opposite side. A raucous crush of townsfolk jostled outside, blocking the entry.

"Merde! Why?' he muttered. "Why must I appear at this trial? Commandant Duval knows all about the death of Monsieur Duplessis; he doesn't need me for that. The magistrate said he may require my expertise of anatomy. What could that possibly mean? And, if I fail to attend, I will receive a fine! And now I am late and cannot even see the door."

He reached the periphery of the raucous huddle, wedged his shoulder into a small gap and pushed ahead, squirming, worming and twisting his way forward. The hustle responded and Pierre flinched at the blows to his body and the pulling at his clothes and hair.

"Stop pushing."

"Wait your turn. We were here first."

"Bloody haut monde, in your smart clothes. Get back."

A guard defending the front door recognised Dr Laurent's head as it popped out between protruding stomachs. "Let the good doctor through immediately! He is required inside and is already overdue."

The crowd parted at the guard's bark and a ruffled Pierre nodded politely at the sneering pack as the officer safeguarded his entry.

Imposing double doors opened into a quiet atrium with vaulted ceiling, depicting an angry Moses breaking the tablets of the Ten Commandments. A court steward ushered him through another door into an aisle between two rear banks of pews. He paused momentarily at the end of the aisle as he scanned an immense chamber filled with the yelling and perspiration of a few hundred men with not a woman amongst them. On either side, ten rows of banked benches reached up towards a soaring, vaulted ceiling where Jesus, bearing his crucifixion wounds, floated on a cloud surrounded by winged angels draped in white sheets. A central area was empty except for a small table and a staircase leading down into an unknown darkness. At the head of the chamber perched an unoccupied, elevated rostrum against a background mural of The Last Judgement. Pierre doubted the mural would provide much comfort to the accused who stood before it. Christ sat high in the centre, handing out judgement to those recently departed. Those having led a good earthly life could stand by his side. Those that had not were cast into a red river of fire flowing down the centre to the bottom of the mural. Here a leviathan and Satan waited just above the rostrum.

Pierre felt the nudge of the steward, who pointed to a space at the end of the first row next to Commandant Duval and a line of black-robed clergy. He nodded to Duval as he took his seat.

A red-robed court official entered from a side door, raised his hand and with the other stamped a silver mace, shimmering with jewels, against the wooden floor. "Silence, silence! Please stand for the judges. Our secular judge and magistrate is Monsieur Louis Deschamps, and our ecclesiastical judge is Bishop Victor Bernard."

The uproar ceased abruptly; the room fell silent and the entire assemblage stood as one.

Judge Deschamps emerged from a side door draped in a long scarlet gown with winged sleeves and an open front from which protruded a white shirted, ample abdomen. A silvery wig atop a bald head cascaded in curls on either side of a round, puce face and onto his shoulders. With laboured breaths, he climbed the four steps and collapsed into his chair on the rostrum. Bishop Bernard followed; almost gliding as his plain black robe fell, unmoving from his ample abdomen. He climbed the rostrum, remained standing and gestured for the audience to be seated.

"A dark shadow has been cast over our lands in recent times. This shadow carries with it more harm than the infidel or the heretic, and even more than the Jew. This is the shadow of malefice, brought to us by Satan's earthly servants. Witches represent the most heinous form of heresy. They have previously received the Faith of the Gospel and have then turned away from God and religion. Thereafter, they have made a pact with the devil, the enemy of the faith. This is apostasy and they are apostates; the greatest of all sins. Therefore, to punish a witch in the same manner as other heretics does not seem sufficient. Life imprisonment may suffice for an infidel. But what of a profane soul that even pays homage to devils by offering them their bodies? If their crime is so great, so must be their punishment."

Bishop Bernard sat down and Judge Deschamps struggled to his feet, breathing deeply. "Today we will trial four accused witches. You will hear and be shocked by their brazen malefice, their carnal lust and their rejection of the faith. But despite the clarity of their guilt, we must abide a fair and just system of law. We, as the devout followers of God, must show fairness and proof of such wickedness. Let the trial begin. Bring up the first accused, Madame Pascale Banzin."

A foreboding silence fell over the galleries. An escaped cough in the top bank was the only sound. Then, muffled footsteps ascending the staircase. The guard's gold rimmed, black tricorne appeared first, followed by a hooded figure with dark hollow eyes peering through cut-out holes. Bruised, naked shoulders emerged, followed by one arm in a frayed sling, and the sagging breasts of a middle-aged woman. Ribs protruded over a shrivelled stomach, bearing the bloodied cuts and bruises of recent torment. Her pubis was clean shaven, and skinny legs portrayed further evidence of her torture. Raw, weeping chain wounds encircled both ankles. The guard continued with eyes firmly fixed forward and, on reaching the top of the stairs, turned to face the rostrum. Next to him, the hooded wretch, forbidden to face the judges, obediently faced the rear galleries. She bowed her head, and the guard removed the hood to reveal the shaven head and blackened eyes of the High Priestess.

Dr Laurent and Duval joined the wave of shocked, indistinct grumbling voices that spread through the side galleries. The rear galleries, targeted by her glare, cowered and shielded their faces with their hands. Both the bishop and the magistrate crossed themselves and, from under their garments, removed and held a small statue in each open palm. One, their Agnus Dei, a lamb bearing the banner of the cross. In the other hand, a small shape of Jesus Christ, composed of herbs and salt, consecrated on Palm Sunday, and embedded in Blessed wax. The bishop, the magistrate and the entire audience spontaneously regurgitated the seven words of Christ on the cross.

"Father, forgive them; for they know not what they do."

"Truly I say unto thee, today, you will be with me in paradise."

"Woman, behold your son! Son, behold your mother!"

"My God, my God, why hast thou forsaken me?"

"I thirst."

"It is finished."

"Father, into thy hands I commend my spirit."

Bishop Bernard, still clutching his spiritual protection, stood and made his way down the steps. He stood, with no sign of trepidation, beside the small table bearing a silver pitcher and a silver goblet. Breaking off a small piece of Blessed Wax from the Jesus Christ effigy, he dropped it into the pitcher, made the sign of the cross and waved his hand across the water.

"The Father, the Son and the Holy Ghost, in thy name, I consecrate this Holy Water. Please help this lost soul to open her heart and confess her sins, so that she may still enter the Kingdom of Heaven."

He poured the consecrated water into the goblet, which he held in his hand. "Madame Banzin, you may now turn and face this shielded servant of God."

Pierre, engrossed by the proceedings, watched as the high priestess slowly scrutinised each face as she turned. Her stinging scowl prompting a wave of swivelled heads and shielded eyes. Her most piercing and unwavering glare came to rest on the bishop. He blinked once and then held her defiant eyes.

"You have not eaten or taken drink for two days, so this Holy Water should quickly enter your body and mind and help you with your confession."

The bishop placed the goblet on the small table and stepped back. The high priestess thrust her hand forward and quickly drained the goblet.

The magistrate rose in the rostrum. "On this, the 10th day of June in the year of our Lord 1670, Madame Pascale Banzin, a spinster, residing at 24 Rue du Chien, is accused of witchcraft. How do you plead Madame Banzin?"

Standing tall and straight, pushing her sagging breasts forward, she announced in a loud, resolute voice, "Not guilty!"

The silent galleries erupted with raucous incredulity at the brazen repudiation of her obvious guilt. Bishop Bernard turned away, clutching his Agnus Dei and climbed the steps back to his podium.

"Bring in the first witness," announced the magistrate.

Pierre heard the door open at the back of the hall, the sound of boots on a wooden floor and the clank of steel. The guard made a wide arc around Madam Banzin and stood below the podium.

"Tell us what you saw on the morning of 25 May, 1670."

"Yes sir, happy to be of service to our God and France. We received information from our watchman, in the schoolhouse near le Pont St Joan, of small groups walking in the darkness towards the Glen. In response, we woke before dawn and together with Colonel Montpellier we made our way to the Glen. We approached and initially silenced a few men who appeared to be guarding entry points. Four of us, including our commander, crept in and observed proceedings."

"And what did you observe?"

"We saw the accused standing here, mark out a circle with a sword and at each quarter, point to the heavens and shout out some otherworldly and fiendish words which I am unable to repeat. Then all the others jumped into the circle she had drawn. A man dressed as a devil then arrived and he proceeded to fuck a young girl on the altar. While they were fucking all the other witches, including this one here, started fucking each other. Then the rest of our company came in under the trees and our commander gave the order to attack."

"Thank you, that is very useful. You may go. Call the next witness, please."

Another guard appeared at the back of the hall, walked around the high priestess, and stood beneath the rostrum.

"I understand you were also at the Glen on the morning of 25 May 1670."

"That is correct, sir."

"Tell us what you saw."

The second guard repeated the same sequence of events as the first guard.

"Let it be known that I instructed these guards to abbreviate the events and to leave out some of the more salacious details. I did not wish to soil the minds of some of the younger attendees. There are two other guards who will describe exactly the same events. But I do not wish to waste the court's time when it is clear that this woman has taken part in a witch ceremony."

The magistrate looked down at the High Priestess. "Madame Banzin, you have heard all the damnatory evidence. How do you plead?"

"Yes, I was involved in an initiation ceremony of our coven. Of that, there can be no doubt. But I ask the court, is it a sin to worship someone other than your God? He is the God of your church, not mine. Your God has done nothing for me. I no longer have a husband. I have lost two children to sickness and starvation and am penniless. When I asked your church for help, I was given nothing more than a fable about a poor woman who gave her last penny to God! The priest said I should be embarrassed to come to ask for alms from God's church. So, when a true saint came to me and offered me real help, it was easy to change to the true path."

The pews were hushed, fidgeting uncomfortably, rubbing their chins and contemplating her words.

The bishop broke the moment of reflection. "Madame Banzin, your guilt is clear. Do not think for one moment that you can influence your sin with melancholy fantasies of your past. But you appear to hold a high rank in your coven. As such, you must know about others of your kind. It may go better for you if you provide us with some names."

"I know no names."

"That is disappointing. You are an impenitent heretic. You have been practising this heresy for several years and have chosen the death of your soul rather than the body of Christ. It is clear that you are infected with this heresy. You will not even renounce your liaison with Satan and return to the bosom of our church and allow us to cleanse your soul. You stand there defiant, even after the tortures inflicted upon you. This could only be so because Lucifer resides in your stubborn heart. I as the representative of God on earth, have done everything I can to persuade you. You leave me no option but to hand you over to the secular court. I pray they can change the sentence of death that hangs over your head."

The bishop sat down and as the murmuring again suffused the galleries, he began conferring quietly with the judge. They sat whispering for a few minutes; the magistrate rubbing his chin and then nodding in unison with the bishop. The magistrate rose from his seat. "After hearing all the evidence and listening to all counsel, I agree that Madame Banzin is a heretic. In fact, she is an apostate, since she once knew the faith and has turned her back on the church. I have conferred with my colleague and we both believe that your stubborn soul cannot be cleansed. A date will be set for the burning of your body and soul. This will take place in a public place to convince others of the futility of the path you have chosen. You can take her back to her cell and bring up the next accused."

Madame Banzin disappeared in the stairwell and an unaccompanied, unshaven, unhooded head emerged. He wore a rough woollen sleeveless shirt and loose leggings, ending above the ankle. His feet were bare and unshackled. On reaching the chamber, he turned to the judges, but his head remorsefully observed the floorboards.

The magistrate stood. "Monsieur August Moreau, you stand here to-day accused of malefice. In particular, you have taken on the form of Satan in heinous rituals and you have had carnal relations with a girl now known to be a witch. How do you plead?"

"I am truly guilty, my Lord. But I plead for penance from the church."

"Let it be known that Monsieur Moreau is a local landowner of significant wealth and standing in our community. It is inconceivable that such a man can find himself in his present circumstances. What is it that led you away from the body of Christ and down this accursed path?"

"My Lord, it all began two years ago when my wife employed a new housekeeper. She was young and tempted me with many salacious suggestions every day for months. I could no longer bear it and one day, while my wife had gone to visit her mother, she came to my room and stood before me completely naked. I took her then, and on many occasions thereafter. She cast such a spell over me. I could not think rationally. She took me to a house where we met some friends and they gave me wine to drink. After a while, they all disrobed and kissed, touched and fondled each other. I was drawn into this web. That first night and on many nights thereafter, I had carnal relations with many women."

"Would you describe these women as witches?"

"Yes, certainly my Lord. During these evenings, they would also chant numerous impious verses, burn incense, meditate and pray to various idols while pouring wine on the ground."

"And what brought you to the Glen on the night in question?"

"These women often told me what a great lover I was, and that I was endowed with a member like Satan. They suggested that I be their devil and in return, they would bring me more beautiful and even younger girls. But before doing this, I would need to be initiated."

"And what was this initiation?'

"To plant the devil's seed in a young virgin at her initiation ceremony."

"I believe it is abundantly clear that this man is guilty of the heresy of witchcraft and he should be given the ultimate punishment. However, my ecclesiastical colleague may wish to question him first."

Pierre contemplated the magistrate as he collapsed in his chair; his face puce as he sucked air through an open mouth.

Bishop Bernard rose. "I believe you have confessed your sin. Is that correct?"

"Yes, my Lord. I have prayed for forgiveness every day since the morning in the Glen. Whilst incarcerated here, I have also lashed myself mercilessly, every day until blood was drawn." He turned and lifted off his woollen shirt to reveal multiple deep wounds over his upper back and arms. "I have also donated much of my wealth to the church, hoping God can witness my pain, recognise my remorse and absolve me of my sins. If God can acknowledge my repentance and once again welcome me back into the bosom of the church, I vow I will forever be his disciple."

"You have consorted with many witches and must know many names?"

"Yes, my Lord. I have provided the name of every one of these horrendous creatures who tempt good men into darkness."

"And how many names have you given?"

"Twenty-one my Lord. And I am hopeful, as God is my witness, that they will all be put to the flame so that we can rid this evil from our lands!"

"It would appear that Monsieur Moreau is truly penitent and the sum he has donated is an indication of his genuine remorse. It would be entirely sufficient for an indulgence from the Catholic Church. I believe, therefore, that he is a confessed heretic who is penitent and therefore does not require the ultimate punishment!"

Bishop Bernard seated himself and engaged in a whispered discussion with the magistrate. In the hiatus, the audience grew restless and sporadic murmuring rippled through the assembly. The ripple developed into a wave and finally a crescendo of discontent and a thumping of fists and stamping of feet on the wooden gallery floors.

"He is the devil incarnate. Why should he be spared?"

"He should go to the fire together with all the witches he fucked!"

"It seems the rich can pay their way out of hell."

The magistrate rose, arms raised. "Silence! Silence! There will be no mob rule in this fair city and certainly not in this court. This trial has been conducted exactly according to the statutes and ordinances of the Holy Catholic Church. Anarchy will not be tolerated. Guards, take anyone who utters the slightest sound to the Tower."

An abrupt hush fell over the proceedings. Not a murmur, not a shuffling of feet, not a smile and not a sideways glance.

"On this day, let it be noted that the events surrounding Monsieur August Moreau and witchcraft have been fairly examined and his guilt has been determined by two high-ranking officers of the court and the church. He has been found guilty of heresy. Because of his sincere confession and his desire to return to the Church, he will not receive the ultimate punishment. For the next two years, he will appear in public, only in the rags he currently wears. On every day he will stand at the door of the church dressed as such and in bare feet so that all who enter may see him. He will hold a candle all the while and during every mass he will carry it and place it on the altar so that all may see him. During this time, the bishop may give him tasks, such as helping a sick farmer sow his fields or provide food for the poor souls who dwell by the river. If he can do this without complaint and without failure, he will be re-assessed by the bishop, who will determine whether there has been sufficient humiliation and penance to be allowed back to the church. Take him away and bring up the next prisoner."

Monsieur Moreau descended, and a tricorne hat and another hooded head appeared in the stairwell. The crowd grew restless and louder as the shoulders and firm young breasts appeared. Then a cacophony, as a flat abdomen, shaven pubis and firm thighs stepped out of the stairwell.

"Silence!" roared the bishop. "Guard, evict that young man in the front row, who is making obscene gestures with his fingers. He can cool off in a cell for the night. The next one will go to the Tower."

While facing the back gallery, the guard removed the hood to reveal Mara's wide, anxious eyes set in a dirt-smudged face and shaven head. A few suspicious spectators in the back rows shielded their eyes, but most fixed their open-mouthed stares on the nakedness in front of them. Mara shivered in her shameful humiliation, her darting eyes searching the rows of lewd faces. Pierre followed her gaze to the middle of the top row, where she fixed on a large blond man. He smiled back and any anxiety, fear or shame seemed momentarily to evaporate. Both judges clutched their Agnus Dei tightly. The bishop again led the congregation through the seven words Christ uttered on the cross. Bishop Bernard again descended the rostrum and at the small table poured the consecrated water into a silver goblet and left it on the table.

"Mademoiselle, you may now turn and face this shielded servant of God."

The crowd remained hushed, preoccupied, and appeared unconcerned that Mara's gaze fell upon them as she turned.

"Drink this holy water. It will help you with your confession."

"Thank you, Father, but I have no need. I will tell this court only the truth."

The magistrate rose in the rostrum. "On this 10th day of June in the year of our Lord 1670, Mademoiselle Mara Mandeville is accused on three counts of witchcraft. The first is that she is the child of a known witch; this count is not on its own sufficient for trial but is damning when coupled with other evidence. The second is that she grows demonic plants in her garden that are used in satanic ceremonies. And third, that she survived the swim test."

Another wave; one of incredulity, spread through the congregation.

"Survived the swim test?"

"Impossible!"

"Useless guards. Cannot even make a good knot?"

"Silence!" roared the magistrate. "How do you plead Mademoiselle Mandeville?"

"Not guilty, my Lord."

"The first count is that you are the child of a known witch by the name of Miriam Mandeville. She has a history of witchcraft from the county around Marseilles, but eluded the constabulary and escaped without a trace. She has lived here undetected for nearly seventeen years, largely because the rise in witchcraft around St Raphael is very recent. It is only since the arrival of Colonel Montpellier, on orders from our king, that we have actively pursued these despicable creatures. Furthermore, let it be known that the accused was borne out of wedlock and is a bastard. Would you care to respond to your mother's guilt?"

Appearing more confident after siting Simon, Mara focused on the judges and spoke with boldness. "My mother is a wonderful, caring person and is not a witch. She has cared for me and her own mother all her life. It was unfortunate that my father died in the service of our king when

I was but a babe. Were this spurious claim against my mother true, I fail to see how that makes me a witch."

"It is well known that witchcraft is passed from generation to generation. This is clearly explained in Exodus 20:5 'Thou shalt not adore them, nor serve them: I am the Lord they God, mighty, jealous, visiting the iniquity of the fathers upon the children, unto the third and the fourth generation of them that hate me.'"

Mara shrugged her shoulders, shuffled her feet, and looked to the ground. "Your honour, I am not a scholar of your book and am unable to comment."

The magistrate smiled down at the beaming bishop. "The second count is that you grow certain herbs in your garden, which you use and sell for medicinal purposes. How do you respond?"

"This is entirely true. But where does it say that it is witchcraft to sell medicines that make sick people well? We do not place curses on our medicines and no-one has ever become severely ill or died after taking them. Furthermore, our practice is to test every medicine we use, not only for safety but also to show that it is effective."

"Yes. Yes. Umm? But we know you grow herbs that are used in witches' ceremonies. I am also told that a guard almost died at your farm because some of these plants poisoned him."

"My Lord. It is true that some of these plants can cause intoxication or a feeling of jubilation, ecstasy or even madness if consumed in sufficient quantity. But this is not our custom. The guard you speak of ignored the protection he required when he went to gather these plants."

"The third count of which there is absolute proof is that you survived the swim test. How was this possible if this was not by some sinister force?"

"My Lord, I did believe I was about to die when I plunged into those icy waters. But as I struggled under the water, a young man appeared out of the turbulence. I can still recall his long black hair trailing with the current as he swam to me and undid my bindings. And then, as suddenly as he appeared, he was swept away. Because my mother had taught me how to swim, I was then easily able to reach the surface and swim to the bank."

"And who was this young man that had the audacity to interfere with a legitimate witch trial?"

"I do not know, my Lord, but I would like to meet him again, so that I might sincerely thank him."

The silent galleries, engrossed with Mara and her story, and unperturbed by the threat of the Tower, broke into sporadic chuckling and commentary.

"It was me!"

"No, it was me. You can sincerely thank me."

"No, me, I am a roper and know about knots."

"Silence!" demanded an irritated bishop, who had remained standing near the table. "We have one further test to carry out to prove that you are indeed a witch. Those that practice this heinous art will somewhere on their body carry a witches' teat. This may be a small nipple like appendage and is often found in the secret parts of the body. We shave every part of their body in the event we need to search for this undeniable mark of a witch. Guard, if you hold her arms behind her back, I will begin the examination."

The bishop took more blessed salt, clutched his Agnus Dei and with the other hand began the examination. The muttering ceased and silence swallowed every sound. At first, anxiety shone out from Mara's blue eyes, but as the examination continued, she stood rigid, eyes closed as the bishop's hands scratched and prodded her scalp, explored her neck, both breasts, back and abdomen. Finally, the soft whimper of humiliation escaped together with a whole-body shudder as the bishop bent down, examined her shaven pubis and touched the upper part of her vulva.

"Aha, I believe I have found it," he proudly announced as he stood, pointing and addressed the audience. "I have seen a few of these and there can be no doubt that she bears the sign of the witch. However, I will ask my learned colleague to come down and verify my findings." He signalled for the magistrate to come down.

Pierre, initially intrigued by Mara's earlier descriptions of her herbal remedies, rose suddenly at Mara's obvious embarrassment. "My Lord, my Lord?" He shouted above the laugher and joviality which had possessed the audience.

"Silence! Yes, doctor?"

"My Lord, this examination of a woman's most private parts is indefensible. I am a man of medicine and have studied anatomy at the University in Paris. I suggest it would be prudent on your part to allow a professional opinion."

The bishop paused for a moment, rubbing his chin. "Please, Doctor Laurent, come forward and confirm my findings."

Pierre stepped down and walked across the floor and whispered to Mara. "Mademoiselle, I mean you no harm and am certain I can end this humiliation." He bent down, had a cursory look, and spoke up to the rostrum and galleries. "I am not surprised that a man of the cloth, who is supposedly celibate and never had the pleasure of a woman, would mistake this appendage for that of the witch's mark. This, my Lord, is a clitoris, a small appendage which most married men in this room know brings their wife significant pleasure. It is not a witch's teat. I do, however, wonder how many poor souls have been sent to the flames for this basic misunderstanding of human anatomy!"

The magistrate, wheezing and panting, had descended the rostrum and was now slowly approaching Bishop Bernard, clutching his Agnus Dei. "My esteemed colleague, it appears my services are no longer required. I am happy to take the advice of this man of medicine."

"Thank you, sir. Now that this amateur examination is complete, I believe we should cover this poor child." Pierre removed his jacket, placed it about her shoulders, and returned to his seat. Mara stood, head bowed, clutching the jacket to herself.

Bishop Bernard wiped a reddening face with his handkerchief and turned to the magistrate. "I will leave you to pronounce judgement, my learned colleague." And quickly returned to the safety of the rostrum.

The magistrate nodded, coughed, and slowly dragged his large, swollen legs and abdomen behind the bishop. He stood on the rostrum, catching his breath. "I find that Mara Mandeville is under grave suspicion of witchcraft and requires further interrogation so that she might confess her sins. However, we should seek clarity about her claim that she can prove that her medicines work and cause no harm. A medicine that is effective could hardly be considered witchcraft. Could you explain this Mademoiselle Mandeville?"

Mara raised her head towards the rostrum, shivered and breathed deeply. "Certainly, my Lord." She paused as the light and confidence returned to her eyes. "All new medicine, we test first on small mice that we catch in the fields, giving them increasing doses of the treatment. We then take small doses for ourselves. These tests will show that they do no harm. Showing proof of effect is difficult and can sometimes be performed on sick animals, but is usually not possible for people. We will normally provide the safe amount to a sick man or woman and wait for a recovery."

"That is interesting. Do you have an example of this?"

Mara briefly considered the magistrate before speaking. "My Lord, I have recently observed an old fox who appeared to have dropsy. Every day, this old fox crawled with great difficulty to a specific plant and ate of its leaves. After about half an hour, he could get to his feet and then run back into the safety of the forest. I took parts of this plant and dried them and left them out for the fox. He ate only the dried plant and ran back to the forest. I have taken increasing amounts and if I take too much, my stomach feels a little queasy. So, I now know the safe dose but have not yet tried it on someone with dropsy."

"That is interesting, but without the proof, you cannot call it successful. Perhaps the leaned doctor may have some patients."

Without waiting for Dr Laurent, Mara spoke. "My Lord, if I am not mistaken, I believe you have dropsy!"

The courtroom fell silent. Not a whisper, not a shuffle, not a cough. Four hundred eyes focused on the boldness of the maiden wearing only a jacket and holding centre stage.

"So, you wish to test this unknown remedy on a magistrate?"

"My Lord, do you not wish to know if the medicine we make is more than witchcraft? What better way to find the truth than right here before this court and before the whole of France?"

Pierre, now suffused with enthusiasm, smiled and nodded to the hesitant magistrate.

Bishop Bernard interrupted. "This is folly. This is an evil witches' plan to do you harm and is further proof of her pact with the devil."

"My dear colleague, I have suffered from this wretched illness now for countless years and can barely climb the stairs to my bedchamber. If there is a cure, I am happy to be the first to try it."

Mara turned to the rear gallery and signalled Simon to come forward. "My Lord, this is Simon. He is the stable hand and works the fields and gardens at our house. I gave him some of the dried leaves before I was taken and I am hopeful that he still carries them with him."

As the back row stood to allow Simon to pass, Mara was relieved to see her belt around his waist. Any trepidation she still had dissipated when he stood, tall and smiling, by her side. Mara took out some of the dried leaf mixture and placed it in a small pile on the table for all to see. She placed the tip of her index finger into the pile, examined it, placed the finger in her mouth, and washed it down with the blessed water. An anxious silence descended on the chamber as Mara stood motionless in the room.

"As you can see, my Lord the plant has done me no harm. Please come and take your portion."

The magistrate wearily descended the stairs and dragged himself across the floor to where Mara stood. Without hesitating, he dipped his finger in the pile and placed it in his mouth and followed with blessed water

"My Lord, it will take about half an hour to take effect."

"Thank you, Mademoiselle Mandeville. While waiting, we will continue with the next case. You can take a seat in the second row next to the good doctor and you Simon can return to your seat. Bring up the next prisoner!" The magistrate trudged wearily up to the rostrum.

The tricorne hat, followed by a hood, appeared in the stairwell. A middle-aged woman, naked, emaciated with sagging breasts and a shaven pubis emerged. The galleries remained silent through the rituals of unhooding, recanting of the seven words of Christ and the pouring of the consecrated water by Bishop Bernard. "Madame Maxine Macon is brought before us today with the charge of witchcraft. How do you plead, Madam?"

Madame Macon, blue eyes still shining through the veil despite signs of torture on wrists and ankle, responded in a loud, unflinching voice. "Not guilty, my Lord."

"Madame Macon, you stand here accused of witchcraft on two counts. First, that you sold cursed medicine, which, among other ingredients, contained the body and blood of Jesus Christ. Second, that you placed a curse on a man who subsequently died as a direct result of that curse. How do you plead?"

"Not guilty, my Lord."

"On the first count, there is evidence that you prepared a potion in your kitchen which you brought to the apothecary, Monsieur Baptiste. He refused to sell your wares in his establishment, and you cursed him in front of numerous patrons. You left the shop and walked to the next corner of the street where you laid out your wares and enticed passer byes to buy your magical cures. Is this correct up to this point?"

"Yes, my Lord. That apothecary is unfortunately so bull-headed, with such fixed ideas he will not try any new and exciting remedies."

"How did you make this medicine and what ingredients did you put in your pot?"

"It is a very simple recipe, my lord. I first bring the water to boil and then add a variety of herbs, the wing of a bat, a piece of skin of a snake, and finish it with some teeth. All the while stirring in the magical words of my ancestors."

"Are you sure that is all?"

"Yes, my Lord."

"Recently, we interrogated a midwife who admitted, that unbeknown to the mother, to causing the death of a newborn infant. She did this by sticking a needle deep into the infant's crown as she brought it into the world. She advised the family that it was a stillbirth and that she would bury the dead child. Instead, she took the dead child to a witches' Sabbat where all those there gathered feasted on the child's body. She was convicted of witchcraft and was burned at the stake."

"Why is this of relevance to me, my Lord?"

"During her interrogation, she provided names of other witches to whom she supplied parts of the dead infant. One of those names was yours, Madame Macon. She told us you requested a portion of the after-birth and the heart, as you believed it had powerful healing properties and could use it in your cures."

"That is a complete and utter lie, my Lord. I have been healing the poor for threescore years and have never used baby parts. Please my Lord, have mercy, you must believe me."

He turned to the court, holding up a sheet of paper. "I hold here in my hand a sworn confession from the midwife, a Madame Celiers. It sets out her complicity in acquiring this infant and in providing you, Madame Macon, with the aforementioned parts."

"I know that witch. Since we were young, she has held a grudge against me, because a man she loved preferred my company to hers."

A surge of laughter and comment erupted from the benches.

"Preferred you!"

"She must have been a werewolf."

"Or he was blind."

"Silence!" roared Bishop Bernard. "As for the other ingredients, I have information that you acquired part of the Holy Sacrament and placed it in your brew. Is that correct Madam Macon?"

"Again, my Lord, this a complete fabrication. How could I possibly acquire something so sacred?"

Bishop Bernard continued. "We have two witnesses to this blasphemous crime. First, as some of you may know, I took the service on the said morning. When I was about to place the Blessed Sacrament on her tongue, she moved it away so that the Sacrament was placed on the floor of her mouth. Thereafter, she quickly escaped the church and was noticed by a passer-by to spit something out of her mouth into a piece of cloth. How do you respond to this, Madame Macon?"

"This is true, my Lord. But I had a very ill child at home and I thought some holy nourishment from Jesus might cure his infirmity."

"To further add to this blasphemous crime, I will present additional evidence to show her renunciation of the faith. Madame Macon, you have plainly stated that you live in St Raphael. Why then do you send your children to the secular village school in St Joan when we have far superior Catholic schools here in St Raphael?"

"The education I received in Paris taught me that non-religious schools produce a more rounded child."

Bishop Bernard smiled up at the silent galleries. "We will continue to the second count, which will be conducted by my learned colleague."

Judge Deschamps descended the stairs, had a brief consultation with the bishop as they passed and took his place in front of Madame Macon.

"Madam, it is here stated that on 18th May, 1670 you knocked on the kitchen door of Monsieur Duplessis. He himself opened the door, and you begged for food and water. His wife, Madame Duplessis, watched the entire proceedings from the kitchen window." He turned to a bedraggled, older woman dressed in plain clothes sitting in the front pew. "Madame Duplessis, could you please stand and recount the events of that morning?"

Madame Duplessis rose tentatively, looking nervously from side to side, avoiding the glare from Madame Macon. "My Lord, after this miserable creature begged for food and water, my poor husband, in a stern voice, told her to go away. I then observed that she walked back to the kitchen gate, turned and then raised her arms in the air, brought them down to her side and pointed to the door and placed a curse on my departed husband. She cursed he would vomit and shit until all life had been drained out of him."

Madame Macon did not wait for an invitation to speak. "This is partly true, my Lord, but my daughter and my son had not eaten in a week. He called me all manner of vile names, which made me furious. I called out in anger. It was not intended as a curse of death. I do not have such power."

"Are you aware that not seven days later Monsieur Duplessis died in his own vomit and excrement just as you cursed?"

"I was not aware of the manner of death, my Lord."

Madame Duplessis, who had remained standing, head bowed in the front row, began to shake and whimper. The weeping became a blubber and then a river of tears.

"Madame, I am also truly sorry that your husband had to leave this world in this manner. He was a model and honest citizen who helped our community greatly. I am absolutely certain he has found his place in heaven. You may sit down."

She didn't sit but stood, wiping her eyes with her handkerchief. "I assumed so too, my Lord, but he held many secrets and, at his death, he left enormous debts. So much so that I have had to sell our estate and move into a humble dwelling on the poor side of town."

"I have no further questions for the accused."

Commandant Duval, who had sat intently following the proceedings, leaped up and addressed the magistrate. "As you are aware, I am investigating this case and was the first officer of the law to inspect the scene of Monsieur Duplessis. I am still trying to fit all the pieces of this unfortunate case together. Can I ask the witness a question?"

"I cannot see how this may be relevant, Commandant, but please proceed."

"Madame Duplessis, I have a very simple question. Do you know to whom your husband owed these monies?"

"I am uncertain Commandant, but I believe a large portion was to the church."

"Thank you, Madame. That is very helpful. Thank you, my Lord." And he sat down.

Bishop Bernard's face reddened, and he thumped his fist down on the rostrum. "Madame Duplessis, it seems you are quick to point a finger at the church. But were you aware of your husband's perilous financial circumstances before he so unfortunately died?"

"No, my Lord. We never spoke about these matters."

"Madame Duplessis, is it also not true that you had developed a friendship with your neighbour, a Monsieur Antoine Bassett?"

"My husband was in St Raphael often, and yes, we became good friends."

"It would seem, Madame Duplessis, that it is quite conceivable that you contrived a loathsome plan to poison your husband, keep all his wealth and thereafter marry Monsieur Bassett."

"How could you even consider that, my Lord? That is a scandalous accusation, without a grain of truth."

"Judge Deschamps, I will not hold up your questioning of Madame Macon any further, but I will question Madame Duplessis again, at a more convenient time."

The magistrate walked briskly across to below the rostrum, whispered a few words to Bishop Bernard, and then returned to face the galleries. "At this point, I would call upon Doctor Pierre Laurent to come forward."

Laurent, distracted by the magistrate's movements, did not respond.

"Doctor?" the magistrate asked again. "Could you please stand and tell us what you saw on the night in question?"

"UUm. Oh yes, my Lord. Yes, the night in question. When I arrived at Monsieur Duplessis' bedchamber, he was almost dead. There was a trail of vomit and faeces from his bed to where I found him on the floor. I do not believe this was because of a witches' curse, my Lord."

"Do you know the exact cause of his death then, Doctor Laurent?" barked Bishop Bernard from the rostrum.

"No, my Lord. But the manner and speed of death suggests poisoning."

"Doctor, my learned colleague does not want you to speculate or give your opinion. He wishes you provide evidence. If a man of your training does not know the cause of death, then it is much more likely to be because of something we do not understand. Such as witchcraft. What is clear from the evidence is that Monsieur Duplessis died in exactly the manner his wife foretold. You may sit down, Doctor Laurent."

Commandant Duval again stood. "My honourable colleagues, we are being too hasty in condemning this woman for the death of Duplessis. I, as the lead investigator, am still following clues related to this death. At this point in time, I concur with Dr Laurent that poisoning seems most likely, but it will take more time to prove conclusively. To pass judgement when these investigations are incomplete would be a blight on our judicial system."

Judge Deschamps conferred quietly with Bishop Bernard and stood straight with his chest out and head held up to the galleries. "The cause of Monsieur Duplessis' death is arguably inconclusive. However, after hearing all the evidence, it is quite clear, Madame Macon, that you have taken part in acts that are gravely suspicious of witchcraft. As you will not admit to this diabolical sin and repent, you will be given one last chance to seek forgiveness from God. You will be sent back to your cell for further interrogation." He turned back towards the rostrum, effortlessly mounted the stairs, and settled in his chair.

In the last row at the rear of the chamber sat a slim, short-haired, boyish spectator with a fire burning in bright blue eyes. In delicate hands, she held a crude model of a priest. As Madame Macon descended the stairs, Francine pulled hard on a piece of twine around the effigy's neck.

Pierre jumped enthusiastically to his feet. "My Lord, Judge Deschamps, over the last ten minutes, you have become much lighter on your feet."

"This is quite true," his round face beaming. As a matter of fact, I have not felt this strong for some time. It is quite miraculous."

"So, my Lord, would you attribute this to the dried leaves that Mademoiselle Mara gave you?"

"I must admit, I can see no other reason for the sudden change in my health. Nothing else I have taken over the last years has ever had quite this effect."

"My Lord, as a man of medicine, I have never seen such a remarkable change in a man with dropsy. This is truly a remarkable discovery. Surely it will serve no purpose to incarcerate and interrogate this young woman. It would be much to our advantage to allow her to do further good work in our city. This is an opportunity for St Raphael to achieve the recognition it deserves and stand on equal footing with Paris as a centre of scientific research. We will be talked about and lauded all over France."

Both the magistrate and the bishop nodded enthusiastically. After a further brief consultation, Bishop Bernard spoke. "We agree, Doctor, that this is an opportunity that should be taken. But where in St Raphael could she do this work?"

"My Lord, I will offer her a room in my establishment. I will set up a small laboratory and she will work under my guidance. I will keep you informed with regular reports."

The bishop and the magistrate again conferred quietly. "Dr Laurent, we agree this plan would be beneficial for us all. We appreciate the offer of your establishment. But you must be warned that you assume an immense responsibility by taking a suspected witch into your care. She will be your entire responsibility. Are you sure you are able to provide the necessary detention? Should she escape, you may well find yourself on trial here."

Pierre looked down at Mara, clutching his coat around her neck. She nodded. "My Lords, I am absolutely certain we can together do some excellent work and I am assured that no attempt of escape will be made."

"Then let it be known that Doctor Pierre Laurent will take the accused witch Mara Mandeville into his care for an initial period of six months. He will provide weekly reports of her progress to Judge Deschamps. If there is no further business, this court is now closed."

15

Sanctuary

10 June 1670

The chamber was silent except for the whisperings of Dr Laurent and Mara. God and all his Judgement Day prophets glared down at the freed witch and the pagan who had negotiated her escape. An angry crowd, cheated of a victim, had initially formed a clamorous mass outside, but as the afternoon crept into evening and she failed to appear, they lost interest and slowly drifted away.

Simon entered through a side door, breathing heavily with small beads of perspiration on his forehead. "I finally located your coachman and your carriage now awaits outside the front door. The crowd has dispersed and there are now only a few traders going about their usual business in the square. With darkness falling, I feel it is safe to leave."

"Thank you, Simon," as Pierre shook his hand. "Hopefully we will meet again soon."

"I am certain we will, Dr Laurent."

Mara, still covered only in Pierre's coat, threw her arms around his waist. "Simon, thank you for everything you have done. I know you will find Maman and Grandmère and tell them I am safe."

"Mara, I do have some news; just a brief note left at our front door. This is the first opportunity I have had to speak with you since you were taken. Your mother and grandmother remain in hiding; they would not tell me where they were. They said that when it is safe to do so, they will contact us both."

Mara, her stomach churning, looked up at Simon with a moist, uncertain stare.

"Mara, always remember, wherever you are, I shall not be far away. If you are in need of me, if circumstances go against you, just wear a flower in your hair when you go about your daily business. I will arrange the rest." Mara nodded up at him while drying her eyes with the back of one hand. Simon undid her other arm and gently pushed her away. "By the way, you may need this." Simon handed Mara her belt, turned and hurried out through the side door. Mara buckled the belt tightly over Pierre's coat, providing some reassuring protection for her underlying nakedness.

Pierre and Mara waited for a few more minutes and under the cover of the fading light, left quietly through the side door into an almost empty square. A few merchants were wearily loading their market stalls and unsold produce onto the tray of a waiting wagon.

A single horse and carriage stood outside, while across the square the towering spires of the cathedral glared down at the escaping heretics. A black suited driver, sitting upright on his box, tipped his top hat. "Good evening, Doctor Laurent. Mademoiselle."

"Thank you, Louis. Jump in," he gestured to Mara. "Do you need assistance?"

Ignoring him, Mara placed one foot on the suspended step, pulled herself up by a handle on the side of the cab, and swung herself into the carriage. Pierre followed and squeezed in beside her. Mara fidgeted with her hands in her lap, conscious of her nakedness under the coat and the closeness of a stranger to whom she was now indebted.

They travelled in silence as the carriage rattled over the cobblestones. Three-storey buildings, painted in various bright colours and partially covered with ivy, bordered each side of the street. Shingles identifying the resident's occupation hung from the doors on the ground floor. A man on a wooden ladder was lighting tallow candles in the lanterns that hung from the dwellings. He tapped his hat to Pierre, who responded as they rode past. "Monsieur Lambert; he and his ancestors have been providing light for St Raphael for generations." Mara nodded, was about to reply, but coughed as the acrid meaty odour of the tallow wafted into the moving carriage. Above the rooftops Mara glimpsed an illuminated steeple against a black sky filled with stars and a low hanging half-moon. The vistas disappeared and reappeared repeatedly as the carriage passed under archways connecting buildings on either side of the road.

Pierre broke the silent claustrophobia. "As you know, my name is Pierre, Pierre Laurent." In the confines of the carriage, he turned awkwardly and shook Mara's hand.

"Thank you, sir. I am not sure how I can ever repay you for your kindness. I have been locked in a putrid cell for six days. I have heard the screams of torture and repulsed the advances of my only visitor; a loathsome turnkey. As you already know, I am Mara, Mara Mandeville."

"It is not only kindness, Mara. Your knowledge and discoveries were truly impressive and I am confident we can together make some genuine progress. I am also just trying to bring some sense to this witchcraft hysteria, which seems to have the entire country and particularly St Raphael in a fearful frenzy."

Rounding a corner, they passed through a high archway under a tower which opened into another square which faced off on all four sides with neat, brightly painted houses. The square was empty except for a few farmers packing unsold vegetable and fruits from a central covered podium.

"Here we are." The carriage stopped in front of a blue three-story house with grey framed windows and shutters. Light poured through the curtained ground-floor windows onto the square outside. Pierre jumped out and offered his hand to Mara.

"Thank you, sir, but I can manage by myself." Mara ignored his hand and jumped effortlessly onto the ground.

"Please Mara, from now on I would be pleased if you called me Pierre."

"I shall try to remember, Pierre!"

Pierre opened a high, ornate door and Mara stood in awe of a large entrance hall. A central chandelier of sweet-smelling beeswax candles illuminated the entry, and a wide, finely engraved staircase rose directly in front of her.

"I make little as a doctor, but I live here because my father is a very wealthy businessman."

"You are a very fortunate son to have such a generous father. Do you see him often?"

"Occasionally. He resides in Paris and disapproves of my career choice. He would prefer that I join his business. My mother passed when I was a child and there are no other children. It is therefore quite unfortunate that we do not agree," Pierre's smile contradicted his remark.

"Well, we have something in common. I am also an only child and my father passed when I was very young."

"Yes, you said that at the trial. It is tragic and I am truly sorry. But enough of this sadness." Pierre, oblivious to Mara's self-conscious nakedness inside his coat, proceeded through a door on the right. "Let me show you where we will work. This is the patient waiting room." Mara followed Pierre through a narrow room, illuminated only with a single wall candle throwing shadows on the ground from the chairs lining each wall. At the end of the room, a solid oak door opened into a larger well-lit room with tall windows at the front and side. "This is my consulting room," Pierre announced proudly. "During the day, the sun streams into this room and provides all the light I need to examine my patients." Under the front window stood a large oak desk covered with an intricately patterned leather inlay. To the side, a solid waist-high examination table and mattress covered with a spotless, wrinkle free white sheet. Two glass-fronted cupboards stood against the rear walls, the shelves filled with a neatly arranged array of knives, scalpels, scissors, clamps, saws and other instruments. Mara's wide blue eyes examined the equipment, but she shivered at their possible uses.

"Yes, they do appear a little gruesome." Pierre opened the cupboard and removed a shiny instrument. "This one is a trepan. This little circular saw is used for cutting a hole in the skull. I can then remove bone fragments that are pressing on the brain. This often happens in head injuries."

"And that one?' Mara pointed.

Pierre replaced the trepan and removed the instrument next to it. "This is a trocar. With this sharp, pointed shaft, I can pierce the abdomen by twisting the handle. Once inside, I can remove the central part, which leaves a hollow cannula through which fluid can flow."

"So, that is for people with big swollen stomachs. Like those that take too much of the drink?"

"Yes, that is correct."

Mara, still clutching the coat against her neck, paused to study a painting of a woman with an outstretched arm. A doctor holding a sharp instrument had punctured her arm, allowing the blood to drip into a bowl.

"Yes, blood-letting. Some say that all illness is because of an over-abundance of blood. Plethora, it has been called."

"I once saw a man on our farm cut into his leg so deeply with a scythe that the blood spurted forth. Simon was unable to stem the flow, and the man died there in the fields. Blood-letting did not appear to do him much good."

"Very insightful, Mara." Pierre smiled broadly below his well-trimmed moustache. "Do not tell a soul, but I share your scepticism and do not use it in my practice. Come, I will show you where you will work."

Through a door beside the instrument cupboard, they entered a long room with floor to ceiling windows. A long wooden bench ran the length of the room under the window. An open door at the far end opened back into the entrance hall. "My mother loved to work in this room, potting her plants and staring out at her garden. It was her sanctuary. The magistrate said she killed herself, but that was not her character. I believe there was mischief afoot; perhaps by my father." Pierre paused for a vacant moment, a tear forming in the corner of each eye as he peered out at the perfectly kept paths and beds. He wiped away the memory with the back of his hand and faced Mara. "This is where I want you to set up your laboratory. Just tell me what is required and I will ensure that we obtain it. I am keen that we do some more work on the dropsy cure, but please talk to me about any other of your promising herbs."

They walked abreast up the wide staircase, which opened onto a large parlour filled with comfortable chairs and side tables. Two floor-to-ceiling windows, bordered by exquisite silk drapes, looked out over the square below. Next to the parlour, they entered an oak-panelled study lined with ceiling-high bookshelves. An iron ladder attached to a high metal rod provided access to the highest shelves. "I certainly have not read all these books, but my father and mother and my grandparents were avid readers and collectors. Please feel free to read whatever you wish."

Back in the parlour, Pierre stopped in mid stride and pulled his watch from his waistcoat pocket. "Oh, how time flies. I am terribly sorry Mara, but I have planned to meet with colleagues tonight. Business, of course. I am sure you can look after yourself. Through that hallway there is my bedroom, and further along is a bedroom with two beds and thereafter another smaller single bedded room. Chose whichever room you prefer. There is no light, so take one of these candles. Up the next flight of stairs, you will find more bedrooms but they have not been used for many years. So, make yourself at home and you should be able to find something in the kitchen if you wish. I am sure you must be famished." He walked away, but turned back and pointed to his coat. "It may be cold tonight, so I may need that. I have packed away some of my mother's clothes in a wardrobe in the larger room. I know it may not be the latest fashion, but I am sure you will find something to wear. Sorry, but I am already late." He considerately turned away and held out his hand for his coat. Mara, uncertain, unbuckled her belt, disrobed and hung the coat over his outstretched hand. She stood with arms and belt clutched around her nakedness as Pierre walked downstairs. When the front door opened and then closed, she let herself go, took the candle and found her way to the bedrooms.

The larger room was sparsely decorated, with bare walls and a full wardrobe. Most of the clothes were elegant gowns, but amongst them she found a simple green dress which fell to her ankles. It was a little loose, but she gathered it in with her belt. In the bottom drawers she found a shift and over this she selected a very fine white silk shirt. She examined herself in an oak framed mirror standing in the room's corner. Feeling more secure in her clothes, she ventured out into the hallway. The smaller single bedded room felt cosy with a small side table and an empty wardrobe. A painting on the side wall of a woodland with a fox in the foreground made the choice easy. She sat on the bed, bounced it up and down, and smiled as her anxiety faded.

Now clothed, it was time to respond to her hunger. The dungeon slop had been her only nourishment since her capture and not a crumb was provided throughout the trial. She ventured downstairs to find the kitchen.

On the same floor as the entrance hall and towards the rear of the house, she found a large stone room with moonlight shining through high windows. A single candle flickered on the central table, illuminating a stone fireplace along one wall. A central pot hung over an open hearth, still containing some glowing embers. An assortment of iron forks, spoons, and pokers hung from the walls. Mara opened one cupboard standing against the opposite wall and found half a loaf of bread wrapped in muslin, a half round of cheese, and some salted pork. The impulse to tear at the bread was quickly suppressed, and she collected a plate and knife and sat in a chair and respectably ate her meal.

With a full stomach, she returned, holding the candle back to her room. She undressed, put on the bedclothes she had selected from Mother's cupboard and blew out all the lights, except those in the front entrance. The day had started ominously; the threat of a guilty verdict, a return to the Tower, torture and the inevitable fire. The young doctor had temporarily dispersed her dread and panic. *Was this genuine kindness, or was his only motive for acquiring her knowledge for his own advancement?* She laid down in her single bed and dropped into a deep sleep.

***

The sound of the front door banging shut followed by a groan and crash on the landing brought Mara back to reality. She jumped out of bed and found Pierre splayed out on the landing floor, snoring. His appearance had taken a turn for the worst since his departure earlier that evening. The jacket lay crumpled and soiled next to him. A stained shirt was no longer neatly tucked into his breeches and he reeked of alcohol. "Doctor, doctor," she called as she bent down, shook him and tried to turn him over.

"Aagh, leave me alone, let me sleep!" he groaned and fell into an unarousable stupor.

Mara grabbed him under both armpits and strained and grunted as she dragged him inch by inch into his room. She ran and took a single mattress from Mother's room and pulled it back next to Pierre. Rolling his comatose body onto the mattress was straightforward. She removed his boots, covered him with blankets from his bed, put a pillow under his head, blew out the bedroom candle, and went back to sleep.

***

The sunshine streaming across her bed woke Mara early. Pierre's snoring poured through the open door as she walked past and down the stairs. The clattering of pots and pans beckoned her cautiously towards the kitchen. Standing beside the stone fireplace, stirring the hot contents of a cauldron, stood a broad, middle-aged woman dressed in simple clothes, protected by a white apron. "Good morning, Madame," Mara proffered quietly.

The woman turned towards the greeting, scowled, looked Mara up and down, and turned back to her chores. "I assume the master brought you home from the alehouse last night. I dare say I have not seen a bald one at breakfast before. Now, I assume you need some nourishment before you go about your daytime business?"

"No, no Madame. It is not like that at all. The good doctor has taken me in to help with experiments in his laboratory. My name is Mara."

"So that is what he tells his girls these days. Experiments! Ha! Well Mara, I am Madame Simmons, but you may call me Claudette. Sit down and I will give you some porridge. The 'good doctor' would expect me to feed you before you went on your way. Besides, you look as if you can do some with some fattening up."

Claudette poured the steaming gruel into two bowls, added a sizeable chunk of butter and a sprinkling of sugar. "Eat up, Mara."

"Thank you very much, Claudette."

Neither spoke as they sat down, and only the clatter of the iron spoons against the bowls broke the silence.

Eventually Mara spoke. "Claudette, you have been most generous this morning, and it appears that we will see more of each other over the coming weeks. So, I feel it is best if I clearly explain my circumstances. I hope we can be friends."

"Weeks!" Claudette laughed a deep-throated laugh. "No girl has lasted here over two nights. But please proceed. I need some cheer this morning."

"Well, I was captured by the guards some days ago and brought to trial on the charge of witchcraft. They shaved me all over when I was in the Tower." Mara ran her hand over her stubble.

Claudette studied her over a spoon of gruel in her mouth. "Witchcraft! Is that supposed to frighten me? I've never heard of such nonsense. But, please proceed."

Relieved, Mara continued. "Well, I am definitely not a witch, but my family has a long history of healing various ailments with herbal remedies." Mara paused, expecting Claudette to respond, but her mouth was full and she signalled with her hand to continue. "While undergoing the trial, I could demonstrate to the magistrate the value of one of these remedies. The good doctor was so impressed with my work that the court agreed with his suggestion that under his guidance, I work here."

Claudette remained silent until she had finished her gruel. "I hear witches are usually naked at these trials."

"Yes, I was." Mara shivered and held her face in her hands.

"There, there Mara," and gently pulled her hands from her face. "You are welcome here as long as you promise not to fly around my kitchen on a broomstick." Claudette laughed another deep-throated laugh and Mara giggled with her.

"Good morning, Madame Simmons; good morning, Mara. I am pleased that you have become acquainted." Pierre walked across the kitchen, clean shaven and immaculately dressed and poured a cup of coffee from a pot standing on a stone in the hearth. He sat down at the table. "Ah Madame Simmons, your coffee is the best in this fine city and just what I need to get me going on this glorious morning."

"Good morning, Doctor Laurent," came the chorus from Mara and Claudette, as they both dried the laughter from their eyes.

"I awoke in the most unusual circumstances this morning. I found myself on a mattress on the floor, so I am hopeful I did not cause anyone too much of an inconvenience last night." Without waiting for a reply, he continued. "Mara, last night I had the opportunity to meet with the apothecary, Monsieur Baptiste, and explained your situation. We agreed it would be informative for you to spend some time learning about our modern medicines before we begin our experiments on promising new ones. So today you will go to his shop, meet with his daughter Isabella, and do rounds with her. That will probably require most of the day, and I will await your return this evening.

"Thank you, sir. I would like that. Isabella is a close friend from school."

"And remember, the court has entrusted you to my care. Therefore, do exactly as Monsieur Baptiste instructs and do not go wandering off. If there is any trouble, you will be back in the interrogation chamber and I will have a lot of questions to answer. Now I must get to work. My first patients are already in the waiting room."

16

La Loire

11 June 1670

Wanting to make an impression, Mara had selected a tasteful selection from Mother's wardrobe. She had dithered with many outfits and was late. Loose fitting, pointed leather shoes provoked an occasional stumble as she negotiated the horse dung littered cobbles. An olive-green, ankle length dress with a low, broad neckline and tight bodice turned heads, but did little to hasten her progress through the morning crowd. A broad-brimmed hat was the only item she felt comfortable with.

Although excited about her good fortune and new opportunity, she could not push the cloud of Maman and Grandmère's absence from her mind. *At last, we have a note. They must be close. They are alive! But where could they possibly be?* Turning a corner, her spirits rose as she recognised Simon standing in the shadow of the butcher's shop. She instantly changed course, but Simon's finger to his lips and a shake of his head reluctantly turned her back on her original path. Curiosity, however, conquered disappointment and she stopped occasionally to browse in a shop window. Glancing back, she smiled at a glimpse of Simon's blond head ducking into a building or his large boots projecting from beyond a doorway.

The bell tinkled as she opened the apothecary door. Francine Macon and Jacques were pleading at the counter with the apothecary. "Please Monsieur Baptiste, this is the finest medicine that this city will ever experience. It contains all the ingredients to cure all manner of ailments. Please Monsieur, could you persuade some of your customers to purchase a mouthful? There is no need to pay for anything now; just a small portion of what you receive. Please Monsieur, we have no money and have had nothing to eat since Maman was taken to trial and now to the Tower."

"Your mother came here countless times, and I bought none of her useless concoctions. Why would I now buy anything from you? The daughter of a convicted witch!"

"How dare you speak ill of my mother! I hope you suffer the eternal agony of purgatory's inferno." Francine turned and walked towards the door with Jacques close behind. She brushed past Mara but failed to recognise her in unfamiliar clothes.

"Francine?"

Francine turned, recognised Mara, and scowled. "My, my Mara, you really have landed on your feet. You may not have recognised me at the trial yesterday, but I observed all your good fortune. You escaped the Tower and now you live in a fancy house with that doctor. I am certain he has given you more than his coat by now," a sarcastic smile revealing a small gap in the middle of her top teeth. "And look at you, with these rich woman's garments. It is not surprising I did not recognise you. Our mother is now having every limb pulled from her body and will soon be taken by the flames. And Jacques and I do not have a single crumb of bread to share." Francine turned, and the bell tinkled louder as she wrenched open the door and walked off toward the square. She held her mother's iron pot tightly under her arm while Jacques trailed obediently behind her.

A frosty silence followed the crash of the door. Monsieur Baptiste's head slunk deeper into his huge journal on the counter. Mara stood rooted, still facing the door, watching her friend scurry away and then turned.

"Good morning, Mara," ventured Baptiste. "Isabella always talks about her best friend at school. It is a pleasure to meet you. You probably don't recall, but I did meet you some eight years ago when you came here with Simon; you still look much the same."

Mara turned, forced a smile and walked towards the counter. "Good morning, Monsieur Baptiste. I cannot thank you enough for providing me with this generous opportunity."

"Think nothing of it. The good doctor spoke so well of you last night, and he and I are close friends and colleagues." He turned his head and called out. "Isabella, Mara has arrived. You have many visits, so I suggest you make a start. Everything is packed and on the counter in the basket."

Mara waited quietly near the counter, studying the rows of medicines, while Baptiste again busied himself in his journal. A few moments passed and a thin teenage girl with red curls falling over her shoulders appeared from behind the curtain. She wore a neat, yellow ankle length dress with a high neck and in one hand carried a basket filled with small packages.

"Bonjour Isabella. It is so good to see you now that our school days are over. So, this is a surprise. Are you well?"

Isabella beamed, a radiant smile accentuating her freckled nose and cheeks. "I am very well. But you! I am so pleased you are safe. So much has happened since school finished. You must tell me everything."

"Come on girls, hurry on, it is already late. The carriage awaits outside. You have much to get through today."

They immediately responded to Monsieur Baptiste's order and scampered out of the door. A grey bearded gentleman in a riding jacket and breeches stood holding the reins of a black horse attached to an open carriage. They jumped into the seat and Isabella took hold of the reins. "Thank you, Gaston. I will return to the stables later this afternoon." And with a flick of her wrists and a shout, "Michelangelo, let's go!" they rattled over the cobblestones, past the rows of tall painted houses and down towards the river.

After passing through the city gate, St Raphael disappeared quickly behind them. They rode in silence as the surge of la Loire raced downstream next to them. The sky was clear and the low sun energised the millions of tiny droplets created by the river spray.

"You are in deep in thought Mara, do you wish to talk?"

"It concerns Francine. I can understand how upsetting it is that her mother has been taken to the Tower. But we are her best friends and I only mean to help."

"I agree Mara, and hopefully this will heal with time."

"I am very concerned for her. If she isn't careful, she herself will fall under the scrutiny of the witch hunters."

"Why do you say that?"

"I thought we all knew. She made it clear to me one day when we were alone. She doesn't like boys. Just girls."

"Oh, I wasn't aware."

"Maybe you're not her type."

The river grew louder and more turbulent as they passed St Joan and its bridge. Maison Diana flickered between the trees and bushes on the opposite bank.

"I am truly sorry, Mara. I cannot imagine how difficult it must be. Just not knowing." Isabella placed one hand on Mara's forearm as she searched the moving landscape across the river. Mara turned and placed her other hand over Isabella's as a stray tear crossed her cheek.

The carriage turned away from the river and up the long hill past the forest of trees which contained the Glen. "That last day of school. I over-heard Celeste ask you to come?"

Mara bowed her head, nodded, and recounted all the events of that shameful and monstrous dawn.

Once over the brow of the hill, Michelangelo broke into a gentle can-ter as the two friends continued their reflections of the recent life-changing events. Almost an hour had passed when they left the road through large, ornamental gates and up a long driveway lined by rows of beech trees. A large, three storey, stone building came into view and they followed the driveway around to the rear of the house.

"We are forbidden to use the front entrance. Servant's entrance only," Isabella explained.

A sturdy, white uniformed maid stood waiting at the back door. "Good morning, Isabella, Welcome to house Martin. How are you this morning? I see you have company this week?"

"Good morning, Charlotte. Yes, I am very fortunate to have Mara with me this morning. She is working with Dr Laurent and wishes to learn everything she can about our modern medicines."

"Hello Mara. But you look familiar. Are you from these parts?"

"Yes, but we have only moved from Marseilles recently," Mara lied.

Charlotte studied Mara, rubbed her chin, and pursed her lips. Then abruptly dropped her hand and led them through into a large kitchen. In the centre of the room stood a long wooden table, on which was placed the master's pill box. "He instructed me to say that he wants exactly the same as last week. He is much improved and says your father is working miracles."

Isabella pulled out three small packets, each one carefully labelled *Monsieur Martin*. She opened the pillbox to reveal seven small compartments. "Mara, this is a weekly pill box, one compartment for each day of the week. This ensures that our patients can easily see if they have neglected to take their pills for the day." Charlotte had moved off to the other side of the kitchen to tend to a large pot hanging on the hearth. "He is an absent-minded old man and was always in the habit of mixing up his medications. Father finally got this for him," she whispered. Then in a louder voice, "Monsieur Martin takes three different tablets every day. So, one pill from each of these three packets goes into each compartment," she explained as she filled the pill box. "There, all in order, Charlotte."

Charlotte turned away from her pot and walked back to the table, and inspected the open pill box. "Good, three pills for each day." She pulled a small envelope from her pocket of her tunic and handed it to Isabella. "You should find this to your satisfaction."

"Thank you, Charlotte. We will visit again next week."

"Yes. Will Mara be with you again?"

"Yes, I hope so."

"I am not sure the master would be happy knowing that I have allowed a witch into his house?" Charlotte looked directly at Mara. "I had heard that Dr Laurent had taken in a young witch."

Mara bowed her head and shifted nervously.

Isabella broke the strained silence. "Madame, you know full well that Mara was falsely accused and that the judge let her go in the care of the good doctor. I also find it strange that someone whose aunt in Paris has recently gone to the fire should stand here and pass judgement. I am certain you would not want Madame Martin to know of your distant relative?"

"Bien. Oui. Oui. I will not mention it to her. But go now. She will return soon from her morning stroll."

A thoughtful silence separated the girls as the road turned back and along la Loire. Michelangelo knew the route and turned into another long drive with a magnificent country house in the distance. "Perhaps it would be better if I remain in the carriage and you go in and make the deliveries," Mara ventured

"How will you learn if you do not come?" Isabella reached across and laid her hand on Mara's. "I have learned that one needs to grow a thicker skin with these rich country folk. If you do not, they will walk over common people like us."

They had only progressed about twenty metres up the avenue of Maison Roux when the sound of growing thunder drifted across from their left. A pack of ten horsemen following three dogs were fast approaching. The lead rider, on seeing the carriage, held up his hand, and the troupe slowed to a trot and stopped in the driveway.

"Ah Isabella, you look as fresh as a rose on this summer's day. And you bring another delightful young maid with you."

"Good morning, Monsieur Roux. Yes, this is my friend Mara. I have your medicines. We will take them up to the house so you can continue with your pleasure."

"No, no. I will not have two delightful young ladies wilt here in this heat. Just give them to me." Monsieur Roux dismounted and strode across to the carriage, where Isabella gave him a packet. He kissed both Isabella and Mara on the back of the hand to the cheering of the troupe. "Now, we must be off. We have a fox to catch." Within minutes, the pack was a just speck in the distance.

Halfway up the next driveway, they observed a gentleman wearing a tartan waistcoat over a white shirt and a tartan skirt. He stood on the lawn next to the drive, swinging at an object on the ground with a club-like stick. He ceased swinging as they approached.

"Monsieur Badeaux, what on earth are you doing with that club?"

"Bonjour Isabella. Yes, this may look strange. But on my recent visit to Scotland, their manner of dress and this delightful pastime took me. They call it golf. The object is to strike this ball here with this club, as many times as you like, and attempt to put it in a hole which is marked by that flag down there." He pointed to a white flag about 100 metres away.

"Well Monsieur Badeaux, I must say I have never heard of this game. Golf?"

"Well, you will see it a lot more. I assume you have my pills."

Isabella handed the packet to Monsieur Badeaux, who placed it in his waistcoat pocket. "Thank you, Isabella. Now I must continue with my golf. I will see you again next week."

After a few more visits, the midday sun beat down relentlessly on the open carriage. Their own momentum provided the only breeze. The long tree-lined driveway of Monsieur Claude Villiers would be their last visit.

Ahead, at the edge of the driveway, stood a middle-aged lady dressed in a white ankle length dress and shaded by a light blue parasol. Initially absorbed in close conversation with a tall, bearded man holding an axe, her head turned at the sound of the approaching carriage. A quick snap back to the young beard saw him scurry off toward a small dwelling at the edge of a line of trees.

"Good day to you, ladies. And thank you, Isabella, for delivering my husband's pills on such a day."

"It is a pleasure, Madame Villiers. If you wish, we will take them up to the kitchen and give them to the maid."

"No, that will not be necessary. They are only his rheumatism pills. You can give them to me. I will ensure they are correctly placed in his box. He is certainly incapable of such a task." She reached into her pocket and removed a dainty purse and withdrew two coins, and waited as Isabella stepped down from the carriage. Reaching out to take the coins, Isabella noted her smudged face powder and a few strands of hair escaping from an otherwise perfectly tight bun.

"Thank you, Madame. This is too much. I will make a note of your credit in my father's ledger."

"Do not worry. I would advise that you girls buy something when you get back to St Raphael."

"Oh no Madame, father would never allow that."

"As you wish, but I know what I would have done when I was your age."

They continued on around the circular driveway and waved to a uniformed maid standing at the front door, and then nodded to Madame Villiers as they passed her again.

"Well, that has saved us a bit more time! That is the third time I have seen that gardener and the madame together. What do you think, Mara?"

Mara tried to suppress her chuckle by holding her hand over her mouth. Taking a breath, she ventured, "they have probably known each other for years. You become good friends when you have been working together all that time. It does not always have to be something naughty."

But all restraint was lost and a fount of giggling and laughter filled the carriage as Madame Villiers disappeared behind them.

Despite the heat, Michelangelo sensed the homeward route and picked up his pace. But as the cart reached a fork in the road, Isabella unexpectedly slowed him down and turned right, off the road and away from St Raphael.

"What! Isabella, the city is that way," Mara pointed back to the left fork.

"It is far too hot to return to St Raphael. Papa will only expect us when the sun is just above the horizon. We are having such fun and I know a place where we can cool down." Isabella turned again, onto a narrow, rutted path which ran through dense bush under a cool canopy of age-old oaks. After another fifty metres, the track opened onto a grassy bank alongside a wider, gently flowing section of la Loire.

Isabella jumped from the carriage and tied Michelangelo to a tree. "Come, take off your stockings." In their bare white legs, they stepped into the cool, gently flowing river and waded until the water reached their knees. Isabella cupped the river in both hands and splashed in over her face.

"Ooh, this is cold." She scooped another handful and splattered it over Mara's dress.

"Oh, you little cow." Mara quickly retaliated with multiple splashes of her own.

The water works quickly expanded into a playful shower of laughter, squeals and cursing. Finally, buoyant but drenched, they crawled back up the bank and lay flat on their backs in the soft grass, soaking up the sun.

"That was much better than bouncing on that road in the boiling sun."

"Oui, and better than dealing with the rich at play or whatever it is they do."

"Yes, but I thought that gardener was rather handsome. And would you not wish to stroke that beard?"

"You are terrible Isabella; you are supposed to think and act like a lady."

"Ha, I am certain you thought the same. As a matter of fact, I guarantee he is doing the Madame."

"I confess, Isabella, I thought exactly the same."

They looked sideways at each and smiled. Isabella closed her eyes and let the sun slowly warm her body. Mara bathed in the warmth and the fragrances of the surrounding woodland. But her nostrils twitched, and she inhaled deeply. Puzzled, she sat up, again sniffing deeply. Standing, she let Isabella doze and wandered off into a faint breeze. Crossing the open field, she entered the forest, where she found a narrow track. Repeatedly raising her nose in the air, a disagreeable smell became stronger and her footsteps quickened. The path led her deeper into the forest, turning first to her left and then to her right. She stopped. The faint smell had grown from unpleasant to putrid. She turned another corner and the source of the repugnant odour lay ahead in the middle of her path. A body covered by a large branch of a tree. The corpse was that of an older, bearded, unkempt man. One branch lay across his shattered forehead, another had slashed a deep gash in his left thigh, and another lay across his bare left foot. On closer inspection, the foot was a reddish black, swollen, and the wound caused by the branch was filled with maggots. Through the torn rags of clothing, a duskiness tracked up the shin and to the knee where it appeared to stop abruptly. Mara took a cloth from her pocket and tied it to cover her nose. She knelt down next to the corpse and tore apart the threadbare trousers. The redness stopped at the knee, leaving white skin up to and around the thigh wound. Intrigued, Mara ripped further at his trousers to fully expose the thigh wound. It was deep with bone exposed. The cavity was filled with a mouldy, moss like substance. She removed the material to reveal clean flesh, ligaments and cracked bone and placed it in one of her belt compartments.

A sudden spine-chilling scream broke the murmuring of the forest and shattered Mara's speculation. "Mara! Help, heeeeelp! Please, please. No! Noo!" The screams ceased abruptly.

Mara sprang to her feet and raced down the narrow path, brushing aside branches with hands, body, and face. At the entry to the field, she stopped. A large broad-shouldered man dressed in a grey soldier's tunic struggled on top of Isabella. With breeches crumpled around his ankles and hairy buttocks exposed to the midday sun, he held Isabella's arms together above her head with one hand and clamped the other over her mouth. Frantically, Mara searched the ground and seized a smooth, fist-sized stone. Breathing heavily, with mouth set, she ran quietly across the field. Approaching the soldier from behind, Mara looked directly into Isabella's wide, terrified eyes. She raised the stone and brought it down as decisively and forcefully as she was able. The stone smashed into the side of the soldier's head. Initially stunned, his hands surrendered Isabella's arms and mouth and he fell to one side, clutching his skull. He stared up in wide-eyed disbelief at his attacker. Before he had a chance to recover, Mara struck him again over his left eye and then repeatedly over his forehead, nose and eyes till his face was a bloody pulp. Wildly, desperately, she continued to strike his motionless head. She stopped momentarily and watched. A flicker of his left eye and a spasm of his body resulted in a resumption of the pounding. Finally, completely exhausted, she collapsed and fell, wasted, in the grass.

"Mara, Mara," Isabella cried as she kneeled next to her and wrapped her arms around her. They lay there, shaking, desperately clutching at each other. As the sun removed the chilling fear and the adrenalin dissipated, their trembling bodies and pounding hearts slowly settled.

Mara was the first to regain composure. "Isabella, we have to get rid of this body. If found, there will be an investigation. And there are several people who can confirm that we were in this area."

"But how, Mara?"

Mara nodded towards the river. "The perfect cemetery for this depraved monster."

Panting and grunting, they dragged the bloodied corpse across the rough ground, stopping every few feet to catch breath. At the edge of the bank, they pushed the body over and watched it roll down to the water's edge. "We must make sure it sinks, otherwise it will float downstream and someone will find it. Those river stones should work." Mara pointed to a small pebbled side stream.

After packing as many stones as possible inside his tunic, they pulled the body towards the middle of the river where the current was running. The corpse was let loose, and it drifted slowly downstream. They stood chest deep in the gently flowing water, holding each other as the soldier of la Maréchausée bobbed around in some rapids and then sank.

"Come Isabella, we must get away from here. Someone may have heard the screams and come for a look."

"We cannot go back like this. We are soaked, and both our dresses are torn."

Isabella's dress had been ripped completely off her left shoulder, and her breast was exposed. Mara fixed her gaze on a small nodule above Isabella's left breast. Isabella, flustered at Mara's focus, quickly tried to cover up. "No, Mara. No! You have seen it. You know my secret. Please, please never mention it to anyone?"

"Isabella, your secret will always be safe with me. You know I do not believe any of that nonsense." Mara smiled and attempted to relieve Isabella's anxiety. "Does it also get excited when you think about a nice boy?"

Isabella laughed, "Mara, you are terrible. How can you say that?"

"I saw the way you examined that gardener."

"Oh Mara, he is not at all my type. But yes, all three of them do."

The laughter burst from their mouths, and the birds in the surrounding trees joined their chorus. But their joy could only briefly blot out the enormity and consequences of this fateful afternoon.

"We can stop at my house to clean-up, change our clothes and get something to eat. Only Simon may be there."

It was late afternoon when they passed back through the city gate, clean and dry and each with a new set of clothes. Simon had not been home. Isabella would tell her father only that they had finished early and went for a swim, if he noticed her change of dress. On her return to the doctor's house, Mara glanced into the waiting room. Doctor Laurent stood at the open doorway of his consulting room, both hands held up, attempting to placate a disgruntled group of patients. A young man with a bloodied cloth around his head, an agitated teenage boy and girl, a bedraggled mother carrying a screaming child and a young man with a bent arm in a sling; all arguing and competing about the urgency of their ailments.

"Mara, please come here. I need your help urgently!" He ushered her past the melee, and into the surgery, and closed the door behind him.

On the couch lay a middle-aged man mumbling repeatedly. "Please, please do not take my leg. My family will starve." The left leg of his breeches was rolled above the knee.

"This is Monsieur Lambert, the street lighter we saw last evening." Mara nodded, staring wide-eyed at his red, swollen foot with a deep, pus-filled wound on the sole. The glowing, tense scarlet extended up to the middle of his calf with angry red streaks extending to just below the knee. "He has had this for a few days and ignored it. He will die of this infection if we do not act immediately. We have to remove his leg here." Pierre marked an imaginary line just below the knee with his outstretched palm. "I gave him a couple of glasses of brandy about half an hour ago. As you may note, he is somewhat intoxicated, but the expected pain will easily break through that." He pointed to a small table under the window. "Pour a bit of the opium onto that cloth and hold it over his nose."

Mara approached the window, and with a trembling hand, lifted the glass bottle and removed the stopper. "Do not take my leg. Do not take my leg. Please!" The bottle shook, and the anaesthetic spattered onto the cloth and onto the plate and table. She turned back to the doctor, who had placed a small cushion under the left knee and immobilised the patient's head, chest and thighs with leather straps. Mara stood frozen, anchored to the safety of the table.

"Mara, come, bring that here! There is no time to waste!" He gestured impatiently with his hand. "Now hold it under his nose."

Mara nodded as her trembling outstretched hand held the soaked cloth against the street lighter's nose.

Within minutes Monsieur Lambert's mumbling ceased, and he lapsed into unconsciousness. "Alright, we must get started. There will be much screaming, but your job is to keep that under his nose and make sure he does not struggle out of those straps."

Pierre lifted a cloth from a small table to reveal an array of knives, saws, and drills. He took a short sharp knife and, without hesitating, drove the knife into the flesh below the man's knee. Monsieur Lambert's eyes sprung open and a chilling scream exploded from his mouth. Pierre ignored the shrieking and quickly and expertly continued to make precise skin incisions marking out the flaps. Once completed, he paused, and the howling settled into a dull mumbling. "Keep the opium up there Mara, the worst is yet to come" Pierre took the scissors from the tray and dug around on the side of the wound. A fountain of bright red blood shot out onto the floor. "That's the artery Mara. Give me that cat gut on the table." He ordered as he squeezed the bleeding vessel with his bare hand. Mara removed the cloth, passed the gut to Pierre, and restored the opium to the patient's nose.

"Alright, that's done! Now hold him tight." He grabbed a short sharp blade and cut the flesh and tendons from the bone, and peeled them back. Monsieur Lambert's back arched as he screamed and strained against his bindings. The forehead binding flew loose, and he threw his head up and from side to side. "Mara, hold his head down, bring your chest down on his head and hold the cloth with your hand." He reached for the saw, placed it on the shin, and moved the blade backwards and forwards across the bone. Monsieur Lambert's head thrashed from side to side and his chest bindings loosened. "Mara, hold his head still. Now!" The bile rose in Mara's throat and the blood drained from her head. Her full weight and breasts collapsed across Monsieur Lambert's face, immediately stifling any further screaming and struggling.

Mara woke laying on the floor as Pierre was bandaging the bloody stump. "You passed out on his head. It kept him down and much quieter. Just lay there until I finish. Almost done."

Mara nodded and mumbled. The room was still swimming but slowly her focus returned and she rose tentatively, holding onto the bed as Pierre completed the bandage.

"Mara, now you must return to the apothecary and get some more rolls of bandages. We will need them this evening. If he is closed, just knock, he will open up. Can you do that?"

"Yes, I think so. I am so sorry I fainted."

"Do not concern yourself. You did everything I required of you. Now off you go."

"But what about the patients in the waiting room?"

"After that fearful uproar, I am certain the waiting room will be empty."

17

The Cloister

12 June 1670

Commandant Duval pulled a woven bell rope hanging beside a high wooden gate and heard the faint response from somewhere deep within the cloister. He stepped back into the road. To one side of the gate, a high stone wall, bedecked with deterrent spikes, extended to the main square. On the other side, the wall stretched and disappeared around a corner. He waited, kicking loose stones and repeatedly checking his pocket watch. Finally, he heard footsteps scurrying inside the gate. A small door, within the large gate, opened to his right, and a robbed, stocky young man with black, unkempt hair emerged.

"Good morning, Commandant Duval. Bishop Bernard awaits you in his quarters. I am Emile. If you would please follow me."

The gate opened onto a large stone courtyard with deep carriage wheel ruts leading around a central fountain and up to the front door. On the far side of the courtyard stood the stables, where a blacksmith stoked some smoking coals. Duval followed the young seminarian through the open front door into a cool, high ceiling atrium. On the wall directly opposite the entry, he was awestruck by a floor to ceiling painting of Moses with the Ten Commandments. The stone tablet was raised high above his head as a lightning bolt pierced threatening clouds. Moses' long white beard and brown cloak flapped with the wind as the crowds below held up their hands in wonderment.

Noting his interest, Emile explained. "God's Ten Commandments are central to all God's teaching and we follow and preach them daily. As we walk, you will observe paintings of each commandment."

They turned left of Moses and then right around a large internal garden separated from the corridor by several stone arches. Priests, monks and seminarians talking quietly in small groups turned and eyed Duval as he passed. On the wall opposite the garden hung three Commandments. Duval slowed and contemplated each one in turn. *Thou shalt not kill*, depicted an assailant running and holding a bloodied sabre while looking back at a recumbent man clutching a bloodied wound. *Thou shalt not commit adultery*, portrayed a partially dressed man, sitting on a couch and pulling a struggling maiden towards him. *Thou shalt not steal*, presented a thief running from a fine mansion and carrying a box under his arm.

The corridor came to a junction, turning right around the internal garden and left up another corridor. The seminarian stopped and pointed to a picture on the facing wall. "This is the first commandment. *I am the Lord thy God and thou shalt have no other gods before me*. As you are aware, this is very relevant to the witchcraft we are experiencing today." Duval stopped and considered the commandment. A man kneeling on the ground, head bowed, arms stretched out towards a golden cow mounted on top of a stone altar.

"Come, we should keep moving. Bishop Bernard is very eager to see you."

They hurried through a maze of passageways and finally entered a large room which opened onto a small, well-maintained, internal garden. Bishop Bernard sat on a small bench, studying some papers. He rose as Duval approached. "Good morning, Commandant, it is not often we have the pleasure, or should I say, the need for the law to visit the House of God."

"You are correct, My Lord. In all my time here, I have never had the necessity of visiting this establishment. But I can see you are busy with your papers, so I will not keep you long."

"Tell me then, how can I be of service to our la Maréchausée?"

"At the recent trial concerning the unfortunate death of Monsieur Duplessis, Madame Duplessis indicated she was destitute. Her predicament arose because her husband had significant debt. You may recall, I asked to whom he owed the money, and she indicated it was the church?"

The bishop's mouth formed a smile, but his eyes stared with contempt. "Yes, it was a most unfortunate sequence of events. Monsieur Duplessis came to me and requested to purchase a large piece of church land that abutted his property. He explained it was for more cows, but also so he could better stretch his horse's legs. Those were his words, I believe. He also wanted to borrow some additional money to pay for a few buildings and fences on the property." He paused and fixed the commandant. "I am a very prudent man with money. I take my responsibility for dealing with church finances seriously. So, we drew up papers to ensure that should he be unable to repay the loan, both the church land and his current land would be handed over to the church. I have all the documentation, if you wish to see them."

Duval concealed his scepticism and waved away the suggestion. "That is unnecessary now, but perhaps later I will send one of my clerks to come and look them over. It does strike me though that the value of his property was far in excess of the loan that you provided him?"

"That is correct, Commandant. But as I have already said, I have an enormous responsibility to the church. I also wanted to impress on Monsieur Duplessis that failure to repay would be extremely detrimental to his financial position. He assured me he had some large business transactions that were almost complete and he would have no problem repaying the debt. Regrettably, these transactions did not conclude as he expected and he returned and begged for an extension, which I granted. Unfortunately, as you are aware, he succumbed to a witch's curse and has left his poor wife with a mountainous debt."

"Who uses the house now?"

"The church arranges conferences there now. We can invite clergy from all over France. We also use the property for respite; some of our senior clergy are sometimes in need of a quiet place where they can talk with God. We have also had a few evenings where we invite local businessmen to discuss financial issues related to the church."

"So, it would appear that the church has profited favourably from the untimely death of Monsieur Duplessis."

Duval watched the feigned smile become a sneer. "Commandant, sarcasm does not befit you, nor does it have a place in the House of God. Can I offer you some tea?"

Duval smiled at the reprimand and held the glare until the bishop looked away. "Sorry, but I have to rush over to the Villiers' household. I have been told that Monsieur Claude Villiers has suddenly died under unusual circumstances."

"Are you suspecting foul play? Why would the Commandant be required?"

"I am unsure what to expect. I have never met the man. But from what I already know, the pieces do not fit well together." Duval rose from his chair. "Thank you for giving me some of your most valuable time."

"It is my pleasure. Emile will show you out and please send your clerk to collect the papers. Good day Commandant."

"Good day my Lord."

***

An hour later, Duval was still reflecting on his meeting with the bishop when he rode down the Villiers's tree-lined driveway. A three-storey country house stood alone on a slight rise with well-manicured lawns sweeping down on either side. Nicolette, a young, olive-skinned girl, met him at the front door. "Madame is out walking in the forest. She said that if you arrived, I was to show you the master's room. Please, if you will follow me."

Monsieur Villiers' room was on the first floor, facing the approach driveway. The sun streamed through the open curtains, baking and amplifying the putrid stench within the room. He lay naked on his back, in the middle of a carpet covered in vomit and excrement. Duval brought a handkerchief to his nose and studied the face. It was familiar. He looked again, searched his memory, shook his head, and then turned and scanned the rest of the room. A waistcoat, breeches and jacket hung on a clothes rack at the far end of the room. The soiled bed sheets had been thrown back. Next to the bed stood a small table on which was placed an open, seven compartment pill-box.

"The apothecary's daughter and another young girl delivered the pills yesterday. They did not enter the house. They gave the packet of pills to Madame Villiers, who met them in the driveway. Madame then placed them in his box."

Duval examined the plain seven compartment box and noted that only one slot was empty. He closed the box and placed it in his pocket. "Take me down to the kitchen." He stepped towards the door and froze in mid stride, looked back at the body, rubbed his chin and nodded. "Ah yes! Monsieur Romero from Maison Claire," he mumbled. Turning to the clothes rack, he ruffled through the jacket pocket and smiled as he pulled out a small, empty brown bottle with a glass stopper. He examined the base and noted a plain pontil scar with no identifying blower's mark. "I think we have finished here. To the kitchen, please."

The kitchen was a large cool cavern in the basement, with filtered light struggling through high windows and kept warm by glowing coals in an open hearth. Duval scanned the shelves and opened all the cupboards and eventually pulled out a small bag of white powder.

"Yes, that is the poison we use for the rats. I am told it is arsenic and you must not let it pass your lips."

"I assume you live here?"

"Yes, I live in the cottage down at the edge of the garden with the gardener."

"Thank you. You have been most helpful. I will just take a stroll outside."

Duval stood at the front door, looking out across the lawns towards a forest that rose abruptly about one hundred meters away. The underbrush suddenly parted and a well-dressed but tousled woman emerged. She bent down, brushed down her dress, fiddled with her bun of hair and walked across the lawn towards the house. She was halfway across when fifty metres to her left, a young man carrying an axe emerged from the foliage and walked purposefully towards a small cottage at the edge of the forest.

Madame Villiers shouted as she approached the front porch. "You must be the Commandant coming to investigate my husband's unfortunate death?"

Duval waited till she was next to him. "Yes, you are correct. Can you tell me what you know of the events last night?"

"Not much, actually. We sleep in different rooms, so I have no knowledge of what occurred. At about midnight, I heard some noise but thought he had a bit too much to drink, which is not unusual for him. The maid came into my room this morning and told me the horrid news."

"You do not seem very concerned."

"He was a bully! He used to beat me, but stopped after I hit him over the head with an empty whiskey bottle. I am glad he is gone. The only time I had some peace was when he spent his nights in St Raphael. He has a house on le Boulevard du Printemps which I have never visited. I would often spend time with my mother to get a break."

"Yes, I made some enquires before departing this morning and learned that Monsieur Villiers has a house in St Raphael. Does he have a kept mistress in the city or does he visit establishments such as Maison Claire?"

Madame Villiers chuckled. "Frankly Commandant, I have no interest in his dalliances but doubt he is capable of such activities."

Duval raised his eyebrows and briefly held the silence between them. "Do you know if he had any enemies?"

"None that I am aware of. He would have friends come to visit when I was away. I heard that from the staff. They said there were some rowdy gatherings."

"Gatherings? Thank you. I shall return if I need any more information. I will just go across and have a talk with the gardener."

"Uh? Why would you wish to talk with him?"

"It seems he is more often here than you. He may have seen something." Duval turned, jumped down the steps and walked towards the cottage at the edge of the forest. As he approached, raised voices reached him.

"You have been with that old slut again, haven't you?"

"She just wished to show me the trees that she wants cut down. It is my job, and she provides us with a roof and a living. You are so suspicious."

"You are a dam… Well hello Commandant, did you have a chat with Madame Villiers?"

"Yes, thank you, Nicolette. But now I need to talk to you, sir." Duval fixed on a muscular young man with a patchy beard. Behind his shoulder length hair, a small ring hanging from his right ear flashed in the sunlight. He sucked on a short stem pipe while trying to light it with a flint.

"Sorry Commandant, I have not introduced myself. I am Gilbert, the gardener." A cloud of smoke left his mouth and nose as he glanced at Nicolette, gave a jerk of his head, and she disappeared inside.

"You, of course, know the purpose of my visit. Have you noticed anything strange here lately?"

"Well, now that you ask, as a matter of fact I have. He has meetings, but only when the Madame goes to stay with her mother. Carriages arrive, some in the afternoon, others after dark, and then leave again in the early hours. Could not see much, but they appeared well dressed."

"No harm in having meetings. Anything else?"

"Well, yes, one of them, I think, was a man of the cloth. I thought he was wearing robes when he arrived, but could not discern any faces." He sucked again and another cloud of fumes enveloped them both.

Duval turned his head and covered his mouth and nose. "Still, no harm in a priest coming to discuss issues relating to the church. Perhaps these men needed spiritual guidance."

"That may be true, but at the last meeting, about a week ago, I heard screaming. So, I got closer, behind those bushes next to the front door. I waited; waited for probably an hour. Four carriages came and lined up directly in front of the door. Then the entrance light went out and the front of the house was in total darkness. Only then did three figures appear; again, the one wearing the robes. They all jumped into one carriage. Then three shorter figures appeared, each covered with a shawl, and each climbed into a separate carriage. All four carriages then left."

Duval's eyebrows raised; his suspicions heightened. "That is all you can tell me. No faces? No names?"

"No nothing. They certainly did not want to be recognised, you know, with the lights going out. I thought it might be useful information, maybe worth a few pennies?"

"What is your relationship with Madame Villiers?"

"What do you mean?"

"I'm not sure. But if I ask around, I feel certain I can find out. It will go better for you if you tell me."

"Alright, alright. We meet occasionally. She gets nothing from the old man, so she's as horny as a bitch in heat. She puts extra in my purse at the end of the week."

"So! She has told me she hates her husband and is glad to see him gone. Maybe you and her cooked up a scheme together. It seems very convenient for both of you now that he is gone."

"No, no, no! He was a good man. Very good to me. I could never be part of something like that." Gilbert sucked again, and this time exhaled the fog to one side.

"How do I know if this story about meetings, priests and short people is just to distract me from the true cause of this unfortunate death? Or just to extract some recompense."

"No! No! It is all true, I promise."

Duval's head nodded. "Will your girlfriend confirm your tale?"

"Girlfriend? Girlfriend? Oh, you mean Nicolette. No, she is always in bed early and sleeps as a stone."

Duval locked Gilbert's eyes. The gardener held them momentarily, then looked away and shuffled uneasily. Duval turned and walked back to his carriage, mumbling quietly to himself, "Lights out? Short people? Robes? A man of the cloth?"

$$18$$

Reunion

14 June 1670

The pitter-patter of rain against the window soothed much of Mara's anxiety about the recent la Loire incident. Singing in a soft voice, she meticulously recorded her latest experiment, occasionally looking out at Mother's refreshed garden. Her reflections turned to the previous nights when Pierre had stayed home. They had sat together talking, mainly about new medicines, but he also seemed interested in learning more about her life. He had been charming, the perfect gentleman. A loud knock at the front door interrupted her contemplation. She continued her writing, but the doorknocker sounded again, and a few minutes later rapped louder. "Claudette must have gone out," Mara mumbled.

When the knocker hammered again, Mara rushed out and opened the door. "What can I do for…... Celeste! What on earth? I, I thought you were in the Tower?"

"As you can see, Mara, I am alive and well. One day I will tell you everything, but right now I am just so happy to see you!" She held her arms out wide and Mara instantly fell into them. They clutched each other in the open doorway, unable to suppress their tears of relief and joy.

"Please, come inside. Look at you! You are soaked through."

"Yes. I clearly need some drying out."

Mara ushered her in and towards the stairway. As they passed the open waiting room, Doctor Laurent stepped out of his surgery to call his next patient. He looked towards them. "This is Celeste, a close friend from school. She has come for a quick visit." Pierre smiled, nodded and guided a dishevelled old man, with a bloodied bandage around his head, into his consulting room.

"Come, Celeste, let me take you upstairs. I have plenty of dry clothes."

They ascended the staircase and once out of earshot; "Mara, he is a very handsome young man. Are you and he the only occupants of this house?"

"Celeste, you are terrible. You always think the worst. It is nothing like that. We have an entirely professional relationship. He has been most kind. He saved me from the torture chamber and the fire by convincing the judge that I could be of benefit to him in his work."

They passed Pierre's open bedroom doorway and Celeste smiled and chuckled at the unmade bed. "Are you certain you do not repay him for his kindness?" Celeste teased again.

"Stop it, Celeste. No! It is not like that!"

Mara led her down the short corridor to the larger bedroom and opened Mother's cupboard. "It may not be the latest fashion, but something should fit. Take your pick. You will be much warmer when you get those off."

Celeste chose a bold red dress and white collarless blouse and continued to chatter while changing. "Well, this is a cosy little room and very convenient. Only a few steps down the corridor from the very kind doctor?"

"Stop it, Celeste, I am only his assistant. Please do not talk of it any further. Rumours like that could be the end of me!"

"Just playing. I promise, not one more word."

"Anyway, you have not told me anything about yourself. As you know, I saw the whole ceremony and arrest in the Glen." Mara paused and bowed her head. "And the river. I am so sorry about Grandmère. It was horrendous what they did. I was certain you would go to the fire."

"I thought the same Mara, but because of my training, I could improve my circumstances. Much like you, I have been fortunate to find a reasonable man. He is the colonel of la Maréchausée. You witnessed him at my initiation. He has heard my story and I have not yet experienced the torture of the Tower or been brought before the court. I just have to assist him with his work."

"Assist him with his work! But his work is hunting witches!"

Celeste held her finger against pursed lips. "It is best not to ask any more questions, and I will not ask any of you. Anyway, how do I look?" She spun around, smiling in the tightly gathered dress with her wet black hair falling to her shoulders. "Maybe the good doctor will find me appealing?"

"Celeste, you are impossible. Enough of that. Come downstairs and we will dry these clothes in the kitchen. Then I would love to show you where I work."

Once the clothes had been laid out to dry, they entered Mara's laboratory from the atrium. A long bench, displaying various devices and containers, stretched the length of the room along the window.

"Well, well Mara! What is all this equipment and what is it you do here?"

"My work is to discover medicines that are effective and so help doctors, like Dr Laurent, rid people of their ailments. My family has used herbs gathered from the forests for centuries to cure all manner of maladies. The doctor wants me to purify some substances that are found in these herbs."

"And how do you do that? Purify?"

Pleased that Celeste was showing interest, Mara smiled and continued. "Well, first we must weigh and grind these herbs here into a powder." Mara pointed out the set of scales and a row of small porcelain cups each filled with differently coloured leaves. "We do this by grinding them with this device called a mortar and pestle. Then I can extract some substances out of the plants using these solvents." Mara pointed to neatly labelled jars on shelves between the windows. "Finally, we can purify some of these substances by using this equipment." She pointed to a glass container perched above three candles and attached at the top to a long glass tube.

The other end of the tube rested on an open jar. "This is called distillation. I have copied the method from a book Monsieur Baptiste gave me."

"Have you made any grand discoveries?"

"We are making progress, but it is slow. I also have a lot to learn and as you can see, the good doctor has provided me with all the latest books." Mara held her outstretched hand towards a tall, full book shelf against the back wall.

"Well Mara, I must say you have been a busy girl."

The door from the surgery burst open, and Pierre appeared. "Mara, can you please give me a hand? I need you to hold down a little girl who will not lie still. Won't take a minute."

"Certainly Pierre," and turning to Celeste, "Just give me a minute." Mara followed the doctor through the open door.

Alone in the laboratory, Celeste's eyes were drawn to an open book on a small desk at the far end of the room. She initially hesitated, but curiosity prevailed, and she moved to the desk and scanned the neat handwriting on the open page. "Hmm, old man, tree branch, foot wound, red leg, deep cut thigh, mould." She placed her hand to turn the page as the surgery door opened behind her.

"Celeste! You cannot look at that. Sorry!" Mara quickly crossed the room and closed the book. "The doctor does not want anyone to know of our experiments until the medicines are ready. We must make sure they are safe and effective. Once all is complete, he will present the work to the College in Paris and then all France can share our story."

"I am truly sorry. I should not have been so inquisitive. But this sounds all very exciting. What does this mould do?"

"I cannot say, Celeste, only that if it works, it will save many lives."

The door burst open again. "Mara, quick, I have a twelve-year-old boy who I cannot hold down. Celeste, I think we could also use your help."

On the table was a trembling, wide-eyed boy laying on his side. His mother stood transfixed next to him, clutching his hand and staring hopefully at Doctor Laurent. "Ruben has an anal tear which has become infected. The abscess needs to be opened so the pus can drain out. Madame Lavigne, we need to turn him onto his stomach so we can lance this abscess. It will be very painful and he will scream. Do you understand Madame?"

The reality of the expected surgery appeared to wake Madame Lavigne from her bewilderment. She nodded and whispered to her son, who whimpered, gripped her hand, and, with prompting from his mother, gingerly turned over.

Pierre carefully parted his buttock cheeks and a red ball appeared at the right anal verge. "Celeste, Mara, each take a leg. Madam, please hold his back down." Pierre selected a scalpel from his instrument tray and, without a moment's hesitation, cut directly into the mass. Ruben's eyes snapped open and a harrowing scream escaped from his gaping mouth as the abscess erupted over Pierre's bare hands. Ignoring the howling, he drew the scalpel further across and into the abscess, and then methodically milked as much pus as possible from the opening. "Mara, pass me that bottle of alcohol and I will try to sterilise this wound." The sobbing boy screeched again as the alcohol entered the raw cavity. Pierre cleaned it out with his finger and waited. The bawling gradually settled. "Mara, I am a little concerned about this redness creeping up that right cheek. Let us pack some of the 'Old Man' in the wound and then place a dressing on it."

Mara looked quizzically at Pierre. "Are you sure? We had planned to purify it further."

"Mara, I have seen this before," and looked up at the mother. "We must use it now!"

Mara quickly left the surgery and returned with a small container containing a clear green liquid.

"Run it into the wound while I hold it open. Celeste, take both legs. This is going to be painful."

Another shiver and tormented scream erupted as the green liquid entered the cavity. "Mara, we will just let that soak in there and cover it with a bandage." The screaming gradually diminished to a whimper. "Madame Lavigne, that part is done. I just want him to drink the rest of the liquid when he turns over. It is essential that I see him again tomorrow. Bring him early."

Madame Lavigne and Mara helped Ruben slide off the couch. Mara gave him the bowl, and he swallowed the green fluid in a single gulp. He rose to his feet, and with a wide-based gait, walked hesitantly out of the surgery.

Pierre rubbed his chin as they departed and called after them. "Madame, just ask Ruben to wait in the waiting room. I require a quick word with you."

Madame Lavigne spoke quietly to her son, then returned, leaving Ruben warily contemplating the row of now empty chairs.

"Madame, have you any idea how this occurred?"

"None at all, doctor. He just came to me and said he had a pain in his bottom."

"Does he have problems with constipation?"

"He has never mentioned it. He goes every day. But he has been a little strange lately, staying in his room and not going out to play with friends. He is usually a very sociable boy."

"Keep a close eye on him and bring him in tomorrow."

"Thank you, Dr Laurent. Thank you very much."

Pierre pushed an outstretched hand through his hair as he watched mother and son leave the waiting room. "Thank you, Celeste, Mara. Hopefully, the rest of the day brings only a few coughs and colds."

"Thank you, doctor for letting me see what you do. It was fascinating. However, I have stayed too long and I must leave before I am missed. I would love to come again if that is possible?"

"I have no objection, as long as it pleases Mara."

"I would be most pleased if Celeste could return."

Mara felt a twinge of guilt as she watched Celeste trudge away in the rain, toward the Tower and towards a most perilous future. On her return to the surgery, she found Pierre sitting with his head in hands. "Is there something wrong?"

"I hope that works, Mara. If it does not, that poor little boy will be dead in a few days. I have seen this before and it will be a hopeless, agonising death."

"It worked for the old man. Let us hope for the young boy."

"Mara, your calmness and confidence are refreshing. Thank you. Now I have one more request. Could you please go to the apothecary for more bandages and alcohol? I will ask Claudette to cook us a grand meal and by the time you get back, we can dine together and talk more about our work."

"Oh? So not going to your gentleman's club tonight?"

"No. This poor young boy and his dismal outlook have dampened any enthusiasm for such pleasures."

As Mara rushed across the square towards the apothecary, she recognised a one-legged man with a bloody bandaged stump sheltering from the rain in a doorway. Monsieur Lambert held a stick in one hand and the other arm was wrapped around the shoulder of a young man. She nodded as she ran past, and Monsieur Lambert responded with a cynical smile.

Isabella was standing at the counter as Mara arrived. "Hello Isabella, I just need a few more of bandages and alcohol."

"Will I see you tomorrow? I have another day of rounds," Isabella asked as she packed the bag.

"I hope so, but Doctor Laurent is very busy and I am uncertain what he may have in store for me."

The bag of bandages was cumbersome and the walk back slow. Fortunately, the rain had stopped. Mara was close to home when she passed an old lady standing by a lamppost. She whispered while looking in the opposite direction. "Turn right at the next alley, second door on your right. You will find your mother." The old lady turned and walked in the opposite direction.

Surprised, confused, but buoyed with hope, Mara followed the instructions and knocked on the second door. It creaked open and Mara slid in. In the dimly lit room stood Maman, smiling with her arms outstretched. Mara crashed into them, clutching her tightly around her waist. Not a word was spoken, not a tear was shed. All that was needed was the closeness of the single person who mattered most in their lives.

Miriam gently prised her lose. "Mara, we have little time. Grandmère and I are in grave danger. If we are found, it is certainly the fire for us. But I do not want you to worry. We will find a way. You, though, are safe at present and according to Simon, the doctor appears to be a good man."

"Yes, Maman, I am safe for the moment, but…"

Miriam cut her off with a raised hand. "I have had little time to talk to you about 'us', but you are now sixteen and need to be aware. As you know, we are healers and do this by what we can find naturally about us. You are already aware of the things we grow and how we use them to cure the sick. But I have not taken the time to instruct you about men. We need them for our pleasure as much as any woman. So, we take, for short periods, the ones we like, to father our children or to provide us with some betterment."

"Why? Why do you tell me this now?"

"That doctor is a good man. An intelligent man and he provides you protection. I have made enquiries and I hear only excellent reports. He drinks far too much, but that a good woman could remedy. I think you could be that woman."

"What are you saying, Mama? What do you mean?"

"Your time has come, Mara. At this moment in your life, you need a man you can trust, one who will always shield you from danger. He is the one. Take him and you will be safe."

"But Mama!"

There was a quick rat a tat at the door.

"That is the signal. Go now, no more time. I wish I had more time to explain all this to you." They again held each other close. Miriam prised her loose again, guided her through the front door and closed the door behind her.

Mara stood, drained, in the darkened alley with the sack of bandages. Then lifted her head, turned and walked back home.

The light was fading as she entered the square. She was surprised to see a group of men busy removing wood from a cart, while others were constructing what appeared to be a small platform. The square was usually quiet in the evening.

She dropped the bag of bandages in the surgery and climbed the stairs. Claudette was in the parlour finishing a table setting near the front window.

"Good evening, Claudette. Will we have dinner here tonight?"

"Yes Mara. The good doctor likes to sit up here when he is home for dinner. As you know, that is not very often."

"Good evening, Mara. I see you have returned."

Mara spun round to see Pierre, no longer in his bloodied work clothes but dressed in a fine suit.

"Oh my, I had no idea this was to be so formal. I will quickly put on something more appropriate."

"That is unnecessary. You look perfect as you are. I also doubt my mother's wardrobe would hold much that would suit you. Please sit."

Claudette departed quietly, and they sat facing each other, looking out through the window across to the houses on the opposite side of the square.

"Some wine Mara?" as he held up a bottle.

Mara hesitated. "I have never taken wine before. Mother says it makes one's head spin and you lose all self-control."

"That is true in some respects, but only if you take too much. I have been guilty of that sin myself. But I promise, not tonight. Here, try half a glass and sip it slowly." He poured the rich redness into both glasses.

Claudette had already cut the pheasant and laid it out on a silver platter together with potatoes, carrots and beans. They both sat quietly, helping themselves to Claudette's fare. Mara trembled. She had known only the rough, wooden table in the kitchen at Maison Diana. There was the occasional pheasant, but never prepared like this or served on a silver platter. Pierre raised his glass and signalled Mara to do the same. He smiled when he saw the light dance in her eyes as she held up the glass. The wine felt smooth in her mouth and the subtle taste transported her to la Loire farms she knew so well.

Pierre broke her reverie. "Mara, there is something I must tell you. While you were at the apothecary, I heard they will burn three witches in the square below this evening. It is the first time they have used this square. I was not aware when I suggested dinner. I am certain it will be very distressing. If you wish, you can go to your room when it starts."

Mara froze, the magic of the evening quickly evaporating. "Do you know who they are?"

"I am truly sorry that this had to happen. You have worked so hard in the laboratory. I just wanted to say thank you. But yes, I have been informed that one is Madame Banzin, the high priestess. The other is Madame Macon, whose crime has been changed to the use of body parts in her brews. It seems that Duval's rejection of the curse as the cause of Monsieur Duplessis death has been upheld. The third is Madame Duplessis, who has been found guilty of poisoning her husband. This confession being extracted in the Tower. Her accomplice, a neighbour, Monsieur Bassett, has disappeared without a trace."

Mara, stunned into a thoughtful silence, gulped a mouthful of wine and could only mumble, "Francine! No, not your mother!"

Pierre held her eyes across the top of his glass. "Mara, you seem to have such strength for one so young. You can stand here and watch when someone you know will go to the fire in the square below."

"Pierre, my heart aches and my stomach turns, but I cannot change anything. I can only take one day at a time and hope my protector is not a charlatan."

"Mara, I can assure….," Pierre hesitated as the noise in the square below grew suddenly louder.

Mara stood up holding her glass and moved closer to the window where she could see the entire square. Three pyres of wood interlaced with bales of straw had been built on the far side of the square. In front of each pyre stood a low wooden cross, in front of which was a small platform. Standing to one side of the gathering crowd stood Commandant Duval; immobile, expressionless and intent on the unfolding tragedy.

Mara took a deep breath, when amongst the turbulent pack, she saw Francine and Jacques huddled together. Mara shivered, swallowed more wine, and fixed on the proceedings below. She felt Pierre stand up beside her.

"Are you sure you want to see this abhorrent spectacle?"

Mara nodded; her eyes focused on the unfolding tragedy.

The crowd roared as a cart rumbled into the square, carrying three bound, white gowned women. The High Priestess stood upright and proud but gaunt and bruised with one arm hanging flail by her side. Madame Macon stood bent, eyes downcast, her bedraggled hair covering her face. Madame Duplessis was hardly recognisable; an emaciated, broken shadow of her former self. Mara took another mouthful to still the dread from creeping in.

To the cheering of the crowd, the doomed prisoners were led down from the cart and one by one tied to their respective crosses. Bound at their feet and each arm hung and tied over the crosspiece, the small platforms were moved away. A loud trumpet hushed the crowd and a court official, resplendent in a bright red coat with gold buttons, stood with his back to the witches. Behind him, a few labourers packed more wood and straw around the base of the crosses.

"Ladies and gentlemen. Tonight, we have three convicted and unrepentant witches. They have had a fair trial and there is no doubt they are servants of Satan who have practised malefice in our beautiful valley. I hereby condemn Madame Pascale Banzin, Madame Maxine Macon and Madame Candence Duplessis to be burnt at the stake for their sins against God and his church."

Three hooded flame bearers ran in from the edge of the square to take up their positions in front of each pyre. The crowd roared as the official gave the signal and the flames were thrust into the base of each pyre. The smoke rose through the straw and into the nostrils of the doomed. Their fits of coughing distracted them momentarily. But as the flames exploded through the smoke and engulfed their feet, the shrill cries of the damned rose above the cheering, boisterous crowd.

Mara shuddered, mouth agape, eyes wide with fright and horror. Francine and Jacques clutched each other and moved to stand directly in front of their mother. Behind them stood a silent, tall, blond man who wiped a tear away with his handkerchief. Maxine held her children's wide, frantic eyes until the flames enveloped her and the acrid smell of burning flesh filled the square. Mara felt their pain, their suffering and the unfairness and injustice welled up inside her. Her horror became anger, her pulse raced, heartbeat pounded, fists balled and a gnawing pain chewed at her stomach.

Pierre placed his arm lightly on her shoulder. "Cry as much as you like. They are your friends and no-one should suffer from such a barbaric practice."

They stood silently at the window until the burnt crosses with their charred remains crumbled into the dwindling flames. The realization that this could be her future drove the fear through her. Her lips and chin trembled and body shook; her face an ashen mask. The need for protection immense; solace was needed. She involuntarily moved closer to Pierre who responded and drew her in. Long minutes passed, and the pain dissipated somewhat and her pounding heart slowed. Mara, broken and lost, looked away from the carnage below and up at Pierre. He bent down and first kissed away the tears on her cheeks and then her mouth. Mara responded, tentatively at first, brushing her lips against his. Pierre pulled her closer and her mouth searched, explored, and she surrendered herself to this new sensation. She placed her arms around his waist and drew her body in further. The closeness of the man and the warmth that welled up inside her could no longer be denied. She pressed herself hard against him and, abandoning all self-control, eagerly, passionately lost herself in Pierre's embrace. Pierre drew back and looked down at Mara.

"Are you certain?"

With her mother's words resounding in her ears, and the inferno seared into her memory, Mara nodded. Pierre took her hand, kissed it, and guided her to his room.

19

Memory Shield

20 June 1670

The nose-less man coughed, spluttered and staggered out of the suf-fumigation box. He wrapped a cloth around himself and joined Monsieur Durand at the counter. Monsieur Baptiste stood; arms raised with palms forward. "I am truly sorry, gentlemen, but I cannot be held responsible if that memory liquid has not eased your suffering."

"But you recommended Monsieur La…..." Monsieur Boucher's voice trailed off as the door-bell tinkled.

"Monsieur Labonne! It is beyond comprehension that you have the audacity to show your face in this shop. These two men tell me they have taken your Memory Shield for the last three weeks with absolutely no sign of improvement. As a matter of fact, they have deteriorated; assuredly because they have not taken the medicine, I usually supply them. You may have provided the first bottle free, but their families starve because of the exorbitant cost of subsequent bottles of your useless concoction."

Monsieur Labonne approached the counter, smiling and not the slightest perturbed by the apothecary's verbal insults or the glare from the syphilitics. "Yes, it is disappointing and I can confirm that this batch has also not been successful for the few patients I have treated myself. However, my work is experimental, and as a pioneer in this field I have carefully thought through my method and now understand the error in my research."

Monsieur Baptiste smiled at the two pox ridden patients. "This should be interesting."

"You may mock me sir, but it is quite clear to me and any educated man that the Memory Shield is too weak. I have diluted it so much that the memory has entirely disappeared. The new batch I am making will have a much stronger memory. As these two gentlemen have already paid for an unsuccessful batch, I would be happy to provide the first week for free."

"Memory Shield! What absolute rubbish. If you have no further business here, please leave."

"I am most troubled you feel this way. You leave these poor gentlemen without my miraculous new cure, for what is until now an incurable disease."

"Do not insult me. Please go!"

"I would like a few bandages, if that is possible?"

Monsieur Baptiste reached below the counter, placed a few rolls of bandaging on the counter, and wrote the items in his ledger.

Monsieur Labonne picked up the rolls, nodded to Monsieur Baptiste and the two syphilitics, and left the shop.

***

In the darkness of a moonless night, Michael and his team again sweated in the graveyard. They had only just begun the dig when a sharp whistle from their scout alerted them to the approaching gendarmerie. Within minutes, they had vanished into the blackness, each in different directions. As arranged, they regrouped an hour later at the river.

"The surgeon is expecting at least one body in the morning. If we cannot deliver, he may take his business elsewhere. I have heard we have some competition; a group from out-of-town bringing in bodies from a potter's field."

"Yes, and I have a screaming wife and a hungry child waiting at home."

"Alright boys, difficult times call for extreme measures. You know what I mean?"

All eyes looked at the ground, but all heads nodded in agreement.

"Good. Let us proceed; the River Tavern will close soon."

Monsieur Durand and Boucher squeezed out of the River Tavern, chatting and laughing as they stumbled home. "Monsieur Baptiste certainly gave that idiot Labonne a mouthful this morning."

"Yes, I doubt very much he will be back for a while. If ever. That bastard deserves a lot worse than a mouthful. His concoction cost a fortune, and we still endure this torment."

They stopped at the corner. "Till our next mercury steam, then." They shook hands and parted in different directions.

Monsieur Boucher continued to lurch and stagger towards his house. Intermittent lamp posts provided some havens of light on the rutted road. But even in the darkness, each stone, each hole, each cart rut was imprinted in his fermented brain. In the blackness between two lampposts, two men fell upon him. They easily brought him to the ground and held his mouth to stifle the scream. After bludgeoning his head a few times, they stuffed a cloth deep into his mouth and covered his leather nose. He struggled initially, but within a few minutes, his legs ceased shaking and breathing ceased.

Michael drew up alongside in the wagon. "Good work, boys. Do not feel bad, consider it a community service. They can no longer spread their clap to those poor river whores who will pass it on to every client at the Tavern. Come on, do not look so glum. Throw him in the back and let us get away."

The cart rattled along the cobblestones towards the River Tavern, where a boisterous crowd poured out onto the street. A large man emerged from the crush and signalled the cart to stop.

"We don't take passengers. Please stand aside," Michael barked as he drove past.

"It is not passage I seek, sir. I believe we may do some business."

"We have no need of your business."

The hulk walked next to the wagon. He pressed the edge of his hand against a full red beard, shielding his mouth, and whispered. "I have a body to sell."

Michael, taken aback, pulled up the reins. "Where?"

"Follow me."

The wagon followed the brute cautiously into the darkness. He stopped next to a tethered horse and closed carriage and opened the door. A canvas sheet lay on the cab floor. Michael jumped down as the stranger removed the canvas. On the floor lay the body of a young bearded man.

"He was involved in a fight and ended up with a blade in his heart. He is from out of town. Not known in these parts. I was about to dump him in la Loire but heard he might be worth something."

"How much?"

"Three livres."

Michael nodded, signalled his men who threw the body in the tray.

Michael handed the brute his bounty. "Good night, sir. Any word of this around town and yours shall be the next body we come looking for."

The stranger smiled, nodded and turned back into the darkness towards the tavern.

They drove in brooding silence via le Boulevard du Printemps towards the university. Michael pulled the horse up at number 28, scanned the street, gave the signal, and William and John hurriedly carried Monsieur Boucher inside.

Labonne smiled when he recognised the man on the table. "That will teach these uneducated scoundrels to laugh at me." He quickly went to work with his quill and soon had a cupful of fresh, warm pus. "Thank you, Michael. A job well done. Here is your fee."

Michael examined the two livres in his open palm and shook his head. "This is not enough! We had an agreement. Double for a fresh body. This one is not dead twenty minutes!"

"Ooh! But are there any guarantees you or I will not be exposed?"

"Do not concern yourself. The surgeon will cut him up within the next two days. No one will even know he is missing until he is just an unrecognisable specimen of muscle, bone, and guts. And besides, if you still think our fee is too high, you should seriously consider the likelihood of ending up like him."

"Ooh! Well here then." Charles handed over another two livres.

The body was again covered with a sheet, and after surveying the street, they carried him outside and dumped him back into the wagon. The wagon was silent as they made their way towards the university.

"A good night's work, boys. The professor should be pleased with these two.

*****

Monsieur Labonne didn't waste any time. Back in his laboratory, he laughed as he held up his treasured jar of purulence. He then weakened the pus as before, but this time only diluted it twice. He held up the slightly cloudy mixture to the light. "That will definitely have some memory in it." He filled ten small brown bottles with the hazy liquid.

He rose early the following morning and fixed a ready-made sign to the outside of his house. *Guaranteed cure for venereal disease. Prepared by Doctor Charles Labonne.* "If Monsieur Baptiste will not sell my discoveries, France will have to learn about them directly through me."

He had just finished breakfast when there was a knock on the door. A middle-aged man dressed in a fine suit stood in the portico. "I saw your sign," he said, pointing up. "I live near to here and have tried everything, and nothing rids me of this cursed affliction."

"Please come in, sir. If you are agreeable, I would first like to examine you before I sell my medicine. I must be sure you have syphilis before we start."

"I understand, and would expect nothing less from a trained physician."

"Good come. My laboratory is down these stairs."

The stranger removed his jacket and waistcoat and climbed onto the couch. Charles examined him, carefully prodding his groin and armpits repeatedly and examining the inside of his mouth. "Yes, you certainly have syphilis, and you certainly have some signs of mercury treatment. Is that correct?"

"Yes, that is correct. I have had this illness for over five years. Caught it from a slut in Marseille."

"Well, monsieur, it is certainly your lucky day. Take this bottle home and place three drops in your mouth three times a day. Come back and see me in a week."

The stranger stared at the little brown bottle. "I hope you are correct, Doctor Labonne. I need a miracle, otherwise I shall not see out the year."

"Good day to you, sir."

20

A Night at the Theatre

21 June 1670

Commandant Duval sat feet up on his desk, hands behind his head, contemplating the day's events. He had been called to the river at dawn with a report of a severed head found at the high-water mark. The eyes were gone, and the rest was so destroyed that recognition of a missing person was impossible. On his return, a visit from Colonel Montpellier, who again remarked about his uniform, did not improve his mood. Later, the bishop made a surprise visit, ensuring him that Monsieur Villiers' death was clearly a result of a curse that Madame Macon had placed. A neighbour, who saw Madame Macon at the incineration, recognised her as the wretch she saw perform a curse at the house of Monsieur Villers three weeks previously. A rotting frog was this morning found in a pot by the front door. There was no need to look further afield.

Duval was about to depart for dinner and thereafter a viewing of a Professor Dubois dissection, when Lieutenant Beaufort appeared in the open doorway. "Commandant, a Madame Boucher is here to see you. She says her husband is missing."

"Madame Boucher's husband often goes missing. He is a worthless drunkard."

"That much is true, sir, but this time, she believes there is mischief afoot."

"Alright, alright, bring her in."

Commandant Duval tidied his desk. Within a few minutes, a rotund, red-faced woman in her fifties appeared at the door.

"Please be seated, Madame Boucher. It has been some months since I have had the pleasure of you or your husband's company. My assistant informs me he is missing again."

"Oh, yes Commandant. He does occasionally go astray, but this time it is different. I have searched everywhere. All the ale houses and even the brothels. I have even been down to the river where they take out bodies. Please Commandant, you must find him. He is wayward, but his butcher business keeps us alive. Without him, I fear I will be on the street.

"Nothing about your husband has come to my attention. He is well known in this city and I would expect most would recognise him. Is there anything at all he said to you on the last night you saw him? Is there anything unusual you can recall?"

"Commandant, last night he said he was off to the River Tavern. He goes there most nights and I am usually grateful for the peace. I am a light sleeper Commandant. Late last evening I heard men's voices near our house, followed by the sound of a cart."

"Is that unusual Madame Boucher?"

"Well, our street is a dead end and there are only a few houses. Most of our neighbours are in bed early. Usually, it is only my Phillipe who disturbs the silence when he makes his way home."

Commandant Duval, uncertain, rubbed his chin. "Thank you for bringing this to my attention, Madame Boucher. It is a little unusual and will need further investigation. We have his description and will begin a search."

"Oh, thank you Commandant. Please find him. He needs to be back in his shop. His customers will go elsewhere."

"We will not leave a single stone unturned. Good day Madame."

Duval had just stepped from the barracks onto the street when he heard his name called.

"Commandant, Commandant Duval."

He turned to see an elegantly dressed Madame Villiers; her blond hair no longer confined to a tight bun but falling freely over her shoulders.

"Good evening, Madame Villiers. This is a surprise. Last time we met, you said you seldom visit this fine city."

"That is true, Commandant, but I have to attend to unfinished business at my husband's residence and will stay the night."

"Yes, there must be much to tidy up."

"Yes, there is. You may not have been aware, but his finances were in a perilous state. I understand he spoke to church for a loan, but they refused. I intend to sell the town house so that I can keep the country estate."

"How can I assist you in that matter?"

"No, that is not the reason I have come to see you."

"So, this is not just a meeting of chance?"

"Commandant, you will remember my gardener, Gilbert. Well, he is missing!"

Duval's eyes widened under raised eyebrow ledges. "Missing! There appears to be a plague of missing men in this city."

"Two days ago, I provided him with a work list. Yesterday he was nowhere to be found, and this morning Nicolette advised me he had still not returned after he had walked into the forest with his axe."

"Perhaps he had an accident. Did you search the forest?"

"Of course, Commandant! All day yesterday. Not a trace."

"Did he have an argument with either you or Nicolette?'

"To the contrary, Commandant, we all have a good understanding and get on extremely well."

"There is not much I can say at this point, but I will send out Lieutenant Beaufort tomorrow to see if he can shed some light on this matter."

"That would be most appreciated. He is an excellent gardener and can turn his hand to most tasks. He would be very hard to replace."

"Good day Madame."

"Good day Commandant."

***

Professor Stefan Dubois stood tall, hands behind his back, ample stomach bulging, beside a table covered with a black linen sheet. He looked up into the steep banks of benches that circled the room and smiled. A line of attendees filed out of a central corridor at the top of the amphitheatre. They fanned out to either side around a circular walkway and then descended the stairs to their assigned seats. The first four levels with the best view were filling with well-dressed gentleman. Dubois smiled and nodded at each one in turn as they took their seats. These were his most valuable clients. The fee for those seats would keep the theatre open for some time to come. Amongst these men sat Commandant Duval, to whom Dubois nodded sceptically. Next to him sat Doctor Laurent, an enquiring and regular attendee, and behind them a row of medical students. The upper galleries were filling fast with members of the public. Expectant mumbling and clatter filled the room as the last seats were filled and doors closed.

Professor Dubois nodded to a group of musicians on a small podium to one side of the theatre. The crowed hushed as the opening bars of Petronio Franceschini's Adagio filled the room. The subdued tones of the violins silenced the crowd as the last rows of the galleries settled. When Dubois was satisfied that everyone was seated and silent, he again signalled to the musicians. Instantly the band launched into the buoyant Sonata in D. The two trumpets slowly built momentum and volume. As the professor placed his hand on one corner of the black sheet, the music ceased abruptly and, with a dramatic flourish, he flung back the blanket. The naked body of a lean man with skinless arms and legs and a head covered with a theatrical mask lay on the table.

"Esteemed gentlemen and members of the public, you are welcomed here today to witness the wonders of science. We have been in the dark for centuries about the functions of the human body. But now, in these modern times, with this technique of dissection, you will marvel at what we have achieved." He paused to let his words sink in

"As is customary, I will provide the background of this body, acknowledging and respecting that anonymity is maintained at all times. This 25-year-old man stole money from his employer, a tailor. When discovered and confronted, he stabbed and killed the tailor with this knife." He held up a blade with a wooden handle. "The employer's son, on hearing his father's last scream, ran downstairs and surveyed the scene. He picked up a large tailor's scissors from a bench." Dubois held up the scissors. "Then after a brief scuffle he plunged the scissors deep into this man's abdomen here," pointing to a wound just above the navel. "He followed the first thrust with an upward strike from below the ribs and into the heart here," pointing to the subcostal wound. "This murderous thief died within minutes." Dubois stopped, stood with hands behind his back, smiling into the galleries as the mumbling and speculation spread around the room.

"Professor?" came a voice from the third row on the right.

Dubois turned, surprised at such an early question from the floor. "Aah, Commandant Duval. I am so pleased a member of our diligent constabulary has again come to one of our viewings. Do you have a question?"

"Yes, thank you, Professor. I concern myself with all the suspicious deaths in St Raphael, but I have not heard of such a murder. A double murder, in fact. I am sure that in my position I would be familiar with such events."

"That is a very perceptive and correct observation. This crime was committed in another district. Our fine city, as you will be aware, has little crime and we do occasionally need to bring in bodies from outside, for our medical students."

"Oh? Thank you for clarifying that matter, Professor." Duval pursed his lips and educed a barely perceptible shake of his head.

Muttering again spread through the theatre and Dubois once more held up his right hand, and the auditorium responded with an obedient silence. "It is summer and this body will decay fast in the noonday heat of the next two days, so let us not delay. This evening we will study the muscles and open the abdomen and the chest. Tomorrow we will open the skull and, most importantly, study the blood vessels and nerves. As you can all see, this body has been skinned so that we can directly look at the muscles of the arms and legs. They are essential for all our daily movements. This muscle here is the biceps and is joined to the shoulder here by this bicep tendon." He carefully cut the tendon close to the insertion. "Now watch, as I pull this tendon, it pulls the arm upwards. This is exactly what happens when you wish to bring a spoon to your mouth. Signals from your brain run through nerves to these muscles, causing this to happen."

Through the next hour, Professor Dubois showed similar muscle movements of the fingers, thigh, foot and toes. When finished, he signalled to the orchestra who recommenced the subdued Adagio. As the violins stilled the crowd, he reached for one of the surgical knives laid out on the table. With the blade held high in his right hand, the trumpets again dominated and, with a loud blast and roll from the drum, he plunged the blade into the upper abdomen. The crowd gasped as his experienced hands made a clean excision down the middle, around the umbilicus and down to the pubic bone. All eyes focused on the necroscopy, not a whisper, only the subdued tones of the orchestra diffused through the chamber. Dubois plunged both bare hands into the newly opened cavity and, to gasps of astonishment, he pulled out some intestines and lay them on the body. "Gentlemen, these are the intestines and from one end to the other," he pointed with his hands, "they are twenty-five feet long." He paused for a moment, picked up his knife, re-entered the cavity and cut the bowel just below the stomach and just above the rectum. Methodically, he dissected out the whole intestine and extracted it completely. The trumpets sounded at his signal and with a swagger, he paraded around the table twice, slowly unravelling and laying the entrails around the body. "This continuous channel starts here at your mouth and our nourishments then travel to these intestines where food is absorbed. What your body does not require is passed out here at the anus." The auditorium was hushed, transfixed and not a person stirred as soul-searching deep tones of the violins permeated the chamber.

Dubois held up a section of bowel, which showed a large opening. "This is where the scissors passed into the abdomen. If this man had not died quickly, the waste products from this bowel would have leaked out into the abdomen and resulted in a long and agonising death."

The professor pulled the opening as far apart as possible. "Hopefully, some of you can see inside." He placed his hand on a large dark red organ in the top right-hand corner. "We call this the liver. We have not fully discovered the purpose of this organ but believe it may have something to do with detoxification. This tube here appears to drain the body's toxins from the liver into the bowel." He pulled the opening back further. "Here and here on either side are the kidneys. These organs are mentioned many times in the Bible and were thought to be the site of temperament, emotions, prudence, energy, and wisdom. We know better now. Look here. There are tubes that lead from each one of these kidneys to this upside-down flask structure called the bladder. This single tube from the bladder leads out to the penis. Our urine is made in these kidneys, then drains into the bladder where it is stored and then leaves the body when we take a piss."

A wave of laughter spread through the audience and brought with it a stream of questions from the upper galleries.

"How many pints of ale can that bladder hold, Professor?"

"Is it bad to hold it in, doc?"

Dubois beamed as he listened and nodded to his audience. He had relieved the tension and replaced it momentarily with some lighter entertainment. They were sure to go back and tell their friends and keep the crowds and money rolling in. He again raised his hands for silence. "I am looking for two members of the audience to give me a hand. Can I have some volunteers?"

Initially sceptical, an apprehensive silence fell. Hands fidgeted, and all eyes locked forward.

"If there are no volunteers, I will have to choose someone myself."

One tentative hand rose in the front row, then another from the top and thereafter one hand after the other till most of the audience had their hands in the air, screaming, "Me! Me! Me!"

With a downward wave of both hands, he silenced the room. "Monsieur Arquette and Monsieur Baize, I see that you have raised your hands. Please come forward. You have donated generously to our university over the years and hopefully, this little experience can, in some way, repay our gratitude." The two men rose from their front row seats and stood beside Dubois. "You look like two fine, healthy men. Are you ready for a bit of exercise? I suggest you remove you jackets and roll up your sleeves."

Both men nodded cautiously. Dubois took a knife and expertly cut the through the skin in the chest's midline and then pulled back the skin slightly on both sides. He reached for a small hand saw and handed it to Monsieur Arquette. "Now start here." He pointed to the bottom of the sternum. "And saw slowly through to here." He pointed to the manubrium. "Do you think you can do that or should I ask Monsieur Baize?"

Monsieur Arquette grabbed the saw and energetically began the sawing. Dubois signalled the orchestra, who began an up tempo beat in rhythm with the saw. "Keep the cuts shallow, as we do not want to damage any of the underlying structures." Monsieur Arquette made good and rapid progress through the soft cartilage and soon reached the manubrium. To the clash of the cymbals and cheering of the audience, he held the saw high above his head in his outstretched, blood-spattered hand.

"Well done, Monsieur Arquette. Now Monsieur Baize, it is your turn. Some of you may know Monsieur Baize has been a very successful butcher in our town for many years. I have therefore entrusted this task to him. Take this knife and cut down through these tissues on either side just below the last ribs and up here along each collar bone. Then you and Monsieur Arquette can pull the skin right down on both sides." Monsieur Baize went about his task methodically and expertly. With their task complete, both men stood proudly next to the body. With hands and clothes bloodied, but extremely satisfied, the galleries cheered them back to their seats.

"Thank you, thank you gentleman. Now we can see the chest wall. There are twelve ribs on each side. They protect what lays inside and these muscles between the ribs allows them to move and expand as we breathe." Dubois again scanned the audience, looking towards the top galleries where the labourers were perched. "Ah, the young man with dark hair and a big beard. Would you like to give me a hand?"

The young man looked down incredulously. "You mean me?" pointing to himself.

"Yes, young man, I mean you. I hope you are not afraid of a little blood?"

The young man pushed out his chest, looked from side to side, and stood up. "Me. Why should I be afraid of a dead body?"

"Good, come down and bring that friend you are sitting next to." A large young man who had been laughing into his hands looked up, wide eyed and shook his head. But the cheering and booing of the audience soon forced him out of his seat and the couple scampered down the stairs to the dissection table. Dubois stood and looked up at his audience. "These two men are going to open the chest with their bare hands."

While the professor spoke, a young man entered the chamber from a back door and, unnoticed by the audience, stood beside an unused harpsichord. Dubois acknowledged him with a nod of his head and held up his hands. "Gentlemen, I have the very great pleasure in introducing my son Paul. He has not followed in his father's footsteps but has pursued a life of music. Recently, he completed his studies at the Academy of Music in

Paris and will play for us tonight. He will play his own composition, les Chevaux, with the orchestra."

Paul sat on his stool and the harpsichord's brittle clipped tones of horse's hooves on stone began softly, with the violins providing a calming backdrop.

Dubois continued. "Now I want you each to take hold of an edge of the rib cage, here, and then pull slowly and steadily upwards and outwards. I will slowly dissect away behind you. Understand?" Both men nodded. "Then let us proceed."

Like two combatants, the two men standing on either side of the body pulled against each other. Vigorously at first, but realising the difficulty of the task slowed to a sustained steady strain. The harpsichord tone increased, the horse's hooves quickened, and the crowd cheered and urged the warriors on. Dubois worked beneath the ribs, cutting away at any unyielding tissue or cartilage. Pieces of muscle, fat and blood spattered the participants and those in the front row. Les Chevaux moved into a headlong gallop and the trumpets and violins filled the auditorium. The cracking of ribs breaking away from vertebrae brought louder cheers, a clash of cymbals and relieved smiles to faces of the flagging gladiators.

The professor held up his hand for silence, and the audience and the orchestra responded instantly. "The chest is now open and we will now see what lies inside. But first, a big thank you to these fine young men who have acquitted themselves extremely well. And please add a cheer for Paul and our orchestra." Dubois clapped his blood-spattered hands, and the galleries responded as the two combatants climbed up to their seats.

"Now gentlemen, within the chest lay some of our most import organs, providing functions that are essential for life. Here on both sides, these large red structures are our lungs." Now I will…"

"Excuse me, Professor." Commandant Duval interrupted. "But those lungs have quite obvious dark patches. Could you care to explain that discoloration?"

"You are very observant, Commandant. This discolouration we see often in people who have been smokers. As I mentioned, this man was only twenty-five, so he must have been a copious smoker from an early age."

Duval nodded, and the professor continued. He took a sharp knife and expertly cut one lung from the hilum to the periphery. "Air enters through our mouth, down through this wind pipe and down here it divides into each lung. It then divides into smaller and smaller branches, a bit like an upside-down tree." He held up the cut edge of the lung. "Finally, the branches end in thousands of tiny cavities called alveoli. These are the tiny chambers which allow us to breathe and, in so doing, continually replenish the lungs with fresh air. We now also know that blood coming from all over the body is purified in the lungs and carries clean air back to nourish the body again."

He scanned the audience. Not a sound. Not a question. "This is the heart. This is really just a pump that pumps blood to the lungs and around the whole body. The blood enters the heart here and is pumped out through these tubes here. He carefully stuck his finger through a small hole at the bottom of the heart. "This is where the scissors entered the heart. The weapon cut right through the heart muscle, so that pumping was inefficient. Most of the blood would then be pumped directly out of this hole and into the chest, and not out of these tubes and around the body. Death would have occurred quickly. Are there any questions?"

Commandant Duval again raised his hand. "From your examination, could you venture to surmise if the assailant was right or left-handed?"

"An interesting question, Commandant. Do you have a specific interest in this case?"

"Not specifically. As you have assured me, this man is not from my jurisdiction. But I am searching for a murderer who may also practice his craft further afield."

"I had not given it much thought. But the wound is to the left of the midline and the track is to the left. As the attack was front on, I would assume he was left-handed." Dubois made a movement with his left hand, moving up and across to his right.

"Thank you, Professor. I would agree with your conclusion."

"If there are no more questions, I would like to end the evening by inviting you all to come down and have a closer look at the body. Starting from the front row, please come and examine the dissection. The medical students can come down after everyone has left."

Over the next hour, the audience steadily made their way past the body. The violins provided a soothing background as the assembly chatted, pointed, and occasionally prodded the various organs.

When everyone had departed, Dubois called down the students who gathered with him around the body. "What you have just witnessed is not how the practice of medicine should be taught. It is just entertainment for our paying guests. Without this income, it would be very difficult to provide you with the very best medical education. Now it is your opportunity. I would like you all to carefully examine this body. Take your time. You can stay as long as you like. Tomorrow we will meet here again and I will answer all your questions. We will also open the skull and examine and dissect the brain and also carefully dissect and trace the blood vessels and the nerves. I will be in my room if you need me."

As he turned to go, Commandant Duval stood directly in his path. "Commandant, I thought everyone had left. You have shown great interest in this villain. Do you still have another question?"

"I am aware the hour is late, but over the last day or so, I have been made aware of several missing men. All have been residents from in and around St Raphael."

"As I have said before, he is not from these parts. His organs and vessels are those of a young man and perfectly fit the description of the man who murdered the tailor."

"That may be so, Professor, but I must be certain. I need to follow up on every clue. I would very much like to see his face?"

"Commandant, I can guarantee you will not find that very helpful. You see, we…"

"Humour me Professor, and show me. It is not a request."

"Very well then." Dubois walked to the head and removed the mask to reveal a skinned head of only bone and muscle. The teeth and eyes had been removed.

Duval, unmoved, searched for something on the remains of the face and briefly held the right earlobe between thumb and forefinger. "Do you do this to all your bodies?"

"Most of them Commandant. It would be a terrible experience if someone in the audience recognised a relative or someone they know."

"It appears he wore an earring?"

"I did not notice one when he arrived."

"I notice that part of his nose is missing?"

"That is correct, Commandant. That part of the nose is cartilage and often breaks off during the dissection."

Duval fixed the professor's eyes, looking for any hint of deception. "Thank you, Professor." He turned, climbed the stairs and departed the theatre.

***

Dubois sighed as he retired to his room. He was certain that the dean would be happy with the full house and his performance, but he could not feel satisfied. Emptiness, guilt and academic destitution enveloped him. He was physically and intellectually exhausted and hoped to quickly tidy his desk and retire. To his disappointment, there was a knock on the door. "Come in."

The door opened, and the dean entered, beaming with his arms raised. "That was a truly magnificent performance. The audience was enthralled, excited and absolutely satisfied. I am sure they will spread the word through all the alehouses and men's clubs in St Raphael and beyond. I am certain we will continue to get more and more requests to observe your excellent skills. Many of these patrons are extremely wealthy businessmen and landowners who will continue to pay good money for regular viewings. This money will go a long way to establishing our university as a centre of excellence in France."

"I understand the need to continue, sir, but the problem we face is securing bodies. At present, we can legally only use bodies from various sources. These include unclaimed paupers, prison inmates, convicted criminals, heretics and those poor souls from mental institutions."

"You must find more!"

"I do, sir. I also obtain bodies from a gentleman who I cannot name, but who gets paid handsomely for his efforts. I do not question the source of these bodies, but believe they may be illegally acquired. I am uncertain what else I can do without destroying the reputation of this fine establishment."

"That is a great pity. I had expected more of you. If you cannot deliver, then I may have to ask one of your colleagues to assist."

A long silence filled the room, and the dean turned to leave. "Sir, I have had some thought on this matter and have a suggestion." Dubois paused, and the dean turned to face him again.

"Well, what do you suggest?"

"You may know there has been a recent and aggressive approach to stamping out witchcraft in this region."

"Yes, that is true, but as they are burned, that would not be a very good source of bodies."

"No, that is correct. But what if there was some other way of making these deaths a spectacle and a deterrent without destroying the bodies? We could then source another five to seven bodies per week."

"That is easily said, but did you have something in mind?"

"Crucifixion!"

"Crucifixion?"

"You are a man of greater influence than I and you might mention it to the magistrate and the bishop. I feel certain they would agree. As you may be aware, these witches are currently placed on a cross and the fire burns them from below. Why not just remove the fire? It would be a longer, more intriguing spectacle."

"Mmm?" The dean rubbed his chin. "That seems to be a reasonable proposal. I do, occasionally, meet socially with the magistrate and will discuss it with him. In the meantime, continue to put pressure on the unnamed gentleman. Pay him more if you must. We can always raise the entrance fee to cover the increased expenditure." He turned and left the room.

21

A Hero's Funeral

22 June 1670

Commandant Duval hesitated momentarily and then knocked on the door of Colonel Montpellier.

"Yes, come in." Montpellier looked up from his journal. "Ah Duval, this is an unexpected surprise. Have you had any success with your deluded theories concerning the deaths of Duplessis or Villiers."

"We have a few clues Colonel but nothing definite yet."

"That certainly doesn't surprise me Duval. You are so pig-headed that you will not see the conclusive evidence that Duplessis was poisoned by his wife and neighbour and Villiers died from a curse placed by that wretch Macon. Both women have been given a fair trial, convicted and incinerated for their crimes."

"Colonel, I have this morning received news that my father has passed and I need to go to Tours to settle his affairs. I will leave Lieutenant Beaufort to continue our investigation."

Colonel Montpellier straightened and held Duval with wide eyes. "That is a great tragedy for one of la Maréchausée's greatest leaders. Please accept my sincere condolences. I have no objections to Beaufort taking charge. From my brief discussions with him he seems to readily accept well established facts. He will probably make good progress and have everything settled by the time you return."

Without another word Duval turned, left the room and made his way down two flights of stairs to the office of Lieutenant Beaufort.

Thomas raised his head as Duval knocked. "Good morning, Commandant, it is not often you come to my office. You must have urgent information."

"Yes Thomas, today I received news from Tours that my father has passed."

"Commandant, that is terrible news."

"Thomas, as you are aware he was in a coma and his death was inevitable. I must go to Tours to tidy up his affairs. Considering the distance, I will be away for about two weeks. I have spoken to Montpellier and he has agreed that you can take charge of our current investigations. We should now however review the current problems and the investigations you need to undertake in my absence."

Beaufort, still with mouth agape nodded.

"First there is Andre Bellamy. We are fairly certain his death was as a result of drowning by a red bearded gentleman. The red beard appears to have gone to ground but I suggest you spend some time in the taverns and ask a few questions. Do not try and apprehend him on your own; he will be desperate if he feels threatened. Take some soldiers with you if you find him."

"That is sound advice Commandant."

"The two pill box deaths are a tangled quandary. I believe they are linked and may in some way also be linked to Andre's death. They both died in similar circumstances and with similar symptoms. Doctor Laurent believes it was poisoning, possibly arsenic but we cannot prove it. They have both taken pills from their pill boxes but the remaining pills have not harmed the rats?"

"If it were the pills then who would be the killer?"

"On two occasions the pills were delivered by the apothecary's daughter, Isabella. She was aided by Mara on one occasion. I have questioned the apothecary and he does seem sincere. I have yet to observe the pill making process but I doubt it will enlighten us. If he were the culprit, he would certainly only demonstrate what he wished me to see. The brown bottles appear innocuous and we have evidence that in both instances they were supplied by the ladies of Maison Clare. Finally, there is the sudden disappearance of Gilbert, the Villiers' gardener; I feel certain he was the body on the dissection table of Professor Dubois. He was killed by a knife wound to his heart. My theory is that he was silenced because of his knowledge regarding strange meetings at the Villiers mansion. I have already described these to you."

"There is not a consistent theme here sir. I am not a believer in witchcraft but we have to accept that Madame Macon was seen by a neighbour to stop outside the townhouse of Monsieur Villiers in le Boulevard du Printemps and place a curse.

"This city is now in the grip of witch hysteria Thomas. We have been trained to methodically collect all available information and construct the possibilities to find logical answers. We cannot allow ourselves to get caught up and influenced by such nonsense. Put it out of your mind and focus on reality. We could add to these theories, the ridiculous assertion, that the wives of Monsieur Duplessis and possibly Monsieur Villiers played a part in their demise. Madame Duplessis has already gone to the fire for the death of her husband and it is not beyond the realms of possibility that the blame for Monsieur Villiers demise also falls on his wife."

"Yes sir, there is much to consider."

"Yes Thomas, there is much to consider. While I am a way forget entirely about witches and search only for indisputable clues. I will be back in two weeks."

22

Alternative Medicine

23 June 1670

Francine sat patiently in the darkened room, awaiting her first customer. Bending forward, she clutched her stomach as another gnawing contraction seized her. She had not eaten for two days. The constant and systematic search for witches had made it impossible to sell the ancient cures found in her ancestor's recipes. With no income, food was required for herself and Jacques, no matter the method. The realisation that the spraying of curses was both useless and dangerous required a significant change in her professional direction. Diversifying was her only option, and she had quickly learned the fundamentals and recognised a ready market for palm reading. An abandoned building in a narrow street just off the main square provided an adequate consulting room. The lock had been easy to pick and a removable sign on the door served as her only advertising. It had not taken long for the word to spread.

A light knock and the door creaked open. A path of light fell across the room and onto Francine and the table at which she sat. Her hollowed eyes squinted into the brightness as she lit the rush candle with a flint and placed it in a pewter cup. "Please come in."

A middle-aged woman dressed in a long gown cautiously moved into the doorway, casting a shadow in the beam of light. "I presume you are Madame La Source, the reader of palms?"

"That is correct, Madame. Please take a seat." She waved towards a chair with a thin outstretched arm. Francine's head was covered by a red scarf from under which black curls fell onto a tattered red piece of cloth covering her shoulders. A small iron ring obtained from the blacksmith's scraps hung from one ear. "How can I be of service this morning?"

"I am terribly concerned about my health and fear for my future. I was hoping you could tell me if my fears are ill founded."

"Foretelling the future is a gift passed down from my ancestors. I am certain I can provide you with a reliable look at the years ahead. But before I proceed, you must first place four sols on the table. On this I must insist, as I have had patrons who have left without payment after I advised them of a dark future."

The customer took out two copper coins and placed them on the table. Francine snatched the coins and stashed them inside her ragged dress.

"I can already see that you are an honourable woman. Please, pass me both your hands?" Francine held the outstretched hands in hers, examining them intently in the candle's glow.

"What is it you see, Madame? Please speak. Is it bleak?"

Francine did not reply, her head bent, studying the hands.

"I knew there was something wrong!"

"Shhh!" Francine pursed her lips. "Your left hand tells us what God planned for you. It is clear that you were blessed with a healthy body and reasonable intelligence. Qualities with which you could well make your way in the world." Francine put down her left hand and examined the right hand. She lightly traced each crease and palpated the palm mounts at the base of each finger with her right index finger.

"What, what is wrong? Please!"

"The right hand tells me what you have made of what God gave you. And also, what the future holds. You have fire hands, which show that you are industrious, confident, and perhaps passionate. However, on certain days, you may lack tactfulness. I believe that this may have alienated your husband on occasions?" Francine looked up and fixed her wide, anxious eyes.

"Yes. At times, I lose my temper, which can cause a frightful argument."

Francine inspected the palm again. "You have a prominent mount of Jupiter here at the base of your index finger. This again shows confidence. The lines of your hand indicate mental strife. Your heart line reflects a contentious relationship, but your life line is long. You will live a healthy life and will have many grandchildren who will care for you in your old age."

Francine looked up into the beaming face of her client. "That is wonderful news. I do not know how I can possibly thank you?"

Francine looked down at her own outstretched palm.

"Oh yes, here, please take another coin."

Francine closed her hand over the coin. "Before you go, I will offer you one further piece of advice. If you wish to keep your husband, you should watch your tongue. If you want to be rid of him because he has a mistress, you have the confidence and intelligence to make that happen."

The visitor stood slowly. "Thank you, thank you Madame La Source. You have been forthright and have given me much to think about." She walked slowly towards the door, pulled it open and, standing in the light, she turned back. "I have a friend who would value your expertise. I will send her to you."

"Thank you, Madame."

Francine blew out the half-burnt candle and turned it upside down in the cup. She waited quietly in the gloom for another thirty minutes before there was another soft knock on the door. A younger woman, probably in her thirties, appeared in the doorway. "Are you Madame La Source, who solves certain personal problems?"

"Yes, that is me. What can I assist you with today? Please take a seat." She gestured with an outstretched hand and relit the candle.

"I have heard that you have had much success in dealing with wayward husbands."

"That is correct. But are you certain that he is wayward?"

"I am absolutely certain. I have heard rumours, which I try to ignore. But I cannot ignore his absence from our bed and complete lack of interest in me in that way."

Francine's gaze remained focused on her next meal and did not respond to the sniffling and tears that sprang forth. "Are you seeking a permanent solution, or perhaps just a minor deterrent?"

"Oh no. I want to keep him, he is a good provider. Just as you say, a minor deterrent."

"That will not be easy, but it can be done without him suspecting you at all. That will cost four sols, but you must pay me before I undertake this task."

"Oh, that is fine, but what guarantees do I have?"

"None, my lady, but the stupidity of an errant husband cannot be overstated. From my previous experience, he will be back clawing at your bedclothes before the week is finished."

The woman placed the two copper coins on the table and Francine grabbed them and stashed them inside her dress. "All I need to know is what ale house he frequents?"

"Oh yes. He is regular at the Laughing Waters Tavern. I am certain he chooses an out-of-town tavern so he can hide his dirty little secrets. He is currently in Marseille on business. Do you not wish to know anything about the young slut who has ensnared him in this depravity?"

"Her name? Nothing else will be necessary."

"I have heard she is of Spanish descent. Constanza is her name, I believe." She got up and on reaching the door, turned. "Thank you for all you have done." The light streamed in as she opened the door and then darkness as it closed behind her.

Francine sat back in the shadows and smiled. It had been a successful morning with enough money for Jacques and her to feed themselves for a few days. She removed her scarf and makeshift wig and gathered her belongings into a hemp satchel. After sliding the latch on the inside of the door, she drew open a curtain on one side of the room and pushed open a small window. She blew out the candle and squeezed through the tight opening into a narrow alley. Stepping toward the city gate, she was distracted by a rumpus behind her. A crowd had blocked the entry to the square. As she approached, the shouts grew louder. "Les Sapphists. Mort aux sapphists."

Francine pushed through the baying tumult, scrambled up the steps of the cathedral and onto the plinth of one column. In the middle of the square, Madame Augustin stood on the tray of a wagon, hands tied behind her back, and a rope around her neck attached to temporary gallows. Madame Blanchette stood next to the wheel, unflinching, her eyes locked on her Clotilde. The horse moved slowly forward. Clotilde's feet dragged momentarily along the wooden tray. Her life slipped away from under her, and then, a sudden drop and wild jerking of legs. As the noose squeezed the carotids and vital nerves and constricted her trachea, she coughed once. Her face flushed, eyes widened and her tongue extruded from her mouth. A violent convulsion consumed her entire body and then quickly eased into spasmodic jerking. Adeline, transfixed, did not take her eyes off her partner. Clotilde soon lapsed into a motionless coma, and the disinterested crowd quickly drifted away.

"Not a pretty sight, is it, Francine?"

Francine turned immediately to the voice, arising from near the cathedral door. The decrepit devil stood holding his candle, with one finger across pursed lips. She hardly recognised him from the man she saw at the trial. She turned and faced the square.

"Celeste spoke to me about you. She thought you were one. Try not to think of this. Just stay true to yourself, as this madness shall one day pass. Just one piece of advice; grow your hair. It is like a wart on your nose. Now go. You don't want to be the last one to leave."

As Francine descended the cathedral steps, she noted Commandant Duval, standing alone and shaking his head at Madame Augustin's lifeless body. He carried a suitcase in one hand.

Francine sauntered, head down alongside the river, occasionally kicking a loose stone. She turned when she heard the rumbling of another cart behind her. The last three carriages had driven by with a sneer and a passing curse. This driver was silent and looked in the opposite direction as he passed. She heard more rattling and held up her arm. She looked hopefully as a small open carriage with a single driver and horse approached. Francine was relieved when the carriage slowed but her anxiety rose as she recognised the driver from her mother's trial; Commandant Duval.

"Good morning, Mademoiselle Macon. I am on my way to Tours and would be pleased for some company."

Her apprehension grew at his knowledge of her name. She considered refusing the passage, but thought it would raise greater suspicion. "I am off to see a farmer who lives about four miles along this road. His name is Tom Allard and says everyone knows where he lives."

"I am afraid I do not know where this Tom resides, but if it is on this road, I am certain we will find him. Please, jump up here." Once on their way, Duval continued talking. "I seemed to have startled you with knowledge of your name. I recognised you from the night your mother was so horrendously burnt in the square. Please accept my heartfelt condolences. I have no belief in witchcraft and am entirely opposed to this witch madness."

Francine's tension dissipated somewhat. Both remained silent as the carriage rattled over the rutted road, making conversation difficult.

Duval broke the silence as they reached a smoother section. "There is one other question I have for you. I have heard that the recent death of Monsieur Villiers has now been attributed to a curse your mother placed: a frog in a plant pot outside his front door. Did your mother ever mention his name?"

Francine sat silently for a while before she answered. "My mother rambled often about people but never told me or my brother anything."

"Did she ever ramble about Villiers?"

Another hiatus. "Yes. She mentioned his name once, followed by, 'pervert, I will make sure you never indulge your vile acts again.'"

Duval's lips pursed, and then a temporary silence as they hit another rough section.

"I saw you with your brother on that fateful night; Jacques, I believe, is his name."

"Yes?" Francine's eyes wide with his knowledge of her brother's name.

"It must be very difficult finding food and lodgings without an income from your mother."

Francine swallowed, startled; suspicious, he was questioning her about her practices. "Well, we certainly do not make any of the miracle cures of my mother. But I make a few sols by reading palms. Fortunately, we still have lodgings in the wall's chasm."

Duval chuckled. "Well, I cannot see how even Colonel Montpellier would have any objection to palm reading."

Francine pointed ahead. "I was told that Tom's place had a lopsided gate; I believe that would be it."

Duval pulled the carriage over. "Mademoiselle Macon, before you go there is something I must say. Your circumstances are perilous, so please be careful. The witch hunters and their informants are everywhere amongst us."

Francine jumped off the carriage and looked up at Duval. "Thank you, Commandant, for stopping and for your advice."

She turned, but stopped as Duval spoke again. "If you or Jacques ever find yourself in difficult circumstances, please come and see me immediately."

Francine looked up, wide eyed and open-mouthed. She nodded, turned and climbed through Tom's gate.

It was past midday, and a relentless sun constrained her pace. The double wheel track led over a steep hill and wound through ploughed, barren fields with not a single shady tree to ease the journey. At last, after rounding a small hillock, a ramshackle dwelling with an equally dilapidated outbuilding appeared in the distance. She walked up to the front door and knocked.

Within minutes, the door flung open and a middle-aged woman with dark grey streaked hair stood in the entrance. Two curious children with snotty noses and ragged clothes clung to her apron on either side. "You must be the witch that Tom is waiting for. He is over there in the shed," pointing to the outbuilding.

"I am not a witch, Madame, but I do have the training and skills that allow me to remove some hexes they inflict on poor souls like yourselves."

"Nonsense!" She turned and slammed the door.

Tom had emerged from the barn and signalled Francine to come over to him.

"Pay her no mind. She is miserable about all our problems. The farm is going to seed and the children are hungry and sick."

"Hopefully, I can be of help. What is your problem?"

"The cows have not provided us with milk for about a month. Every crop I put in the ground starts, but just when it looks as if we will get a harvest, it all shrivels up and dies. I cannot understand why. I am certain a hex has been placed on my land."

"What makes you think that?"

"Well, an old witch, bent with wild hair, came here begging about a year ago. I told her to go away."

Francine swallowed for a moment at Tom's likely description of her mother, but held her head up and pushed her shoulders back. "Go away; that is all you said?"

"Well, I gave her a real telling off."

Francine rubbed her chin and surveyed the dry fields again. "Yes, it could be a hex, but if so, it has been here for some time, which is unusual. Some witches often hide things on properties to perpetuate the hex. I can have a look around and see what I can find."

"Good, you go ahead. I will just be busy with the kiln if you need me."

"You must pay me before I begin my work. My experience has taught me that once the hex is lifted, farmers seldom pay. My fee is six sols."

"Alright," and pulled the coins from his pocket and placed them in Francine's outstretched palm.

While Tom continued with his work in the shed, Francine strolled around the farmyard, head down, occasionally stooping to look under an old log or a discarded farm implement. She looked up from time to time, back to the barn and to the house, where she glimpsed Tom's wife at the window. About an hour passed and Tom left the barn and walked back towards the house. Francine, continuing her slow, searching pace, arrived back at the barn door and entered. She searched in boxes, behind straw bales and under an old wagon. She returned to the barn door, stopped and bent down at the entry. With her back to the house, she brushed away some loose dirt, then paused. Got up, reached for a spade just inside the door and gouged out some of the compacted soil. Back on her hands, she removed more dirt and pulled an object from the hole.

"Tom, Tom, come quickly. I have found something."

The kitchen door burst open, and Tom came running across the yard.

"This is prolonging the hex!" In her palm, she held a small effigy of a figure made from sticks and dressed in a scrap of red cloth with a rusty spike through its abdomen.

Tom reached out to take it. "No Tom, do not touch it. It will contaminate you. I know how to eliminate this hex and dispose of this evil thing. We need to burn it as soon as possible. It must be destroyed at the site it was laid."

Tom nodded, drew his hand away, and stepped back. "Come inside. The kiln still has a flame."

Francine threw the effigy into the kiln, closed her eyes and began a long incantation of which Tom only recognised a few words. "Destroy this evil thing that has been placed on Tom's threshold." Then raised her arms up in the air, continuing with the gibberish. Lowering her arms, she walked slowly around the hearth. "Banish this curse to whence it came, back to the darkness, back to the evil that sent it." She did two circuits, stopped and stared into the flames and looked across at Tom. "The curse is stubborn; it remains in the fire." She went around again, repeating the chant. "Banish this curse from whence it came, back to the darkness, back to the evil that sent it" On the fourth circuit the fire crackled and spat. "There!" She held up a finger. "It leaves this place, never to return." Her finger and eyes followed the curse as it ascended the chimney. Satisfied that it was on its way, Francine completed one more circuit and stopped, breathing deeply. "It is done. The curse has been lifted."

Tom stood wide-eyed, mouth agape. "Is it true? Oh, thank you, thank you. I do not know how I can ever repay you."

"This is what I am trained to do. But if you know of any other farmers with similar problems, I would be happy to help."

"Yes, yes, I shall do that."

Without a further word, Francine turned and began her walk back along the track. The return journey was not as successful. She hailed many carriages and wagons, but the only response was a snigger, an insult, or a spray of spittle. Three hours later, she reached the stone bridge and the Laughing Waters Tavern. The noise and smoke billowed out of the front door. She took a deep breath and pushed and squeezed through the crush, ignoring the lewd propositions and brushes against her breasts and buttocks. On reaching the bar, she bought a pint of mead and a crust of bread. She found an empty seat at a table occupied by only men, except for two young girls who occupied the laps of two older farmers. The conversation moved from person to person and subject to subject but invariably returned to the conquests or sexual exploits of those seated. Francine sat quietly, occasionally sipping her mead and savouring her bread, but listening intently to every word of the babble. Finally, she seized on a single sentence. "Yes, that little Spanish trollop, Constanza. She is just a teaser."

"Oh, that is not true. I know her well." Francine interjected.

Instantly, the table fell silent, and all eyes turned to the stranger.

"So, I assume if you know her so well, you are in the same profession." A spontaneous burst of laughter erupted from the seated farmers.

"Maybe, but I doubt very much any of you could afford me."

"Judging from the rags you wear, I suggest you lower your price. Maybe you would get some more custom."

"I'm not sure who your clients are. That boy's haircut suggests customers of a different nature."

Again, the laughter enveloped the table.

With all eyes now focused on her, Francine stood and slugged down the remains of her flagon. "Goodbye gentlemen. I have more important things to attend to than waste any more time listening to the gibberish of yokels. But if you want my advice, stay away from Constanza. She is usually under the care of the local doctor for a very contagious condition." She turned to leave.

"What do you mean? What condition?" The table spoke as one.

"I am not exactly certain, and it is not my business to start false rumours."

The table pondered silently as they watched Francine turn and push her way to the door.

***

Later that evening, Thomas Beaufort, in the clothes of an ordinary citizen, reached the Laughing Waters Tavern. He coughed as the pipe smoke wafting out of the front door reached him. Hesitating only for a moment, he pushed in through the clamour, purchased a tankard of ale from a passing maid, and mingled with the crowd. He casually asked a few revellers if they had seen an old friend with a red beard who he was trying to locate. After an hour, he returned to the city and visited two other taverns with a similar lack of success.

At about midnight, he entered the River Tavern through the usual crush standing outside in the road. On reaching the publican, he bought his fourth tankard for the evening. He mingled with a group of rowdy farmers and allowed the festivity of alcohol to overtake him as he watched the front door. He was about to go home as he drained the last of his fifth tankard when, over the shoulder of a customer, he saw a tall, redheaded, bearded man enter the tavern. The red beard eyes widened with recognition as he saw Beaufort and immediately turned and hastily pushed his way back outside. Beaufort jostled through the melee, and on reaching the road, the cold air cleared his thoughts. *He knows who I am?* He looked left, then right, and watched a tall shadow disappear up an alley. He followed, swaying slightly, and reached the alley entrance. With blunted senses, he proceeded tentatively into the darkness, feeling his way along the alley wall. A shape suddenly loomed to his left. He grabbed blindly. Then a sharp pain to the back of his head, and then blackness.

Dawn was seeping into the alley when Lieutenant Beaufort was stirred by the scuttling of small rats over his bare hands. Brushing them off, a silver button fell from his hand. He retrieved it and in the dim light discerned an engraving: a closed coach pulled by two horses with a uniformed driver, holding the reins in one hand and a book in the other. Gingerly, Beaufort struggled to his feet, felt for the pain behind his head and found a raised, tender lump. He stumbled out of the alley, but dizziness overcame him and he fell unconscious against the closed door of the River Tavern. He was still delirious one hour later when the publican found him and delivered him to Dr Laurent.

23

A Curious Button

4 July 1670

Commandant Duval had returned from Tours the previous evening; drained, both physically and emotionally. He forced the personal tragedy back into a subconscious recess, entered the barracks, and made his way directly to the office of Lieutenant Beaufort.

Beaufort sat fiddling with an object in his hands and lifted his bandaged head as Duval stood in the door. "Thomas, what on earth have you done to your head?"

Thomas felt the bandage and smiled proudly. "Yes, it has been an eventful ten days. I had a minor altercation with our mysterious red beard and came off second best."

Duval's eyes sprung open. "Well, tell me more."

Beaufort relayed the night of the taverns, the sighting of red beard and his tracking to the darkened alleyway. "Then blackness and I awoke in Dr Laurent's surgery."

"Thomas, I warned you of that fiend. He is a desperate criminal who will stop at nothing."

Thomas held up the object in his hand and smiled. "But I must have pulled this off his jacket as I fell."

"A button!" Duval examined it carefully. "A closed carriage pulled by two horses? Is this a book the driver carries in one hand?"

"Yes, I believe so. I was about to begin investigations when my head cleared. I thought we should start with the coach houses along the west wall."

"Yes, I agree. This may be a critical clue, and you are to be commended. But you will return home and rest and only return when your head settles. I will continue these investigations this very morning."

Most of St Raphael's stables and carriage houses were along the west wall on la Rue des Chevaux. Semi-circular arches above stable entrances punctuated the almost solid walls that bordered the street. Between the arches stood stone drinking troughs interspersed with sandstone mounting blocks and iron tethering rings.

A somewhat musty, somewhat sweet smell reached Duval as he stood under one of the largest arches bearing the name *Babineaux et Fils*. Entering a darkened cobblestoned horse walk with deep cart ruts, he smiled as he tested the clean air; confirming the reputation of the west side stables. The repetitive clang of metal on metal drew him into a tunnel which opened into a large central area. A rotund man, sweating profusely over a metal wheel rim and glowing coals, looked up, recognising Duval. "Good morning, sir. I don't believe I have ever had a visit from la Maréchausée before. I usually keep my nose clean. What crime am I guilty of?"

"No crime, my good man. I am Commandant Duval and have a minor problem which you may be able to help me with." Duval pulled out the button and handed it to Monsieur Babineaux. "Is there a stable or carriage house whose horsemen would wear a tunic with such a button?"

Monsieur Babineaux turned it over in his hand and smiled. "Commandant, can you see this book that this driver carries in his hand?" Duval nodded. "Well, this book is a bible. These are the buttons on the tunics of those employed by the cloister."

Duval's brows knitted, and he cleared his throat. "Are you certain?"

"Yes sir, the cloister. They do not have many permanent horsemen, but I have seen this from time to time over the years."

"Thank you Monsieur Babineaux, you have been of great help to la Maréchausée." Duval nodded, turned and walked back as the clash of hammer on steel again reverberated through the horse walk.

Duval pulled the cord at the cloister gate and heard the bell somewhere in the distance. A minute later, the small gate opened and Emile appeared.

"Good morning, sir. We were not expecting a visit from la Maréchausée this morning. I assume you wish to see the bishop."

"No, that will not be necessary. I just wish to speak to your blacksmith."

"Well, please come in. Emile pointed across the yard at the stables. You will find him in there."

Duval had almost reached the stables when he heard a voice from behind. "Commandant. Commandant." He turned to see the bishop scurrying to catch up. "Commandant, how can we be of help this morning?"

"Good morning, Bishop Bernard. Yes, perhaps you can help. This button was found in an alleyway and I believe it belongs to one of your drivers?"

Bishop Bernard turned the button over in his hand. "Yes, it is one of ours; on the shirts and jackets of our horsemen."

"Well, this button came from a large red bearded gentleman. I wish to question him. Could you provide me with his name and place of residence?"

Bishop Bernard shifted slightly, averting Duval's gaze while still turning the button in his hand. "Er. Yes. I recall such a man; he drove me occasionally but not recently. I am unaware of his name or his place of residence."

Duval, with a tilted head, eyed the bishop and then turned towards the stables. "Perhaps your blacksmith has more information." He walked across to the blacksmith, leaving the bishop standing in the yard. "Good day, sir. I am looking for one of your horsemen. A large red bearded man?"

The blacksmith hesitated, looked towards the bishop, and then back to Duval. "Yes, an excellent horseman. He goes by the name of Remy Gauthier."

"And his place of residence."

"He is a drifter. He only comes here occasionally; when he requires coin, I assume. As a matter of fact, I have not seen him for some weeks. I am unaware of his place of residence."

"Thank you, sir. If you remember anything, please come and find me at the barracks." Duval turned, nodded as he walked past the bishop and left the cloister through the small door in the gate.

24

The Fifth Commandment

5 July 1670

A crowd roared and chanted in the square below as Bishop Bernard and three senior clergy sat closemouthed with heads bowed, fearful of attracting the glare of Archbishop Chevalier. He stood towering over them, his resplendent gown and jewelled hands glowed in the single beam of light from the only window in the musty room. A wooden door, the only exit, was shut and bolted.

"Why is it that in this canton, witchcraft is only just emerging and growing? In my city of Paris and the rest of France we have contained it. Colonel Montpellier works tirelessly to bring witches to trial, but it seems convictions and burnings are scarce." His flushed red face scanned the four bowed heads and fixed on their leader. "Bishop Bernard! You have presided over this heinous rise in devil worship. What have you to say?"

Bishop Bernard lifted his head slightly, careful not to make eye contact. "My Lord, I agree with all you say. But we have worked night and day to rid this bourgeoning scourge from our land. In the last month, we convicted twenty witches by fair trial, and they have all lost their souls in the fire."

"Twenty! Is that all? You cannot let a seed like this grow and fester. You must pluck each and every seedling out by the roots and throw them into the fire. If you let even the smallest seedling survive, they will grow, multiply, and finally control this whole canton with their malefice."

"My Lord, we would have convicted more, but we are having some problems with the secular judge. He seems more concerned with finding the absolute truth rather than following the words and directions of our Lord and his Holy Bible. He has even sent some manifestly guilty witches out into the community under the watchful eye of some of our respected citizens."

"Back in the community! Not back to the torture chamber? And you allowed this to happen. Who is this judge? What is his name? If you are so incompetent that you cannot ensure that these witches get their deserved punishment, I will have to deal with it myself."

"My lord, I would be happy to……."

The archbishop's fist crashed onto the table. "Stop! I have heard enough. Your ineptitude galls me. I will see that you do not rise above your present position. You will languish here for the rest of your useless life. Can you all hear that crowd out there? They shout my name. These good citizens see the devil's work every day in this fair city and county. They desperately want a solution to the devilry and bewitchment that permeates and grows in their canton. Now, all of you, get out of my sight!"

The four clergymen jumped up, silent, heads bowed, and scurried across the room. The archbishop's glare burrowed into their backs as they struggled with the bolted door and then escaped down a passageway.

Archbishop Chevalier smiled, turned and parted a set of curtains, allowing the light to fill the room. He opened the double doors and, with arms outstretched, paraded through the doorway and onto a balcony. The crowd erupted at his appearance and he raised his hands higher above his head, bathing in the adulation of the masses below. Once fulfilled, he brought his hands down and gestured to the assemblage to be quiet. "Disciples of Christ, I welcome every single one of you here today. Our Lord will look down on you all gathered here in his name and will bless you and protect you for supporting his work. Let there be no doubt in your minds as to the purpose of my visit here. The scourge of Satan has fallen on your lands. It has been allowed to germinate and grow. Some progress has been made to eradicate the Prince of Darkness and his concubines, but they remain a festering ulcer." He again raised his head and arms upward.

"Dear Lord, give us the strength and the unfaltering conviction to cut out this sore."

The crowd held up their hands as one and chanted, "Dear Lord, please help us cut out this sore! Dear Lord, please help us cut out this sore! Dear Lord, please help us cut out this sore!"

Within the crowd stood Francine, her head covered with a shawl. In her hands, she held the effigy of the archbishop dressed in a brightly covered tunic. With a needle, she pierced the effigy's eyes, mouth and heart and cursed softly under her breath, "The devil will take you soon, you false prophet." Glancing momentarily to one side, she caught a young man's stare. She promptly put the effigy in her pocket, but while squeezing away through the baying crowd, her head shawl fell to her shoulders.

The chanting stopped abruptly as the archbishop again raised his hands. "I have made arrangements with the constabulary and the magistrate to double our efforts here. No stone will be left unturned, no devilry will be tolerated, and no servants of Satan will escape. Every single witch and devil in this canton will be found, tried and burned in the square for all to see. We cannot do this alone, and we require the help of everyone who claims to be a true disciple of our Lord. Be watchful, trust no-one, there are witches and devils amongst you. Report anything suspicious, no matter how insignificant it may appear. Your mothers, your wives and even your children may have been infected by them. Do not underestimate their cunning, their deceitfulness. Do not be tempted by the flesh of women. This is their chief weapon. With vigilance and persistence, we can exterminate this scourge from our land."

Archbishop Chevalier raised his arms for the last time, waved and turned to walk inside with the crowd wildly chanting. "Dear Lord, please help us cut out this sore. Dear Lord, please help us cut out this sore."

He closed the door behind him, dampening the uproar in the square below. He exhaled deeply and slouched as he made his way to his quarters; physically and mentally exhausted, he needed rest. A tall, dark-haired seminarian approached him as he turned the knob of his bedroom door. "Archbishop Chevalier, I am Dominic, one of the seminarians. We have prepared some food and wine in the courtyard for you. We know you may be weary, but we would truly appreciate the opportunity to speak with such an esteemed cleric from Paris."

The archbishop stood straight and proudly pushed his shoulders back. "I will always have time for fine young men like yourself. Men who forego the worldly pleasures to dedicate their lives to God and his church. Lead the way, Dominic."

A few glasses of wine in the company of spellbound young men made the time pass quickly. Two hours later, he opened his bedroom door and sat exhausted on the edge of a large canopied fourposter bed. On his bedside table stood his oak pill box with an ivory inlay of the crucifixion on the lid. He opened it, swallowed his daily pills, took off his robe and lay down; a quick nap was required. Thereafter a warm dinner and a hot bath before he retired for the night. He would require a good rest needed before he began the long journey back to Paris in the morning.

Archbishop Chevalier woke in the darkness, the room spinning wildly. Attempting to reach the door, he felt a stabbing pain in his abdomen, forcing him to buckle over and fall onto the floor. The gall rose in his throat and he vomited over his underclothes as he hopelessly felt excrement run down his leg. He desperately sucked in air and called out, but no words passed his lips. He collapsed, unconscious on the floor.

***

Duval had just completed his report on the identification of the red beard as Remi Gautier, when a black-robed, breathless young boy appeared in the doorway.

Duval recognised him immediately. "Emile, what brings you here so early?"

"Commandant, you must come to the cloister immediately. The visiting archbishop from Paris lies dead on his bedroom floor. The bishop is extremely eager to see you."

Duval rose immediately and followed Emile through the narrow streets till they reached the main square and the cloister. Emile pushed open the gate and Duval followed across the yard and into the cool of the atrium. Duval looked up at Moses. Those piercing, angry eyes looked disdainfully back at him and appeared to follow him as he passed. The garden of huddled groups of black-robed men seemed more animated, louder, and turned as one as he walked along the corridor. Duval glanced momentarily at the fleeing man with the bloodied sabre in Commandment V. *Could he have inspired a resident of this cloister?* He followed the seminarian through the winding corridors, but before they reached Bishop Bernard's door, he appeared and came hurrying towards him.

"Commandant, a tragedy, a terrible unforeseen tragedy. Our archbishop from Paris is without breath in his room and is undoubtedly now already with his maker. Come, please follow me."

They turned away from the bishop's door, through unfamiliar corridors and stairs. A steep climb up a spiral staircase opened onto a large light filled atrium with an open door at the far end. The smell of vomit and excrement filled Duval's nostrils, and he thrust a handkerchief to his nose and entered. In the centre of the room, the archbishop lay on his back, dressed only in his underclothes. Vomit and excrement smothered his body and dripped onto the ruined carpet. Pierre Laurent stood to one side; a clenched fist held under his chin as his eyes fixed the body.

"Good morning, Dr Laurent."

"Ah good morning, Commandant. Another death characterised by vomiting and diarrhoea. And, of course, another open pill box." Laurent nodded towards the bedside table.

"Has anything been moved?"

"No, everything is just as we found it," replied Bishop Bernard.

Duval studied the room, which was in perfect order with no evidence of a scuffle. He inspected the open pill box and noted that three compartments were empty. He closed the wooden box, noted the ivory inlay of the crucifixion, and placed it in his jacket pocket. "Was there a small brown bottle on the bedside table?"

"No Commandant. As I said, everything is exactly as we found it."

"Are you aware of anyone who would wish him ill?"

"No. As you know, he is a visitor here and should have no enemies. He was a dedicated and vigilant witch hunter and it is possible that a few of them may have placed a curse on him. Particularly after the speech he made in the square yesterday."

Commandant Duval knelt down and carefully lifted the undershirt. The body was cold and livedo was already apparent. "It appears that he died last evening. Did he not come down for supper?"

"No, we found it strange that he did not appear on his last night. But this servant here," he held his hand towards a young man standing silently to one side, "advised that he knocked on the archbishop's door with no response. Knowing that he had had a busy day and was probably sleeping, he knocked no further. The archbishop had had a tiring journey from Paris and has been extremely busy while here. Understandably, he must have been exhausted."

Duval turned to the young man. "Is there anything you can add to the events described by Bishop Bernard?"

"No sir. It is exactly as the bishop described. I knocked and when there was no reply, I returned downstairs to the kitchen."

Duval, together with Laurent, turned towards the door. Duval hesitated and turned back to the priest. "By the way, you know well that Monsieur Claude Villiers died about three weeks ago. You speculated it was as a result of a curse placed by the late Maxine Macon."

"Yes. A most unfortunate death at the hands of pure evil. But it is more than speculation, Commandant. As you know, the curse was witnessed and a decaying frog found at his front door."

"I heard from his wife that he was in some financial difficulties and sought help from the church."

"That is true. His state of affairs was so parlous that we could not risk lending him any money."

"Did you ever visit him at his country residence?"

"I cannot say that I have. Which is unfortunate, as I believe it is quite magnificent."

"I heard a rumour that he had meetings there with the clergy."

Bishop Bernard blinked, but held Duval's stare. "That may be true Commandant, but I can assure you they would not be of the St Raphael clergy."

Duval's moustache twitched as he studied the bishop for a few seconds, then turned and left the room.

Duval and Laurent walked silently through the corridors, and once outside, Duval spoke. "So, what is your medical opinion, Pierre?"

"Poisoning! The short time period and the severe vomiting and diarrhoea would suggest a highly active poison. The symptoms and time line are identical to the two previous deaths. This time, no brown bottle."

"Thank you for confirming my thoughts, Pierre. And again, another pillbox, but this I assume is his Paris pill box?"

"Yes, I agree. Three compartments are empty; two days for travel from Paris and one compartment this last evening."

Duval nodded in agreement and they turned and walked together towards the square.

25

Draw the Veil

7 July 1670

Celeste stared through the bars of her Tower window. The daily activity of unfettered citizens continued below, oblivious to her plight. The red roof tops, spires and squares stretched out, ending abruptly at the city wall. Beyond lay the freedom of the river, the fields and the distant blue mountains. A tangled, coarse mess of hair fell onto a dirty gown, hanging open at the front and revealing unclean nakedness. Dry, scabbed skin from the bites of a thousand unseen creatures itched constantly. A small low bed with a broken straw mattress occupied one wall and a simple chair and table stood next to the window. It was an improvement to her previous squalor, but the cost had been her soul. Her mood was as sorry as her cell. The bitter taste of frustration in the pit of her stomach had crushed her gratitude for avoiding the fire. A jangle of keys and a lifting latch stirred her from her dark contemplation. The door opened and Colonel Montpellier filled the doorway.

"I have little time. It has been an especially busy morning," he muttered as he undid his tunic.

Celeste remained at the window, fixed on the activity below. "I can only dream of a busy morning. But pray tell of your adventures."

"Well, the body of one of our missing soldiers was found by the river downstream from le Pont St Joan. His head shattered to a pulp. Undoubtedly, a brutal beating. There was also the body of an old man nearby; apparently killed by a falling tree branch." He pulled off his boots and undershirt and, approaching from behind, pushed his nakedness against her and placed his hands around her waist.

231

"Well, while you walked in the sunshine, I have remained caged in this hellhole." Celeste's gaze remained locked on the distant mountains.

His hands found their way under her gown and onto her breasts. Celeste stood rigid, staring at the horizon.

"You should go out for the day again. The fresh air will replenish your spirits. But a warning; if you fail to return by the afternoon, you will be tracked down, tortured and sent immediately to the fire."

With the negotiations complete and her day of freedom won, Celeste turned, threw off her grubby gown and pressed herself against him. Valentin effortlessly lifted her and laid her on the straw mattress. He wasted little time with kisses and caresses and was soon inside her. Celeste endured the encounter with feigned ecstasy and had learned what was required to ensure the ordeal was promptly concluded.

Once finished, the captain rose quickly and dressed. "I must return to the soldier as soon as possible. I believe Duval will be there and I would like to see him." He made for the door, but Celeste stood in his way and held out her hand. "Oh yes, I almost forgot. He placed his hand in a tunic pocket, drew out a key, and placed it in her hand.

"I was thinking of going to visit Mara and the doctor today. Could you arrange that?" Without waiting for a response, she added, "I cannot go dressed and smelling like this."

"Certainly. Your key will fit the devil's old room two doors down. You can freshen up and will find some clothes in the cupboard. I will inform the guard. My sources have advised that Mara is quite settled now. A Monsieur Lambert has a score to settle with Dr Laurent for losing his leg and his income. He provides us with regular reports about his and Mara's movements. No suspicious activity has thus far been observed. See what you can find. We must have something with which to prosecute her. I also need this information to show your usefulness. Questions are being asked about your continued incarceration and failure to present for trial. The bishop has advised he has set a trial date for you in one month. Some damning information concerning Mara or sinister material about their ex-periments might save you." He opened the door and turned around to face her, standing naked against the wall, smiling. "Yes, you have a right to smile. By now, you should have been burnt to a cinder. I am relying on you. I need something with which to bring her in. That little witch has been out there far too long."

Celeste almost skipped along the streets, her washed dark hair bounc-ing on an ill-fitting dress. She stopped occasionally to look at fashions in shop windows and greeted anyone who passed her by. Today was her first day of freedom in three weeks. She would savour every moment and experience whatever the day presented. On entering the doctor's square, she halted. Paralysed. On the opposite side, workers were busy sweeping up the debris from the previous night's fire and unloading wood from a wagon for the next sacrifice. Tentatively, she stepped closer. Amongst the carnage lay a pile of charred bones and three skulls. The breath caught in her throat when her mother's horned ring on a charred toe flashed in the sunlight. As she stooped down and removed it, a shadow fell over her and a large leather boot kicked the foot to one side.

"Sorry sweet-heart but this is my turf. Scratch somewhere else."

Celeste jumped up clutching the ring in her hand; wide brown eyes nervously contemplating a bearded brute towering over her.

"But you are a pretty young thing. Perhaps we can come to an arrangement."

Her trepidation faded when she realised he was not aware of the ring. She straightened, threw back her head and sneered. "Do you tru-ly believe that a woman of my standing would have anything to do with scum like you? Curs who grovel in the remnants of dead men's bones. God forbid! I have business with the doctor across the square." She turned and walked upright and briskly across the square with not a backward glance. Grandmère was lost to the water, and now Maman to the fire. That chapter in her life was now closed. She was entirely on her own.

Celeste reached the ornate door but didn't knock immediately. She stood shaking, and with trembling hands, wiped the tears from her eyes. Once composed, she reached for the brass knocker and gave two firm knocks against the door. Within a few moments, the door opened and Doctor Laurent appeared, his hair dishevelled and white sleeves rolled up to his elbows.

"Oh Celeste! What a surprise. It has been weeks since we saw you last. Mara has been fraught with worry; she will be so pleased you have come."

Celeste's face lit up with a wide smile and fluttered her eyelashes. "You are most kind, Dr Laurent, but I hoped you might also be pleased to see me."

Pierre fumbled with his hands, but managed a stilted reply. "Celeste, if you were not such a good friend of Mara, I might think you serious. Now come in, you will find her in the laboratory."

"Thank you, doctor." She smiled and brushed against him as he held the door open.

She softly opened the laboratory door and observed Mara standing at the far end of the room, humming quietly. One hand writing in her notebook and the other stroking her abdomen. "Hello Mara," she ventured in a low voice.

Mara spun toward the door, her mouth fell open and blue eyes smiled. "Oh, Celeste! At last! It has been three weeks. I, I was so fearful that something had befallen you."

"You mean the fire? As you can see, I remain alive and well," as she spread her arms, palms up, from her side.

"Oh Celeste, it must be horrendous in that Tower." Mara straightened her dress, took a few quick strides, and they crashed into each other's arms.

Wet eyed Celeste prised Mara loose. "I remain in wonderful spirits. My colonel keeps me in reasonable comfort and food. But yes, I am fed up with being locked up and unable to come and go as I please. But I should not complain, it keeps me from the fire." Celeste's smile faded; she could no longer maintain the façade hiding her inner pain. Looking at the ground, she fiddled with her hands and shuffled her feet. She opened her mouth to speak, but her mouth quivered and no sound passed. From wide, moist eyes, a single tear fell on her left cheek. Mara reached out for again and held her.

"Celeste, what? What troubles you so?"

Through increasing sobs, she blubbered; "the bishop is fed up with the delay. He has insisted on a trial date in one month. So, my days of relative comfort and the ability to breathe may soon end!"

"Oh, Celeste!" Still clasping her. "Maybe there is something Pierre can do?"

"I am a big girl now and on my own in this world. There is no need for you or your Pierre to worry. I have already conceived a plan."

"Please do not say all alone. I am here whenever you need me. Have you any news of your mother?"

Celeste instantly crumpled in Mara's arms and sank slowly to the floor.

"Celeste, what, what is wrong? Please tell me." She knelt down beside her.

Without speaking, Celeste held up her right hand with the large ring dangling from her fourth finger. Mara's eyes sprung open and her hand masked the scream that tried to escape. "But! But! Where did you get that? No! It cannot be? No! Not the fire?"

Celeste nodded with her head bowed. "Yes, they were sweeping up her bones when I arrived in the square. I thought you might know, as this injustice occurs just outside your door?"

"Oh, no! No! I am so sorry. I watched once. It was Francine's mother. It was horrible and I can no longer bear to look. Now both of you have lost your...."

They sat together on the floor, clutching each other until the sobbing slowed. Celeste managed a smile as they helped each other up. "I think you may have some news that will brighten up my day. Is there something you are not telling me?" She rubbed her hands over her own belly.

Mara's eyes widened, her mouth agape, her secret gone. "Oh, Celeste! How do you know? But yes. It is only three weeks since our first time, but I have not had my courses and am usually very regular. Celeste, please, please do not tell anyone. It is not only me, but Pierre would also be for the fire."

"Do not worry Mara, your secret is safe with me. But I agree, a doctor and a pregnant witch would break all the rules that they continually quote from that stupid book, The Malleus Mal… something."

"Yes, I am fearful. Every day I despair that someone will notice and now you have. Pierre seems to think everything will work out. He has a plan to send me to my mother near the end and leave the child with her."

"Well, I wish you luck with that plan. But please, stop stroking your stomach and start wearing something looser. Anyway, on an entirely different matter, this morning Valentin told me they had found a dead soldier downstream from le Pont St Joan. Head bashed in and face all out of shape. He also said that nearby he found the decomposed body of an old man where a tree had fallen on him?"

Mara's eyes widened, but displayed no other signs of understanding. "That is frightful news, but why should that interest me?"

"Well, if you recall, last time I was here, I peeped at your book and noticed that it mentioned a branch falling on an old man's leg. It struck me how unusual but similar these two stories were and wondered if Valentin and you saw the same thing?"

"Yes, there was a man, but that was north; upstream from St Raphael."

"Well then, they are probably not connected." Celeste raised her eyebrows and smiled at Mara.

The sudden opening of the doctor's door broke an uneasy hiatus. "Come quickly. I have another troublesome case. Come, both of you."

Inside the room, a man lay on the couch mumbling incoherently and holding his head in both hands. A piece of linen covered his face.

"Please stand on either side, ladies. The cloth covers his eyes. If I remove it, he screams and his hands quickly cover them. Look at both his groins. See those lumps? Those are signs of syphilis. It would seem he has had this illness for some time."

Without warning, the man suddenly stopped moaning, and his whole body, arms and legs stiffened. The rigidity remained for a few seconds, and then his mouth clenched in a spasm, followed by full body jerking and shaking.

"Quick, hold him down. I will prepare the opium."

Celeste and Mara grabbed his arms and legs and placed their full weight over him as the body writhed and shook underneath them. Pierre arrived with the opium-soaked cloth and clasped it against his nose. The man initially struggled against the cloth, but gradually his shaking slowed and then ceased. Pierre held the cloth for a few minutes longer and then removed it. His breath, steady at first, slowed and eventually ceased. Pierre, immobile, watched patiently.

"But Pierre, is there nothing that can be done?" Mara gasped.

"Mara, there is no point in any drastic measures. The syphilis has consumed this man's life for many miserable years. I would guess that it has finally attacked his brain. I doubt he will wake up as the same man that went to sleep. We will let him rest in peace. You can release him now and go about your business. I will inform the commandant."

As Celeste left the room, she turned back. "Thank you, doctor for letting me help you again."

Pierre nodded. "Thank you, Celeste."

"I love to help and only wish I could spend more time here with you and your little family to be."

"Oh! Oh, yes!" Pierre looked across to Mara, who shrugged her shoulders. "It is good news but we have not yet announced it, so please let it be a secret. And please, there is no need to be so formal. Please call me Pierre."

"We witches need to stick together. Your secret is safe with me."

"Thank you again, Celeste. If you girls will please excuse me. It has been a long day and I now have a serious matter to attend to."

Back in the laboratory, Celeste wasted no time. "Mara, it is so exciting to work like this with this very handsome doctor, or should I say lover?" Mara was about to speak, but Celeste continued. "Do not worry, my lips are sealed. But I have one further request. I am truly interested in those recipes that you have in that book. Is it possible to have a copy of those to read? I promise I will not show a soul."

Mara's eyes widened and searched Celeste's face. "I will talk to Pierre and if he agrees, then I am sure you can keep them to yourself until he presents them at the college. He hopes to travel to Paris next month for the presentation."

"Thank you, Mara, I will return as soon as I am able, but I have stayed too long and am expected back in my cell."

Mara showed Celeste to the door. As they waved goodbye, Mara noticed Monsieur Lambert standing in the square on one leg with a crutch under one arm. His wife, teenage son and child stood beside him. All were emaciated, dirty, and sparsely covered with rags. He nodded at Mara, who returned the gesture and quickly closed the door.

Mara returned through the waiting and into the surgery to find Pierre placing a white cloth over the dead man. "Pierre, there is something I need to speak with you concerning Celeste."

"If it concerns her flirtatious behaviour, please do not worry. I am flattered, but find it all rather immature."

"No, certainly not that. She asked if she could have a copy of our experiments."

Pierre was silent for a few moments. "Mara, I believe she requires information about what we are doing here to show her usefulness. Montpellier probably wants to know what manner of demonic concoctions we are brewing here so that he has reason to send you to the Tower."

"Yes. But there is nothing there that should lead them to think that."

"Correct. But just in case Celeste or Montpellier have the intention of stealing some discoveries we have made, I believe we should adjust the method in each case. Make her a new copy with recipes that will fail."

Mara smiled back at Pierre. "You have kept that devious streak well-hidden up to now. It makes me love you just that little bit more."

***

Celeste walked quickly through the winding streets toward the Tower. She had the information Montpellier required to further suspend her torture and trial. As the Tower loomed larger above the rooftops, she glanced around, saw no-one watching and suddenly changed direction. The laneways, initially confined and bordered on each side by narrow, four-storey dwellings, widened and through the spaces between the buildings the cathedral spire appeared. She hurried across the square and up the cathedral steps towards the entrance. A gaunt, barefooted devil in a rough, ragged woollen shirt and loose leggings to mid-calf stood to one side, holding his candle. His unkempt, thick hair fell to his shoulders and a thick, dark beard covered most of his face. Celeste stopped at the entrance and, with head fixed forward, whispered to her master. "My Lord, I find myself in a most difficult quandary. I have been told that I will go to trial within the month. Colonel Montpellier confirmed that if I can provide damming information on Mara, I will avoid that trial. I have that information, but she is my best friend and I cannot find it in myself to break that trust."

"Do nothing at present. I have learnt much as the watcher of this square and from the whisperings of the clergy. I believe I will soon have a plan to rid us of Montpellier. You are safe for the moment. Now go, another parishioner approaches." Celeste continued into the cathedral, crossed herself, mumbled a few words, then turned and left the cathedral. Ignoring her commander, she descended the stairs and continued toward the Tower.

26

A Twisted Sin

7 July 1670

Commandant Duval pushed through the undergrowth, while above, massive oaks shut out the midday sun and provided some relief. The rush of water showed he was close. He pushed another bush to one side, revealing the river and two soldiers sitting on a fallen log. After a few more paces, he noted the body on the rocks, just below the bank.

The soldiers jumped to attention as he approached. "Good morning, Commandant, we have not moved the body as instructed. Colonel Montpellier left about an hour ago. He asked us to apologise for his absence as he had urgent business to attend to."

Duval grunted and clambered down the bank onto the rocks. The tattered uniform remained in place on his torso, but an unbuckled belt hung loosely from breeches around his calves. He knelt next to the corpse. The misshapen head displayed a long deep gash along the left side through which broken bone was visible. The nose was bent to the left, and both eyes were gone. A small river crab scuttled out of an open mouth, which revealed several missing and broken teeth. Duval opened the tunic, allowing a few small stones to fall out. He singled the two soldiers to come down.

"Let us get this body up on the bank."

As they dragged the corpse, more rocks fell from the tunic and trousers. The left hand was clenched into a tight fist, while both arms were slashed with multiple scratch marks. Duval lifted the left hand, inspected it and then slowly, one finger at a time, prised it open. Laying in the palm was a small fragment of faded, yellow cloth. He carefully removed it, held it up to the light, and placed it in a leather pouch.

"What do you think, sir? We believe he was battered, busted up and then dumped in the river. The stones were probably there to make him sink, but that clearly did not work." The soldier beamed smugly, confident that he had solved the crime.

"Yes, but that is the straightforward part. Who did it? And what was the motive? These are the real questions."

The soldier smiled and pushed out his chest. "Probably a beggar or vagrant who was after his money."

Duval grunted again while methodically examining his tunic pockets. He pulled out a wallet, opened it and withdrew two copper coins. "Mmm, does not appear that your robbery theory fits. Did you ever find his horse?"

"Yes. Our horses carry a distinctive saddle. A local farmer recognised it and returned it to the stables about three weeks ago. We looked everywhere but could not find him."

Duval stood up and again searched the river. "Where did you first find the body?"

"Just down there, sir," pointing to where the river made a sweep to the right. "Just among those reeds. He probably got caught there, as the river makes a turn. We then dragged him out and onto those rocks." He fumbled with his tunic and looked to the ground. "We have been taught about disturbing crime scenes, but were afraid the river might take him away again."

Duval considered the flowing river and traced it upstream. "Wait here. Do not touch the body." Turning, he found a small path through the undergrowth. He followed the track for about 200 metres till it opened onto a cleared circular field alongside the river. He walked around the periphery and knelt to inspect some indistinct hoofprints in the soft ground. *Possibly two different prints from two different horses?* Further along, faint grooves from carriage tracks randomly criss-crossed the broken parts of ground and led out along a narrow trail through the woods. Next to the trail, a length of bandaging, swaying in a soft breeze, hung in the high grass. On closer inspection, it revealed no blood; just smudges of soil. He rolled it up in a ball and continued around the periphery, moving slowly inwards and focusing on the ground. Pausing, he bent down and picked up a fist sized rock; a dark stain, enhanced by the sunlight, became apparent on the sharp side. He placed it in his pocket. The grass was everywhere at an even length, with no evidence of a scuffle. "Not surprising if it happened some four weeks ago," he mumbled to himself. Duval stood contemplating at the river's edge, noting the small sandy beach with reeds on either side. *Nice place for a swim or a picnic on a hot day. Probably frequented often by the locals.*

He walked back along the river track to the soldiers. "You men seem to think you are excellent investigators. There are some hoof prints and carriage tracks on the edge of a clearing about 200 metres from here. I want you to examine them and see if they fit the soldier's horse and any of your carriages. The prints are not very clear, so have a very close look."

"Yes sir. Our horse's shoes all bear the royal crown. That should be easy."

Duval nodded and smiled. "This body will have to go back to the university and arrange for the professor to do an autopsy. Track down his family and give them the bad news. The body cannot be used for public dissection. And do not ask the professor for money!"

Commandant Duval turned to go but was stopped by the soldier. "Sir, there was also another body just a short distance up the trail. An old man, a branch, had fallen on him. He is badly decomposed and has a rotten smell. Would you like to see him before we bury him?"

"An old man? Tree fell on him, you say? Does anyone know him?"

"Yes, sir, he is known around these parts. He does odd jobs on farms and sleeps wherever he can lay his head."

"It does not sound related, but we should consider all the evidence. Take me to him."

One guard and Duval pushed along a path until a faint smell alerted them of the body. The corpse, now shrivelled and devoid of most flesh lay under the branch of a fallen tree. The skull was cracked, and the left femur broken.

"Yes, it certainly seems a tree fell on him, possibly while he was sleeping."

"We thought the same, sir. We have searched around the body and found nothing. There was no coin in his pockets. As we have already said, he is well-known and does odd jobs around this community."

"Get him out from under that tree, wrap him up and take him, together with the soldier, to Professor Dubois. Once you have removed him, search the area carefully for anything unusual."

***

Duval passed through the city gate and was turning right towards the barracks when his head suddenly swivelled to the left. A woman in a red dress with blond hair bobbing on her shoulders strode across the street. He recognised her instantly; his heart skipped a beat as "Giselle" escaped his lips. He prepared to get out of his carriage but hesitated, shook his head, and sat back in his seat. *No! No. It was I who was deemed unworthy. That chapter of my life is over.* He flicked the reins, and without a backward glance, soon entered the barracks.

Duval strode, head down through the corridors, oblivious of passing soldiers, and almost crashed headlong into Lieutenant Beaufort. "Oh, sorry Thomas, my mind must be occupied with the morning events by the river."

"Sir, Mademoiselle Macon and her brother are her to see you. They have been waiting in your room for almost one hour. She seems most anxious and says it is an urgent matter."

"Thank you, Thomas." Duval continued down the hall to his office. On entering, the sight of Francine and a ragged, dirty, wide-eyed young boy forced him to drag his thoughts away from Giselle and the events at the river. "Good morning to you, Mademoiselle Macon, and to you too, young man." Duval held out his hand. "I am Commandant Duval. And you must be Jacques?"

"Yes, this is my brother Jacques." The urchin, closemouthed, nodded and his trembling hand took Duval's. "You said I could come and see you at any time."

"That is correct, Mademoiselle. Please be seated. I attended your mother's unfortunate trial and am thus aware of your circumstances. Unfortunately, if it concerns that matter, there is very little I can do. I could speak to the church about some financial assistance, but in view of the conviction, I feel certain they will not be at all sympathetic."

"No Commandant. We are here on an entirely separate matter."

Duval raised his eyebrows. "Well then, please tell me of your problem."

"It concerns my brother." Francine held Jacques around the shoulders as he became tearful, and bent over with his head in his hands.

"Do not worry, my boy. This is the barracks of la Maréchausée. It is a safe place. You have come here on your own free will, so no harm will come to you. No judgement will be made of you and nothing will be made public unless you wish it to." The words appeared to reassure Jacques, and he wiped his wet, blue eyes and focused on Duval. "Please continue, Mademoiselle."

"When I arrived home, about a month ago, Jacques was not home. I noticed some dirty breeches on his bed. I picked them up to wash, and a coin fell out of his pocket. Naturally, I was surprised, so I confronted him when he returned home later that evening. He refused to tell me. But ever since he has been acting strangely, brooding, and occasionally I have found him crying. It was only last evening that he was so distressed that he blurted out the events that have caused his torment." Francine turned to her brother. "Jacques, will you tell the good commandant how you came about this money?" The urchin hesitated, the tears welled again and his face shifted to scarlet. "Jacques, I know you feel ashamed, but you must tell him what you have told me."

Jacques nodded. "Sir…, sir, I… I was walking along the street about a month ago when a carriage passed slowly by. I remember it was a few days after Maman was taken." Jacques hesitated, wiped his eyes with the back of his hand, and continued. "I could not see inside. The carriage stopped some twenty paces ahead. As I got closer, the driver jumped down and waited for me. 'You look as if you could do with a bit of extra money,' the driver said. I asked him what the work was. 'Helping in the kitchen,' he said. 'We are having a party tonight. Money is very good,' he said. The work seemed simple, and the payment was good. So, I agreed. We eat scraps and Francine goes out every day to get some money. I wanted to help too."

"So, what happened next?"

"The driver said he would pick me up in the carriage at 6 o'clock in the main square. He then climbed up and drove off."

"Was there anyone in the carriage?"

"I am uncertain. The curtains were partially open, but I saw them move. Perhaps it was just the movement of the carriage."

"Would you recognise the driver again?"

"Yes, I have seen him before. He was a tall, big man with a bushy red beard."

Duval's eyes widened. "Where did you see him before?"

"I saw him once standing near the Temple of Miracles opposite my friend Andre's house."

"And then?"

"I quickly went inside as he was looking my way."

"Alright. Let us return to the evening in question. So, what happened next?"

"Not much. I was picked up at six as arranged, but there were another two boys my age also there. We all got into the carriage. I did not know any of them, but would remember their faces. We were all very excited because the money was good. The carriage drove out of the city and arrived at a beautiful, big house in the country. We were shown to the kitchen and then spent the next couple of hours helping prepare food and cleaning pots and plates."

"Was anyone else in the kitchen?"

"Yes, there was a maid, Nicolette, who was telling us what to do. She left soon after and some other maids arrived. We finished at about 9 o'clock and were given our pay as promised. We were all very happy. They gave us something to drink and eat and told us to wait in the kitchen. Someone would soon come to take us back to St Raphael. These maids then also packed their bags and left by the kitchen door."

"Then what happened?"

"Well, as we waited, things became a blur. I remain confused and vague about exactly what happened. It was as if I was in some kind of trance. The others boys were blurred and seemed to giggle a lot."

"What parts of it can you remember?"

"Well, I…." he hesitated and looked at his sister and then back at Duval, who nodded. "Well, I remember I was in a room and there was a naked man. He was quite fat." He stopped, unable to speak, tears again beginning to roll down his cheeks.

Francine again put her arm around his shoulders and pulled him in close. "It is alright Jacques; the commandant will not judge you. Just tell him what you told me. Use the same words."

Jacques pulled away from Francine, but his head remained downcast. "It…It was so painful. I tried to scream. But I could not. He. He. He fucked me!" The release of the confession brought a painful wail and a flood of tears as Francine held him again.

Duval sat up stiffly in his chair. "Jacques, that is very good. You are a very brave young man. You have nothing to feel ashamed about. Your secret will not leave this room. That I promise. You have said enough and hopefully those words will bring this monster to justice." Duval waited as the sobbing slowed and came to a halt. "Jacques, I have only one more question for you. Would you recognise this man again?"

"I do not think so. It was such a haze. It was like being in a dream. One moment I was floating on clouds and the next an incredible pain and strange demons floating around me." Jacques stopped for a moment as his eyes widened. "Yes, I remember only one thing, an image that has recurred in my mind and will haunt me forever. I am not sure if it is part of the dream or something real."

"Tell me anyway. Let me be the judge."

"Well, there, there was a big black birthmark on his bum." Francine again grabbed him and held him as the sobs resumed.

"Jacques, you have been very brave and your information may help me solve some strange events that have occurred in this city. I will see that you and your sister get the care that you both require. Mademoiselle, please take this coin, get some good food and go to your dwelling. I know where it is. If you need anything, anything at all, please do not hesitate to come and see me; even at my home if the hour is late or if you feel endangered here at the barracks."

Once Francine and Jacques had left, Duval sat in his chair, lit his pipe and stared out of his window. He put his feet up on the desk and contemplated Jacques' account. *The maid was Nicolette, the same as Maison Villiers' maid. Could it be the same maid? This adds some truth to the gardener's story. In fact, I wonder if he has returned. I feel quite certain that it was his body at the dissection; the lungs of a young smoker and the earing hole in his right lobe. I will have to question that Nicolette again. And what of the red beard in Jacques' account? He rode in a carriage. He must be Remy Gauthier.*

27

Small Brown Bottles

8 July 1670

Commandant Duval arrived at the Villiers house and was met by Nicolette. "Good day, Commandant. What brings you back here today?"

"Good day, Nicolette. Yes, it is an issue of some urgency and I will get straight to the matter. About one month ago a young lad describes coming to a country house to help prepare for a party. He mentioned the maid's name was Nicolette."

"Yes, that is correct. I helped three young lads prepare and clean up in the kitchen. Then at 6 o'clock I left and saw another carriage arrive with two other girls."

"Did you notice the driver of the boy's carriage or the girl's carriage."

"I only saw the girl's driver. A large man with a red hair and a beard."

Duval nodded and continued. "Had you noticed similar events previously?"

"Yes, on at least two other occasions over the last year."

"And from your dwelling did you see or hear anything unusual during the most recent evening?"

"No, nothing. I had some scraps for dinner and went to bed."

"Anything else? Where was Gilbert? Was he with you?"

"Yes. As usual that bastard had his way with me before he let me go to sleep. After that I don't know what he saw or heard. I am glad he hasn't returned."

The door opened behind Nicolette and Madame Villiers entered, her long blond hair hanging freely over her shoulders. "Good day, Commandant. What brings you here on this beautiful summer's day."

"Good morning, Madame Villiers. I was just concluding some questions for Nicolette concerning one of your departed husband's parties. I believe he usually had these when you visited your mother."

"That is entirely correct. As I told you before, we lived very separate lives and I had no interest in his business. I am glad he is gone."

"And I assume you have still have no news of Gilbert?"

"That is entirely correct Commandant. But I have found an excellent replacement with whom I am very satisfied. In order to give Nicolette some privacy I have housed the new gardener in some accommodation here, just off the kitchen."

"Thank you, Madame, thank you Nicolette. I will return if I have further questions."

After passing through the city gate Duval negotiated his way through the busy streets to the house of Doctor Laurent.

Claudette answered the door. "Commandant! Good evening. It is not often we require the services of the constabulary. Do you....?"

"Doctor Laurent asked me to come as soon as possible," he cut in sharply.

Laurent appeared at the door of the waiting room. "Good evening, Commandant, please come in. Thank you, Claudette."

Once in the consulting room, Pierre closed the door behind them.

"I am most pleased to see you again Doctor Laurent. But please, the message I received seemed very urgent. How can I be of help?"

"Commandant..."

"Please! Call me Bertrand."

"Yes, and please call me Pierre. Well Bertrand, some three weeks ago a young lad of twelve came to me with a grossly infected anal tear. I feared for his life but fortunately with some new medicine, we were able to stem the infection and save the lad. These tears are often due to constipation, but he and his mother assured me he was not troubled by straining.

I indicated that this was strange. Well, I did not hear from them till this morning when the mother arrived here without the boy and provided me with some very disturbing news."

"Disturbing! How so and why call me? It sounds like a medical problem."

"Well Bertrand, the mother, a Mrs Lavigne, explained that her son Ruben had been acting very strange lately. Not his usual self; quiet, not eating with outbursts of anger and tears. His mother begged him to talk to her and finally early this morning he disclosed this horrific news." Pierre wiped his brow with a handkerchief.

"Well come on young man I do not have all night."

"Yes, yes. The boy said, to use his own words, that he had been fucked in the bottom by a man at a house in the country."

Astounded, Bertrand wide eyed, sat back in his chair. "That is most intriguing. Is there anything further?"

"Mrs Lavigne said that Ruben would not talk any further. But she asked if I could talk to him. I agreed to go there tomorrow. However, it seems like a legal matter and I thought it best if you accompany me in the morning?"

"Thank you very much Pierre. That piece of information confirms another similar tragedy. It may help me put a few pieces of a very perplexing puzzle together. I will see you in the morning." He stood up to go. "I am sorry that that I cannot talk longer but I have arranged to go to another dissection by Professor Dubois this evening."

"Well, Bertrand, that is most convenient. It seems we share the same interest in the human body. I am attending the same dissection: the body is that of a man who died in my rooms yesterday. Can I share your carriage?"

"Certainly. My carriage awaits outside."

***

"Please do not touch the exhibits and please keep moving along. The dissection will commence in ten minutes." A uniformed official stood pressed against the wall in the corridor, directing the squash of chattering patrons towards the theatre.

Bertrand and Pierre marvelled at the specimens lining both walls as they jostled their way forward. Pierre stretched out to feel the smooth hand bones of a full-length skeleton which stood guard on one side of the entry. Beyond the lifeless sentry, wall to ceiling shelves displayed skulls of grown men, children and tiny babies. Skulls with gross deformities, Siamese twins joined at the head and even an ape skull comparing the differences with man. Cabinets held preserved specimens embalmed in a clear liquid. There were livers, lungs and kidneys, all possessed with tumours. Dissection demonstrations of hands, feet, arms and legs were meticulously laid out behind the glass. Pierre stalled, and examined the gross malformations of a preterm baby. Bertrand stopped, fascinated by a section of a skull with a steel blade entering the eye and exiting the crown.

The attendees entered at the top of the amphitheatre and fanned out to either side and down the steps to their allocated seats. The small orchestra played softly as Professor Dubois looked up with a satisfied smile as the jabbering banks of seats quickly filled. He nodded to his invited guests as they took their seats. Commandant Duval, Dr Laurent and Monsieur Baptiste, had received a special invitation and were seated together in the front row. Five rows higher, he frowned but nodded in recognition to Charles Labonne who smiled back politely. Once all seats were taken, he signalled to the small orchestra and his son, who again immediately silenced the crowd with Les Cheveaux.

With their attention secured, Professor Dubois held up his hand and the band stopped. "Thank you all for gracing us with your presence this evening. This morning my students and I dissected and examined the muscles, abdomen and chest of this poor soul. Now we will publicly open the skull and perhaps solve a mystery concerning the cause of death. This man died suddenly of an unknown illness at the rooms of my esteemed colleague, Dr Pierre Laurent. Dr Laurent would you please come forward and tell the audience what happened to this man on that unforgettable and tragic evening."

Pierre squeezed past some patrons and stood next to the Professor. "Thank you, Professor. The evening of which you speak was at the end of a busy day. I was about to close the door when this poor gentleman was brought in by a friend. He was initially extremely confused, agitated, and shielded his eyes with his hands; like someone who finds the light too bright. However, after we got him onto the examination table, he suffered violent spasms and fits. With the help of my assistant, we managed to hold him on the table. We administered some opium and the spasms and fits seemed to settle. However, as his fitting declined so did his breathing and within a few more minutes he stopped breathing completely and perished. I then examined him and the only unusual findings were the lesions of late-stage syphilis in both groins. I was unable to examine his mouth as his spasms had closed it tight."

"So, Dr Laurent, would you be able venture a reason why this man expired so suddenly?"

"I must admit Professor, I am most perplexed. I can only postulate that he had some form of brain complication related to his syphilis."

"Thank you, Doctor. You may sit down. Monsieur Baptiste is our esteemed apothecary. Would you care to come forward and tell us about your dealings with this man?"

"Thank you for inviting me Professor. I have little to tell other than that I was treating this man for his syphilis with mercury for numerous years, but have not seen him for a least four months. I would venture to say that I was able to keep his late-stage illness at a steady state but over the last months without my treatment he probably deteriorated; possibly with involvement of his brain. Like my learned colleague Dr Laurent, I remain puzzled by his sudden death."

"Thank you, Monsieur Baptiste. You may sit down. I am hopeful that this dissection today may shed some light on this mystery and demonstrate the marvels of this technique. So, let us not speculate any further but rather search for the real truth in this body. Before we open the skull, we will examine the arteries and veins." He nodded to the orchestra and the trumpeters started softly but rapidly built to a bright, vibrating crescendo of anticipation. They stopped abruptly and the Professor gripped the sheet and with a flurry removed it to reveal a man with an open abdomen and chest and carefully skinned legs and arms. The violins took their cue, with a soothing background melody.

"We will the trace some of the large arteries from the heart on their journey through the abdomen, into the thighs and down into the legs." Over the next hour Professor Dubois methodically dissected away the muscles of one leg to expose the track of the arteries and the veins. "Gentleman please marvel at the wonders of dissection. This large artery which we call the aorta leaves the heart carrying blood through this tube through the abdomen and then divides here to go down each leg. We can now follow it down past the knee and down to the foot where it divides repeatedly into tiny little tributaries which feed the muscles and tissues with nutrients. Now here you can see these larger darker vessels, called veins. They arise here from the foot and through these tubes carry blood all the way back to the heart."

Professor Dubois stood back, scalpel in bloodied hand and looked up at his audience. "Are there any questions about these precious vessels here described? Vessels that provide each and every one of you with the gift of life."

Not an arm was raised or a question asked. Only the violins filled the silence. "Well then, let us return to the aorta where it leaves the heart." He held his hand on the bulging vessel. "This aorta is unusually large here, where it leaves the heart, and narrows again only one hand length beyond. This man's syphilis infection has invaded the vessel wall, weakening the wall structure. The weakened portion has then slowly expanded and would eventually burst. This would have caused his death at some future time if the current problem had not taken him."

His hand still on the vessel he surveyed the audience for a question. Again, only the subdued, mellow violins.

"We will now proceed to the cause of death. You have heard that our learned doctor speculates that this man was suffering from a severe illness in his brain. He bases his theory on the man's fitting, spasms and his delirious state. Is he correct or will he be proved wrong? Let us now open the skull. Perhaps we can explain this strange behaviour just prior to his sudden death."

The muffled whispers of curiosity spread through the audience as Professor Dubois proceeded to the head of the table. "Before I remove the top of the skull, I would like to point out some findings which will not be clear at a distance." He placed one hand on the chin and the other on the nose and slowly opened the mouth as wide as he could. A metal rod was inserted into the mouth to hold it open. He held a small candle in front of a mirror to illuminate the man's orifice. "Now gentlemen, here on the tip of his tongue is a small ulcer. It looks new. Also, here on his upper and lower gums are fresh erosions. And here on his palate and at the top of his throat are also multiple similar ulcers. These I am sure are those of early syphilis. We know this man had syphilis for some years. Our apothecary has already attested to this. It would therefore appear that this man acquired a new syphilis infection through his mouth; possibly from the ladies of the night or perhaps from elsewhere?"

The buzz of multiple speculations and theories rippled around the theatre.

Professor Dubois raised his hands again. "That is enough guesswork. Let us open the skull. We have already cut through the bone. It is a tedious process which I did not want to waste on your entrance fee." He held his hands on either side of the head, just above the ears and gently lifted off the skull vault revealing the brain. The normal shiny convolutions of the two hemispheres were absent and in their place was a dull flattened brain surface encased in a slimy film. "This brain should normally be devoid of these secretions and it indicates that a disease process has taken place in this poor soul's head. This would adequately explain and be responsible for his strange behaviour and ultimate death." He scanned the tiers looking for a question but the room remained silent.

The Professor was about to open his mouth when a young student in the front row tentatively raised his hand. "Professor, considering the ulcers in the mouth could these secretions on the brain surface be an extension of this new syphilis process?"

Professor Dubois smiled. "Monsieur Vidal is one of our youngest but also one of our brightest students and it comes as no surprise that he has found the correct answer. Yes, this looks like involvement of the brain by the syphilis disease. It is my hypothesis that this dull film over the brain is not due the disease he has suffered over the last years but part of a newly acquired infection. This however raises an even more perplexing question. How would he have acquired this new syphilis infection? He is well known in this town and no women of the night would have anything to do with him. They certainly know how this devastating illness is transmitted."

The buzz again permeated the theatre. With another nod of the Professor's head a drum roll commenced as he walked to one side of the room. He stopped and stretched an open palm towards a jacket hanging from stand. The drum roll quickened as he placed his hand inside the jacket and pulled out a small brown bottle with a glass stopper and held it up to the audience. Duval's, Laurent's and Baptiste's eyes snapped open in unison. The drums ceased. "This, gentlemen, was found in the pocket of this poor man. It is unlabelled, but I have it on good information from his close friends that he sipped at this regularly during the day and in the evening. I have given it to some mice and await the outcome." At this point he shifted his gaze momentarily towards the third gallery where

Monsieur Labonne shifted nervously in his seat. "I have been informed by Monsieur Baptiste that there are charlatans in our town who are espousing medicine with miraculous cures for the syphilis. This may be one of those devastating hoaxes. Unfortunately, I cannot provide you with any definite results now, but I hopeful that the mice will provide the answer within the next week." He walked across and handed the bottle to Duval. Another signal to the orchestra and the calming background of the violins commenced. "Thank you all for coming. As usual my students will remain behind to study the body in more detail. The apothecary, our good doctor and Commandant Duval are also welcome to stay behind to examine the body more closely.

As the audience stood and slowly filed out Duval, Baptist and Laurent remained seated and conferred quietly.

"A Monsieur Labonne provided the same bottles to two of my syphilitic patients who I was treating with mercury. It did them no good but also no harm. I am not sure they are relevant to this man's death?"

Duval added. "Similar bottles were found on the bedside tables of Monsieur Duplessis and Monsieur Villiers. They were provided by the ladies of Maison Clare who advised they were supplied by a man named Charles. But my information is that these ladies gave them to numerous clients but only Duplessis and Villiers perished. However, I will follow up with questioning Labonne tomorrow."

"Yes, I also saw the brown bottle at the bedside of Duplessis, but in my medical practice I have seen similar bottles provided by other establishments; not only by Labonne. If each of these bottles has the same unique blower's mark, then that might be a better clue but even then, not a conclusive one."

Duval added while viewing the bottle base. "That is a good point, Pierre. I can confirm that the base of both bedside bottles and this one has a simple pontil scar with no unique blower's identification. Raphael, can you comment on your two syphilitic patients?"

"Unfortunately, I did not look at their bottles in any detail. At the time there was no indication of a connection with murder. As I said it did my patients no harm."

Pierre stood up. "It seems like a red herring. It is highly unlikely that pus taken from a syphilitic lesion, once diluted will have any surviving contagion after one or two days. The likely failure to demonstrate syphilis from the bottle would exonerate Labonne completely. On the contrary however, the specimens from the active brain infection may certainly kill the mice but this alone would not condemn Labonne. I believe we should await Bertrand's discussion with Labonne and now go and examine this brain."

***

Monsieur Labonne melted into the crowd and steadily worked his way forward. The theatre crowd spilled out into the quiet, cool evening, mixing with townsfolk out for a stroll. Charles was relieved to escape the incriminating atmosphere of the theatre and immediately turned right in the direction of the le Boulevard du Printemps. He stopped at a begging street urchin, whispered in his ear and placed a coin in his palm. The boy quickly disappeared into the darkness as Charles continued home.

He walked briskly contemplating his move in light of the revelations of the dissection. *Yes, I recognised the corpse, and the medicine bottle held up for all to see. Will the mice show the signs of syphilis and prove conclusively that the medicine contained the infection? Could my theory of stronger memory be incorrect? Surely not! Everything about my theory made perfect sense and fitted with my life-long observations.*

Young couples, arm in arm, walked laughing and chatting towards him. Greetings were exchanged as they passed. He felt suddenly very vulnerable and very alone. He needed someone to talk to, a confidant, a partner, someone with whom he could consider the options for his next move.

He had never completely allowed that someone into his life, although he had his admirers and numerous brief affairs.

Another couple walking arm in arm approached him, talking softly to each other. Their total indifference to his presence deepened his isolation and encouraged his envy. He had almost had that once before. She was a beautiful and vibrant woman, but very poor and far beneath his station. They both had a profound interest in medicines. Their opinions varied and sometimes clashed but they agreed that the current course of medicine was flawed. They had confided together, laughed and loved but differences in their social standings had proved too great and he had abandoned her. At this low point in his life, he wished he could talk to her. But that was no longer possible. He had watched her burn to death.

He reached le Boulevard du Printemps and opened the blue door. Wasting no time, he quickly set about dismantling his small laboratory and collecting all the medicine bottles that were identical to the one on display at the dissection. He packed a bag and took off his fine clothes and replaced them with poorly fitting breeches and a coarse jacket. In his desk he opened a secret compartment and retrieved a key. He removed a large painting of the 1348 Plague of Paris behind which he opened a small safe with the key. He removed all the documents and cash and placed them in a tweed sack.

He was busy writing a note when he was interrupted by a knock on the door. He scanned the room and satisfied that all was in order he climbed the stairs and opened the door.

"Sir, your horse and carriage are waiting. Where would you like me to take you?"

"Good, I see that little rascal found you. Nowhere my good man. I will take the carriage myself. Here are ten gold coins which should cover the full cost of the carriage and the horse. I am sure you will find it satisfactory."

The man stared at the fortune he had just been handed. "So, this is a sale? You do not wish to hire the horse and carriage?"

"That is correct." Here is a deed of sale which outlines our arrangement. It just requires your signature. If you disagree with the sale or the price please leave immediately and I will contact another carriage merchant."

"No, no that is satisfactory, I was just clarifying an unusual transaction." He dipped the pen in the ink and signed the paper. Without another word he turned and walked into the darkness.

Charles quickly loaded all his goods on the carriage, locked the door behind him and rode slowly and as quietly as possible down the boulevard. He turned into the main avenue of the city towards the city gate. Just before the gate he hesitated, then instead of escaping through the exit he turned left along the wall. The fine houses gradually gave way to more broken and decrepit tenements and the cobblestone road became narrower and finally degenerated into a hard-packed, rutted, dirt track. He slowed as he passed a loud group of young men loitering outside the Temple of Miracles. In the breach of the wall, he stopped outside a small wooden shanty on the opposite side of the road. He jumped off, with his bag in one hand and knocked on the door.

There was initial silence with no sign of light inside. He knocked again. Finally, a shuffling inside and then a young girl's voice. "Who goes there? What is your business at this late hour?"

"I would like to speak to Mademoiselle Macon."

"I do not know what rumours you have heard sir, but this is not a house where one comes to visit in the cover of darkness."

"I am aware of that. I mean you no harm. A gentleman who knew your mother instructed me to deliver some things that belong to her."

There was the noise of a useless latch on the door, and Francine's face appeared in the small gap that she allowed. "Alright but be quick; what is this business?"

He held up the bag. "This bag contains some money he owes your mother. Also, there are title deeds for a house in le Boulevard du Printemps which he wishes to give her. He is aware of her unfortunate death and has put the deeds in your name."

"What sort of trick is this? I have never heard of such nonsense. Who is this person who knew my mother?"

The boys from the Temple of Miracles had become curious and began to move across the road towards the carriage.

"This is no trick Mademoiselle. Please take the bag. I am in a hurry and need to start a long journey." He pushed the bag through the gap in the door, turned and walked quickly to the buggy.

The boys, holding sticks and knives, had gathered around the carriage. "I hope you have no sinister intentions for that poor young girl and her brother? Are you alright in there Francine? Do you want us to give him what he deserves?"

A faint voice came through the crack in the door. "No, he means me no harm. He is just a friend of my mother offering his condolences."

Charles climbed onto his buggy, the ring parted and he disappeared into the darkness.

28

The Finger of Suspicion.

9 July 1670

The bell tinkled and Monsieur Baptiste looked up from his ledger at a sombre Commandant Duval. "Good morning, Commandant. How can I be of service this fine morning? I have not fallen foul of the law, have I?"

"Of that one can never be certain. But I have known you to be a law-abiding citizen for many years, so I think it unlikely. Can we speak here? I will be brief."

"The shop is currently empty except for Isabella and myself, and it is early. Please proceed."

Duval nodded to Isabella, who had just appeared through the curtain. "I will get straight to the point. Two days ago, we found the body of a soldier in the river beyond the southern bridge. The injuries would show that his death resulted from head injuries inflicted by a rock. Furthermore, the evidence points to involvement by a woman. I was drawn to this con-clusion because the soldier's breeches were around his ankles and his belt was unbuckled. This theory, however, may prove incorrect."

"Commandant, this is indeed a terrible, but possibly deserved, death. But I fail to see how this could possibly involve me?"

Duval withdrew a package from his pocket. From it, he pulled a rolled-up bandage. "I found this near to where the soldier may have been slain. It was laying unravelled in the bushes by the side of the track. As you are a supplier of such bandaging, I hoped that you may recognise it."

Monsieur Baptiste took the bandaging and rubbed a section between his thumb and forefinger. "Yes Commandant, this is good quality ban-daging, exactly the type I stock in my establishment. But there are other apothecaries in this town that attempt to emulate my quality. Furthermore, many customers come into my shop and buy bandaging. Even if it came from this store, it would be impossible to determine who purchased it."

"I thought that might be your response, but as you are aware, I must leave no stone unturned. Thank you for your time." Commandant Duval turned and let the door tinkle behind him.

***

Duval walked from the apothecary to the house of Dr Laurent. He knocked once, and the door opened. "Good morning, Bertrand. I have no patients for the next hour, so as discussed, let us go and see Reuben. He resides on Rue du Quai which is near to the River Tavern."

As they walked, Duval related the events of Jacques Macon's encounter with the child molester in a country house. "Pierre, I am suspicious the same monster has perpetrated Reuben's abuse. Hopefully, this interview will provide some identification." The avenues and fine houses mutated slowly into narrow streets and dilapidated tenements. They passed a sleeping tavern and turned up a narrow side alley. They knocked at number four; a small single storey dwelling squeezed between and shadowed by two, three-storey buildings.

Madame Lavigne opened the door almost immediately. "Please come in Dr Laurent, and this must be Commandant Duval who you advised was to accompany you."

"Good morning, Madame Lavigne." Duval and Laurent replied in unison.

She showed them into a small but neat front room where Reuben sat quietly, staring down at his hands.

"Reuben, you know Dr Laurent, and this is Commandant Duval. As you and I discussed, they have come to speak with you."

Reuben's expressionless eyes, ringed by dark shadows, looked up at both men in turn and nodded.

"Reuben has not been himself for some time. He is not playing with his friends. He cannot sleep and eats very little. But he has agreed to speak with you about the events that led to his visit to your rooms, Dr Laurent; with that terrible infection of his bottom. Go ahead Reuben."

Without hesitating, Reuben began a rambling, monotonous narration. "In the late afternoon, four days before I came to see you, doctor, a carriage stopped as I walked through the main square. A large red bearded man asked if I wanted to make some good money. I agreed, and I jumped into his carriage. We arrived at a large house in the country where I met one other boy with black hair; we did not share names. Together we helped in the kitchen, till it was dark, with a maid who called herself Manon. We were given some food and drink and after a while the room started to spin and I was seeing all manner of strange colours and shapes." Reuben stopped and looked at his mother, who nodded and rolled her hand for him to continue. "I can't remember much else other than a fat naked man being on top of me. He fucked me in the bum. Then they took me home."

Duval seethed inwardly, but remained unmoved. "Would you recognise this man again or is there anything else that might help us find him?" asked Duval.

"He had a big black birthmark on his right bum. That is all I can remember"

Failing to hide the linkage, Duval's mouth fell open. "Thank you Reuben. Thank you very much. You have been most helpful."

Without another word, Reuben got up and shuffled, head down, from the room.

"Reuben is not his usual self. He used to be such an active boy with many friends." Madame Lavigne's dejected face unveiled her inner torment.

Duval opened his mouth to speak, but Laurent intervened. "Madame Lavigne, it is clear from his emotionless dialogue and his dejected posture that he suffers from severe depression. This can be extremely serious, but expected, considering the circumstances. I would urge you to let me see him again as soon as possible. There will be no charge. Not in my rooms, but somewhere less daunting. I will get back to you within a day or two."

Duval and Laurent walked back up out of the squalor of the riverside. "Pierre, the date would be the 10 June, which does not coincide with the Villiers episode on 5 June. There was also only one other boy with black hair: Jacques is blond. The maid's name was Manon, not Nicolette. It must be a different encounter with the same red-beard; Remy Gauthier, I assume, and the same fat man."

"I agree entirely, Bertrand. But that poor boy has bottled up so much pain. Self-loathing, self-harm or even suicide are common with such depth of depression. I fear terribly for his life."

***

It was almost midday when Mara entered the coolness of the apothecary. Isabella looked up through wide, troubled eyes, as the three customers she was serving turned briefly towards Mara.

"Good morning, Isabella. How are you?" asked Mara.

Isabella forced a weak smile with a fixed forehead frown, nodded and then continued to serve her customers. Mara waited patiently, taking time to study the mural of the four horsemen.

The bell tinkled as the customers departed and Mara approached the counter. "Why so glum today? Are you ill? Is your father unwell? I do not see him here."

"He is out. I am very busy. What do you need this afternoon?"

"Just some more bandages."

Isabella quickly retrieved the bandages, handed them to Mara, and without another word, turned to make the entries in the ledger.

"Well, you are clearly not in the mood for conversation today. So, I may see you tomorrow?"

Mara had only gone as far as the next corner when Isabella suddenly appeared from a side alley, panting. "Mara, I could say nothing while you were in the shop. My father may have arrived at any moment. But something terrible has happened. The commandant came by and spoke to father about a dead soldier they found by the river, beyond the bridge. His head was badly smashed. He thought a woman was involved because rape was suspected. He asked if father had any knowledge of it. Father said no. But, but why on earth was he asking? He showed father some dirty bandaging and asked if it came from our shop."

Mara opened her right hand and contemplated the small scar in her palm. "It must have fallen off as we rode up the track." This confirmation of Celeste's recent account of the dead soldier by the river rattled Mara, but only raised eyebrows betrayed her inner turmoil. "Do not worry Isabella, there is nothing to link us to that pig's death. Now go back to work and I will see you tomorrow."

As Mara crossed the square, her apprehension heightened as she noticed a ragged and emaciated Monsieur Lambert leaning on his stick. This time, he was only with his wife and teenage son. His child was not with them. Mara nodded politely and walked past.

"I hear your days of freedom may soon end," Lambert chuckled as Mara walked away.

Shaken, Mara fidgeted nervously with the lock, entered the front door, then closed it quickly behind her. She passed an empty waiting room and entered the laboratory to find Celeste and Pierre standing together, engaged in lively conversation.

"Hello Mara, you look a little flushed. Is everything alright?" asked Pierre.

"Yes, yes, everything is fine." She held up the parcel of bandages. "Hello Celeste, how are you? I did not expect to see you here so soon."

"On my last visit, you were so welcoming and Pierre so gracious that I wished to return as soon as I was able. But Mara, look at you, you are the perfect picture of health. Any nausea or vomiting?"

Mara shook her head, opened her mouth to speak, but Pierre intervened. "As you can see, Mara's well-being is excellent. Now, I have some things to attend to, so I will leave you ladies alone."

"Thank you, Pierre, for giving up your precious time to talk to me while we waited for Mara."

"It has been a pleasure. Now I must go."

"Well, Celeste, it appears to be quiet here today, so we might go for a stroll and you can tell me all your news."

"That would be delightful, but I am only allowed a brief visit. Have you finished the copy of the recipes you promised me? I am expected back in the Tower within the hour."

"As a matter of fact, I finished them last night." Mara walked across to the rack of books and pulled out a notebook, and handed it to Celeste. "This is a copy of all the recipes we have."

"Thank you. By the way, do not worry, your little secret is safe with me. But be careful, someone may notice soon if you don't start wearing loser clothes."

Mara smiled. "Sorry it has been such a quick visit, Celeste, but please come again. Anytime."

"Goodbye Mara." She put the book under her arm and walked out of the door.

As had become their custom, Pierre and Mara sat down for dinner against the window in the parlour. Mara's pent-up anxiety could not be contained. As soon as Claudette left, Mara poured out the events at the river and the visit by the commandant at the apothecary. "I am truly sorry, Pierre, that I did not confide in you. It all happened just after I came here. I was unsure of you then. I thought that brute would never be found and the total nightmare would be erased. I am so sorry. I should have trusted you." She held her head in her hands as the tears dripped from her fingers.

Pierre pulled his chair closer and held her around her sobbing shoulders. "Mara, Mara, my dear Mara. What a terrible ordeal for you and Isabella. Under the circumstances, what else could you have done against such a rogue? I am absolutely certain the commandant would understand."

"Under normal circumstances, the judges may see the truth, but I am an accused witch who is here with you on borrowed time. If I and Isabella admit to this death, then we will both go to the fire. To kill a soldier of la Maréchausée is an unacceptable crime."

"Yes, what you say has truth. And to add to the anxiety, I hear that the archbishop's speech has created an even more zealous band of witch-hunters. And his own death has intensified that frenzy. Now I hear that a young witch standing in the crowd was sticking pins in an effigy of the archbishop. She is yet to be identified. With all this hysteria, the best approach at the moment is to lie low. How could he possibly tie you and Isabella to that soldier's death? I feel he is working on some very dubious intuition."

"Pierre, I hope you are correct. But if anyone hears of this pregnancy, then I fear for both of us. And what of Monsieur Lambert? I have seen him with his family on three occasions outside in the square, watching this house. And on my return today, he commented that my days of freedom may soon be over. Why?"

"Mara, I did not wish to worry you about this matter. But he is very distressed about the outcome of his leg. He can no longer light the streetlights, and therefore cannot feed his family. And to make matters worse, his child died recently from a combination of hunger and illness. He would not permit me to tend to his sick child. I have spoken to him and even given him money. But he cannot forgive me and says he will have retribution."

"Retribution? What could that possibly mean? Pierre, I feel everything is closing in. This pregnancy will be noticed in another month. I do not trust Celeste and her association with Colonel Montpellier. And now Monsieur Lambert; a perfect retribution would be for him to alert the colonel to my confinement when it becomes harder to hide."

"You may be correct, Mara. You have given this some thought. What do you suggest?"

"I truly believe it is best if I disappear. That way, you will not be held responsible and life would continue as normal for you. Then, after a time when this insanity is over and if you still love me, we can meet again."

"If I still love you? Mara, I hope you do not think this is just a passing fantasy. You bear our child and I will always love you."

Mara smiled, and some of her fear seemed to subside. "But Pierre, I worry that this nonsense will go on for some years. What then? Would you close up your practice and your entire career and meet me somewhere else? Maybe in another country?"

"Mara, I have told you many times how much I love you. Of course. I would follow you anywhere. Of that you can be certain. But right now, I would like to think on it some more."

Mara smiled. She had grown to love him. Despite his faults, he was a good man, someone whom she had grown to trust. "I noticed that you and Celeste were quite close and comfortable with each other when I walked in. What was her proposal?"

"Is that a touch of jealousy I detect?" He smiled mischievously but with eyes as warm as sunbeams. "But yes, she gets a little close and makes her intentions clear. She wanted to know if she could also come and work here with you and I."

"And how did you respond?" Mara asked teasingly.

"I said I did not think I could manage two witches under my roof, let alone one."

Mara laughed, her anxiety dissolving. She put her arms around his neck and kissed him. "I think it is bedtime."

29

Monsieur Baptiste

10 July 1670

Commandant Duval and Lieutenant Beaufort sucked in the fresh dawn air and watched the oarsmen in two boats straining against la Loire's current. The River Tavern's publican had sent word that there were two more floaters in the river. Behind each boat trailed a rope attached to a floating body. Large river rats scurried over the naked, bloated corpses and jumped off as they approached the shore.

"Well, Thomas, these two will probably just add to the many unsolved deaths in this city. That soldier with the smashed skull and trousers around his ankles puzzles me greatly. The soldier himself I have little concern for. I think there was a struggle, and he got what he deserved. I have the sense that there is more to it than a rape gone wrong. Even so, it remains our responsibility to seek the truth."

The first boatmen dragged a body across the pebbles and then higher up the muddy bank. He stood, hands on hips, panting, waiting for the commandant's instruction.

"Let us examine this poor soul."

As they approached, the stench of decay reached their nostrils, and they brought their handkerchiefs quickly to their nose. The rats had already devoured the eyes, lips and nose before their meal was confiscated. There was no obvious cause of death. "What do you know of this skinny man, Thomas?"

"Not much, sir, although I have dealt with this fellow previously. He is a frequent visitor to the River Tavern. Rumour has it he regularly beats his wife when he gets home. Probably just an alcohol fuelled tavern argument about a gambling debt or money owed. Who knows, when the ale takes hold of your senses, your mouth becomes loose and brain turns to jelly. Or just drunk and fell into the river and drowned," ventured Thomas.

"And why is his hair cut so short?" Commandant Duval took a stick from the bank and partially opened the mouth. A few small river crabs scurried out. "Look Thomas, no teeth?" Duval examined the man's hands and fingers. "I think if we find the wife of this poor fellow, she will confirm he wore a ring. What do you think now, Thomas?"

"Probably the body snatchers again, Commandant."

"I agree Thomas," and rubbed his chin again. "But if they were responsible for his death, then this body would already be dissected at one of the professor's performances. So, it is more likely he died by drowning; be it forced or accidental. The body initially sank, but as the gases of decay filled the tissues, the body rose. The body snatchers then fished him out of the river and took whatever they could sell. By then, the body was probably not up to the standard required by our professor and they threw him back to feed the fish and rats."

The second body of a large red-bearded man with a torn shirt was dragged up next to the skinny corpse. Duval, mouth open and eyes wide, knelt down beside him. "Is this our man, Thomas? Remy Gauthier?"

"It certainly is Commandant." Beaufort considered the body and ran his fingers over his own healing head wound. "Definitely the man from the River Tavern."

"The smashed temple and this small knife wound under his left ribs would certainly show there is mischief afoot." Duval focused on the left wrist. "Look, Thomas, these scars on the thumb side of his wrist. Together with the red hair and beard, I would confirm he is the rogue who abused and drowned young Andre. And probably the coachman who took Jacques Macon and the two other boys to the Villiers' mansion."

"Yes Commandant, it certainly accords with our theory. But why has now been murdered?"

Duval handled the man's shirt. "Look Thomas, one button missing; and the same coach buttons as the one you grabbed. I would venture his minders wished to keep him quiet. Your recognition of him at the River Tavern and your subsequent pursuit and investigations would suggest to his superiors that he has become a liability."

"He was in the employ of the cloister; are you suggesting that they could be his minders and his assassin?"

"Thomas, to suggest that our own house of God is involved in such a crime is almost unspeakable, but we will have to delve deeper into this connection. Thomas, stay here for a while and examine these bodies carefully. Make sure we have missed nothing. Also, visit the family of the thin man and see what you can find. I wish to visit the apothecary again. As with the deaths of Duplessis and Villiers, the recent death of the archbishop also appears related to a pillbox; but it was his Paris pill box. On this last occasion, there was no brown bottle, which makes this a less likely source of a possible poison. It is high time we spoke in more detail about these pills."

***

Monsieur Baptiste looked up from his books when he heard the knock on the door. He pulled out his pocket watch. *Only 7.30! An hour before opening! Who could that be so early?* As he walked towards the door, he recognised Commandant Duval and his irritation changed to alarm as he hastily undid the latch. "Good morning, Commandant, it is always a pleasure to see you. But what emergency brings you here at this hour? Are you in urgent need of some medicine?"

Duval held up his hand to stop the chatter. "Nothing of that nature, Monsieur Baptiste. I was busy with some business down by the river and thought I would see you before going back to the office. Hope you do not mind?"

"Definitely not. Nothing should stand in the way of our gendarmerie."

"Well, I will get to the point. As you know, the deaths of Monsieur Duplessis, Monsieur Villiers, have something in common. They both had pillboxes, filled with pills supplied and delivered by this establishment. The archbishop appears to have brought his pills with him from Paris." Duval locked on Monsieur Baptiste for any hint of deception.

"My God sir, I hope you are not suggesting that I had anything to do with these tragic deaths!"

"At present I assume not, Monsieur Baptiste. But so that I can fully discount this possibility, I would like to know how you make these pills and how you dispense them?"

"Absolutely Commandant! That will not be a problem. I am glad you are here before my customers arrive, so you can have my undivided attention. Come, please, follow me."

Commandant Duval followed Monsieur Baptiste through the curtain into a short corridor which led up a flight of stairs. On the left of the corridor, a door opened into a spacious room.

"This is my dispensary where we prepare all our medications. It also serves as a laboratory where I can experiment with different ingredients."

The side walls were lined with floor to ceiling wooden shelves filled with an orderly display of different shaped glass and metal bottles, pots and jugs. In the middle of the room stood a long wooden bench, on which a complex series of interconnected flasks and tubes had been erected. The back shelves contained an assortment of funnels, and next to them was a rack with various sized mortars.

Duval sniffed and held his hand over his nose. "Yes Commandant, it is an unusual smell, somewhat sour, and perhaps somewhat acrid and stale, but one that I have become accustomed to. All these wooden shelves have absorbed a multitude of chemicals over many years and they continually leech back, providing this room with this delightful aroma." Duval nodded and dropped his hand. "Commandant, our ingredients come from many sources. From as near as local farmers to as distant as the four corners of the world. We may receive prepared ingredients which require no further processing. Or we may start with herbs or plants and grind them first with these mortars and pestle and then possibly extract the desired ingredients with this still." He nodded to the complex series of connected flasks and tubes. "We only use herb and plant extracts that have a scientifically proven effect. This separates us from the many charlatans and country folk that make brews from all manner of herbs with no proof of effect." Baptiste paused and pointed to a large flask filled with a cloudy liquid. "This method is that of precipitation. Ingredients from plants can be extracted with water and then the active ingredient can be brought out of solution with the addition of various chemicals. In this case, precipitation is with alcohol. After using these various methods, we then store all our active compounds in those containers. As you will notice, they are all labelled with the contained ingredient."

"Who does this?"

"Only I have the authority to prepare the compounds."

"So, what happens when you receive a prescription?"

"From the prescription, I calculate the total active ingredient and weigh it out on the scale. I then mix this with a binding substance, such as a sugar syrup. From this, I make a paste and roll the paste into a tube. I can then cut the tube into several equal discs which I then allow to dry. These discs are the pills. Occasionally I may coat the pills in sugary coating for a more tasteful swallow. The children happily swallow those pills." Baptiste paused for a moment. "From my description, you note pills are made in batches. This would make it very difficult to explain how a single poisonous pill could find its way into a single patient's pill box." Baptiste spread out both arms and looked around the room. "You are free to search my entire establishment for a small batch of poisonous pills, if you wish."

Duval's eyebrows narrowed as he fixed Baptiste for a moment. "Then what happens to the pills?"

"They are often packed directly for a prescription or if I make a large batch, the pills are placed in the appropriately labelled jar, where they can be stored until we have to fill an order."

"And who fills the order?"

"That Isabella usually does. She did this before and after school. But now that her schooling is complete, she also does deliveries. I always check that she has filled them correctly."

"That is very helpful. So, what you are describing is that if any of these pills contained poison, only you could have prepared them?"

"My good sir, how could you suggest such a thing? I have run this business for thirty years and no-one has ever questioned my methods. I am deeply offended by your remark, Commandant!"

"Monsieur Baptiste, I am sorry for any affront, but you must understand that the nature of my work demands that I look under every stone. By the way, what is that big container in the corner?"

"That is where we throw any unused ingredients, unwanted prescriptions or old stock." He paused as the commandant nodded. "Is there anything else you wish to know? If you wish you can return this afternoon, I have six prescriptions to fill and you could observe the entire process?"

At that moment, footsteps descended the staircase and Isabella walked past the open dispensary door. "Isabella, this is Commandant Duval. He is here to gain some knowledge of the workings of an apothecary." Duval tipped his hat in her direction and Isabella nodded and continued into the shop.

"The offer to observe the pill making process is generous. But that will not be necessary. Thank you for your time." He opened the curtain and had almost reached the front door when he turned and pulled a piece of faded yellow cloth from his pocket. "Oh, by the way, many people pass through your doors. Would you know anyone who has a garment made of this material?"

There was the briefest pause and a flicker of the eyes. "No, I cannot say that I do." Monsieur Baptiste rubbed the material between his thumb and forefinger. "It seems like excellent material, not something worn by those close to the river."

"Yes, that was my thought as well. Good morning to you sir, and thank you for your time." He again tipped his hat toward Isabella, who was busy packing shelves behind the counter.

"Hopefully, I have been of some assistance to the gendarmerie today. Gooday to you Commandant."

As Duval departed, three customers entered the shop to pick up pre-scriptions. Thereafter Monsieur Durand arrived for his mercury suffumi-gation. Bishop Bernard dropped in and engaged in a lengthy conversation with Monsieur Baptiste. There was even a visit from Colonel Montpellier, requiring something to boost his energy. After Isabella departed for her rounds, the hustle settled and Monsieur Baptiste spent most of the after-noon preparing prescriptions in his dispensary. When finished, he packed each prescription into a labelled paper bag on the central table for Isabella to deliver to clients the following day. It was only after closing time, when Isabella returned, that Monsieur Baptiste related the visit and his discus-sions with the commandant.

"Isabella, I recognised the fabric. It was the dress that you got for your birthday last year."

"Oh Papa! Please, do not be angry. I wore that dress on the first day I did rounds with Mara. Something horrible and frightening happened on that afternoon. Something that I shall never be able to forget." Isa-bella collapsed forward, shoulders shaking. "Sorry father, I should have told you."

He wrapped his arms around her as she cried and her body trembled. "There, there, calm yourself. When you are ready, you can tell me what happened." As the sobbing continued, Baptiste held her with one arm around her shoulders while stroking her hair with the other.

Gradually her shoulders becalmed, and the sobbing became a whimper. Isabella pulled herself up and faced her father with dripping, bloodshot eyes. "Oh Father, on that day after we had finished our rounds, Mara and I went to cool our feet in the river. I am so sorry, father. I know you said I should never tarry. But it was so hot and Mara and I had become such good friends and it seemed so innocent."

"I will not judge or scold you, my darling. Just tell me what happened."

Isabella recounted the drive to the isolated clearing near the river. Then Mara's walk away, the arrival and attempted rape by the soldier, Mara's return, and bashing the soldier to death. Finally, their attempt to sink him in the river. "Father, I did not want to tell you for fear that you would do something. I had hoped that it could just be mine and Mara's secret and that it would just go away."

Baptiste's head bowed. "Isabella, my darling, my heart is broken. What that fiend attempted to do was disgusting. The fear and the hurt it must have caused you can hardly be imagined. That man deserved his death and you certainly have nothing to apologise for."

"Oh Father, I am so sorry."

"Isabella, it has been terrible for you to relive this event. Please go upstairs and try to get some sleep. We will talk no more of this tonight. I need to consider all the consequences of your link to this soldier. Where is the dress now?"

"After the attack, we both swam to clean up and then went to Mara's home to change into clean clothes. Simon was not home, so we were not seen by anybody. I then carried the dress in the medicine bag and have stored it in the back of the drawer, in my room."

"Please bring it to me before you go to sleep."

Although it was the middle of summer, Baptiste prepared a fire in the hearth and poured a glass of wine. When the flames flickered up the chimney, he threw the yellow dress in and watched it burn. He sat quietly, watching the flames and occasionally sipping the wine. He rose from his chair, entered the laboratory and removed a sheaf of blank paper from his desk and began to write. When finished, he folded the letter, walked up the stairs and silently pushed it under Isabella's door. Returning to his laboratory, he removed one filled prescription from the centre table and threw it in the discard bin. He picked up the flask with the cloudy liquid and poured it down the sluice. Opening three jars, he removed three pills from each and swallowed them in rapid succession. He sat back down in the dispensary, gulped the remaining wine, and waited.

***

As usual, Isabella woke early, almost elated. Her confession had lifted the tremendous burden of her secret. She noticed the paper on the floor and snatched it up. Her eyes darted across the page, becoming wider as she read. Her heart began racing within a tightening chest. She looked up and her trembling hands let the letter slip to the floor. "Papa, Papa, where are you? What have you done?" She charged down the stairs, two steps at a time, and stopped as she passed the dispensary. "No. No, Papa. Please. Please don't leave me." A sudden weakness in her legs forced her down next to his lifeless body. Dizziness transformed into blackness, and her head fell into his lap.

The constant knocking at the front door brought Isabella back to consciousness. She peeped through the curtain to see a customer with his nose pressed up against the front door. She stepped back, waited and looked again. He was gone. With head spinning and body trembling, she re-entered the dispensary, bent over her father, kissed his cold forehead, stroked his hair and shed a tear on his cheek. Still shaking, but with some focus, she ran up the stairs and retrieved the letter. Then crossed to her father's room and hid the letter in a drawer. Returning to the shop, she straightened her dress and wiped her eyes with her hand. Peering out through the door, she noticed Lieutenant Beaufort walking, as he occasionally did, from the barracks toward the river. Isabella shut out the risk, placed her hand on the doorknob, and hesitated. *Should I? Is this the right thing to do? What would father do?*

She opened the door and ran across the small square, sidestepping some early residents and waving her arms. "Lieutenant Beaufort, Lieutenant Beaufort."

He lifted his head and smiled. "Isabella, what distresses you so? What brings you out so early?"

"Lieutenant, it, it is my father. I fear he is dead."

"Dead! Where?"

"In his laboratory."

Beaufort turned, entered the apothecary, pushed the curtain aside, and entered the dispensary, where he found Monsieur Baptiste slumped in his chair. He felt the coldness of his skin and the absence of a pulse and proceeded back to Isabella.

"I will return immediately to the barracks and inform Commandant Duval, whom I am certain will wish to return and investigate the crime scene. Please go inside, lock the door, touch nothing and let no one enter."

30

The Witches' Mark

10 July 1670

His face puce and breathing heavily, Beaufort reached the barracks and found Commandant Duval's office empty. While waiting at the door, he noticed Colonel Montpellier swaggering across the courtyard and rushed out to meet him.

"Colonel, Colonel Montpellier, could I please have a word?"

Montpellier stopped mid stride. "Yes Lieutenant Beaufort, you seem most troubled at this early hour?"

"Colonel, I have just returned from the apothecary, where I found Monsieur Baptiste dead in his chair. His daughter found him so, and she is most distraught."

Montpellier stiffened, staring at Beaufort. "Baptiste dead! You are certain?"

"Yes sir, dead, in his chair."

"Lieutenant Beaufort, it would appear that this is a very serious criminal matter which requires complete and prompt investigation. However, it appears at first glance unrelated to witchcraft. The criminal arm of la Maréchausée is entirely in Duval's hands so that I can focus on more pressing issues. I am already late for a meeting with Bishop Bernard and suggest you wait for Duval and ensure he urgently attends to this matter. Now I must press on."

"Thank you, sir."

***

Father Nicolas pushed the exhausted, sweat drenched horse up a long dusty incline. Once over the crest, he smiled at the sight of St Raphael cradled in a light morning mist beside la Loire. Once through the city gates, the spires guided him through quiet, empty streets to the cathedral and the cloister. He pulled the cord and heard the muffled sound of a bell somewhere deep within. No-one immediately responded. Tired, irritated, and thirsty, he rang again. The door finally creaked open and Emile stuck his head through the opening.

"Good morning, sir. I see you are a man of the cloth. I am truly sorry that you have been kept waiting, but we were all at morning prayer. How can I be of service?"

"I have travelled from Paris with some important information for Bishop Bernard."

"Paris! Certainly, sir. Please come in. I will have your horse stabled and fed."

The welcome coolness inside the cloister dissipated some of his irritation and he followed the seminarian through the corridor of the Ten Commandments. He nodded to the groups of curious clerics gathered in the courtyard as he passed. After a few more twisting corridors, he was shown through a door and entered a small private garden.

"Please wait here. I will inform Bishop Bernard of your arrival. You will find water in the jug; you must have a great thirst after such an arduous journey."

A few minutes later Bishop Bernard appeared, panting, at the door. "Father, please excuse the delay, but it has been an extremely busy morning. I am most pleased to see you have been made comfortable. I am Bishop Bernard. What is it that brings you so unexpectedly from Paris to St Raphael?"

"My Lord, I am Father Nicolas. I have been despatched from Paris as the bearer of some very important news." He held up a scroll of paper. "It is all contained in this official document, but rather than a full reading, I will get straight to the point. After much consideration of the many candidates from all of France, you have been selected as the new Archbishop of

Paris. You will replace our recently and sadly departed Archbishop Chevalier. Despite the spread of witchcraft in your canton, Colonel Montpellier has convinced our king that you have made significant progress in curbing this burgeoning plague. Your qualities of fortitude, diligence, and steadfastness could not be surpassed by any of the other nominees." He held out the scroll for Bishop Bernard.

The joy welled up inside and Bishop Bernard could not contain the grin that escaped across his flushed face. Everything he had worked so hard and long for, all the sacrifices and the sometimes-difficult choices he had made, had all been worth it. The culmination of all his prayers had finally been answered. "Thank you, Father Nicolas. It is indeed a real privilege to have been awarded such an honour." He reached out and claimed the scroll. "May I ask when this position will begin?"

"I feel certain that you will have many things to tie up here and Paris has considered this. You will, however, be expected in Paris in one month."

"Thank you, sir. I am sure you are exhausted from your journey. One of our seminarians will take you up to your quarters, where you can rest and freshen up. Then you must join us for some breakfast. Is there anything specific that you desire?"

"Thank you. Yes, rest is exactly what I need. Would a bath be too much to ask after such a long journey and perhaps someone to help me?"

"I will arrange the bath and will send someone up to assist. How long will we have the pleasure of your company?"

"Unfortunately, I cannot tarry long and will start my return journey after prayers tomorrow morning."

As soon as the door closed, Bishop Bernard's suppressed delight escaped in an uninhibited jig as he circled the room, humming and waving his hands. He collapsed in his chair and poured a full glass of wine. After savouring his success with a mouthful, he picked up a bell on the table and rang it twice.

A seminarian opened the door. "Yes, my Lord. How can I be of service?"

"Could you ask Robin to come and see me? I have some tasks for him."

"My Lord, I was about to inform you, but Colonel Montpellier is here to see you."

"Oh yes, our weekly meeting. What a pity. Please bring him in."

Montpellier and the bishop sat together for the next half hour cross checking reports from informants. These betrayers and their motives varied, and included neighbours with a grudge, lifelong friends and even family members fearful of association. They examined confessions from the torture chamber and follow-up reports and rumours of individuals who had been acting strangely. They selected a dozen of the most compelling suspects; these would require capture, interrogation and an interim trial date.

"Thank you, Colonel. It appears we are making steady progress. It should not be that much longer before we rid this pestilence from our land." The bishop paused and sipped some water. "I must thank you for recommending me for the role of Archbishop of Paris." Montpellier smiled, was about to speak, but the bishop held up his hand and continued. "You, of all those in the King's service, certainly deserve a promotion for your determination and commitment to this laborious task. I would be honoured to recommend this to your superiors when I arrive in Paris."

"That is most kind, my Lord and much appreciated. However, there is one further piece of information that one of my soldiers brought to me just this morning. I have heard that the apothecary, Baptiste, died last night in unusual circumstances. His daughter found the body this morning in his shop. I have heard through my contacts that Commandant Duval was seen speaking with Monsieur Baptiste early yesterday morning. As you are aware, the commandant is pointlessly pursuing the deaths of Monsieur Duplessis, Monsieur Villiers, and the archbishop. I wondered whether their meeting had anything to do with those deaths; and then not long after Monsieur Baptiste is dead."

"Yes, those deaths of good innocent citizens are certainly not a mystery to the church and the constabulary. It is hard to understand why the commandant pursues them so persistently. And what on earth would the apothecary, a good upstanding citizen, have to do with them?"

"That may remain a mystery."

"It is co-incidental that this should happen now, as I have recently heard rumours from fellow clerics about his daughter. I have heard that she is a witch."

"We have certainly not heard any whispers in this regard, my lord. On what evidence or information do you make this conclusion?"

"I am told she bears the witches' teat here." He pointed to an area above his left nipple. "A priest advised me that an elderly woman confirmed this in the confessional late last evening. She had occasionally cared for Isabella as an infant and believed it was a sin against God to now withhold this information."

"Truly! It would be the first such mark we have seen. I would never have expected it from her. She works tirelessly in her father's shop. She has few friends and seldom plays or talks with other girls of her age. The one person with whom she spends time is the suspected witch, Mara."

"Well, there you have it. That may just be the link, Colonel. Witches are everywhere amongst us and can hide in the most unexpected places. You should go there immediately. To examine her, of course."

"And if she bears the mark?"

"Bring her directly to the Tower. She will go to the next trial and then straight to the fire. There should be absolutely no reason we cannot convict her forthwith with such damning evidence."

***

The apothecary door was shut. A CLOSED sign hung on the inside. Through the curtain, Isabella watched curious townsfolk wander past, some pressing their nose against the window, then walking away with shaking heads. She stifled a scream as Colonel Montpelier and four guards rode into the square. He dismounted, knocked repeatedly on the locked door and pressed his face against the glass. She shivered and stumbled from dizziness, causing a slight movement of the curtain. Montpellier knocked harder and longer. Isabella, with trembling lips and chin, hesitantly emerged. A few more tentative steps forward, her pulse pounding in her ears, she froze in the middle of the room. Then, reconsidering, she turned and scurried back through the curtain.

"Bitch," shouted the colonel and turned to his men. "You! Go around the back and catch that witch. And you, break down this door!"

A few more curious citizens stopped at the presence of the soldiers. But when the crash of glass on the cobblestones and the screams of a young girl penetrated the morning calm, the crowd quickly expanded. The two guards dragged the struggling, hysterical victim through the broken door and into the square. Montpellier stood smiling, with legs apart and hands on his hips. "Hold her down and remove that dress!"

"Colonel Montpellier, what on earth are you doing with that poor child?"

Montpellier turned to the source of the interruption and smiled as he saw Duval and Beaufort rushing across the square. "Back away Duval! This is no business of yours."

"This is unfathomable. This child has just lost her father. Now these two brutes are about to rip off her clothes for a public display. This behaviour is inhuman. You should be ashamed."

Montpellier's smile contorted into a sneer and his cold eyes burrowed into his second in charge. "Duval, you are an insult to your esteemed family name, and your father would now surely be turning in his grave. You are sorely testing my patience." Montpellier pointed to two guards. "You two stand between the girl and these frauds, who dare call themselves soldiers. You can use whatever force you want if they attempt to interfere." Then to the other guards, "hold her down and remove that dress!"

As the guards moved in, Isabella screeched again. She twisted and turned and kicked one guard in the crotch as the other fumbled to tear off her clothes. Irritated by the delay and conscious of his diminishing authority in front of the growing crowd, Montpellier took one step forward and slapped her savagely across the face. Isabella fell silent as she tasted the blood in the corner of her mouth. "No more noise, bitch! Do you understand?"

Duval launched himself at a gap between the guards but was held back. "Have you no shame, Colonel. She is but 16 years of age. This is despicable conduct for a man on the King's business."

Montpellier glared at Duval and nodded to the largest of the guards, who immediately drove his right fist straight at Duval's nose and his left into his abdomen. As Duval buckled and sank to his knees, gasping for breath, a final fist crashed into the back of his head. Montpellier smiled and turned his scowl back to Isabella and slapped her again. Defeated, her body sank and her head slunk forward. First her father and now the shame. She knew what they were looking for; the secret she had hidden her entire life. She did not struggle as she endured the last piece of clothing being ripped from her body. The colonel's sting had removed any remaining fight or life.

"It is true! Look there, this witch bears the mark." The soldier pointed to the small nipple above the left breast and beckoned the growing crowd closer.

The mob pushed in, examining the mark and every other part of her nakedness. "Yes, yes! It is true. She has the teat, as was described by the bishop!"

Some in the crowd backed away with their hands over their faces. "Be careful! She must be a powerful one. Do not get too close and do not hold her eyes. A grave ill could befall you."

Colonel Montpellier stepped forward. "Alright. That is enough, gentlemen. There is only one place for this little devil's whore. Take her to the Tower."

Naked, down cast and numb, the clamour of the crowd hardly reached her consciousness. The soldiers bound her hands together with a coarse rope, the other end held by Montpellier. The unruly procession departed the square with Duval on his knees, holding his nose, and Beaufort standing beside him.

The colonel, leading on his white stallion, pulled Isabella through the narrow streets while the two soldiers rode on either side. The news of the witch circulated swiftly through the city and crowds spilled out of every side street and alley to line the road. The burgeoning mob squeezed in closer; their abuse spraying her nakedness and the smell of hatred flooding all Isabella's senses.

***

Mara heard the distant rumble and commotion as she stepped out of her front door. The cacophony grew louder as she made her way through the winding streets towards the apothecary. She quickened her steps and from the far side of the square she froze at the broken glass door hanging open and the figure of Commandant Duval getting gingerly to his feet.

"Commandant, Commandant, what has happened?"

"Mara, the news is grave. Monsieur Baptiste lies dead inside and Isabella is being led to the Tower." Duval pointed toward the noise.

Mara's hand went to her mouth open. She hesitated briefly, looking back to the apothecary and then toward the commotion. Struggling to contain the alarm and terror surging through her body, she turned and bolted towards the source of the tumult. The frenzy grew loader and clearer as she ran. After turning a few corners, she could hear the distinct humiliation.

"So, this is the devil's favourite little slut."

"Yes, I bet he had his fill of that copper pussy."

"Look, look. The scarlet harlot has the witches' teat."

"This fire will be an inferno, seen even in Paris!"

Mara reached the back of a thick pack that had completely blocked the street. The colonel and the two guards bobbed ahead above the pandemonium. She pushed through the crush, ignoring the knocks, groping and abuse, until she emerged next to the soldier's horse. Isabella's long red hair, naked frame and outstretched arms lead by the colonel were directly ahead. Working her way forward, she could jostle to a position just in front of her friend. Isabella's usual expressive and lively face was empty. Her eyes fixed, dead ahead, blank, devoid of any life or awareness of the mayhem surrounding her.

"Isabella." Mara called, quietly at first, but louder and repetitively until she broke through the din and Isabella's shield. Her head turned and her searching eyes found Mara. A flicker of life appeared in her wide green eyes and the semblance of a smile transformed her face. That connection, that link to happier times, seemed to provide some inner fortitude. She stood more upright, her gaze not wavering as Mara walked just in front of her, till they reached the Tower entrance. The soldiers halted the throng and Mara could go no further. As she passed under the iron gate, Isabella's head turned and craned backwards as she tried to hold on to her only friend.

31

The Ledger

10 July 1670

Duval, bent forward and with tentative steps, moved towards the apothecary door; a blooded handkerchief held to his nose.

"Commandant, we should go to Dr Laurent; to attend your wounds?"

"Lieutenant, I will not allow a minor altercation with our deluded superior officer to distract us from finding the truth. My time in la Maréchuasée may be short, but I intend to exhaust every minute that remains." He paused, removed his handkerchief from his nose and felt with thumb and index finger; no break and the bleeding had stopped.

The renowned front door with its now silent bell hung on one hinge and shattered glass lay strewn across the cobblestones. Several curious townsfolk peered through the opening but had not as yet dared to cross the threshold.

"Thomas, please go back to the barracks and bring some men to board up this door and make it fast. I will have a look inside." Duval, mindful of disturbing any potential evidence, stepped cautiously through the debris. The shop was much the same as he had seen it on previous occasions. But there was something different; a smokiness irritated his injured nostrils. He ignored the odour and walked past the counter, noting the ledger of sale and accounts open and in its established place. He pulled the curtain aside and entered the laboratory. Monsieur Baptiste sat fully dressed and slouched in his chair. Now a different musty smell, disguised the usual laboratory odours; Duval recognised it as the decay of death. The body was cold, the fingers and the knees were stiff and flexed. Lifting an eyelid, he noted a cloudiness over the pupil. With both hands, he pulled down Baptiste's breeches, exposed his buttocks and viewed the purple discolouration of livor mortis. He pressed his finger into the non-blanching discolouration. "Sometime last night?" he mumbled. Duval straightened slowly, pushed his fingers through his hair, and surveyed the room. A glass with a residue of red wine stood on the counter next to three open pill containers. On the centre table was the precipitation flask, now empty, and a row of five packages containing the medicines for that morning's deliveries.

Duval returned to the salesroom. Again, ignoring the smokiness, he was drawn to the open ledger, sat on Monsieur Baptiste's stool and began scrutinising the pages. There was a page for each day, divided into a debit and credit side. Methodically, he opened every page and ran his finger down the multiple entries. On the credit side were all the purchases of pills, medicines, and bandages; nothing out of the ordinary. On the debit side, there were accounts for ingredients, equipment, and salaries. He noted the entry from Khan Abas Hassan, the trader from the east. But otherwise, there was nothing unusual. His eye caught one entry that occurred monthly, always on the first or second day of the month. It was to a Monsieur Leroy, 25 Rue d'Or, Moulin. He jotted the details in his notebook.

Satisfied that there was no further useful information in the ledger, he proceeded back through the broken curtain to the laboratory and found the formulary book. Turning through the pages, he found the last entries for Monsieur Duplessis and for Monsieur Villiers, but could not discern any suspicious ingredients. Then suddenly, his head pulled back from the page. He rubbed his eyes and looked again. An entry titled Visiting Archbishop stared back at him. The date of 5th July was that of Archbishop Chevalier's visit. The batch listed all the ingredients, none of which seemed suspicious. *I thought he brought his own pills from Paris?* He went back to the salesroom, opened the ledger for 5th July and ran his finger down the credit side. He found an item for 'Monsieur Durand: payment for mercury suffumigation.' His address was included.

He looked slowly around the room and then proceeded upstairs. He pushed open the door of a small room on the left to find a single unmade bed and a rack of clothes, which he shuffled through. *No yellow dress here*. Leaving the room, he crossed the narrow hall into Monsieur Baptiste's bedroom, where a neatly made bed confirmed that it had not been slept in. A chest of drawers stood under the window. The top drawer contained only socks and undergarments. The second drawer contained his finely pressed shirts, on top of which lay a folded sheet of paper. Duval picked it up and, from the first few lines, realised it was Monsieur Baptiste's last words to Isabella. His eyes widened and his head nodded as he read further. He folded the letter and placed it in his inside jacket pocket. The bottom drawer contained an array of clothes and shoes, but underneath was a small, embossed, silver jewellery box. He held it up and on the front was a single inscription: *Anna*. Bertrand undid the tiny clasp and opened the box. Inside, a single key rested on a simple red silk inlay. Duval held up the key. *What could this possibly be for?* He tried the key on every drawer and door upstairs and then downstairs on anything with a keyhole. The key did not fit a single lock. Puzzled, he placed the key back in the box, which he placed in his jacket pocket.

He suddenly stood upright. "Five? Not six?" he said aloud. He re-entered the laboratory and looked inside the large discard drum, half full with discarded pills, solutions, ingredients and a few packets. Laying on top was a small packet labelled Monsieur Thomas. Inside were seven pills. "Why would Baptiste make six packets of pills and throw one away and then kill himself?" He placed it in his inside jacket pocket. Turning to leave, Duval paused, picked up the empty precipitation flask, held it up to the light, noted there were drops remaining and carried it out of the laboratory.

Back in the salesroom, the smell of smoke again distracted him and proceeded to the hearth, which contained burnt wood and ash. He placed his hand against a charred log. *Mmm, still warm; must have had a fire last night. In the middle of summer?* He took the poker from its holder and pushed the wood to one side, then stopped. There amongst the ashes were the charred remains of a yellow garment. He inspected the unburnt patches. *Same material as in the dead soldier's hand.*

Duval left the apothecary and headed toward the River Tavern and turned into a narrow ally; Rue du Pêcheur. He found number 16 and knocked. Within minutes, a dishevelled man, his face covered with bumps and sores, opened the door. "Good morning, I am Commandant Duval. I assume you would be Monsieur Durand?"

"Yes, that is I. I haven't fallen foul of the law, have I?"

"No, definitely not. I have just a simple question for you. On the afternoon of the archbishop's speech, were you in Monsieur Baptiste's apothecary?"

"Yes, I remember it well. I could hear the chanting from the apothecary. I was having my mercury steam."

"During your time there that day, did you see a man of the cloth enter the store?"

"Yes, Bishop Bernard entered the shop. He seemed rather agitated."

"Bishop Bernard, not the archbishop?"

"Definitely our bishop. He wanted his pills and asked for his special pills in one packet and the others in a separate packet. He was only there for a short period, then left with two packets. As I have already said, he seemed most agitated."

"Thank you, Monsieur Durand. That is most useful information. Could you please write down all the events that transpired at the apothecary that day? Please include how you can clearly view the whole apothecary from your steam box. I will send someone to pick up your statement tomorrow."

"Most certainly Commandant. Good day to you."

"Good day Monsieur Durand."

32

Escape

11 July 1670

To dull the pain of Baptiste's death and Isabella's incarceration, Pierre had suggested a day in the country. They had spent a glorious sunny morning pick-nicking next to the full blossomed elderberry bush. A few glasses of wine had had the desired effect. The wily old fox's nose had appeared, sniffed the breeze, then disappeared, presumably awaiting their departure. On return, their brief enjoyment evaporated at the sight of Commandant Duval waiting at the front door. Pierre drew the reins and jumped down to greet him. Mara alighted and followed a few yards behind, carefully adjusting her skirt.

"Bertrand, I hope you have not waited too long? But my God Bertrand, your face? It appears more serious than Mara described. Your nose may be broken? Come into my surgery so I can have a better look."

"It is nothing serious, Pierre, and not the reason I am here. It was just a minor disagreement with Colonel Montpellier."

"Minor! Montpellier?"

"Pierre, one day I will tell you the entire story. Now there are urgent matters to discuss. I have questions for you both."

"Oh, I hope nothing too serious. We do try to keep our noses clean. Please come inside." The door opened and Claudette appeared. "Claudette, we are honoured to have Commandant Duval for a visit. Could you please prepare some refreshments and bring them up to the parlour? This way Bertrand." Pierre held out his arm towards the stairs.

Once seated and refreshments served, Duval came straight to the point. "As you both know, the apothecary has committed suicide and Isabella has been taken to the Tower on the suspicion of being a witch."

Mara could not hold back. "She is innocent, sir. You must believe me. I have known her for many years and she has a beautiful heart and would never, never take part in witchcraft."

"Calm yourself Mara. I have not come here to discuss her witchcraft, as I have no belief in such absurdity. She will, however, face the judges, and who knows what she will endure in the Tower before the trial begins."

"Oh please, please! Not the torture! I have heard such horrific tales."

"I will do all I can in that regard. But I am here today because I know that you have on occasions accompanied Isabella on her rounds in the country. Is that correct?"

"That is correct, sir." Mara's quivering lip unmasked her guarded fear.

"Well, as you may be aware, the body of a soldier has been found by the river." He paused, searching her transparent face. "The evidence I found at the river places Isabella at the scene of the crime. I have up till now not been able to question her, but wondered whether you had any information." He pulled something from his waistcoat pocket and displayed the faded yellow scrap of fabric in his open palm.

Mara's eyes widened. The memories rushed back and engulfed her. She buried her head in her hand, whimpering. Pierre shrouded her with a comforting arm. "Bertrand, please, you must understand. It was a frightful experience for two innocent young girls. That beast of man tried to take Isabella and received a deserved punishment."

"I fully understand, and the evidence at the scene points to a vicious struggle, but I must confirm my theories. It is unlikely to go any further. Mara, please recount the events of that day."

Mara lifted her head from her hands. She faced the commandant with swollen, bloodshot eyes. Her voice choked with tears as began her story of that fateful day. First the visits to the country houses, the heat, and then the grievous decision to go to the river to cool their feet in the water. How she had wandered off to trace a strange smell and found a dead tramp laying under a fallen tree.

"Ah, that solves that mystery. I felt the dead vagrant was unrelated; thank for that confirmation. Please continue."

"I heard screams and ran back as fast as I was able. There on the grass was a soldier, his trousers down, on top of Isabella. I picked up a rock and smashed it against his head many times until that beast fell off her. We then dragged his body into the river, filled his tunic with stones and watched that monster drift downstream until he sank to a deserved grave."

"Thank you, Mara. Were you aware of these events, Pierre?"

Before he could answer, Mara blurted, "I told him absolutely nothing. It was mine and Isabella's secret. We thought it best not to talk to even you, as we did not believe a fair hearing was possible."

"Well, I believe your story clears up those loose ends. Hopefully Isabella will corroborate your story, when I am permitted the opportunity to see her. I have one other matter which I wish to discuss. It concerns Monsieur Baptiste, so I hope it does not cause too much upset."

Mara wiped her wet eyes and nodded. "Please ask, if it helps Isabella at all, I will tell you all I know."

"Well, you have confirmed that you accompany Isabella on her rounds and also spend time at the apothecary?"

"That is certainly correct, Commandant."

"I have been told that you were with Isabella on the morning you visited the house of Monsieur Villiers."

"That is correct."

"Could you tell me in your own words what happened that morning? How were the pills delivered?"

"Yes, I recall that morning clearly. We met Madame Villiers on the way to the house and she asked for the pills. We gave them to her and then turned around and drove back."

"So, you gave her the pills in a brown paper bag and did not place them in the pillbox?"

"That is correct, Commandant."

"Thank you, Mara. That confirms the account of Madame Villiers."

He raised his hand as if to say goodbye, but instantly brought it down. "There is another matter that requires some clarity with which you may help."

"Hopefully, I can assist."

"Did Monsieur Baptise ever leave the apothecary for an extended period? Perhaps a whole day."

"Monsieur Baptiste never left his shop. It was his whole life. His only concern was to ensure that his patients received the best possible treatment. I still see him standing behind his counter, talking to customers or buried with his head in his ledger. He was always there."

"Are you absolutely certain? Did Isabella talk much about him?"

"We spoke mostly about girl's things. Not much about our families."

"Thank you both. I best be on my way."

"Wait Commandant. Yes, Isabella mentioned once, on a Monday, that her father had been away the previous day. A Sunday."

"When was that?"

"It was two Sundays passed."

The Commandant raised his head and smiled. "So that would be the last Sunday in June."

"That is correct, Commandant."

"And Isabella, did she perchance tell you where he went?"

"Yes, I remember it clearly now. Maman and Grandmère took me there occasionally to visit friends. It is a beautiful town with the most wonderful windmill in the central square. Moulin! Yes, the town is Moulin."

The commandant rose from his seat. "Well, that has been most help-ful, and I suspect may help solve a tangled mystery. That will be all for me this afternoon. I hope I have not been too much of an inconvenience."

"It has been a pleasure, and I am pleased we could help." Pierre shook Bertrand's hand. Mara stood up, nodded, and curtsied.

"Thank you again, Mara, for all the information. By the way, you are certainly flourishing. I am pleased to see the doctor is feeding you well. You appeared somewhat undernourished at the trial."

Mara blushed. "Thank you, sir. Glad to be of service."

"I will see you out, Bertrand."

Mara listened to the parting pleasantries and when she heard the door close, she collapsed in the parlour chair, shaking and staring blankly out of the window. Within minutes, Pierre sat down beside her and again wrapped her in his arms. They remained silent and attached for some long minutes before Mara broke the silence. "Pierre, I have to go and so do you. The commandant's visit confirms the net is closing around us. He now knows that I killed the soldier. He cannot keep that a secret. It is his duty to pursue it. I am also certain his parting comments about my health were not polite chatter. Possibly a warning, even at this early stage, that my, our secret is out and that soon we will get a visit from Colonel Montpellier."

"Mara, it saddens me greatly to hear you talk about leaving. But I agree we are playing with fire if you stay any longer. The baby will become more difficult to hide. But where will you go? Will you be safe and when will I see you again?"

"I will be safe if I leave tomorrow. Maman and Simon will know where to hide me until the child is born. But what will become of you? You remain at significant risk. They will accuse you of negligent supervision of a witch entrusted to your care. Or even worse, that you assisted a witches' escape."

"Mara, I have thought about this moment for some time. What would I do? Could I just let you walk away? The answer was simple. I can no longer think about my life without you being part of it. I have told you I love you, and wish to spend my life with you." A smile lit up Mara's face, and she flung her arms around his neck and kissed him. She had often agonised about this moment. Would he choose his comfortable established life or would he stay with her? Pierre gently pulled away. "I will spend a few days tidying up my affairs and then I will follow you. Just let me know where I can find you."

"Let us not talk of this any longer. Let us make the most of our last night together." Mara stood up, took him by the hand, and guided him to the bedroom.

The following morning, breakfast proceeded with the usual informality. Claudette scurried around them with coffee and food while the chatter moved from Claudette's children to the day's patient list.

Pierre pulled his watch from his waistcoat pocket. "Almost time to start. So, Mara, what are your plans for today? I assume you will go to the apothecary first, to get those medicines we talked about?"

"That is correct, Doctor, but because of Monsieur Baptiste's untimely death, his apothecary has closed. So, I will have to go to Monsieur Rousseau who is further away. He is on the main entry road almost at the city gate. Do not expect me back for a couple of hours."

"Oh yes, Monsieur Baptiste, that is unfortunate. And his lovely daughter Isabella, in the Tower. What a tragedy."

"I will see you back in the laboratory when I return." Mara got up from the table, picked up her leather satchel, opened the front door and stepped out onto the square.

As was usual, a group of young boys and girls were playing a race and tag game before going to school. Mara walked across the square towards them and they quickly gathered around her. "You look pretty today, Mademoiselle Mara. Is that a new dress? And what a pretty red flower you have in your hair. But why are you going this way? You always go that way." One boy pointed in the opposite direction.

Mara responded in a voice louder than was necessary. "Our regular apothecary is closed now, so I am going to Monsieur Rousseau by the city gate."

"I see. Well, have a good day, Mademoiselle Mara."

"Have a good day Mademoiselle Mara," the rest of the group echoed and returned to their game.

As Mara walked off the square, she noticed Monsieur Lambert, alone, emaciated, in rags and leaning in a doorway. Head down, she avoided his scowl and continued, nodding politely at ladies and gentlemen walking in the opposite direction. She stopped occasionally to look at fashions in a shop window and glanced up and down the street. There was no sign of Simon. She continued through the busy streets and initially ignored a faint background tapping against the cobbles. However, the tapping became more persistent and seeped into her consciousness. She stopped again to look in a window and caught sight of the lurching figure of Monsieur Lambert. After picking up her pace for a few streets, she stopped and looked again. He was not there. She breathed a sigh, but was just about to proceed when he appeared around a corner. Ducking into a small side street, she took a long detour, running through narrow streets and many twisting alleyways. She felt certain Simon had seen the red flower and was watching her and any moment would appear in a doorway as he had done many times before. But anxiety churned her stomach as she got closer to Monsieur Rousseau's shop and Simon failed to appear. She turned a corner onto the main entry road and could see the south gate directly in front of her. A horse and carriage stood outside the apothecary, but there was still no sign of Simon. As she reached the apothecary door, she heard the whisper she was waiting for. "Mara!" She turned to see a well-dressed man with a wide-brimmed hat low over his forehead. For Mara, the disguise was futile. She didn't hesitate and jumped in and within a second, the horse was off in a trot. She looked back; Monsieur Lambert was not there. She smiled, waited, looked again and her smile faded as the peg leg and stick appeared in the main street watching the departing carriage. Mara whispered in Simon's ear. They were soon through the gate and then immediately broke into a canter along the river, heading south. Mara again looked back and saw that no-one was following.

"Simon, you had me so worried. Why did you take so long?"

"I will always be there when you need me. You gave me the sign when you were in the square. You never need to worry."

The carriage turned left over le Pont St Joan and as they drove past Diana, four thought filled eyes reflected on what was once home.

***

After Mara had left, Pierre sat at his desk, attempting to write some notes while waiting for his first patient. Distracted, he put down his pen and stared out of the window. They had talked long into the night about the future, their future. What had started as a mutual interest in medicine had become a powerful attraction and from there had developed into an intense emotional bond. He loved her. Of that, he was certain. She had only just left, and he already missed her. She would not be back later to work beside him. To exchange ideas, to laugh together, to touch in passing, to feel her closeness or to steal a warm kiss. "Why would he wait a few days? Why am I not with her now?" he mumbled. The knock of his first patient forced him from his reverie.

With a newfound energy and sense of purpose, Pierre methodically worked through his patients during the morning. By midday they had all been treated and he closed his doors and hung a closed sign. He gathered his important belongings, did not say goodbye to Claudette, and walked out of his front door where a carriage was waiting.

"Thank you, sir. I will drive it myself and will be away for a few days." He jumped into the seat and was just about to release the brake and flick the horse when, from behind, he heard the clattering of hooves on the cobblestone square. He did not need to look around to see who they were. The reins fluttered in trembling hands and his elation and future sank as the horsemen surrounded his carriage.

Colonel Montpellier rode up beside the carriage on his white stallion. "Good day, my good doctor, and where would you be off to this afternoon?"

"Good afternoon, Colonel. I am off to see a patient in the country who is late with child and is in terrible pain. So, I would be pleased if your men could please move out of the way so that I can proceed with what is very urgent business."

The colonel ignored his request. "Is the lovely Mara in at the moment?"

"No sir, she left this morning to go to the apothecary but has as yet not returned. It is some distance, but she should be back any moment."

"That is strange, Doctor. I have reliable information that she was seen early this morning in a buggy with another man leaving the city by the south gate."

"That explains it then, Colonel. I cannot understand a recent change in her Colonel. Things were working out so well. She was helping with the patients, doing valuable research with new drugs and going on rounds with Isabella, the apothecary's daughter."

"And fucking you, Doctor?"

"Whatever could you mean, Colonel? That is a disgusting suggestion. To think I would do such a thing to a young maid entrusted to my care."

"Doctor, we have information from an unnamed source that she is with child."

"I believe this source is just passing on a malicious rumour Colonel with the hope she can obtain some favour with you. She has regained some weight since her incarceration, but this is entirely the result of the excellent food and care she receives here. This source, most likely a woman, probably just needs something to gossip about."

"Doctor, I have now heard enough of your lies and denials. You will be taken to the Tower to await trial. You will be charged on two counts. The first for letting a suspected witch under your supervision escape and second for fornicating with a suspected witch. Men take him away.

Pierre was led out of the square, hands tied in front by a rope held by Colonel Montpellier. Already a small, inquisitive crowd was gathering around the procession. At the edge of the square, he passed a smiling Monsieur Lambert who drew the edge of his open left palm across his neck.

33

A False Dawn

12 July 1670

Francine hummed a tune as she packed her remaining valuables into a large bag. She moved uneasily in her new red dress and leather shoes. A wide, collarless blouse was comfortable, but she felt constricted in the tight-fitting bodice. The shack, their home for many years, stood empty except for the kitchen table and dresser. She would leave them for the next inhabitants who would not be as fortunate as her. Her eyes moved repeatedly to a small pewter mug perched on top of the dresser. It had been there, unmoved for as long as she could remember and was beyond her reach. She had already decided to leave it. Curiosity, however, overcame apathy. She pulled the table closer, struggled to climb on in her tight-fitting clothes and reached for the mug. Something sparkled inside as it caught the light. She pulled out a silver, heart-shaped locket attached to a silver chain. On opening, it was empty but on the back was the simple inscription, *Love Charles*. "Charles? Charles?" she pondered aloud, shook her head, jumped off the table and placed the locket in the bag.

"Jacques, have you got all your things together? The carriage will soon arrive?"

Jacques opened the door and stepped inside, his wide-brimmed hat just passing through the narrow opening. "Yes, I am ready. Is it really true? Are we going to live in a fine house on le Boulevard du Printemps?"

"Yes, and with enough money not to worry about our next meal."

"Must I wear these clothes? The boys at the Temple are laughing at me?" He tugged at the tight blue jacket that fell to mid-thigh over blue, loose-fitting breeches. "And these stockings and shoes are silly."

303

"When we live up on le Boulevard, all the boys will be dressed the same. You will see."

The clatter of hooves on the cobblestones could be heard in the distance. They became louder and then softened as horses trod the dirt road.

"It is somewhat early, but that must be our carriage. Let us leave this wretched place."

Francine flung open the front door and stepped outside. Her expected future evaporated when Colonel Montpellier and four horsemen rode into the square.

"Are you the daughter of Madame Macon, the convicted witch who went to the fire?"

An outward composure disguised her tightening chest and churning stomach. "She was not a witch. She was a wonderful mother and was unjustly convicted. It was an outrage that she was burned."

Colonel Montpellier ignored her response. "Did you, some months ago, visit Monsieur Thomas Allard, a farmer some three miles from town, and attempt to remove a curse from his farm?"

"Yes, that is true. I found the curse that some person had laid on his farm and then removed it. That is not witchcraft. That is the removal of a witch's curse and should be applauded."

The presence of the horses and the guards attracted some inquisitive residents from the Temple of Miracles who crowded around the horsemen. "Hey, what is your business with this young lady and her brother? They mean no harm and just try to get by from day to day."

Colonel Montpellier turned to the voice, placed his hand on his sword, and stared with a smirk that morphed into a cynical smile. "First, this is no lady," his hand outstretched towards Francine. "Second, you boys had better tend to your own business. Another word, and I will send a contingent of thirty armed men to that distasteful establishment and close it down. We all know what goes on there. Up to now, we have turned a blind eye. But right now, I am beginning to see a little clearer."

The boys looked uneasily at each other, mumbled softly, and slowly drifted back and watched from across the road.

Colonel Montpellier turned back to Francine. "Madame Allard, Tom's wife, watched your deceit from her kitchen window. She saw you place the curse in a hole and claim that you had found it there. That is both deceitful and witchcraft. Furthermore, you were seen sticking a nail into an effigy of the archbishop as he gave his speech."

"Yes, I was at the archbishop's speech. It was an immense crowd. How could anyone have fingered me amongst all those people?"

Montpellier sat tall in his saddle, cocked his head and smiled. "You were described as a young girl with short, black hair." Francine, silenced, bowed her head and shuffled her feet as Montpellier's sneer continued to mock her. "We have known of this offence for some two weeks, but rather than make an arrest, we chose to keep you under observation. During our surveillance, we have noted, on several recent occasions, that you visited la sapphist, Madame Blanchet. Finally, you are also the daughter of a proven witch. On each of these aforesaid counts alone, you are unquestionably a suspected witch and will go to the Tower and await your trial. Men take her away."

"No! No, please sir, I have to look after my little brother. He cannot be left on his own."

"Those lads over there seem to have an interest in your welfare. Judging from their manner of dress and place of residence, I am sure they with turn him into a fine young gentleman."

Ignoring the dread that consumed her, Francine bent down and held Jacques tightly to her. "The carriage will be here soon. Take the bag which I left inside. You know where to go. We have talked about this. Go immediately. Stay there and wait for my word." She wiped a single tear off his cheek, stood up straight, and walked along the street with the horsemen forming a guard around her.

34

Retribution

12 July 1670

Monsieur August Moreau's bedraggled hair fell across slouched shoulders and over a threadbare, woollen shirt. An unkempt morass of a beard sprawled across his chest. Stained leggings gave way to mud spattered legs and filthy scabbed bare feet. However, behind the veil, bright blue eyes flicked from side to side scanning the square. Resolutely, he held the candle in his right hand while his left hung by his side. He spoke to no-one who entered the cathedral but occasionally nodded if spoken too. Outwardly he presented an empty shell of man submissively working through his sentence, but this manifest desperation belied his inner dedication and purpose. Having studied and memorised the clockwork movements of the clergy, he knew exactly when he could slip away. He had gained a thorough understanding of everything that transpired and everyone who walked within the square. He had watched Mara conscientiously go about her daily rounds and the tall blond gentleman who watched her every move from the shadows. The naked Isabella, dragged across tied behind Colonel Montpellier on his white stallion; her witches' teat for all to see. The recent capture and parading of Madame Macon's daughter did not gain as much attention. Evening did not bring inactivity, as the drunks, ladies of the night and the body snatchers emerged for their business.

His most puzzling observations were those of Colonel Montpellier. For the last two Friday evenings, as the cathedral bells tolled seven, he had swaggered across the square. Not in his sparkling uniform on his white stallion, but walking in the attire of an ordinary gentleman. Intrigued, Monsieur Moreau had on both occasions followed him down a street off the square and into a side alley, where he knocked softly on a red door. Through a narrow opening, as she let him in, Monsieur Moreau recognised her. Mademoiselle Giselle Lafonte had recently become a regular attendee at church on a Sunday morning, but also practiced with the choir on a Thursday evening. Moreau's sentence prohibited all conversation except with the clergy. By asking a few covert questions, Bishop Bernard had been happy to disclose that Mademoiselle Lafonte was an unmarried woman under suspicion as a witch. Although the evidence was nominal, the bishop was confident that she would soon be incarcerated and sent to the fire.

The devil's plan was bold and needed to be executed with stealth and precision or he would find himself in the Tower. He chose his time well. As usual, on this Thursday evening, Mademoiselle Lafonte crossed the square. She nimbly climbed the stone steps and made her way to the cathedral door. Moreau waited till she was directly opposite and with eyes fixed forward, he whispered, "Good evening, Mademoiselle Lafonte."

She stalled and glanced across at the sad soul. "How could you possibly know me? How dare you speak to me? Everyone knows who you are. You are the devil."

"I know everything and everybody that passes this church. I know also that Colonel Montpellier visits you every Friday evening at seven."

She froze, open-mouthed, momentarily silenced, with eyes fixed directly forward into the church. "Please do not speak of this. I do not wish to see that pig, but if I refuse, he will find reason to send me to the Tower and extract a confession."

"Calm yourself Mademoiselle, there are people who wish him gone and you can be of help."

"How?"

"On Friday, tomorrow evening, when you let him in, do not lock the door. I will see to the rest. Now go inside. You have stood here long enough and there are others approaching from across the square."

It was the usual daily observance that all the clergy had their evening dinner together at six and thereafter retired to a central study to discuss the weeks' events. On Friday, this usually included planning for Sunday mass. During these times, Moreau could slip away unnoticed to prepare for his planned mission. It was essential that he return by nine when one cleric returned to close the cathedral.

Punctually, on Friday evening, Colonel Montpellier walked briskly across the square. On this occasion, his usually serious visage was replaced with a wide smile, and he tipped his hat to greet the evening strollers.

"Probably been a successful witch hunting day," Monsieur Moreau mused through his beard.

Just before he reached the edge of the square, Colonel Montpellier stalled, as he usually did, turned and scanned the square. Appearing satisfied with his surveillance, he turned and disappeared down a side street.

"The only person watching you is me," mumbled Moreau. He waited ten minutes, feeling the cold blade against his thigh inside his ragged woollen trousers. And then, with a quick look back into the cathedral, vacated his position. He hurried down the steps, across the square and into the side street until he came to the house with the red door. It swung open with a gentle push and he entered; his bare feet silent on a stone floor. He found himself in a small atrium with a kitchen and sitting room to his left and a narrow staircase to the right.

He heard voices above and softly climbed towards them. On the landing were two doors; one closed and the other slightly ajar. Through the gap, he heard an authentic theatrical performance by Mademoiselle Lafonte. He removed the blade from the inside pocket and gripped it in his right hand. He pushed the door gently to view the colonel's bare, white, bobbing buttocks. The wide eyes of Mademoiselle Lafonte stared directly at him over the colonel's shoulder.

He moved slowly forward, blade in hand, waiting for the moment. Then, as Montpellier groaned and released, Moreau jumped onto him and jammed the knife twice, deep into his back. A mixed cacophony of pain, orgasm, and disbelief erupted from deep within Montpellier. He turned to face his adversary. Moreau was waiting and drove the bloodied blade to the hilt, up and under his bottom rib and into his heart. The colonel stared open-mouthed at his attacker and, with one last effort, grabbed the devil around his throat. But as the blood pumped from his body, his grip weakened and he collapsed on top of Mademoiselle Lafonte.

"It is done. Quick, a blanket to wrap him in and some cloth to insert into the wounds to stem the flow of blood. We must not leave any evidence."

She threw on a night robe and did as instructed. Together they worked swiftly and soon pulled him off the bed, onto the blankets, and tightly wrapped the body. Moreau rifled through his pockets and found some coins and a set of keys. He passed the coins to Mademoiselle Lafonte and placed the keys in the pocket inside his woollen trousers.

A sharp whistle broke their busy silence, and Moreau moved to the window and peered through the curtains. "They are here already; they will be up in a minute. Let us finish."

Within a few minutes, Moreau heard the whisper of two men on the staircase. He greeted them when they appeared at the door. "Good evening, Michael. Glad to see you are on time."

"Always on time for a fresh body." Michael held out his hand.

Moreau pulled a silver ecu from his pocket and handed it to Michael. "A good night's work for you. Double the pay for a single body."

"This is perilous business, and you will find no one as efficient or as discreet. I know also that those rags you wear a not a reflection of your true wealth."

"Alright, alright. He is naked. We have put all his clothes in this sack. Throw it in the kiln at the stable on your way to the university. And do not forget, he is well known and easily recognised. Do something about that before you hand him over to Professor Dubois. Not even he will take a chance with this one."

"No problem, the good professor will pay just as much for a body without a head."

Moreau, Michael, and William carried the wrapped body down the stairs, stopped briefly at the door, and looked up and down the empty street.

"Let's go."

At the corner of the street, a shadow waited silently in the darkness with a horse and cart. They bundled the colonel's body into the tray and the body snatchers jumped on. "I have not had the pleasure of doing business with a devil before," whispered Michael as he tipped his cap. "You seem pretty good with that knife. We could make a good team and rid this town of a few more scoundrels."

"Thank you for the offer, but I must decline. Do not forget to burn those clothes and discard the head where it can never be found."

"Do not concern yourself. Hiding heads is all part of the service we offer." Michael gently flicked the reins, and the cart rumbled slowly into the darkness.

On his return, Moreau found Mademoiselle Lafonte slumped in the kitchen chair with her head buried in her hands

"What is wrong now? You wanted him gone, and that is done."

"Yes, but what if someone saw him here? What if we are exposed?"

"Nothing will happen, as long as you do all I ask of you. Be sure that everything here is spotless. Check everywhere for traces of blood and clean them. Keep nothing that belongs to him. Someone may come forward and say they noticed the colonel visited here regularly on a Friday. Do not lie about that. Your response should be that he used to come on Fridays to check on you, but failed to arrive this Friday. I will give you some further advice. You are a suspected witch and these miscreants are trying hard to get their quotas up. It will not be long before you are in the

Tower and they extract a confession from you. Get away from here. Visit a relative far away."

"Thank you, thank you. Yes, I will. You are most kind, thank you."

Moreau crept stealthily, staying in shadows of the dimly lit streets and around the periphery of the square. He reached the front of the church, picked up his candle and stood resolute with eyes fixed forward. The church was silent, the square empty, the task complete. He smiled through the veil of hair. One of their greatest enemies had been silenced. An hour passed and Moreau heard the bishop enter the church and perform his evening prayers; he waited patiently for the incantations to cease. Then, as was his practice, he entered the church and approached Bishop Bernard. "Good evening, my Lord. Is there anything else I can do for you tonight before I close up?"

"No, that will be all. Just close the front door and I will let myself into the cloister."

"Good night, sir."

The bishop turned towards the cloister but stopped and turned back. "By the way, August, we had some discussions concerning you this evening. You have behaved admirably during your terrible ordeal and we are considering significantly shortening your servitude here. The substantial additional donations you have made as penance have certainly been considered."

"That is very generous, my Lord. I have learnt much about servitude and forgiveness during my time here, but an early release is something I certainly had not expected."

"Good night, August."

"Good night my Lord."

The night air felt fresher, and the chill did not bother Moreau as he took the church steps two at a time and almost skipped across the square.

The death of the colonel and now the news of an early release gave him hope and a future. He did not go directly to his straw bed in the cloister stable, but turned towards the Tower. The keys jangled in his pocket as he pranced over the cobblestones. The Tower loomed ahead; usually a symbol of pain, dread and persecution, but tonight it held no fear. He reached the external door and pulled the colonel's keys from his pocket. Methodically, he tried each in the lock and sighed with relief as the third key fitted. He felt the latch lift and the door open. A dimly lit spiral staircase wound endlessly upwards through the landings. From his time in the Tower, he knew that there were seldom guards about at this late hour. Two steps at a time, he moved silently, quickly, stopping briefly at each landing and surveying the corridors that led off deep into the darkness. Reaching the third floor, he again tried the keys on a heavy wooden door. On the second attempt, the latch lifted, and he pushed it open. Celeste sat on her cot and Francine on a small chair in the corner. Two open mouths and four sunken eyes focused on the devil.

"Oh August, I thought you had forgotten me!" Celeste jumped up and threw her arms around him.

"What is she doing here? I was not expecting two," replied August.

"This is Francine Macon. You may know her mother, who was at the same trial as you?"

"Yes, I remember, but this is unexpected. I expected only you."

"I asked the colonel if I could have some company. She is due for her first visit to the rack in the morning. If they find her here with me gone, I fear it will not go well for her. She must come with me tonight."

"Celeste, I do not know how you can trust this fiend." Francine interrupted. "I was at his trial where he escaped the fire by providing a list of twenty-one suspected witches."

Celeste, silent, mouth open, turned to the devil. Moreau stroked his beard and looked at Francine. "What Francine says is true, and her hatred of me is to be expected. But what she does not know is that each one of those twenty-one souls was drowned in the river or killed in the Glen that fateful morning and their bodies burnt beyond recognition. I have heard that Colonel Montpellier has wasted much time tracing those names. I can also add that the Colonel is now dead."

Francine bowed her head, averting the devil's gaze as a stunned silence filled the cell before Celeste spoke. "Does that mean we are safe and escape is unnecessary?"

"No. Montpellier was only the hatchet man. His minders in Paris will soon send someone else. But quick, it is time to go. I suppose, in a way, Francine is one of us. We must depart before the guards come on their rounds."

They put their few belongings in a small hemp bag, which Celeste threw over her shoulder. Silent but vigilant, they descended the three flights of stairs. Once outside, Moreau locked the door behind him.

"Quick! Follow me, and not a sound."

They followed a rutted path through long grass in the shadow of the Tower until they reached a rough track that led towards la Loire. Moreau stopped near a tree on a low ridge overlooking the river. "This is as far as I go. From here, you are on your own. You will find a small boat down by the quay. There is enough light with this half-moon for you to find it. Just push it off with the oar and the current will take you downstream. Get off on the left bank before the bridge. The current is too strong under the bridge and you may be noticed as you pass Laughing Waters. Walk in the shadows of the forest. Beyond the bridge, you will come to a small sandy beach. Wait there. An old man with a long, white beard and a horse and cart will find you. He will take you to a safe house where you will wait until it is safe to venture further. You will be his granddaughters."

"What about my brother?"

"I hear he is in the trustworthy hands of Commandant Duval. I will arrange for Jacques to meet you at the safe house within a few days. Now go!"

Moreau remained in the darkness and watched till the boat departed the quay and glided silently across the water in a beam of moonlight. He took the knife and keys from his pocket and looked around. Satisfied that he was not being observed, he first threw the knife and then the keys into the middle of the river. When the ripples reached the bank, he turned back towards the cloister.

35

Justice

16 July 1670

Duval eased the carriage to a canter through the city gate and then to a trot as he negotiated the cobbles towards the main square. Relieved, he turned to a wide-eyed, older gentleman sitting beside him, bouncing in his seat and holding his hat. Simon sat silently crouched behind them. "Finally, we have arrived, gentlemen. I hope it was not too uncomfortable, Francois?"

"It certainly has not been my most pleasant trip. But I understand the need for haste. I may seek an alternate mode of transport for the return to Moulin. Will we be on time?"

Duval pulled out his pocket watch. "According to my timepiece, the trial has just started." He pulled the carriage up beside a crowd jostling outside the courthouse. The three men elbowed their way through the clamour and obscenities till they reached the door where they were stopped by a guard. "I am Commandant Duval, and these gentlemen are critical witnesses for the trial taking place inside." The guard checked the names against a scroll in his hand, nodded, and they made their way into the chamber to three vacant seats in the front pew.

The formalities, already complete, Bishop Bernard stood upright on the podium with the river of fire and the waiting devil and leviathan towering menacingly above him. Judge Deschamps sat quietly beside him, studying a manuscript.

"We were to put on trial five suspects here today. But three have slipped through our net. The young Celeste who fornicated with the Devil some months ago, and held in the Tower, has disappeared without a trace. Francine Macon, who we only recently apprehended, has also escaped the

Tower. She is the daughter of the proven witch, Maxine Macon. Finally, Mara Mandeville, who has been impregnated by her court approved guardian, Doctor Laurent, has also escaped. Let it further be known that Colonel Montpellier, the illustrious leader of our Maréchausée and relentless witch hunter, has also disappeared. I suspect that he may have met his fate at the hands of these three escapees."

An initial whisper, "Montpellier dead?" starting in the top corner, soon spread and consumed the whole chamber. "Montpellier dead?"

"Celeste? Fucked by the Devil?"

"Mara, impregnated by Doctor Laurent?"

"Francine Macon?"

"Find them! They should all burn in hell!"

"Silence, please silence!" Bishop Bernard waited for the uproar to settle. "So unfortunately, today we have only two suspects and they have such indisputable guilt that I doubt today's proceedings will take much time. Let the prisoner Isabella Baptiste come forward."

There was some patter on the steps and the gold rimmed, black tricorn appeared followed by a hooded figure peering through cut out holes. Long, bedraggled, red hair fell from under the hood onto pale, freckled shoulders. Continuing the ascent, small firm breasts, flat stomach, a red crotch and pale thin legs arose. She reached the top of the stairs and stepped to one side. The guard removed the hood and Isabella's startled, tear-filled eyes scanned the rear galleries who immediately shielded their faces. Bishop Bernard and the magistrate crossed themselves and clutched their Angus Dei. The whole assembly then followed the bishop through the seven words of Jesus on the cross. Descending the stairs, the bishop consecrated the holy water, poured it into a silver goblet, and stepped back. "Mademoiselle Isabella Baptiste, you may now turn and face this shielded servant of God."

Isabella turned slowly, trembling with head bowed, avoiding the chamber's leering eyes.

The audience in the side galleries buzzed.

"Look, look, she has the teat."

"There can be no doubt."

"Do not look at her. Her power must be immense."

The bishop was about to silence the crowd when Simon rose to his full height and shouted above the babel. "Silence! Silence! Have you no shame? Can you not see the fear, the embarrassment in this young girl's eyes? The next person who makes a filthy comment about this girl will have to deal with me outside this courtroom. I will find you!"

The crowd fell silent. Simon had lived his whole life around St Raphael. His reputation was established. He was not one to argue with.

The bishop stood; stunned and quizzical. "Well, well, it appears we have a defender of witches in our midst. Perhaps you would care to introduce yourself, sir?"

Simon, still standing, pushed out his chest and spoke resolutely. "I am Simon, Simon Baptiste, the brother of the apothecary, Raphael Baptiste, and the uncle of Isabella."

A curious low drone spread through the chamber.

"The apothecary has family?"

"An uncle of a witch."

"Is he part of this witch treachery?"

The bishop stood patiently, waiting for the banter to subside. "This is interesting. I was not aware there were other members of the Baptiste family in this city. Let me remind you Monsieur Baptiste, this is a witch trial and I would ask you to refrain from speaking unless you have something meaningful to contribute."

A large, unkempt, black-haired man rose from the back row. "I am Michael Baptiste and am also a brother of Raphael. Another word about my niece Isabella and I will find you and ensure that you never open your foul mouths again." Many had heard rumours about how Michael earned a living. The chamber was silent.

The bishop, intrigued by the support for the accused, turned to the magistrate on the podium. "It is interesting that both these men have now only declared their allegiance to this witch. I do wonder why it has been such a secret? Perhaps we will need to question these men when this trial is over. Could you please write these two names in my ledger?" He turned back to face Isabella. "Let us continue with the proceedings. Mademoiselle Baptiste, you have not eaten or drunk for two days. This holy water will quickly enter your body and allow an easy confession. Please drink."

Isabella grabbed the goblet in two shaking hands and, without taking a breath, drained the holy water.

"Isabella Baptiste, you stand here today charged with being a witch. How do you plead?"

"I am not a witch, my Lord. I am an ordinary girl, wrongly charged."

"It is absolutely clear to all of you here today that this young girl bears the witches' mark. Is there anyone else in this room who has any doubt that she is a witch?"

A rumbling spread through the crowd as the bishop returned to the podium. All heads looked to the ground and no-one ventured a comment as Simon and Michael scoured the galleries.

"Is there a learned man amongst you who would wish to question this?"

Commandant Duval rose in his seat. "Sir, I wish to call the esteemed Professor Stefan Dubois. He is a highly respected man of medicine and his opinion on this matter should be heeded."

The grey bearded Professor Dubois rose to his full, imposing height from one of the middle pews on the opposite side of the chamber. "Your honour, I am here to comment on what we in the profession call accessory nipples. We have known about these for centuries and they occur in at least one in every hundred women. I am sure that considering the size of this city, there are many more innocent women with an extra nipple walking along our streets."

"Thank you, Professor. That is extremely interesting. To be made aware that these witches are roaming our streets in such numbers has only fortified my resolve. It is no wonder we cannot expunge this curse. We must double our efforts, examine every woman if we have to, until we rid this scourge from our lands. Your words professor in no way absolves this girl of her witchcraft. The Malleus Maleficarum clearly shows that such marks identify a witch. You may sit down."

Without sitting down, Bishop Bernard conferred briefly with Judge Deschamps and made some notes in his ledger.

"Not only does this witch bear the teat, she also stands accused of murder. Commandant, I note your tardiness this morning, but am pleased you have given us the pleasure of your company. This is your investigation. Please outline the case against Isabella for the charge of murder."

"Thank you, sir. In brief, there is no case for murder but only one of self-defence. This will become apparent when Isabella describes the events of that day to this court. Please proceed Isabella."

Standing naked in the middle of the courtroom, Isabella hesitated at first, but fixed on Simon's bright blue eyes. With a trembling voice, she outlined that fateful day's events; beginning with the deliveries of medicines, the heat and the detour down to the river. How Mara walked off, followed by the soldier's attack. "He was a big powerful man and held me tightly by both arms and forced me down to the ground. He ripped at my dress and my underclothes and also pulled his breeches down around his ankles. I screamed and screamed, but that did not stop him. He was about to put his thing in me when he howled and blood spattered all over my face and body. He fell off me and then I saw Mara hit him over the head. Again, and again, she struck him, until he lay motionless on the ground."

"What did you do then?"

"Together we pulled his body into the river, filled his tunic with stones until he sank."

"Why did you not report this incident?"

"He was a soldier of la Maréchausée and we did not think we would be treated fairly."

"Isabella, what were you wearing that day?"

"A yellow dress, sir."

Commandant Duval reached inside his leather case and pulled out a torn, partially blackened yellow garment. "Is this the remains of your dress?"

"Yes, sir."

He faced the judges and then looked up at the audience. "This blackened and torn yellow dress I found in the fireplace at the apothecary on the morning after Monsieur Baptiste's suicide. He was attempting to hide the connection between Isabella and the soldier's death. The identical fabric was found in the clenched fist of the dead man." He held up the piece of fabric and laid it on top of the remnants of the dress. "This torn garment confirms the story of her struggle with the guard and proves her self-defence. Furthermore, I have spoken to witnesses, some from his own regiment, who will testify that this guard was found with his trousers around his ankles. This all corroborates Isabella's version of events."

The bishop stood red faced. "You are very presumptuous, Commandant. She clearly has a part to play in this death. By declaring her innocent, you destroy the reputation of a member of la Maréchausée by accusing him of rape. And to add insult, you have accused him of fornicating with a witch. Is that the legacy you wish to leave this young man and his family?"

"The evidence speaks for itself, my Lord. It is not my task to shield la Maréchausée from this heinous crime. A crime that was corroborated by her friend Mara before she unfortunately disappeared."

"Yes, yes Mara, another witch of whom we shall hear more of later. And you expect me and this court to believe a tale told by these two witches?"

Bishop Bernard turned and sat down to confer with Judge Deschamps. Their conversation was whispered, although animated. The bishop's face reddened, and he threw both hands in the air while the judge shook his head. In the hiatus, the assembly grew impatient and a restless murmuring spread through the galleries. Finally, the secular judge stood and held out his arms to silence the court.

"On the count of being a witch. There is no argument concerning the witches' teat. The presence of Satan's mark is a well-established confirmation that the bearer is a witch. The Malleus Maleficarum, used as our guide for witchcraft for centuries, confirms this as absolute proof. However, on the second count of murder, both girls acted in self-defence against a soldier who committed a crime unbefitting his station. The prisoner's fate will be decided at the end of the trial. She can return to her cell."

Commandant Duval rose again and raised his hand. "Your honour, if it pleases you, I wish to call her as a witness on another case and request that she remain in the courtroom?"

"This is a very unusual request, Commandant, but I see no harm. Please give her something to wear. Bring up the next prisoner."

Footsteps in the stairwell silenced the chamber. Pierre's head appeared; his hair ruffled and his usually well-trimmed moustache in need of attention. His now rumpled clothes were the same as he wore on the day of his arrest.

Bishop Bernard continued proceedings with his customary aggression, unperturbed by the dismissal of the murder charges. "Doctor Laurent, you are accused of fornicating with the suspected witch, Mara Mandeville, and have implanted a child in her womb. How do you plead?"

"Yes. I am guilty of laying with the young Mara, but she is not a witch and therefore I cannot be guilty."

"The case against Mara as a witch is significant and was conclusively dealt with in her previous trial. She was placed in your custody because you convinced the court that there was some benefit in her medications. In order that we follow appropriate protocol, I will remind the court of the case against Mara. Her mother and grandmother, who are both in hiding, are both witches and hence the child of a witch can be tainted. She is born out of wedlock, a common practice among Satan's servants. Evidence heard today shows that she has formed a strong relationship with a proven witch, Isabella Baptiste. I would now also add that the strength she has shown to beat a powerful guardsman to death could only be possible by someone of such small stature, if she were Lucifer's handmaiden. If we could find her now, I have absolutely no doubt that a trial would prove her a witch and she would go straight to the fire. So strong is the case against her. You, our fine doctor, have admitted fornicating with this devil's harlot, who was entrusted to your care."

Pierre glanced first at Simon and then focussed on those on the podium who determined his future. "Sir, she was entrusted to my care. A more intelligent, thoughtful and kind person I have yet to meet. I fell in love with her and she with me. I had hoped to spend the rest of my life with her. I have nothing further to say, my Lord, and I throw myself at your mercy." He glanced back at Simon, who nodded.

Bishop Bernard sat down and conferred softly with Judge Deschamps as all eyes in the Day of Judgement looked down threateningly at Pierre. Both heads nodded in unison, and Judge Deschamps stood to announce the verdict. "Doctor Pierre Laurent, you have been found to have consorted with and given a child to a suspected witch. There are absolutely no extenuating circumstances that can absolve you of such a heinous crime. This is unfortunate. I have heard that you and Mara Mandeville have made good progress with new medicines in your rooms. I also remain extremely grateful for the continued supply of the plant powder; it has been life changing. Now please sit down and await your sentence."

The bishop rose. "Gentleman, at this stage our other three accused cannot be found, but I can assure you we will hunt them down and bring them to justice. For today, therefore, our proceedings are complete. We will confer for a few more minutes and return with the sentencing."

Commandant Duval rose from his seat. "Judge Deschamps, if it pleases the court, I would like to bring another case to this court."

"This is unusual practice, Commandant. Is it a case of witchcraft?"

"No, your honour. Not directly, but it may clarify some witchcraft convictions. I understand that this is an open court and any significant issue can be brought if there is sufficient evidence."

"What is the charge you wish to bring?"

"Murder and incitement to murder, your honour."

Whispers trickled down from the top galleries and quickly reached a crescendo as the incredulity spread throughout the hall of justice.

"Silence! Silence! Well, this is unusual, but as you are a respected man of the law in this city, I will assume you bring with you sufficient evidence with which to present your case. Please call out the accused."

"I call Bishop Bernard to the stand to answer to the crimes of murder, blackmail, and incitement to murder!"

The crowd, initially dumbstruck, erupted in a torrent of dissent. They rose in their seats, screaming abuse and banging their fists against the wooden benches.

"Impossible!"

"Outrageous!"

"How can you humiliate this man of God?"

"Stop this at once!"

"The Commandant is Satan's messenger!"

The bishop jumped from his chair wide-eyed, red-faced and hands outstretched to calm the upheaval. "Commandant, both this jury," he stretched one hand across the assembly, "and I believe this is ridiculous and totally against all protocol. I advise you to put an end to this immediately. If you apologise now in front of all gathered here, I promise I will be lenient."

Judge Deschamps had remained standing. "Bishop Bernard is correct. This is against all protocol and you should be very wary of anything further you wish to say. However, as you have brought the case, I will confer with you briefly, privately. Doing so, I can assure the public gathered here that these accusations carry no substance and your rumour will not blacken Bishop Bernard's good name." He hurried down the steps, breathing easily, and conferred in whispers with Duval for some minutes. Judge Deschamps rubbed his chin, occasionally asked a question, perused a single sheaf of paper and then nodded. He comfortably climbed the steps again. "I have heard some disturbing information from the Commandant and believe that this material should be tested in a court of law."

"But your honour, I am shortly to be the Archbishop of Paris. This is extremely embarrassing and totally unwarranted. This must stop now! What gives this man the authority to question an archbishop?"

Duval held up a piece of paper and addressed the podium. "I will answer the bishop's concerns about my authority. In the absence of Colonel Montpellier, I have assumed command of la Maréchausée in St Raphael. In this position, I am honoured to have direct contact with King Louis."

Absolute silence fell on the galleries and the judges sat open-mouthed on the podium, looking down at the king's entrusted servant.

Duval continued. "I had expected this response from Bishop Bernard, so I wrote directly to King Louis, outlining the charges against the soon to be Archbishop of Paris. I despatched this with overnight horsemen and the response from his Majesty arrived yesterday." He walked across to the podium and handed the paper to Judge Deschamps.

The judge quickly scanned the letter and passed it to Bishop Bernard. Judge Deschamps stood up and addressed the court. "This letter bears the royal seal and clearly gives Commandant Duval the authority to question Bishop Bernard before an appropriately appointed court. The accusations are grave and we must test the evidence. But make it short. If the evidence is weak, I will stop immediately. I have no particular wish to embarrass my esteemed colleague." He turned to Bishop Bernard, who sat red faced staring at his sovereign's seal. "Sir, it would be best if you were to sit below next to the other accused. So that there is impartiality, I would ask if the most qualified of the clerics come up here and take Bishop Bernard's seat as the representative of the church."

The six seminarians in the front row all turned as one to a dark young man who immediately stood, chest out, to full height. "Sir, I am Father Dominic and I am the most qualified of my colleagues. I have recently been ordained, and Bishop Bernard has taught me everything about the proceedings of a witch trial."

Judge Deschamps look down at the dejected bishop, who nodded his approval.

"Thank you, Father Dominic. I appreciate that these are difficult circumstances, but your unplanned assistance is greatly appreciated. Please come and take a seat next to me. Please continue Commandant."

"Thank you, your honour. Many of you recall that over the last eight weeks Monsieur Hugo Duplessis, Monsieur Claude Villiers and the Archbishop of Paris have died under strange and unexplained circumstances. You would also know that both witches and wives have been sent to the Tower and fire for these crimes. However, I believe I now have the evidence that will reveal the actual killer." He held up a letter. "This letter is from Monsieur Raphael Baptiste, our apothecary, who you are aware recently took his own life. In his own hand, he clearly states that he was responsible for these deaths and achieved this by providing pills to these gentlemen which contained an unknown poison. Although he is guilty of these atrocities, I will show that he committed these murders because Bishop Bernard threatened to expose his daughter Isabella as a witch. I will read his suicide note in its entirety.

'My Dearest Isabella.

There is a secret I have been hiding from you for many years. I think you may remember the priest who molested you on a few occasions when you were much younger. I so hoped these memories would be extinguished with time. At the time, I spoke to the priest and told him to leave you alone.

He did, I think, mainly because his interest moved to young boys. However, he said that I would forever be in his debt. I would have to do him a small favour from time to time, otherwise he would expose you as a witch because of that remarkable extra nipple. I have done some bad things at his request, including poisoning three people. Although you have delivered the pills, you did not know what they contained. However, he recently requested a fourth victim, a Monsieur Thomas. I could no longer live with the guilt and that my actions would taint me and my family. I could no longer go through with it.'" Duval paused, eyed the bishop and continued.

"'I have thought this through carefully and believe the best way forward is to leave this world. With me gone, he can no longer use me to do his dirty work and I doubt he will bother you, as you are no use to him with me gone. Please do not destroy this letter, keep it and, if needed, give it to Commandant Duval, as it will exonerate you from any involvement in my crimes. He is currently asking questions, and I fear I will soon be exposed. I suggest you pack a small bag and visit my brother Michael or Simon Baptiste. You do not know of this family, as we decided many years ago, that our connections should be kept a secret. Both will stand by you and care for you.'" Duval nodded in turn to the brothers.

"'Isabella, I love you more than words can say, and truly believe this is the only way to protect you. Be strong. You are a beautiful and intelligent young woman. Never, ever doubt your own strength and ability.

Goodbye, Papa.'"

Duval turned his head to the silent, intrigued audience. "You note he refers to his brothers Simon and Michael, who you have seen earlier. Simon, could you please stand and read the letter you received from your brother five years ago?"

Simon rose and was about to address the crowd when Father Dominic asked, "For the record, could you please state your full name and place of residence?"

"I am Simon Baptiste, and I have lived and worked as a farmer on my family property since I was a young boy. Maison Diana is situated just on the eastern side of Pont St Joan." He paused and when the judge nodded, he read the note. "'Dear Simon, my dear Isabella has been molested by Bishop Bernard. When I confronted him, he promised to stop but said that she bore the witches' teat and would expose her if I did not do as he asked. Please store this letter in a safe place.'"

"Thank you, Simon. Please sit down. His brother Michael has an identical letter, also given to him five years ago. I submit the suicide note and both letters as evidence before the court."

The young priest spoke again. "Could you Michael please state your full name, place of residence and employment?"

"Certainly, sir. I am Michael Baptiste. I am a dealer of legal bodies and reside at 20 Rue du Chien."

Both judges studied each letter, verifying signatures and dates. Both nodded and Judge Deschamps addressed the court. "Yes, it would seem that three letters held by three different people are conclusive. However, is it not possible that these three brothers formed a family pact and conspired five years ago with the ultimate aim of bringing down an innocent man of God?"

"I did give that some thought, but I have been able to find one more piece of the puzzle that confirms the blackmail of the bishop."

"Please proceed!"

"At the suicide scene, I found this." Duval pulled a small silver container from his satchel and held it up for the assembly to see. "It was in the bottom drawer, in the room of Monsieur Baptiste. It bears the inscription Anna, which I have discovered was the name of his departed wife." While holding it up for the audience, he undid the clasp, opened the lid and slowly turned around, displaying a key inside. He took out the key and held it up. "This key did not fit any of the apothecary doors or any of the cupboards or drawers in the shop. A most intriguing puzzle? However, as

I methodically worked through the apothecary's account book, I noticed a monthly amount paid to a Monsieur Leroy in Moulin. Most of you know that this is a small town, not more than two leagues from St Raphael. I visited this town yesterday afternoon and found that Monsieur Leroy is a goldsmith." Duval paused, swept the galleries, and let the word permeate.

"A goldsmith?"

"Why would an apothecary pay a goldsmith?"

"All the way in Moulin?"

"Silence! Please Commandant, no more theatrics. Get on with it."

"Monsieur Baptiste was a simple man, not interested in gold or trinkets. Why would he pay a monthly fee to a goldsmith? To answer this question, I have brought this goldsmith here with me today. Please stand Monsieur Leroy." The goldsmith rose to a mumbling chamber. "You may not be aware, my Lord but a goldsmith will keep valuables for paying customers in their gold vaults for safekeeping. As it happens, this key, from a small jewellery box, kept in the bottom drawer in Monsieur Baptiste's bedroom, fitted another small box in the vault of this goldsmith, in a town some two leagues away. Monsieur Leroy, would you elaborate on your dealings with our apothecary?"

"Gladly sir. Monsieur Baptiste came to me about six years ago, requesting that I store such a box. I observed he placed a single piece of paper in the box, locked it and placed the key in his pocket. I placed the box in my vault. He visits me occasionally, about every six months. I do however, receive his monthly payments by means of a courier."

"Well, I am certain the judges and this court find this all rather intriguing. But pray, what does the note say?" asked Duval.

"I will read it to the court. 'Monsieur Baptiste, I have certain knowledge of your daughter, which will remain a secret between you and me. However, I may, from time to time, need your valuable and expert apothecary services.

Bishop Bernard.'"

Judge Deschamps spoke from the podium. "Well! It would certainly appear that all the evidence points to the certain conclusion that the bishop has been involved in serious blackmail, resulting in the death of three innocent men at the hand of the apothecary. But there is no evidence that he was directly involved in the crimes. Bishop Bernard, what have you to say on this matter?"

"My dear sir, and to all you gathered here today, what you have heard is complete nonsense. This is all pure fabrication, and I have heard absolutely no reason why I would want three people dead. What would be my motive for committing these heinous crimes?"

"If it is a motive that Bishop Bernard requires, I would be happy to provide that in each case, my Lord?"

"Please proceed Commandant."

"In the case of Monsieur Duplessis. You lent him money, but unfortunately, he fell further into debt. When he asked for a further loan, you refused. The agreement of the loan stipulated that should he die prior to the loan being repaid, you would receive the surety as stated in the agreement. Sir, would you tell the court what that surety was?"

"Yes, yes, of course. I had to ensure that if some misfortune befell him, the church would not be left with his debt."

"The surety, Bishop Bernard?"

"The title to all his lands"

"The title to all his lands!" Duval paused, challenging the audience. "Would anyone here wish to guess the value of this surety?"

The mumbling again started and grew until the judge shouted from the podium. "Please, Commandant! This is the last time. No more theatrics. Please get on with it."

"This surety is worth fifty times the value of the original loan. Yes, it is hard to believe, but fifty times! Certainly, it was stupidity that Monsieur Duplessis would sign such a surety. But are you aware that upon his death he left his wife a beggar? She wandered the streets in her rags before also being convicted of poisoning her own husband, accused of witchcraft and sent to the fire. The church now owns these properties and uses them as respite and a venue for festivities for their priests. We may hear more of this later."

"But Commandant, the good bishop made it clear in the surety of his intentions and it was signed in good faith."

Duval looked up at the galleries, watching the questioning, nodding heads, and smiled. "Yes, my Lord, but the bishop asked for motive. If the good bishop had a hand in this man's death, then he certainly had an excellent motive. Not so?"

"Yes, yes, this is true. Please continue."

"In the case of Monsieur Villiers, you and he arranged evenings together with other like-minded men. And it is at these evenings that you molested young boys, some as young as ten."

The audience erupted.

"Evenings together?"

"Molested young boys?"

"Commandant, you go too far."

"This is not possible. It cannot be true!"

Amongst the pandemonium, Bishop Bernard sat, mouth open, red-faced and shouted to the judge high on the podium, "This is preposterous and insulting to a man of my position! Please, you must put an end to this ridiculous nonsense."

"I agree that this has the ring of malicious rumour and I certainly hope that you have good evidence, Commandant. If not, you must cease immediately."

"I do indeed, my Lord and will provide proof of these molestation charges later. What has been asked for is motive. Monsieur Villiers threatened to expose Bishop Bernard of molestation of minors unless he assisted him with some financial difficulties. This would be ample motive if the molestation charges could be proved."

"Yes, Commandant, but at this point, you have made some serious assumptions. I await your proof, but please continue."

"I will turn to the case of the Archbishop of Paris. Prior to his public speech, he made an announcement to the bishop and other clergy, some of whom have provided written statements which I hand over to the court." Duval turned and eyeballed the bishop. "The archbishop indicated that because of your inability to control the witch problem, you would never be elevated above your current position. This would mean the end to your dream of attaining your archbishop's status. Therefore, you could not allow him to return to Paris with such an order."

"Please sir, this is absolute fantasy made up in the mind of a simple officer attempting to rise above his rank. Clearly, he is trying to make a name for himself."

"Sit down Bishop Bernard. There is ample evidence here to convict you. There is more evidence here than there has been against the witches that you have sent to the fire. Please do not interrupt the proceedings again! Now Commandant, you must return and provide proof of these child molestation accusations."

"My Lord, there are two young boys who I can call to this court to testify that at different times, this bishop molested them. However, for such boys to be recognised and recount these lurid details in this open court would be an extreme embarrassment and taint them for the rest of their lives in this city."

"Clearly, sir, this information is vital. How do you suggest we deal with this?"

"Thank you, sir, for obliging. Both the boys will be most grateful. Both have unnamed, handwritten statements which I hand to you. In there are the full descriptions of the events. More importantly, both have independently identified a specific mark on the accused. It is a large birthmark on his right buttock. I suggest that if you wish to verify these boy's observations, we ask the bishop to disrobe here in front of this court."

"But, sir, this is a bishop, a man of God. How can we ask him to disrobe in public?"

"My Lord, how can a man who has perpetrated these heinous crimes be considered a man of God? You have today paraded this poor girl naked before this court, and plenty of others before."

"Yes, yes. Guards! Pull up this man's frock and show the court his right buttock."

Bishop Bernard jumped to his feet, red faced, legs apart and arms raised, ready to resist embarrassment and his attackers. Two guards initially approached head on, and not expecting the strength and ferocity of the bishop, were easily despatched. The crowd, enthralled by the unfolding spectacle, cheered on the three gladiators. The bishop stood ready for a second foray. The guards, humiliated, regrouped, this time attacking the priest from both sides. With full force, they tackled him into his empty chair, which shattered to the accompaniment of the cheering spectators. Once on the ground with both guards on top of him, Bishop Bernard breathed heavily and, realising the futility of his efforts he meekly surrendered. They pulled up his frock to reveal stout hairless legs and loosely fitting drawers tied at the waist. The guards hesitated and looked up to the judge, who nodded impatiently. A unified howl of laughter filled the chamber as the flabby buttocks were exposed. Silence and amazement immediately replaced the merriment as a large black birthmark on his right buttock was there for the whole chamber to see.

Duval stood with one hand outstretched towards the evidence while scanning the galleries and then fixing on the podium. "Sir, it would appear that this is the molester of the two boys I have described."

Judge Deschamps stood rigid and wide eyed at the evidence before him. "Bishop Bernard, there is enough evidence here to convict you many times over. You are a disgrace to God and your church. Sit with the girl and the doctor to await your punishment. Now, Commandant, you have provided much information and presented a strong case. There is still, however, one last unresolved question. How did the late Monsieur Baptiste kill these three people?"

"Yes, your honour, that is a question that puzzled me for some time. But the clue came in his suicide note where he stated he aborted his planned killing of Monsieur Thomas. To me, this suggested that he had started the process but did not complete it. At the apothecary, I located a bin in which he disposed of any returned drugs, partially prepared scripts, or out-of-date medicines. This bin is emptied and disposed of weekly. I searched this bin and found a packet for Monsieur Thomas. It contained seven pills, one for each day of the week. We gave one pill to each of seven rats and only one rat died. In the three deaths previously described, we tested all remaining pills and none killed the rats.

Duval stopped briefly as the questions, and theories raced around the chamber.

"I think it is clear that only one pill in each prescription contained the poison. It did not matter which day of the week Monsieur Duplessis or Monsieur Villiers took the poisonous pill. But in the case of the archbishop, it was essential that he not return to Paris to deliver his damning report on Bishop Bernard. His death was best achieved while still in St Raphael, or perhaps on his trip home. I am not exactly certain how this was achieved, but I am aware through a regular client of Monsieur Baptiste that Bishop Bernard was in the apothecary on the afternoon before the archbishop's death. There was a heated discussion between the two men and the only words the customer could hear clearly were, 'I need some more of my pills urgently and please mark the best one.' The apothecary then disappeared into a backroom for a short time while the bishop paced impatiently around the shop. When Monsieur Baptiste reappeared, he handed Bishop Bernard two small packets, which he snatched and then rushed from the shop. I can produce the witness who was in the shop that day, but he is so frightfully disfigured from syphilis that he would horrify most of the people in this room today. I have his written statement here which I submit to you. I have assumed that the one packet contained the poisoned pill and the other packet contained the harmless pills."

Duval paused briefly, allowing the chamber to digest the information. "The only unanswered question is, what is the poison? I and my colleagues doubt it is arsenic as the speed and severity of all three illnesses were both swift and deadly. However, Monsieur Baptiste acquired medicines from traders from the east. It remains possible that this potent poison is one not yet seen in Europe; a theory which I believe has some merit. Let me explain. In his laboratory was an empty flask which the morning before the apothecary's death contained a cloudy liquid. However, the morning after his death, there was only a film on the inside of the glass which I could remove with a small amount of water. This was given to two rats who both died within four hours. I am certain Baptiste was preparing this poison but am uncertain of its origin."

"Thank you, Commandant. That seems to fit most of the puzzle together. But the timing concerns me still. How did Bishop Bernard find the time and the opportunity to get to and from the apothecary and into the archbishop's room to fill the pill box if the archbishop was there?"

"Yes, that puzzled me somewhat. But directly after he left the meeting with the archbishop, the bishop arranged for the seminarians to meet with the archbishop and keep him busy for a few hours. These young gentlemen in the front row will attest to this hastily arranged meeting."

Father Dominic spoke from the podium. "I can confirm that Bishop Bernard asked me to arrange this meeting at very short notice."

"Thank you, Commandant. That appears to tie up most loose ends. Bishop Bernard, you have heard all the evidence. In your own words, have any explanation concerning these last two packets and what you did with them?"

"They were my regular pills."

"Your honour, I have looked carefully through Monsieur Baptiste's ledger and there is no evidence that Bishop Bernard received regular medication."

"Can you respond to that, Bishop Bernard?"

The bishop cupped his head in his hands, his silence affirming his dishonour and guilt.

Judge Deschamps conferred briefly with the young priest, who then stood tall on the podium. In a loud and confident voice that belied his age, he addressed the court. "Bishop Bernard, you have committed some heinous crimes and all in the name of our Lord. This is unforgivable. Please stand. You are hereby convicted of the following crimes. One, you have, by your own hand, murdered the late Archbishop of Paris. Two, you have committed at least two counts of blackmail, which have resulted in the deaths of Monsieur Duplessis and Monsieur Villiers. And three, you have sexually molested at least two young boys. Now please sit next to the other convicted criminals. My colleague and I wish to retire to another room so we can vigorously debate these cases. We will return in about fifteen minutes for sentencing. Guards, please maintain some order in the court."

As soon as the judges departed the mumbling and speculation spread around the chamber. Isabella, covered in a black cloak supplied by one seminarian, sat alongside Pierre and Bishop Bernard in the middle of the chamber. No insults were hurled at the accused. The favoured, usual suspects somehow seemed less culpable than the town's beacon of truthfulness, innocence, and godliness. A hushed silence filled the room when the judges took their place on the podium.

Father Dominic rose to deliver the sentence. "The evil of witchcraft has spread like a plague throughout our lands. Unstoppable, it seems, despite vigorous witch-hunting, various forms of unspeakable torture, rigorous trials and horrendous death. These processes would be expected to discourage any sane human being from following that path. But no!

Despite all this we are still exposed, almost daily, to these evil deeds. It is our genuine conviction that we need to set an even harsher punishment. Something that will turn our brothers, sisters, mothers and fathers away from Satan. We are left with no other choice." He paused, scrutinising the galleries and ensuring he had their attention. "These three criminals will be subjected to public crucifixion within six days."

36

Reconciliation

16 July 1670

Duval pushed through a raucous mob outside the courthouse. The solution of the baffling crimes and the sentencing of Bishop Bernard provided some satisfaction. However, the planned crucifixion of Pierre and Isabella weighed heavily. "Five days! That is all! There must be something I can do; something I have overlooked," he mumbled, oblivious to the surrounding commotion.

"Commandant Duval," a deep voice interrupted his contemplation.

Duval turned, "Oh bonjour Simon, and Michael, I believe?" His shoulders sank as he exhaled. "Simon, I know how your heart must ache for Isabella and Pierre. I still have five days. But please, call me Bertrand."

"I understand Bertrand. On behalf of my family, I wish to thank you for all you have done. No-one could have done more. Michael and I are extremely grateful. It requires considerable courage and personal risk to stand up to this established order."

"Thank you, Simon. There is, however, something you should have." He pulled the small jewellery box from his satchel and held it out for Simon. "It should remain in your family."

"Thank you, thank you Bertrand. It will forever remind Michael and I of our brother and niece."

Bertrand turned to Michael. "You referred to yourself as a dealer of legal bodies?"

Michael's eyes widened, and his mouth fell open in a forest of black hair. "Er, yes? That would be correct, Commandant."

"No need for formalities; please call me Bertrand. Do not concern yourself. I will not interrogate you regarding your employment. But there is one matter you may be able to help me with."

"Please Bertrand, go ahead."

"About four weeks ago, the Villiers' gardener disappeared under unusual circumstances. I suspect that his final destination was the Professor's dissection table."

"How could I possibly be of any assistance in this matter?"

"I understand your hesitancy and fear of incrimination. So, I will ask you only one simple question. Have no fear it will go no further than we three. Do you recall a young bearded man with a small earing in his right ear?"

Michael stood unmoving and eyed Duval. "Yes. I purchased such a body from a large red-haired man with a bushy beard."

Bertrand nodded. "Have you seen the red beard before, or is he a complete stranger?"

"Yes, occasionally. He sometimes drives the bishop's carriage and has been seen in the bishop's company."

"Anything else?"

Michael looked to the ground and shuffled his feet. "Rumour in the taverns is that he also has an interest in young boys."

"Thank you, Michael. Thank you very much. It would seem the missing gardener talked too much, and perhaps the red beard knew too much. Michael, Simon, I feel we will still meet again sometime, but at this moment I have other business to attend to. So, I must say goodbye."

They shook hands in the middle of the square as the audience continued to spill out of the courthouse. Bertrand watched the brothers depart, heads bowed, examining the small silver box in Simon's hand.

There was still one more task Duval needed to complete. He should have settled it earlier, but had fabricated many reasons to avoid the confrontation. Dragging his feet across the square, he entered a small side street and stopped in front of a red door. He hesitated, turned to go back, but stopped again and strode purposefully up to the door and knocked. Almost immediately Mademoiselle Lafonte, her blond hair falling neatly on her shoulders, opened the door wearing a long red dress.

"Oh Bertrand, it is a pleasure to see you again after all these years. I was expecting a visit from the constabulary, but am most pleased to find you at my door."

"Good day Mademoiselle Lafonte."

"Bertrand, you knew me previously as Giselle. There is no need for formalities."

"Ah yes, Giselle. So, it would appear that you realise my visit is in connection with the disappearance of Colonel Montpellier?"

"It is disappointing that yours is not a social visit. But yes, I have heard of his disappearance. But why would I have any knowledge of that?"

"I have information that the colonel visited you mostly on a Friday evening." Bertrand paused, waiting for a reaction, but Mademoiselle Lafonte stared straight back through wide green eyes; a frown replacing her initial smile. "He has not been seen since he was last observed crossing the square just before 7 pm last Friday."

"Yes, he did visit me regularly. He wished to keep a close eye on me. You may know I am under suspicion as a witch."

"I have heard so, but I understand the evidence is extremely weak and unsubstantiated. As a result, it is highly unlikely that you will proceed to trial."

"Well Bertrand, it appears that you have been taking a keen interest in my case."

Bertrand's face flushed. "Er... Yes. Yes. I am aware of many fabricated cases of suspected witchcraft."

Giselle smiled at his embarrassment. "Sorry Bertrand, but I have forgotten my manners. I have left you standing there on the threshold. Please come in and share a cup of tea. We used to be such good friends, so please, please come in."

Bertrand entered the small downstairs room and noted the suitcase at the bottom of the staircase and drapes over the furniture. "Are you about to travel somewhere?'

"As a matter of fact, yes. I can no longer stay here and am to visit with my mother in the country. At least till this inquisition settles down in St Raphael."

"Yes, yes, I agree. This witch hunt business is frightening. The three this morning will face crucifixion. Burning was apparently not a sufficient deterrent."

"Yes, I wondered what would become of that poor doctor and that child whom I saw paraded through the streets."

"Mademoiselle Lafonte……"

"Bertrand please, Giselle."

"Yes, yes. Of course. Giselle. I need to ask a few questions. You have said that you know absolutely nothing of the colonel's disappearance?"

"That is correct. Absolutely nothing. This last Friday evening I was expecting him and he did not arrive."

"So, somehow, between the main square and your house, some ill fate found him. We have an unresolved mystery. Unresolved mysteries do not sit well for someone in my line of work?"

"There are many rogues about in the evenings who would silence a man for the sake of a few coins. And, as every corpse has some value, those that take them away are easy to find."

"Well, thank you, Giselle, for your time. And thank you for the kind offer of tea, but I best be on my way." Bertrand tipped his hat and turned towards the door, hesitated and turned to face her again. "Giselle, I will travel to the country in the morning and will pass by your mother's house. I am taking a young boy back to his family. I would be happy to take you."

"That is a most generous and fortuitous offer, Bertrand. I was to leave this morning but the transport I had arranged failed to arrive. I fear it was related to the rumour that surrounds me. I would be most pleased to accept."

Bertrand beamed. "Excellent, excellent. I will see you in the morning." He tipped his hat, turned and walked out of the door. With a spring in his step, he made his way home with the memories of their past flooding back. They had met ten years previously. Her poise, beauty and intelligence had been an instant attraction. Her family, however, were local landowners and frowned upon Giselle's friendship with a mere officer and, after a brief courtship, forbade any further contact. He had been so scarred by the rejection that he was never again seen in the company of a woman. As time passed, he had heard how her father drank heavily and gambled away most of their fortune before he died under mysterious circumstances. Poisoning it was rumoured. Giselle's mother had fallen under suspicion but avoided conviction. However, the stain could not be removed and led to a spiral into poverty and rejection by friends and the community and finally exile to their country cottage. More recently, he had information that Giselle's mother was again under suspicion for witchcraft.

***

Jacques appeared from his room as soon as Bertrand opened the door; the picture of innocence in his blue jacket and breeches. Not the dejected, angry, streetwise child who had knocked on Bertrand's door five days previously. "How are you today, Jacques? Did you eat everything I left for dinner last night and breakfast this morning?"

"Yes, thank you Bertrand." Bertrand had insisted on first names. "Will you be going away again?"

"No Jacques, that is a promise. I am sorry, but it was urgent business that I had to attend to before court this morning. I do have some good news from the trial. It finished today and you do not have to attend. No-one will ever know about your ordeal. And that priest will never bother you again."

"Is that fucking bastard going to the Tower?" Jacques' angelic exterior could not hide his previous beggary, the scars of his mother's death, and his own recent anguish.

"Much worse than that. I am sure he will burn in the fires of hell! Bertrand crouched down to Jacques' height and held his shoulders with both hands. Jacques let us not talk of that fiend any more. I want you to forget those detestable events and know that most of the people you will meet have good hearts and wish you no harm."

Jacques nodded, his wide eyes finding their way directly into Bertrand's heart.

"You must be tired of being locked up in this house. So, this afternoon, we will go down to the river, take out a boat and try some fishing. We may even have a swim." Bertrand paused and then continued. "Jacques, there is a young boy, Reuben, who has been through an ordeal similar to yours. If you are agreeable, I would like to take him with us?"

Jacques eyed Bertrand; initially hesitant but then teased. "Yes, someone of my age might make it even more enjoyable."

Bertrand smiled. "Good, and tomorrow we will see your sister."

***

Jacques rose early, humming a tune as he packed his meagre belongings in the bag that Francine had given him and joined Bertrand in the kitchen for breakfast. His departure from Bertrand partially tempered the elation of reuniting with his sister. The previous afternoon had been the most memorable of his short life. They had basked in the sunshine on a placid section of la Loire. Bertrand had patiently shown him and Reuben the intricacies of the hooks and bait for the various species in the water below. The excitement and achievement when he pulled a large perch into the boat, and the joy of a swim when they docked on a sandy beach, were sensations he had seldom before experienced. Reuben, initially closed, opened up slowly and, when he caught his perch, the first glimmer of a smile appeared. By the time they reached Reuben's home, the boys had agreed to meet again. But for Jacques, his most enduring memory would be the shared warmth and companionship while preparing his catch for their evening meal.

***

"Good morning, Bertrand. But you have dressed well for a ride in the country to see my sister." Bertrand's coarse rumpled jacket had been exchanged for a fitted, red one covering a matching waistcoat. Instead of his comfortable ankle boots, he walked awkwardly in buckled, leather heeled shoes.

"Er, er, yes. I do occasionally get out of my work clothes for social occasions."

The conversation at breakfast was stifled, each preoccupied with thoughts about the impending day. Both heard the knock at the door and they gathered their belongings and hurried outside to the waiting carriage. Bertrand led the horse across the square in the opposite direction of the city gate.

"This is not the way to the city gate?" queried Jacques.

"No, we must pick up a friend; a Mademoiselle Giselle Lafonte, who is to meet her mother in the country."

"Ah, so that is the reason for the fancy clothes?" Jacques chuckled.

"Jacques, that is very cheeky. I think you have spent too much time with the boys from the Temple of Miracles." Bertrand could not contain the laugh he tried to swallow.

Giselle, dressed in the same finery as the previous day, looked radiant in the morning sunshine. Bertrand's heart skipped a beat and Jacques elbowed him in the side, smiled and nodded his approval.

"Jacques, let me introduce you to Mademoiselle Giselle Lafonte."

"Good morning, Jacques."

"Good morning, Giselle," replied Jacques.

They had soon passed the city gate with la Loire rushing and crashing beside them. The road was rough and the carriage clattery, with little point in conversation. After an uncomfortable three hours, they turned off onto a narrow, rutted path which ended at an old crumbling farmhouse. An elderly man with long white hair and beard working in a vegetable garden stood up and stretched his back as the carriage approached. Bertrand jumped down and walked across the yard to meet him.

"Good morning, sir. I am Bertrand Duval, and I bring Jacques, the brother of Francine Macon."

"Who is the lady?" He nodded towards the carriage. "Is she to be trusted? I was told there would only be you and the boy."

"I can guarantee her silence; she is also under observation."

The old man rubbed his beard. "Bien, bring the boy and follow me. She will remain here with me."

Bertrand explained the arrangement to Giselle, who nodded. He, with Jacques carrying his bag, followed the old man down a narrow, overgrown path till they reached a small stream. They continued beside the burbling water until an expansive bramble bush completely blocked the path. The old man parted some low shrubs in front of the bramble to reveal a low tunnel.

"Crawl through. On the other side you will find a simple shelter. Wait there. She will approach when she feels it is safe."

The brambles ripped at their clothes and skin as they crawled and slid on their stomachs through the narrow tunnel. They stretched and dusted themselves off on the other side. The shelter was about fifty metres ahead, leaning against a massive oak; a rudimentary three-sided structure made from an assortment of timber and branches with pine bark filling in the gaps. They waited quietly next to the dwelling, as instructed. The wind rustled gently through the oak. A nightingale sang in some smaller trees to the left, and the brook babbled steadily in the background.

Then the nightingale stopped, and to their left, the bush parted. Two bedraggled, gaunt faced girls emerged. Their filthy rags hung from bony shoulders as they walked across the rough ground in bare, scabbed feet.

Jacques saw them first. He dropped his bag and ran towards them. "Francine, Francine, Francine!" He jumped up onto her as she grabbed him in both arms. Celeste stood back quietly; her eyes fixed warily on Duval. Francine whispered briefly to Celeste and then took Jacques by the hand and led him back through the bush from which they had appeared.

"Good morning, Commandant Duval, I am Celeste. I have heard much about you and am pleased to make your acquaintance."

"Good morning, Celeste. Yes, I have followed your case since your time in the Glen."

"Francine would like some time alone with Jacques."

"That is a little strange. I thought I was bringing him to her."

"Let us just sit here quietly and be patient."

Celeste sat on the ground, and Bertrand followed. No words were spoken, and the nightingale resumed his song from a more distant tree as the stream continued its perpetual journey.

Fifteen minutes passed. Then half an hour. Finally, after an hour the bushes parted and the dishevelled Francine and the dapper Jacques appeared and sat down with Bertrand and Celeste.

"Commandant…"

"Please call me Bertrand."

"Bertrand, my brother and I have spoken at length about our future. I am a suspected witch. I have been in the Tower and have heard the torture.

If I am caught, I will certainly be burnt. Celeste's future, particularly now that the colonel is gone, is also dire. We must stay in hiding, and to be safe will need to leave St Raphael. It is not the life for a young boy. I cannot possibly take him with me. If I am caught, what will become of him? He needs a better future. School is essential. He must break out of the poverty we have been in."

"Yes. I can understand that it will be difficult for you to look after him. But what is your proposal?"

Francine took a deep breath, looked at Celeste, who nodded. "He likes you. He feels safe with you and, above all, you have protected him and brought his worst nightmare to justice. He admires you. He never had a father. And now, he chooses you."

"He chooses me?" Bertrand looked into the wide, wet, searching eyes of Jacques. "He is a wonderful boy. But, but, I do not think I can be the father he needs. I work for very long hours. I leave early and come home late and hardly ever eat a proper meal."

"He will take you just as you are. He needs nothing more. At this moment, his life is an empty shell. You have been his only ray of hope. The only sunshine and happiness that he has ever had."

"I do not know what to say. Perhaps I could… Maybe if…. I only hope he will not be disappointed."

With a slight shove from Francine, Jacques stood and threw his arms around Bertrand, who clutched him tight while nodding at Francine over his shoulder.

"Good. That is settled." Francine pulled across the bag that Jacques had been carrying. To Bertrand's surprise, she removed a small cloth sack and emptied many gold coins and a silver locket and chain into her palm. "This bag contains many valuables from a wealthy benefactor who I believe may be my father; but not Jacques' father. I understand he is also on the run. Celeste and I will use the money to clothe and feed ourselves while we travel and stay in hiding. What remains in this bag are title deeds to several dwellings. One is on le Boulevard du Printemps. My suggestion is that you transfer these deeds into your name and move into the house with Jacques. There is enough value in the bonds and properties for you and Jacques to live a comfortable life."

Bertrand looked stupefied. "I am a man of the law. Where does all this come from? I cannot……"

A shrill whistle broke the afternoon heat.

Celeste and Francine jumped to their feet. "We must go. That is a warning. Someone has approached the house. Goodbye!" Celeste grabbed Francine's arm and dragged her away. Francine held Jacques' eyes until she disappeared through the bushes from which they had first emerged.

Bertrand and Jacques sat quietly for a few minutes, listening. Bertrand got up first. "We should go," and held out his hand to pull Jacques up. They walked in silence towards the bramble tunnel, Bertrand holding the bag in one hand and Jacques' hand in the other. After sustaining a few more scratches and ripped clothing, they dusted themselves off on the other side. The bush path was clear, and they ventured back cautiously along the track towards the house. At the edge of the clearing, they froze and Bertrand put his finger to pursed lips. Jacques nodded. Another horse stood next to their carriage. Next to the house, the old man and Giselle were in conversation with a grey jacketed soldier. They lay flat on the ground, daring not to move but watching the meeting through the shrubbery. The uniformed officer towered over the old man; his face flushed. The grizzled farmer stood his ground, responding calmly to the soldier's questions. Giselle interrupted occasionally, pointing to the carriage and to the hills in the east. The interrogation proceeded for fifteen minutes, after which the guard nodded, turned, mounted his horse, and rode back out along the rutted track.

"What did he want?" asked Bertrand when they arrived back at the house.

"He was following up on some information that Colonel Montpelier had been sighted in this area. Both I and my niece here ensured him we had not seen him."

Bertrand smiled and nodded. "Yes, I did wonder how you would explain the carriage and Giselle. That is a relief."

Giselle bent down and gave Jacques a hug. The old man looked on and nodded.

"It is getting late and we still have a long journey ahead of us. Thank you, sir. I did not get your name."

"It is best that you do not know my name."

All three were soon on the carriage and back on the road. There was a slight detour to Giselle's mother's cottage, where Bertrand pulled the horse up outside the garden gate. No words were spoken as he helped Giselle with her luggage to the front door. The garden was wild and overgrown. There were large gaps in the thatch and the shutters hung askew on each side of the windows. Giselle knocked nervously at the door. There was no reply. She knocked again and then again. Her hand trembled and beads of perspiration appeared on her forehead as she knocked one last time. No response! Giselle turned, rushed around the side of the house to a large pot filled with herbs. She pushed her hand under the edge of the pot and found the key that was always there. With a trembling hand, she pushed it into the lock and opened the door. A strong mustiness and rat smell flowed out through the opening as she clutched a handkerchief to her nose. The furniture was placed much as she remembered it but ruined from the leaking roof. The signs of a hasty departure were clear. In the bedroom stood an unmade bed soiled with rat droppings and a chest with open drawers and clothes strewn over the floor. On the kitchen table lay a plate with a few clean chicken bones and beside the table, a wooden chair, pushed hastily aside. In the centre of the table, she found what she was looking for. The note was short and concise.

To the person who finds this note.

I have had to leave suddenly. The events in this county have been building up against me. My healing practices, of which you are aware, were brought to the attention of la Maréchausée and I have had to disappear. Please do not try to find me.
Louise.

Giselle passed the note to Bertrand, who stood beside her. He glanced over the note and then back at Giselle, whose tears were wet on her cheeks. "She wrote this note for me. She, she, she did not wish to mention my name for fear I would be implicated." Covering her eyes with her hands, the sobbing shook her body and tears fell to the floor. Bertrand floundered, fumbled with his clothes, uncertain. But as Giselle's helplessness reached his heart, he could no longer hold back. He grabbed her tightly in both arms as she continued to mumble. "Oh Mama, what has become of you? And what now will become of me?"

Bertrand spoke softly. "Giselle, please, please do not worry. You cannot live here. I will not leave you here. You will come and live with Jacques and I until such time as your circumstances improve."

"But, but Bertrand, people will talk; what of your reputation? And now, you have just acquired a new son who will require all your attention. I could not possibly impose."

"Giselle, Jacques and I have just acquired a large house on le Boulevarde du Printemps; there is plenty of space for all us and Jacques and I would welcome an improvement in our food." With his arm around her shoulders, he guided her out of the derelict cottage and helped her into the carriage. Jacques followed with her suitcase.

37

Diana and Artemis

17 July 1670

Mara woke again with nausea. Her recent heightened smell immediately detected last night's left-over food and aggravated the queasiness. She dressed and stepping outside immediately improved as the fresh morning air reached her. A basket of dirty laundry stood on a table near the barn and she began the tedious process of scrubbing, rinsing, and wringing, being careful not to knock her tender breasts against the scrubbing board. The washing continued for the next hour, interrupted by occasional visits to the toilet. Once complete, she hung the washed rags on a rudimentary line stretched between their small dwelling and the branch of a tree; the bile rising in her throat each time she bent down to pick up another item from the basket. With the last article hung, she breathed a sigh, stretched and absorbed the surrounding countryside. The mountains rose majestically in the east and somewhere beyond the western horizon lay la Loire and her home. She tensed as a flock of larks suddenly flew out from a tall pine. *Someone was approaching. Soldiers?* Then she heard it, the distant rumble of a cart, maybe two. She listened again and could now discern the hooves of a single horse. Relieved, she waited as the rumble of the cart grew louder along the potholed track. The horse came into view first as it rounded the last bend, and then, a blond-haired driver, waving at her. She walked as fast as possible towards the cart shouting back, "Mama, Mama, come quickly! It is Simon. Simon is here!" She soon reached the cart, climbed up next to Simon, and wrapped her arms around him.

"It is so good to see you, Mara."

Mara pulled in tightly next to him. "What news is there? What of Pierre and Isabella?"

Miriam appeared first from the cottage, followed by Grandmère, hobbling slowly and panting. "Simon, what news have you? How are Doctor Pierre and Isabella? What happened at the trial?"

Simon jumped down and the three women gathered around. "Yes, there is much news, but I am afraid it is grave. Pierre was declared guilty of fathering a witch's unborn child and allowing her to escape his custody." Simon pulled Mara in tightly as she wiped the moisture from her eyes. "Isabella was found guilty of witchcraft because of that extra nipple. The bishop called it a witch's teat." Simon gently pushed Mara away and turned to face her. "Mara, there is something I have never told you, and I must tell you now."

Her wide, wet eyes bored into Simon's. "What, something worse?"

"Not worse, but a long, held secret. Monsieur Baptiste is my brother and, as such, Isabella is my niece. I am Simon Baptiste."

Mara pulled away, looking first in disbelief at Simon, and then at Maman and Grandmère. "Why? Why? Why the secrecy? Why was I not allowed to know?"

Mother was about to speak, but Simon jumped in. "Our whole family was aware of Isabella's mark at the time of her birth. We all knew its significance. This included my brother Michael, as well as Miriam and Grandmère. It was agreed that during these difficult times, we would support each other steadfastly, but our connections would remain a secret. Sadly, Isabella herself was never aware, but during the court proceedings, I made it known that I was her uncle."

Maman and Grandmère stood silently as Mara absorbed the news. She didn't speak, and shook her head as her gaze shifted from Simon to Maman, to Grandmère, and back.

Simon broke the silence. "There is some surprising news of the bishop. He has been found guilty of blackmailing my brother Raphael with Isabella's mark. This resulted in Raphael poisoning Monsieur Duplessis and Monsieur Villers. The archbishop, the bishop poisoned by his own hand. The bishop was also convicted for molesting two young boys."

Mara, having listened in silence, interjected. "But Simon, what is the punishment?"

"Mara, it hurts me to say this, but the punishment is grave. Isabella, Pierre and the bishop will be crucified in public in four days."

"Crucified, crucified! That has never been performed in this canton before. Why crucifixion?"

"The judges felt that the current punishment of burning and hanging did not provide a sufficient disincentive for witches to cease practising their craft."

"That is monstrous! What are we to do, Simon? We cannot just let Pierre and Isabella die. No! No! Simon, you have always known what to do. You must have a plan," Mara pleaded.

"I have ridden all night and have thought long and hard on this and believe that escape from the Tower is virtually impossible. It would also be extremely risky for any of you three to attend!"

Grandmère interjected. "I agree, Simon, but this is the father of Mara's child and your niece. We must all go to this crucifixion so that we can at least comfort those we love."

Simon nodded in agreement. "The additional news is that Colonel Montpellier has disappeared and has possibly been murdered. The perpetrator is unknown. Also, Celeste and Francine escaped the Tower just prior to their impending trial."

"Thank you for all the news, Simon," Miriam responded. "But you have driven all night and need some food and sleep. We will all leave this evening. Simon, you will find a comfortable bed in the barn. I will see that you have what you need."

Mara picked up the washing basket and walked back towards the cottage with Grandmère. She heard a brief laugh from her mother and looked back to see Simon and her walking closely together towards the barn. For a moment, the fingers of their hands touched and lingered till they reached the barn. She had noticed similar instances over the years and perhaps in the innocence of childhood, had regarded them as part of a close relationship between friends. Mara saw things differently now. She had experienced similar intimacies with Pierre. Little secrets in public, just as the one she had now observed.

Mara and Grandmère spent the next hour gathering their belongings and sufficient food for the journey. Mother appeared through the doorway, slightly flustered. "Simon is sleeping, so let us make sure we can leave when he wakes in a few hours."

The packing continued in silence, but thoughts swirled uncontrollably through Mara's head. She had to know. She could no longer be silenced. "Mother, there is something I have to ask. Something I had wondered about from time to time but never knew how to ask."

"Well, go ahead child, speak!"

"It concerns you and Simon, and possibly even me. I feel certain you know what I am asking."

Grandmère chuckled from her chair in the corner. "Ha! Ha! Ha! My daughter. I told you this moment would come. Tell the poor girl. It is so obvious. You can no longer hide it."

"Oh Mara, I was trying to protect you, but also Simon, through these terrible witch hunt times. Yes, Simon and I have been together and unmarried for all these years. And," Miriam hesitated and took in a deep breath. "Yes. Yes, Simon is your father."

Mara stood frozen, silent, mouth agape. She trembled and the blush of anger rose from her neck and enveloped her face. The words erupted from deep within. "Mother! How could you? How could you? How could you keep such a secret? You have robbed me of my father for sixteen years. That is shameful. The most wonderful and loving father a young girl could wish for. I do not think I will ever be able to forgive you. And what of Isabella? She only recently became my close friend. She is now my cousin! We have missed so much together and may never get another chance."

"I am truly sorry, Mara. But to understand this silence, you not only have to understand the horrific times in which we live, but also must know who I and your grandmother really are."

"What sort of nonsense is this? I know exactly who you are. You are my closest people who have kept a life-changing secret from me. There is nothing more to know."

"Please Mara, please sit so I can try to explain."

Reluctantly, Mara sat in a chair facing Maman and Grandmère. "Alright, speak! Let me hear this mysterious family secret."

"Thank you, Mara. Momma, please fill in if I miss anything. We belong to a gathering of women who still follow the path of the Goddess Diana. To fully understand this, I need you to know about this goddess. Diana was a Roman goddess and the ancient Greeks had a similar goddess called Artemis. As they had very similar attributes, over time they were combined into one; the Goddess Diana. Diana is the goddess of the hunt and nature and took on Artemis' additional qualities of healing with herbs. We do not follow any satanic rituals but meet regularly to talk about a range of things, such as helping women in pregnancy and during childbirth. We also exchange herbal recipes and advise women who feel the wrath of a violent husband or who just wish to improve the drudgery of their subservient role."

"Is that why our farm is Maison Diana?"

"Yes, and no. First, the farm is not ours. It belongs to Simon, Michael and Raphael. Their mother, who was also a follower of Diana, named it thus."

"But if that is what you do, why should that be such a secret?"

"Yes, that is true, and the explanation is complicated. First, some in the church consider the following of any goddess as witchcraft, as it conflicts with their first commandment. *Thou shalt have no other gods before me.* Certain worshippers of Diana have raised her to a triple goddess and combined her with Luna and with Hecate. Hecate is associated with magic, witchcraft, ghosts, necromancy, and sorcery. It is this connection that the catholic church considers as dangerous and hence all worshippers of Diana are considered witches."

"But if you had married Simon, that would have put you under much less suspicion?"

Miriam was silent and looked across at Grandmère for help.

Grandmère was more direct. "Our coven does not allow marriage."

Mara's face reddened and her eyes burrowed into her mother. "What! So, because of your silly coven, I have not known my father for the first sixteen years of my life."

"Yes, that is true, but he has known you and will always protect you."

A nervous silence fell on the room as the door creaked open and Simon bent down to enter the room. "I am well rested. I have fed the horse. Let us load up and go!" His enthusiasm was met with a stony silence from the three generations seated in a small circle. "Well? What is wrong with you all? I thought we were leaving."

Mara could not contain herself and with tears streaming down her cheeks, she jumped up and flung herself into Simon's arms. "My father! Papa, I have missed you so much. Do not ever let me go."

Simon wrapped her up in his powerful arms and smiled contentedly over her shoulder at Miriam and Grandmère.

The sun had sunk below a red western sky by the time they departed. Mara sat up front, shoulder to shoulder with Simon, incessantly recounting her memories of childhood, her days at school, and her time with Pierre. Simon, content to sit and listen to all his daughter described, beamed. When she spoke of Pierre, Simon could finally ask the questions that had burdened him. "Did he treat you well? Did he ever hurt you? Do you love him?"

"Oh Papa, he has been wonderful. He did drink some when I first arrived. But of late, he only has a glass of wine with me when we have dinner together. He is a true gentleman. He has not once hurt me and never forced himself upon me. In that regard, I was the first to move, as he was so hesitant. Papa, I love him dearly. Please! Please do not let him die."

"I am pleased you have told me Mara, because we may have to take a terrible risk. In fact, we may all be caught and find ourselves in the Tower awaiting our own punishment."

"I do not care Papa, we must try."

The evening turned to night, and Mara swopped places with mother in the tray. The joy of having found her father completely negated the rough road, and she fell into a deep and contented sleep.

Maison Diana was bathed in the early sunrise when Simon pulled the carriage to a halt. Maman, Grandmère, and Mara jumped off and entered the garden. Generations of knowledge allowed them to quickly gather all that they needed, including ingredients from the locked garden. All eyes watched their past disappear as they crossed le Pont St Joan. Covering their faces as best as possible, they passed through a lifeless hamlet of St Joan. The only human, a patron, sleeping at The Laughing Waters front door. They climbed the small hill and St Raphael lay before them. Simon pulled up the horse. "My ladies, this is where we part. I will see you here again at sunset. Agreed?"

"You may not recognise us, Papa," Mara countered, smiling.

"We must go. There is no time to waste. And what will you be up to, Simon?" asked Miriam as she walked to go.

"I have a few things to arrange but also hope to go fishing with a friend."

Miriam raised her eyebrows, shrugged and followed Mara and Grandmère. With shawls draped over their heads and eyes downcast, they strolled along the approach road ignoring eye contact with any passer's bye. No-one paid any attention to the three simple country folk that passed through the city gate. They turned immediately right along the river wall and soon approached the chasm and the Temple of Miracles. The usual gang of mischief, about to start their days' assignments, loitered outside, considering the three approaching peasants.

"Well, well, boys, what do we have here? One little rose between two thorns."

The Mandeville's ignored the provocation and prepared to move through the pack towards the Temple. The huddle closed, halting their progress.

"Come now, just one kiss from the little rose. You may pass for just one kiss."

Grandmère had no patience and snarled from deep within her shawl. "If you wish your member to fall off in the middle of the night, you had best move aside. Which one of you wishes to tempt the curse of an ancient witch?"

Suddenly silent, the crew looked tentatively at each other, shrugged their shoulders, detached and let them pass.

"And where would we find a woman who goes by the name Madame Dumasque?" growled Grandmère

"Madame Dumasque can be found on the third floor."

Intricate engravings on a grandiose front door and portico suggested the Temple of Miracles had once enjoyed a more distinguished past. A wide staircase with broken steps and balustrades rose in front of the three peasants and divided the entry. The cries of children and an oppressive smell drew their attention to a door on the right. Through the smoke-filled dimness, a mass of cramped, partially clad, hollow-eyed adults and naked children peered inquisitively back at them. The source of the haze was a small iron pot standing over a fire next to a window on the far side of the room. Behind the stairs, another two open doors revealed further wretchedness, which spilled out into the hallway.

A sharp command drew their heads to the left. "No! If you do it like that, you will be in a cell for the night." A lean, grey-haired man with a beard hanging over his hollow stomach stood in the centre of a ring of teenage boys. "Never work alone! Always work in pairs and with two or three distractors. Let the one with the softest hands take the goods. At the moment, that is Martin, but as you learn, you will all get your opportunity. As a team, you will win and as a team, you will share the spoils. Now, we will all try it again. Let us get it right this time."

On the next floor, the wretched crush and smell of humanity again poured out of the rooms on the right. In a large, open area to the left, an assortment of sick and disabled young men gathered around a boy on the floor. His body shook, his limbs writhed, his face contorted as he frothed profusely from his mouth. The encircling, afflicted crew clapped at the performance. He stopped, stood up, smiled and pulled a small piece of soap from his mouth. To one side of the room, another juvenile with a blindfold negotiated various objects with a stick but crashed into a chair. "Again!" growled a tall tattooed man with a patch over his left eye. On his next attempt, all the objects were avoided. He removed the blindfold and displayed a wide toothless smile. "Excellent William, now go up and see Madame Dumasque. She will need to fix your eyes before you take to the streets this morning." The tattooed man turned his attention to two other ruffians, each with a stick in one hand and one leg tied up behind the thigh. They stumbled and fell repeatedly around the periphery of the room. "You cannot go out today. You will be exposed. Keep practicing."

They followed William to the third floor, again with crowded, squalid and fetid side rooms. Opposite the rooms, an attentive group of men and women sat in chairs in a circle facing inwards. An elderly woman, her face partly obscured with grey, straggling hair falling over a flowing red gown, moved from person to person. She was attending to a large, disfiguring growth on the left cheek of a young girl. Next, she moved to a man dressed as a soldier with an horrific burn involving the left side of his face, a missing ear, and a head devoid of hair. "That looks very good, but it is not just what they see. Do not forget to mention the battles you have fought for your fatherland." Next was a man with a conspicuous hunchback. The silver illusionist adjusted it slightly. "Always sit with your right side facing the street. It is more realistic from that side."

"Thank you, thank you Madame Dumasque. I do not know how I can ever repay you. My family could not survive without the artistry you provide," bowed the hunchback.

Madame Dumasque smiled and moved onto a dishevelled, young man and with a brush touched up one of his multiple, syphilitic lesions. She then created William's cataracts, followed by some finishing touches to a hole in the side of a man's head with part of his brain exposed. "This is excellent Marcel; this is definitely our best work so far."

Madame Dumasque was about to move on when she noticed the three women rivetted at the edge of the room. "And what can I do for you three? I do not recognise you. If you are here to spy and learn some of our techniques, you should leave at once. If you refuse, I will instruct some of these boys to deal with you."

Grandmère responded immediately. "No! No! Madame Dumasque. Everything we heard about you appears to be true. Your work is truly exceptional and we wish to make use of your services."

"So, you think you can just walk in here and ask for a disguise? These are my family, my regulars. They take substantial risks out on the streets so that we can all share the daily profits. I have no time for outsiders. Please leave or I shall ensure that these poor souls here evict you."

Grandmère opened her palm to reveal a silver coin.

Madame Dumasque's expressionless face focused on the coin. "Three people, three coins."

"We accept your offer, but require it done today."

"Four coins."

Grandmère sighed, pulled out another coin, and handed them to Madame Dumasque.

Without speaking, she closed her palm tightly and turned to her family. "You boys and girls are ready to go. You should all do well this morning." She turned back to the Mandevilles. "You may call me Sophia. Now, who do you wish to be?"

***

Simon waited till the Mandeville's disappeared beyond the city wall, flicked the reins and drew the carriage up beside the city gate. He signalled to a loitering urchin; his head turning repeatedly, looking for opportunity. The urchin immediately rushed across to the wagon. "I want you to take this note to Colonel Duval, and only to Colonel Duval. Ask him to meet Simon just down there by the river for some fishing." Simon pointed to a short sandy beach at a bend in the river. "Don't speak to anyone else. You must return with him and I will give you twice what I give you now. Can you do that?" Simon held up one sol and the urchin's wide eyes sparkled.

"Yes, that will be easy. I know where he works and his place of residence."

Simon watched the waif run off through the gate and disappear down a side street. He proceeded towards the beach, tethered the horse and prepared his fishing lines. It was an hour later when Simon watched Duval and Jacques being led by the juvenile.

"Well, Simon, this is a very pleasant surprise and is much appreciated by Jacques. Jacques, this is Simon. I am sure he can teach you more about fishing than I."

"Good morning, Jacques. Glad to make you acquaintance." Simon held out his hand, and Jacques took it enthusiastically. Then to the urchin, "here is what I promised and not a word to anyone."

The boy clasped his hand tightly around the coins. "Thank you, sir. Please let me know if there is anything else I can do for you." Simon nodded, and the boy went back to his position at the gate.

"Throw those lines in. I have already caught this little perch."

After another half an hour of fishing with Jacques totally engrossed, Duval broke the impasse. "Simon, I am certain you have arranged this meeting to know if there is anything I can do about the planned crucifixions."

"Please Bertrand, is there anything we can do? The death of Isabella and Pierre will be a cross the rest of us cannot bear. I have not told you before, but Mara is my daughter."

Duval raised his eyebrows and smiled. "Well, that is news, but I noticed how close you and Mara were and have speculated on how you and Madame Mandeville passed your time at that farm over the last sixteen years. But let me answer your question. I have communicated with King Louis by messenger about this, and the news will not be what you wish to hear. The king made it clear. The verdict of a properly constituted court should not be overturned. To do so in one case would result in many, possibly hundreds requesting the same treatment. The courts must be seen to be the final adjudicators of the law. If not, anarchy will reign."

Simon's disbelieving eyes held Duval's. "I understand Bertrand. I am certain that if anything could be done, you would already have done so."

Bertrand stretched out his hand on Simon's shoulder. "I will be at the crucifixion as the head of la Maréchausée to ensure all appropriate processes are in place. The best I can do as colonel is to ensure that they do not suffer long. I will also speak to Professor Dubois. As you are aware, they are now proven witches and cannot be buried. He will want the bodies in good condition for dissection, so he will be keen to pronounce death early and not let them hang endlessly." Simon's dejected eyes continued to fix Bertrand, and for a very moment, he thought he saw Bertrand's right eye blink.

"I got one!" Jacques shouted, and both men broke their contemplation and reached out to help him reel it in.

38

The Crucifixion.

21 July 1670

The sun sank below the western mountains, painting a canvas of orange and red in a cloud filled sky. Isabella, naked with hands fastened behind her back, stumbled on her bloodied, bare feet across the cobblestones. A pressing crowd walked alongside, baying for more pain and punishment. Behind Isabella Pierre, naked and bound, walked upright with eyes fixed ahead. Bishop Bernard followed, panting, stumbling repeatedly, as rivulets of sweat ran down his obese nakedness. A cordon of fully armed guards shielded the condemned souls from the clamorous crowd. Inside the cordon, Father Dominic and Elias walked on either side of the bishop, chanting from their open prayer books. Simon, in step beside Pierre, spoke quietly. Michael walked shoulder to shoulder with Isabella, talking continuously and catching her when she stumbled.

The cacophony grew as the procession approached the city gate. Waiting crowds had taken up prime positions on the wall on either side of the gate. The confines of the gate amplified the press and abuse, which was accompanied by a shower of decaying rubbish onto the cortege below. Once through the gate, Isabella drew a sharp breath and fell against Michael as three low crucifixes menaced on top of a distant hillock.

Beyond the gate, the cavalcade left the road to follow a narrow, rugged path cutting across an open, uneven field of boulders, trees and waist high grass and flowers. The crucifixes, menacingly palpable, stood silhouetted against the last remaining light of the doomed lives. With every step closer to the structures of torture, Isabella's heart beat louder and faster. Her mouth was dry, her throat tight, and an unrelenting tightness and pain permeated her chest and belly. Her fear largely obliterated the noise of the crowd. In this vacuum of sound, she tried to exclude the persecution and shroud herself in the smell and beauty of the surrounding pale lilac flowers of the tall rocket.

Pierre had blotted out the crowd's torment. The tears that trickled down his cheeks were not the fear of death, but losing the woman he loved and his unborn child. A familiar sound, however, gradually, incessantly, penetrated his shield. "Tap, tap, tap." He turned to his left to locate the intrusion and saw that Simon had heard it as well. Monsieur Lambert hobbled along next to them, smiling spitefully.

At the hillock, the procession joined a smaller crowd who had arrived by horse and cart along a side road which connected to the main south road. The crosses were low to the ground and a small platform with steps was placed in front of each. Bishop Bernard was taken first. Without a struggle, he climbed the steps and placed his arms over the crosspiece, to which the guards tied him securely. When fixed, the guards jumped off the small platform and, in one quick motion, pulled it from under the cleric. A loud groan and deep breath escaped as his arms took the full weight of his fleshy body. His stout legs jerked uncontrollably, searching for the illusion of support. Isabella shivered as she watched and vomited onto the ground.

Pierre was next. He looked straight ahead into the crowd as he was tied to the crosspieces. He ignored the satisfied smile of Monsieur Lambert but fixed on a young, dark-haired gypsy, with a large birthmark on her left cheek. His eyes widened with the recognition of a red ribbon in her hair. He smiled and held her as the platform was pulled away.

Isabella screamed and struggled as two guards dragged her up the steps. As they tied her arms over the cross pieces, the pain in her stomach intensified and a trail of excrement ran down her pale legs. The platform was removed and her dead weight jerked beneath her stretched arms as she fainted.

The troupe of soldiers formed a cordon around the crosses, allowing only the registered carers of the condemned inside the ring. An old, bent,